Thanks to Ewan Crawford
(http://www.railscot.co.uk) for his prompt and
efficient help in checking the details of Irish
railways of the period. I have hundreds of
reference books and not one gave me the
necessary information!

PART ONE
Lancashire, July 1848

I

Dora sighed in relief as the final siren went and the mill machinery began to slow down and switch off. She picked up the broom and swept her area, then set everything ready for the following morning. The overlooker came round and peered suspiciously under her rows of spindles for fluff, but was unable to fault her on anything. He'd have liked to, though. Benting loved to fine people. You'd think the money went into his own pocket.

It had been hot and stuffy all day, so bad inside the mill that the women tending the spinning bobbins had removed any clothes they decently could. But even that hadn't been enough to make them comfortable, it never was, because *he* refused to let them open the windows. He never seemed to suffer from the heat so that pale face of his was never marked by a flush like the women's were.

Outside the air was fresh, getting cooler now that it was past seven o'clock. Dora breathed in deeply, walking along for a while with one of her friends, not saying much, just feeling pleased that the working day was over. When they parted company, she decided to take the longer way home by the river. She could see a man walking towards her along the curve in the riverbank, moving even more slowly than she was, but apart from that distant figure she was blissfully alone.

The grass was soft and green beneath her feet and the shallow water sparkled as it flowed over the pebbles. She glanced long-ingly up at the moors which overlooked the small town. They were dotted with sheep on the lower slopes, with gentle curves of dull green above. Perhaps she could persuade her little sisters to go for a walk on the tops with her on Sunday. The bracing air up there would clear her lungs of cotton fluff and you could see for miles, something she craved after being shut up in the steamy heat of the mill all week.

She stopped to breathe deeply again, half-closing her eyes. And then she heard it, the sound of voices jeering and taunting further along the river, followed by a yelp of pain. It was coming from a clump of trees and bushes, so she couldn't see who it was, but lads could be so cruel. She couldn't bear to think of them hurting some poor creature on a lovely evening like this, so she turned in the direction of the sounds.

When she saw what was happening she began to run, shouting, 'Stop it! Stop it!' at the top of her voice.

The three youths spun round in surprise as she shoved one out of the way and ran past them, bending to pick up the puppy that was tied to a stake. It had been huddled down, quivering with fear, blood showing on its brown and white coat where the stones had hit it.

'What do you think you're *doing*?' she demanded, untying the rope from its neck and flinging it aside as she cuddled the shivering creature to her bosom. 'Get off home with you at once!' And then she recognised the leader: Huey Benting, eldest son of the overlooker at the mill and just as much of a bully as his father.

'I'm only doing what Dad told me. It's been coming round the houses trying to steal food and leaving its messes on the foot-path. It don't belong to anyone, so he said to kill it.'

Her heart sank. Interfering in this would make yet another reason for Benting to pick on her at work, she was sure, but she wasn't going to give in. 'So you decided to torture it.' Anger made her voice louder than usual. 'Brave, aren't you? Three big lads against one little pup. Well, I won't let you do it.'

Huey took a step forward, scowling. 'It's none of your busi-ness what I do an' I reckon I'm stronger than you, so it's you as can get off home. But you can give that dog back to me afore you go so that I can finish what I started. If I don't, my dad will belt me.' He took a step forward, hands reaching out to take the puppy.

She turned to run, but his friends had moved to either side of her to prevent escape. Her heart was thudding now because they had a gloating look on their faces and there was no one within earshot if she called for help. But she couldn't, she just couldn't give them back their victim, which was still pressed against her in a warm, shivering bundle.

And then someone stepped out from behind a nearby tree and shoved Huey away from her. 'Leave the lass alone!' ordered a deep voice.

She looked in relief at the man now standing between her and the three bullies, a man who looked as if he could take care of himself. He was tall, his dark hair sun-streaked and his skin tanned, as if he'd spent a long time in the sun. He was almost good-looking, but his nose was too long for that and there were deep creases in his cheeks. His clothes were shabby and hung on him as if he'd lost weight, but they were well cared for, and he was clean shaven, unlike most men, without even a hint of side-whiskers.

The three lads moved closer together and Huey opened his mouth to answer back but at a glare from the stranger, he closed it again. That surprised her. Not many folk could face down a bully with only a look, especially when it was one against three, for these were well-grown lads of fifteen or so, not children.

'Be off with you,' the stranger repeated.

Huey hefted the stone in his hand and all hung in the balance for a moment or two, then he hurled it towards the river. They shuffled away with occasional backward scowls and when they were out of reach, Huey turned to yell, 'You'll be sorry, Dora Preston!'

She could guess that she'd be at the receiving end of rubbish thrown in the street for some time to come. She'd seen these three do it to others, usually people weaker than themselves. Once it had been an old man who hadn't got out of their way quickly enough. The police constable had stopped that eventually and had a word with them. Well, she didn't care if they did pick on her. She'd saved the puppy and that was what counted. She smiled at the stranger. 'Thanks ever so much. I don't know what I'd have done without you.'

'It's a good thing I heard you shouting. You were foolhardy to stand up to them on your own, lass.'

She looked down at the puppy, now nestled trustingly against her as if he knew there was no longer anything to fear. 'I couldn't let that Huey kill him.'

'He's hurt. Let me have a look at him.'

As the man took the puppy from her, she saw that his right hand was missing parts of the first three fingers and the injury still bore the fading red of skin healed recently. She could tell that he was waiting for her to flinch away from it as other people had probably done.

'I had an accident. Doesn't hold me back much,' he said off-handedly.

'We're used to accidents like that in a mill. One of my friends lost part of her little finger when it got caught in the machinery. She said it didn't hurt till over an hour afterwards. It stopped her working for a week or two, though. How did you do yours?'

'I was in the Army. A rifle exploded.' He looked down at his hand and a bitter smile twisted his face. 'This stopped me for longer than a week or two because it got infected. They thought I was going to die.' He stared at it, then added in a low voice, as if talking to himself, 'Sometimes I wish I had.'

She didn't know what to say to that. You couldn't ask too many personal questions of a complete stranger.

He glanced at the river then back at the pup, changing the subject completely. 'We could wash its injuries, if you like. It's best to keep wounds clean.'

'Oh, yes. The water will be all right here because we're upstream of the dye works. On the other side of the mill where I work the river was bright red today with the run-off.'

He stopped at the edge of the water to look sideways at her. 'My name's Gideon. Yours is Dora, I think that lout said?'

'Yes.' She pulled a face. 'Such a silly little name, Dora.'

His smile warmed his whole face and quite took her breath away, and somehow now he seemed good-looking. 'What would you like to be called if you could choose?'

'Anything except Dora. It's short for Theodora, which is even worse. My mother chose stupid fancy names for all of us girls.'

'I think Dora suits you. It's a nice, neat name.'

She didn't know what to say to that, but wished he hadn't described her in such an ordinary way – nice, neat! – she'd rather he'd said she was pretty. She held out her hands for the puppy, but he moved with it to the edge of the water.

'I'll wash him. You'll get your skirt wet, and my boots are fairly waterproof.'

'It doesn't matter. These are only my working clothes and they're all sweaty today. It was so hot in the mill.'

'It must be hard work keeping those bobbins going.'

'Yes, and boring, but there's not many other ways for lasses to earn their bread in Hedderby – unless you go into service, and I don't fancy that at all. They watch you all the time in service. At least your free time is your own when you work in a mill.' She couldn't hold back a sigh. 'I'd love to do something more interesting, though. One of my older sisters works in music halls, in a comedy act with her husband. Imagine travelling all over the country and wearing pretty clothes every day. She has some lovely clothes.' She looked down at herself and grimaced. 'She used to work in the mill, too, but what she's doing now is a lot better.'

'Travelling's not always pleasant, especially in winter. Anyway, you'll probably get wed one day, then you'll be able to stop working at the mill.'

'Hah! There are lots of married women in the mill. They have to keep working there to feed their children. They come in tired in the mornings and they go away even more tired at night. And when they get home they still have their families to look after. I don't want to live like that.'

He crouched in the shallow water, immersing the puppy,

calming it when it panicked and gently cleaning the blood off with the fingertips of his left hand. 'I don't think there's any serious harm done, just cuts and bruises.' When he'd finished, he held up the little creature eye to eye and smiled at it. 'Now, young fellow, I hope you're duly grateful to Miss Dora.'

The puppy let out a shrill bark and tried to lick his nose, which brought another of those wonderful smiles to his face. Dora sighed, wishing she could stay here talking to him, but the light was fading and it must be tea time. 'I'd best be getting home. They'll be wondering where I've got to.'

'What shall we do with this little fellow?'

'I'll have to take him with me. I'm not leaving him here to be killed.' As she spoke she caressed the puppy, who licked her hand and bared his sharp white teeth in what looked like a grin. Her movement brought her close to Gideon and she found herself staring up at him, her breath catching in her throat again. He was such a fine figure of a man and kind with it. She wanted to know him better. And she could tell that he too felt that instant attraction between them from the way he was looking at her.

Then his smile faded and he took a step backwards. 'Don't!' His voice was harsh now, no hint of a smile.

'What do you mean?'

'Don't look at me like that. I'm not for young girls like you. I've seen too much, done too much . . .' His voice cut off abruptly and he closed his eyes, taking a deep breath and letting it out slowly. When he opened his eyes again, he seemed cool and distant, the smile gone completely. 'I'll walk you back to the streets where you should be safe from those three louts.'

He did so in silence then handed her the puppy. 'Here you are. You'll be all right now.' After a nod of farewell he strode off along the main street.

She stood and watched him go, wondering why he had said 'Don't!' to her in such a way when all they had done was look at one another. *All!* Her cheeks grew warm as she thought of how it had felt being close to him. None of the lads she knew had ever made her feel like that.

Then she realised why he'd said it. He was older than her, so of course he'd be married. Yes, that would be why. All the best men were.

She wondered where he lived, what sort of woman he'd married. She'd never seen him before and she knew most people in Hedderby by sight. Now that she came to think of it, he hadn't spoken like someone from her town, either, though he didn't have a southern accent as some of the performers at her brother-in-law's music saloon did. Strange.

And why she was standing here thinking about him instead of making her way home, she didn't know.

That same morning Eli Beckett received a letter he'd been waiting for impatiently. He tore it open right there by the door, read it quickly, then went to find his wife. 'Carrie, love, that architect we wrote to in London wants to see us to discuss building our music hall.'

She turned from spooning food into their little daughter's mouth, her face lighting up. 'That's marvellous.' Then she noticed his arm. 'Eli, what's happened to your sling? You know the doctor said you should still support that arm till it's properly mended.'

He pulled a face at her. 'It's all right now. He said it was only a simple fracture, though it hurt like hell at the time.'

'As soon as I've finished giving Abigail her breakfast, I'm going to find that sling and you'll wear it if I have to knock you out to fit it on you.'

He grinned. 'You wouldn't win, but we'd have fun trying. Look, love, I'm favouring that arm, not picking anything up with it. I'm not stupid. But I'm going mad with nothing to do. The sooner we get the Pride rebuilt, the sooner we can start bringing in money again.'

'You're a stubborn man, Mr Beckett.'

'And you're a wonderful woman, Mrs Beckett.'

'Oh, go on with you! Read that letter to me while I finish feeding this young madam.' Expertly she used the spoon to catch the food now decorating her daughter's chin and slipped the mush into Abigail's mouth again.

My dear Mr Beckett,

I found the letter from you and Mr Jeremiah Channon very interesting and am sorry for the troubles you've had with your music saloon. I don't like to think of someone impersonating a member of my profession like that and building the sort of theatre that falls down. I'm glad you caught the miscreant.

I'm very busy but I do want to help you. I haven't the time to design a new theatre for you, but I could modify a previous design. Since your neighbour Mr Channon is a responsible architect, he would be able to supervise the day-to-day work.

I wonder if the three of you could come down to see me in London to discuss it, bringing measurements and site plans? For the coming week you can find me any afternoon at the above address, but after that I shall be travelling part of the time.

Yours sincerely,
Saul Barton

Eli and Carrie beamed at one another.

'No fear of him cheating us like that other fellow did,' she said. 'Barton has an excellent reputation, Jeremiah says. When do you want to go to London?'

'How about today? Then we can see him tomorrow.'

She gaped at him in shock. 'Today? But . . . what about Abigail?'

'Someone in your family would have her for us. There are many advantages to being part of a big family. It wouldn't take a minute to throw some things into a travelling bag. We wouldn't need much for a couple of nights in London. And I know Jeremiah has already made new site plans, so we can just up and go.'

She reached out one hand to clasp his briefly. 'I'm still getting used to having the old Eli back, the one who's always impatient and wants to do things yesterday.'

He shuddered. 'I'm glad I can't remember those months after the Pride burned down, from what you tell me about how I behaved. Getting hit on the head when the new building collapsed was a blessing in disguise.' He looked at her expectantly. 'Well? Can we go down to London today?'

'Why not? You go and see Jeremiah, ask if it's convenient for him, and I'll nip round to Gwynna's to see if she'll have Abigail. If we bustle, we can catch the midday train. I just hope we can find somewhere decent to stay. It'll be quite late when we arrive and—'

But Eli had already left.

As she went into the house Dora braced herself for arguments. In the kitchen savoury smells filled the air and made her mouth water. There was no sign of her stepfather Nev, but her step-mother was stirring something on the stove and her little sisters were setting the table. Raife was sitting in his usual corner reading a newspaper. He was a great one for reading newspapers. She smiled just to see him. Nev's father was like a kindly grand-father to them all, though he wasn't really a relative, and she was hoping desperately that he'd be on her side about the dog.

Essie turned to greet her, spoon in hand, and stared. 'What have you got there?'

'It's a puppy. He is, I mean. That Huey Benting had him tied up and was trying to kill him by throwing stones at him, so I rescued the poor little thing. Then Huey and his friends turned on me, but a man came along and sent them away.'

'No need to bring the puppy home with you,' Essie said sharply.

'He doesn't belong to anyone and if I let him go, those three will catch him again and kill him. Anyway, he's a lovely little fellow, aren't you?'

By that time her sisters had come over and were stroking the puppy, making cooing noises at him. Dora looked at Raife plead-ingly over their heads and he winked at her, so she said it straight out, 'I thought we could keep him and—'

'Oh, no! We definitely don't need a dog,' Essie said at once. 'They're a lot of trouble and they make a right old mess of the floor in wet weather. Let it loose on the other side of town then that Huey won't find it.'

'He will. I know he will. And anyway . . . I don't want to let the puppy go. He's the dearest little creature.'

Essie sighed. 'Look, love, you're not here most of the day. It'd be left to me to deal with the puppy and I don't have the time or inclination with three toddlers in the house as well as you lot.'

'I could look after him for you,' Raife said in a mild voice. 'I'd like a puppy to keep me company. I had a dog when I was a lad. They make good friends if you train them properly and you know I'd do that, Essie.'

Dora held her breath, willing her stepmother to change her mind. 'Please,' she said softly when the silence continued. 'He's such a little love. Look at the way one ear flops over at the top.'

'He may be little now but he'll grow bigger,' Essie said. 'They always do.'

'I don't think this one will grow very big.' Raife took the puppy out of Dora's arms to examine it more closely. 'Look at his feet. They're small and neat. Puppies that are going to grow big have much larger feet compared to their bodies. I think this one will be quite a small dog.'

The puppy swiped a quick lick at his chin then looked round, bright-eyed, from one person to the other, as if he knew they were discussing him.

'He must have a nice nature. If he's been ill-treated, it's not made him snap at anyone. And see what an intelligent look he has in his eyes.' Raife looked at Essie. 'I'll see to him in the daytime, love. Time hangs a bit heavy for me since the music saloon burnt down, so I'd be glad of the company. Eh, I miss playing the piano there, I do that.'

Essie threw up her hands. 'On your own head be it, but what my Nev will say when he gets back, I don't know. Just make sure you keep that creature from under my feet, clear up after him out back and don't let him traipse mud into the house when it's wet.'

'We will.' He winked across the room again.

'What are you going to call him?' Grace asked.

'I don't know.' Dora took the puppy from Raife. 'What are you called?' she asked it.

The dog put its head on one side, then gave her finger a small, experimental bite.

'Ow!' She looked at him and then slowly smiled. 'Are you telling me we should call you Nippy?' When he let out a soft woof and gave her another of his doggy grins as if to approve, everyone laughed.

'Nippy it is, then,' Raife said. 'Now, Essie love, I reckon this young fellow needs something to eat. Have we got any scraps?'

She sighed and spread her hands in a gesture of surrender. 'Yes. Get two of those old tin bowls off the shelf in the scullery and give him a drink of milk first. Better wait a bit then to give him food if he's been clemming or he'll make himself sick. He's very thin.'

'I'll get it for him,' Gracie said at once.

'No. He's your sister's pet so she must be the one who looks after him when she's at home,' Essie said firmly. 'And we'll get one thing straight from the start. When you get married, Dora, the dog goes with you.'

The girl looked at her in amazement. 'I'm not even walking out with a fellow, let alone thinking of getting wed.'

'You're nineteen and pretty. It's bound to happen within the next year or two, and I'm not being left with a dog.'

Dora pulled a face. There was yet another reason for not getting married, though she didn't say it now. If she was anything like her mother, she'd have one baby after the other. Eleven of her mother's babies had lived and a few others had died, but bearing the final one had killed her mother and it was a good job Nev had married Essie because she was raising the child. Dora's earliest memories were of minding a little brother or sister, or changing a dirty clout, and she'd had enough of it, thank you very much. To her relief, Essie turned her attention to someone else.

'Gracie! Hurry up and finish setting that table. I'll be serving the meal as soon as your brother gets home.'

'Aren't you waiting for Carrie and Eli?' Dora walked across to the scullery for the old bowls.

'They've gone off to London for a couple of days to see an architect about rebuilding the Pride, so your niece has gone to stay with Gwynna. Eh, it'd never have been possible to gallivant about like that when I was young, but now people can set off for London by train without thinking twice about it.'

Nev came in just then, smiling round at everyone then going to hug his wife. 'That smells good, love. I'm a bit sharp-set tonight. Eh, who's this?' He stared across the room at Nippy, who was far too busy gulping down the last of the milk and polishing the empty bowl with his tongue to pay the newcomer any attention.

'It's Dora's dog,' Raife said. 'But I reckon we s'll all enjoy having him.'

Nev beamed at them. 'Eh, yes. I've allus wanted a dog.'

Dora heaved a sigh of relief. Essie would do anything to keep Nev happy. The two of them had married late in life after Dora's mother died, but were more like young lovers than old ones, showing fondness for one another in word and deed. Her younger brother and next sister Edith came in shortly afterwards and by the time she'd explained Nippy's presence to them, the food was on the table. And good food it was too. No going without in this house, thanks to Nev's ability to turn a penny into a shilling.

Essie waited till everyone had been served to continue her explanation of why their eldest sister was missing. 'Carrie and Eli had a letter today from some architect in London who builds theatres and it seems he can design them a new one. So they went down to see him and Mr Channon went with them. He's going to oversee the building and do it properly this time, so that it won't fall down. Eli was that set up about it. Now he's better, he's itching to get his music saloon up and running again.'

'Music halls they're starting to call those places now,' Raife reminded her. 'And this one's going to be much fancier than the old one.'

'We'll all be glad to have our shows back, shan't we?' Nev said. 'There were so many clever folk playing at the Pride – singers, acrobats, minstrels, even dogs.' He looked across at Nippy who was standing by his now empty bowl, sporting a milky moustache and wagging hopefully. 'Would you like to go on the stage, young fellow?'

This time the dog came across to sniff the newcomer's feet and look up at him with a bright, expectant air.

'He looks hungry.'

'No feeding him scraps from the table,' Raife said firmly, 'else he'll be a pest at meal times. Our Nippy's going to be the best-behaved dog in Hedderby.'

'He'd better be,' Essie said. But she found Nippy some scraps after the meal was over and smiled as he ate them, so everyone could see that she was gradually being won over.

Later on they all sat drinking their usual cup of hot milk and honey before they went to bed. Dora watched happily as the puppy sighed in its sleep and turned over, snuggling down in the old basket Essie had found for him, warm and comfortable on top of the ragged blanket Essie had provided without anyone asking.

'We must agree on the words we use to train that dog,' Raife said, following Dora's gaze. 'We don't want to confuse him by one person saying something and another saying something else.'

His son looked at him across the fire. 'Mother would never have a dog in the house, but you had one while you were living with my brother, didn't you, Dad? I don't rightly know how to treat them or what to expect, so you'll have to show us.'

'You treat puppies as you would any of God's young creatures, son, with firmness and kindness. Everyone responds to kindness, but all youngsters have to be taught what's right and wrong.'

Dora edged closer to Nippy, putting out one hand to stroke him.

'Let him sleep, lass,' Raife said. 'He's had a confusing day.'

So had she, Dora thought, taking another mouthful of warm milk and remembering her reaction to Gideon. She couldn't seem to get him out of her mind . . . but she didn't want to share that information with anyone.

'I'm not for young girls like you,' he'd said.

Was he married or was there some other reason for him saying that? And what was he doing in Hedderby? She very much wanted to know.

2

When he left Dora, Gideon Shaw felt guilty about treating her so harshly. What had got into him to say that when she'd only looked at him? He stopped walking for a moment as he admitted to himself what it was: fear. He was afraid of the sudden attraction he'd felt for her, because it was the first time he'd noticed a woman in that way for over a year. Though why he should be so attracted to Dora was more than he could work out. She must be ten years younger than him – and had that open sunny look to her that said life hadn't treated her badly. Maybe that was what attracted him, but it wouldn't be fair to bring his dark memories and present problems into her life.

Annoyed with himself for letting the thought of her distract him and telling himself she was just another pretty young lass, nothing special about her – he went back to the main street to get directions to his aunt's house. She'd moved to Hedderby while he was in India and he'd never visited the town before. He'd felt so twitchy after a long train ride that he'd gone for a walk first. It was good to have so much energy again, even if he wasn't quite his old self yet.

He soon found someone who knew where Gill Farm Cottages were and set off in that direction. Walking slowly and enjoying the scenery, he made his way up a side road that led towards the moors, looking for a white gate and then a turn-off just beyond it.

He found the lane quite easily and followed it down to the row of four cottages, which sat neatly on top of a small rise looking down into the town. They were whitewashed and the roofs were tiled in slate, charcoal coloured, with a few newer slates showing here and there. They looked capable of withstanding the wind and weather, nothing fancy, just solid dwellings for farm workers, built before the town grew so big.

His aunt was his only surviving relative and he was looking forward so much to seeing her. After his parents died he'd joined the Army and his aunt had written to him, telling him to come and stay with her whenever he got leave. The words had been printed out carefully as a child's, because she'd learned to read and write late in life, but the warmth of her affection had still showed through. While he was in India she'd written to tell him of her second marriage and given him her new name and address. Sam Haskill, it seemed, was a prudent man and was well set up in his old age, owning these cottages.

Gideon had written back, promising he'd come to see her again as soon as he returned to England. But his posting overseas had lasted longer than he'd expected, nearly ten years in fact. His last message from her, smeared with tears, had been to tell him that her Sam had passed away suddenly.

He was a little nervous of just turning up at her house, but every time he'd tried to write a letter, he'd got in a tangle of explanations, so in the end he'd decided to explain about his life in person. She was the only person left to care about him, his only close relative in all of England. Suddenly he couldn't wait to see her.

He knocked on the door of Number One, surprised at how dull the windows looked because his aunt usually kept everything sparkling clean. There was no answer, so he knocked again, but still no one came.

A woman peered out of the door of the next house. 'He's not there. He's gone away for a few days.'

Gideon took off his cap and nodded to her. 'He? I thought Mrs Haskill lived here.'

'She did, but she died a few months ago, poor soul. Her nephew inherited the cottages and he's living there now, for part of the time, at least.'

Dead? His aunt was dead? Grief pierced him and it was a

moment before what the woman had said sank in. 'Nephew? But—' Gideon was the only nephew she had. He knew that for certain. What's more Sam Haskill had been childless, last of the Haskills, his aunt had told him, so there was no one on his side to inherit. Biting back the hot words of protest because he'd learned the hard way over the past few years not to rush into anything heedlessly, he asked, 'What's his name, this nephew?'

She gave a sniff. 'Gideon John Shaw, it said on the piece of paper the lawyer sent us. He doesn't make anyone free of his first name, though. We have to call him *Mr Shaw* because he's the landlord. Polly and Sam weren't uppity like that with their neighbours.'

The world spun round and Gideon clutched the door frame for a moment. That was *his* name! It didn't take much thought to work out that someone must be pretending to be him. But he didn't say that, only asked, 'It was her lawyer who sent you the letter, was it, the one about her nephew?'

'Yes. Mr Hordle, he's called. He's well respected in the town, has rooms on Market Street, at the far end from the station. You can't miss his place. It's a big house with a brass sign on the wall near the door.'

He nodded, unable to think what to ask next. Surely he should be asking questions? But his mind seemed to be going round in circles. The worst thing of all was that his aunt was dead. He'd never see her again, never feel her arms round him. And he hadn't even been here for the funeral, hadn't said a proper farewell.

The neighbour came along the footpath that led along the front of all four cottages and put a hand on his arm. 'Are you all right, love? You look a bit pale.'

'Yes.' He swallowed hard. 'I was just – um – shocked to hear that Mrs Haskill was dead. She was kind to me once or twice when she lived near my family, and she said I should come and see her if I was passing through Hedderby.'

'Aw, what a shame! Shall I tell Mr Shaw you called?'

'No. No, it was her I wanted to see. I've never met the fellow. How did she die? Do you know?'

'Yes. She'd not been well and I'd been popping in to help her. Then one morning I found her dead, just lying there in bed, really peaceful she looked. The doctor said her heart had given out and she'd have felt nothing. It's how we'd all like to go, that, isn't it?'

'Yes. Um – where is she buried?'

'In the cemetery, against the back wall. You can't miss it. She's buried with her husband. She bought a plot for two when he passed away. The lawyer arranged the funeral and had her name engraved on the headstone next to Sam's. It's just a simple square headstone. She wasn't one for fancy things.'

'Thank you for telling me. I'll call in at the cemetery and pay my respects.'

'That'll be more than the nephew has. He hasn't looked after her grave. I went and weeded it for her last week, couldn't stand seeing it like that. All *he* was interested in was the cottages and our rent money.'

Gideon made a non-committal noise in his throat, jammed his cap on his head and began walking back towards the town centre. He stopped once he was out of sight of the cottage to sit on the dry-stone wall that bordered a field and try to work out what to do. He felt angry. He wasn't greedy, but the cottages should have come to him. Some impostor had stolen his name and inheritance. Only . . . after what had happened to him since his arrival in England, how was he to prove who he was and get it back?

Someone had taken his personal possessions during his long illness during the voyage back to England. He'd come with a group of sick men from different regiments and the paperwork that had come with him had been lost, so no one at the infirmary had known for certain who he was.

He'd been out of his senses for days, hadn't even known they'd landed, and when he did recover he'd found himself in a military hospital, too weak to do anything. And as he hadn't been formally discharged, he hadn't been able to leave the infirmary. *He* had known who he was, once he'd recovered, but they wouldn't take his word for it when he claimed to be a sergeant. As a result, they hadn't even paid him the full amount they owed him in back wages, only what a ranker would earn. They said he could be cheating, pretending to be someone else. He still grew angry every time he thought about that.

They'd promised to send away to India for proper identification and he'd given them his aunt's address so that they could let him know what happened and maybe pay him the rest of what they owed him. But that was as far as they would go. And now he'd have to send them another address, because any letter sent to the cottages would fall into the hands of that damned thief.

With a sigh he got up off the wall. It was getting late and the first thing to do was not chase after impostors but find somewhere to stay for a few days. He still wasn't his old self and he felt weary now.

In the morning he'd think what to do next. Surely there must be some way of reclaiming what was his?

In a small Irish village Ishleen Milane watched stony-faced as they buried her infant son. The tiny coffin had been fashioned out of scraps of rough wood by one of her neighbours and she'd prepared Danny's body herself, pressing a last loving kiss on his cold cheek.

Her husband had been no use. Milo had wept a few easy tears when informed that his son had died, then gone out and got drunk – which was his answer to everything. And where he'd found the money to buy the illicit poteen was more than she could tell, for he'd had nothing to give her for food this week.

She wrapped her arms round her body and stared blindly into the hole in the ground. Twenty-five years old, she was, and felt ninety-five today – ancient, weary, worn out. It had been a stranger's face that stared back at her from the mirror hanging on the side wall at church, a gaunt, hollow face framed in dark hair, with eyes that seemed too big for it. It had shocked her, that face had, then she'd shrugged. What did it matter? What did anything matter? The way things were going, she'd be lucky if she was even alive this time next year, they all would.

Two years old he'd been, her Danny, and not strong from the beginning so that other women had warned her not to get too attached. How could you help loving them, though, when they nursed at your breast? It had hurt to lose him, hurt so much she didn't dare start to cry because if she once did, she'd never stop and she still had a daughter to look after. On that thought she looked down at Shanna, who was holding her hand. Her little girl was too thin by far, like all the children in the village.

And yet, if they shared food out fairly in this world, her son might still be alive. Everyone knew that Mr Maltravers up at the big house had a table loaded with food every single day, three times a day, and his agent ate just as well. Their English servants, God forgive them, threw the leftovers to the landlord's plump pigs, while down in the village people were more than half starved.

It had been different when Mrs Maltravers was alive. She'd helped the poorer tenants through the first two years of crop loss due to the potato blight. Then she'd died suddenly and her husband had stopped providing free soup and bread, though they'd begged him to continue with it for the children, at least. Even so, they'd thought they'd manage – just! – because last year the potatoes had grown again, not well, but at least the blight hadn't rotted them. Only no one had the money to buy seed potatoes, so the crop they'd grown hadn't been big enough to see them through till the next harvest, not if they kept some for seed. Well, a new crop was growing in the fields around her now, the plant tops green, not that dreadful sickly yellow, and soon they'd be able to lift a few early potatoes. *Please, God, keep that crop safe!* she prayed.

Her husband put his arm round her shoulders and she shook him off, walking away from the churchyard without a backward glance and taking Shanna with her. There'd be no wake for her son, no gathering of friends and neighbours, because her cupboard was as bare as theirs, and even so Milo had still wasted money on drink. She couldn't forgive him that.

He continued to walk beside her. 'We'll manage somehow.'

'How?' she demanded. 'You've not found work and I can't now.' She pressed one hand against her swelling belly. 'I told you not to start another baby, but you would have your way, couldn't do without my body, you whined. Who but a fool would bring new life into the world when they can't feed the mouths that are here already?'

He fell back then and she was glad, could hardly bear the sight of him since he'd started forcing himself on her. Let him try to force her again after this one was born and she'd take a knife to that part of him, so she would.

If she'd had her way, they'd have gone to England three years ago, to her relatives in Lancashire. The Heegans had written a couple of times, saying they'd be happy to help her and her family settle over there, that there were jobs in the town. But Milo hadn't wanted to leave his bit of land, said he couldn't abide living in a town and didn't want to be dependent on *her* relatives. What he really meant was that he'd have to work harder in a town than he did here and didn't want to leave his drinking friends.

She should have gone on her own with the children. Milo wouldn't have dared to stop her, not if she set her mind to it. But she'd taken her vows in church, couldn't bring herself to dishonour them, even though she'd long ago lost any fondness for such a feckless man.

When they got home she could have wept as she looked at the bare shelves in the kitchen. Unable to settle, she decided to go and pick some nettles to boil up with the two shrivelled potatoes which were all that remained in her wooden storage box. She left Shanna with her neighbour, not trusting a four-year-old child to Milo, who had had little to do with his children. She went into the landowner's woods, not caring if they arrested her for trespassing, because they'd have to feed her in gaol at least.

But she saw no one and since most of the villagers were too frightened of the keepers to forage here, she was able to gather a good, big bundle of nettles which would make soup for tea. She handled them carefully, getting only a few blisters, and carried them home in her shawl. She even sat for a while on a log that tempted her because it lay bathed in sunlight. Holding her face up to the warmth, she enjoyed a rare moment of peace.

Back at the house she found the two potatoes missing, with a patch scraped among the ashes where Milo must have cooked them. She felt sick with disgust that he'd take the last mouthful from their child and when he came in she flew at him, attacking with nails and feet, whatever she could find to hurt him.

'You took the last of the food! Your child will go hungry tonight. What sort of a man do you call yourself?'

Even as she spoke Shanna came in. 'Did you find some nettles, Mam?'

He stared from her to their daughter, then down at the bundle of wilting green plants as it got through to him what he'd done. Ishleen could see the realisation dawn on his face, and with it regret. Well, regret wouldn't fill their daughter's belly.

'I'm sorry,' he muttered. 'I didn't think. I was just so hungry I ate them half raw.'

'The whole village is hungry. But we try to feed our children, at least. Ah, get out of my sight, will you. I can't bear to see you. You're acting like a greedy gossoon, not a man grown!'

She went to get some water. It'd be nettle soup and nothing else tonight for her and her daughter, and she wasn't giving him any. She didn't care for herself, because she didn't seem to feel hungry any more, but she cared for Shanna, who deserved a better chance at life than this.

Dusk was turning into night as Gideon approached the town centre. When he heard the shouts and whimpers echoing down an alley that led off the main street, he hesitated. He'd rescued one person today and that was surely enough. Besides, it sounded as if there were several people involved in this scuffle and he'd no mind to risk a beating.

But a shrill cry of pain which sounded as if it came from a child went straight to his heart and cursing himself for a fool, he turned abruptly to investigate. No need to walk quietly up the alley. Whoever was round the bend in it was making too much noise to notice his approach.

When he got to the other end he groaned. Same three louts. Did they do nothing but hurt others? Why had no one in the town taught them a sharp lesson or two? He'd guess this second attack would be to make them feel better about the failure of their earlier one on the puppy and girl. Bullies were like that. The trouble was, they were out of sight of the street here and this time, his loud Army voice might not be enough to make them back off.

Just as he'd made up his mind to intervence anyway, another man came rushing down the alley from the upper end yelling, 'Stop that, you young devils!'

They turned towards the newcomer, fists clenched, bodies tensed in that mindless way that said their blood lust was up and they'd not be stopped easily. Gideon didn't hesitate now but went to help, grabbing the nearest youth by the back of his jacket and hurling him to one side, so that he hit the wall hard and slid to the ground, winded.

The other man was tall and well built. He made short work of sending the other two louts clattering off up the alley. The third one got to his feet and rather than face two grown men, stumbled away down the hill in the other direction from his friends rather than pass the two men.

Gideon bent over the victim, a thin youth with a badly bruised face. He helped him to his feet. 'Are you all right, lad?'

'Yes, thank you, mister.' The words came out thickly and as he spoke, the lad's arm jerked in an uncontrolled way. Gideon had seen others like that, with a palsied arm, some of them idiots, but this one had a bright, intelligent look in his eyes.

The stranger clearly knew the lad. 'Let's be having a look at you, Barney,' he said with a marked Irish accent as he brushed down the shabby clothes. 'Your grandma will have to mend that jacket for you. Eh, that's a bad bruise on your cheek. What made them attack you this time?'

The victim spoke in a halting way, as if his voice was being strained through a piece of cloth. 'Don't know. Shouldn't have – come down Crookit Walk. Should have taken – long way round. Safer.'

'I stopped those three killing a puppy earlier on today,' Gideon said, 'so they were probably ripe to take out their disappointment on someone else.'

The other man turned to him. 'Thanks for coming to my help.'

'I doubt you needed it.'

'It's always good to end a fight quickly.' He stuck one hand out. 'Declan Heegan.'

'Gideon – um – Potter.' The one thing he'd decided was not to reveal who he was until he found out more about his legal situation, but he hadn't worked out a new name for himself, so grabbed at the first one to come to mind.

Declan's eyes rested on him for a moment as if he'd understood the reason for that hesitation, then he looked down at the hand he was shaking. 'Looks like you've been in the wars yourself.'

'It's an old injury. Doesn't hold me back much now,' Gideon said automatically.

The big man looked at him searchingly. 'You're a stranger to the town?'

'Yes. I'm looking for work and a place to settle. Just been invalided out of the Army. Not got any family left.' He held up the injured hand again. 'You can't fire a rifle without a forefinger, can you?'

'What kind of work are you seeking?'

'Any kind, as long as it's honest.'

'Can you read and write?'

'Oh, yes.' He smiled wryly. 'Actually, I was a sergeant in the Army, for what that's worth.'

'Better and better. I can probably find you work, but it'll come and go, won't be steady.'

'I'd be grateful for a start till I get used to things here.'

'Where are you staying?'

'I've yet to find lodgings.'

Declan looked at Barney, who had stayed close to them and kept looking anxiously over his shoulder. 'Do you think your grandmother would find a bed for Mr Potter?'

'Front room's empty. Gran had to pawn the furniture when I was ill. She could do with the money, though.'

'Then I'll walk you back home and introduce Mr – um – Potter to her, after which we'll find him a bed.'

Gideon saw him grin as he said that 'um', so it was clear he'd guessed it was an assumed name.

'Granny Horne runs a clean house and is as honest as they come.' Gideon nodded.

It wasn't far to go and they stopped at a narrow house in a terrace of similar dwellings partway up the hill. Barney went inside first, calling, 'It's me, Gran. Mr Heegan's with me.'

They walked along a narrow corridor past a room that was bare of furniture and into a rear kitchen that was sparsely furnished.

'Eh, Barney, love! What's happened to you?'

'Fell over.'

'That you didn't. Someone's been attacking you again. Who was it? I'll give them what for.'

'Huey Benting,' Declan said, 'and his two nasty little play-mates.'

Gideon watched the anger fade from the old woman's face, to be replaced by apprehension, and wondered why.

'I'll have a word with them for you,' Declan said.

'You already did and it didn't last long. Them rascals have stopped listening to anyone lately. If no one's around, they do what they want. Someone broke my front window last week and I reckon it was them. They've got a real down on my Barney, I can't understand why.'

Declan shook his head. 'Well, we may all be able to help one another. My friend here came to Barney's aid and it turns out he's new to the town, looking for lodgings. You've an empty front room. How about letting him have it? He knows how to handle himself and if he's here, you'll be safe at night.'

She looked at him sadly. 'If I still had the furniture, I'd say yes like a shot.'

'I can get some furniture of my own,' Gideon volunteered, liking the look of her. 'Or we can redeem yours.'

She brightened. 'That'd be champion. I'm a good cook when I have summat to cook. And I can do your washing for you, too.'

'We've a bargain then.' Gideon looked out of the window. 'It's getting late. I'd better fetch my things from the station. I can sleep on the floor tonight if you have a spare blanket.'

She flushed and shook her head. 'They were pawned too.'

'I can lend you a couple of those,' Declan said. 'Do you need a hand with your things?'

'No. I've only a bag to pick up. The stationmaster let me leave it with him.' His voice became mocking. 'All my worldly possessions are in that bag.'

The Irishman grinned. 'I'll come with you in case those young devils are still on the prowl. Look, Granny, we'll go and get his stuff and on the way back we'll buy some pies for tea.' He hustled Gideon out of the house as tears filled the old woman's eyes. 'She hates people to see her crying, but you're a godsend to her. Your things will be safe here. She's as honest as they come.'

'She seems a nice woman. The place may be bare, but it's clean, which matters to me.'

'Salt of the earth, Granny is. She's brought up Barney single-handed because her daughter wasn't married and ran off after she had a crippled baby.'

As the two men strode down the hill, Gideon asked, 'Can we do something to stop those louts attacking Barney?'

Declan grinned. 'I'll see that they leave him alone and I have a few friends who'll keep an eye out for him. Having a word with Huey wasn't enough, clearly. This time I'll have to hammer my instructions home.'

Gideon didn't argue. He'd learned in the Army that there were some fellows who only seemed to understand brute force.

'When do you want to start work?'

'Not tomorrow, if you don't mind. I'll need to get my bearings and help Granny get the room furnished again. Maybe the day after?'

'Barney will show you where to find me. What I'll be wanting you to do is help out at the markets, in case you're interested.'

'That's fine by me. I'll do anything honest.' Gideon had enough money to tide him over for a while, but it'd look strange if he didn't get some sort of job. And anyway, he wasn't one for idling around.

3

The next day, as he walked through the big yard that sep-
arated his house from the mill, James Forrett looked idly
up at the windows of the huge building full of spindles and noise.
He hadn't felt like doing much lately, not since the death of his
infant daughter, though he'd made sure his stupid damned wife,
who'd accidentally killed their child in her permanent state of
laudanum-induced fog, was locked away safely in a home for
ladies who didn't know what they were doing.

But today things seemed different somehow. The sun was
shining brightly and it lifted your spirits, made you want to get
busy.

He'd walked nearly to the door of the office where he spent
most of his time during the day when something occurred to
him and he turned to squint up at the mill again. The windows
were all closed. That wasn't right. There should be a few open
on a day like this or the lasses inside would be too uncomfortable to work properly. He didn't believe in pampering his operatives, had always felt scornful of the morals of the noisy women
who worked here, but lately his feelings towards them had
changed. He smiled. All due to young Gwynna, who had worked
for him as a nursemaid and a nicer, more caring lass you couldn't
hope to meet, for all she'd a clouded background. She had made
him realise you shouldn't judge folk till you knew them.

As he entered the mill the stifling humidity hit him in the face
and made him gasp, bringing sweat instantly to his brow, for he
was one who couldn't cope with too much heat. What was going
on here? Were there no windows open on either side?

He could see no sign of his overlooker so he walked across to the nearest bank of windows and used the long winding pole to open the top ones himself.

'Thanks, mester!' one of the older women called. 'I were nearly fainting wi' the heat.'

He walked across to her station. 'Can't have you doing that, Betty, can we? Who'd do my work for me then?'

'There's a few have fainted in here lately,' she said bluntly, trading on the fact that she'd worked here longer than anyone else and known him as a lad. 'The heat's been getting us all down lately, I can tell you.'

He looked at her flushed face in concern. 'Well, I shall have to see that the windows are opened from now on whenever the weather's warm, shan't I?'

'*He* won't like it.'

But that was going too far. He wasn't trying to undermine the overlooker's authority. 'Get on with your work now, lass, and don't waste any more time gossiping.'

A voice roared from the other end of the long room, 'Shut them damned windows!'

James moved to the side of the room to stand near the windows, where he wasn't hidden by the machinery. 'I think we'll have some of 'em open today, Benting,' he said mildly as his over-looker joined him. 'We don't want the lasses fainting on us.'

'You can work the cotton better if the air's warm and moist.'

'I know. But the lasses don't work better if it's too hot and without them we'll get no cotton spun. Now think on, I want them windows opened every warm day.'

They began walking towards the front of the building. 'You don't usually come in here,' Benting said in an aggrieved tone.

That also was going too far. 'I hope you aren't suggesting I should stay out of my own mill?'

The overlooker shrugged. 'You've your own problems. I can run things for you in here, you know I can.'

'I'll hand over the running of this mill to someone else when I die, and not until.' James turned to stare round. 'About time I had a good poke about, I reckon. You've got to keep them on their toes.' But he meant keep his overlooker on his toes, too, and from his scowl, Benting understood that hidden threat perfectly well.

'I'll come round with you, Mr Forrett.'

'No need. I know my way. You get about your business.'

On the next floor he found a lass just recovering from a faint and it came to him that life was hard enough and there was no need to make it harder for these workers, as long as they did what he needed. And if he wanted to be softer with them than he had before, who was to say him nay? He was master here and everyone had better remember that. Everyone.

James visited the three other floors of his mill one by one, opening windows on each and nodding as the lasses called out their thanks to him. When he came back down to the ground floor, he stopped near one bright-eyed lass who was a friend of Gwynna's. 'How's my former nursery maid going on with her new husband?'

'She's well.'

'Happy, is she?'

The lass looked at him. 'Why don't you go and ask her yourself, Mr Forrett. She allus speaks kindly of you. She'd be right glad to see you.'

He pursed his lips at this novel idea. 'I might just do that, Dora.'

She darted off to attend to one of her bobbins and he watched, enjoying the speed with which she dealt with the broken thread, her fingers deft and sure. He nodded approval and walked away. Maybe he'd been wrong to consider these young lasses to be of low morals, just because they were more independent and outspoken than women usually were.

Eh, he was getting soft in his old age. He'd better watch himself.

Benting went round after his master had left, annoyed about the windows and the sly smiles of the women. What had got into Forrett to interfere like that? It made Benting look bad in the eyes of the operatives. He'd have to do something to show them he was still a man to be feared.

He saw Dora mouthing something to the lass on the next set of spindles. She was getting prettier by the year, that one. He'd had his eye on her for a while. Maybe it was time to act. Bringing her to heel would be a salutary lesson for the others to mind their step with him.

Dora didn't like the way Benting was looking at her this morning, like a cat about to pounce on a poor helpless bird. 'What's wrong with him today?' she asked the woman working next to her.

Her companion hesitated, then looked over her shoulder before saying, 'He's been nowty for a week or two. He's allus in a bad mood when his wife's close to her time. I overheard him telling one of the draymen that he'd have to start getting his bed rations somewhere else. And the way he's been staring at you . . . Well, I wouldn't go out to the necessary on your own, if I were you.'

Dora stared at her aghast.

Her friend tapped her nose. 'I never said a thing, mind.'

Dora went on working, but the other woman's words kept echoing in her brain. When Benting chose a mill lass, heaven help her if she didn't give her body to him. He seemed to have a knack of choosing those who'd cave in to his demands. Most of the time, anyway. He'd tried it on her sister Marjorie and when she'd refused very forcibly, he'd found an excuse to sack her.

Since he'd never really looked at Dora before, she'd hoped he didn't find her attractive, or had learned that the girls from her family weren't easy in their ways.

It seemed she was wrong.

In the past Mr Forrett had done nothing to stop the overlooker pestering the girls, but lately there had been signs that their employer was taking more of an interest in his workers. Look at the way he'd had the windows opened. And he'd had the necessary cleared out last week, as well as a new tap put in the corner of the yard, one you could get water from at any hour of the day. A godsend that tap was, because some taps or street pumps only gave water at certain hours of the day, and you got thirsty with all the cotton fluff. He was letting them fill buckets with it before they went home, too, and some of the women had bought new ones with lids. It was good clean water brought in along pipes by the town's new Water Corporation, perfect for drinking. Some of the lower cottages down the far end of town still relied on wells and the water from those tasted horrible.

For the next two days Dora was very careful not to go to the necessary on her own, but the third day she had a bit of an upset stomach and she couldn't wait any longer. She looked round and made signs to her companions, but no one else wanted to go, so she checked that Benting wasn't around and rushed off.

When she came out, she found him waiting for her at the door to the yard, barring the way back into the mill, smiling.

'I've asked May to keep an eye on your spindles while you're with me,' he said grasping her arm. 'I've something to show you in my office.'

She pulled back, knowing exactly what he meant by that. 'I'm not going in there and I'm not doing it with you. If you try to force me, I'll tell my stepfather and he'll have the law on you.'

His smile windened. 'It'll be done by then and I'll deny it was me, say you've been going with all the lads – and my son and his friends will bear me out on that. They're very unhappy at you interfering with their pleasures.'

'Pleasures! Killing a puppy!'

His voice took on a coaxing tone. 'You'll find it to your advantage to behave yourself, Dora. I can make things easier for you here.'

He tried to pull her along and she resisted. 'Mr Forrett won't let you force me.'

'Mr Forrett is out. He won't know what's happening till too late and then he'll believe me, not you. He doesn't think much of mill lasses' morals anyway.' This time he tugged her hard and jerked her forward a few steps.

She kicked and struggled, screaming at the top of her voice. But she knew that only the women who worked near the door would hear her because of the noise of the machinery, and they were the ones who'd be most afraid to lose their jobs if they helped her. He'd stationed them there when he first started preying on the lasses.

He wasn't a tall man, but he was much stronger than she was and for all her struggling he continued to drag her towards his office step by step.

Then suddenly he jerked and let go of her, so that she fell over, bumping hard against the wall. Rubbing her elbow, she looked up to see Mr Forrett standing there.

'What the hell are you doing, Benting?' he shouted.

'Having a bit of fun.'

'The lass didn't seem to be enjoying herself.'

'Aw, she was just playing, weren't you, Dora?'

She thrust herself to her feet and heaven help her, she hesitated for a moment, knowing her working life would be made miserable if she didn't agree with him. But she couldn't do it. 'No, I wasn't. He was going to force me and I've never been with a man, Mr Forrett, never. You shouldn't let him do this to the girls.'

There was silence in the narrow corridor, then James said quietly, 'Get back to work, lass. And say nowt about what happened.'

'They'll have heard me screaming. They'll guess.'

He frowned. 'Why didn't they come and help you, then?'

'They wouldn't dare. He puts the ones who'd have helped a lass in trouble on the upper floors where they can't hear anything.'

He stiffened. 'You mean – this has been going on for a while? The forcing.'

Benting took a hasty step forward. 'Don't listen to her. She's a liar, that one is. I've only gone with lasses as were willing. This one's been leading me on for weeks.' He lunged for Dora.

Forrett held out one arm to keep him back and for a moment the two men glared at one another. Then the millowner turned back to Dora. 'Answer me, girl. Has this been going on for some time?'

Her eyes met Benting's defiantly. 'Yes, sir. It's been going on for years, though some lasses have been willing. But he's forced two others that I know of and he tried to force my sister once. When she wouldn't go with him, he sacked her. He'll probably sack me now.'

Forrett took a deep breath and muttered, 'And I've let it happen. I didn't want to believe . . .' His voice trailed away, then he said, 'Get back to work, lass, and say nothing. This won't happen again and he'll not be sacking you.'

When she'd gone he turned to Benting. 'If you ever try this again, you're out. You can find your fun outside my mill. Them lasses are here to work, not lift their skirts for you. And leave Dora Preston alone.'

'Are you taking her word against mine?'

'I'm taking the evidence of my own eyes. I've seen lasses struggling with you before and told myself they were just larking around, pretending to be reluctant, because they didn't complain to me. But they weren't willing, were they?'

'They're fair game, women as work in the mill,' Benting said sullenly. 'You know how rough they are.'

'I thought I did, but I've had my eyes opened to a few things lately. Any road, I meant what I said. If you do owt else to Dora Preston or try to force any of the others, you'll be out on your ear.' He turned on his heel and went away, scowling blackly.

Dora got back to her work as quickly as she could.

'What happened?' her neighbour mouthed.

'Nothing.'

'I didn't dare come after you when I saw him follow you outside. Sorry.'

Dora didn't even bother to reply to that one. A complete stranger had come to her rescue down by the river. *He* hadn't hesitated to help her. These women were supposed to be her friends and they would have let the overlooker force her.

Shame on them!

Why did men like Benting do such things?

She had no faith whatsoever in Mr Forrett saying this wouldn't happen again. The overlooker would be more careful in future but he'd find a way to get back at her, she was quite sure of that.

What she wasn't sure of was whether to tell Nev. Her step-father was such a kind, soft man, a bit shy. She didn't want him getting beaten up.

It might be best to wait a bit and see how things went. If Benting did nothing further, she wouldn't tell.

Gwynna fed Abigail her dinner, speaking softly to the child, who was missing her mother and still a bit uncertain about being suddenly taken away from her home. She looked up as her husband came through the workshop door. 'Are you hungry, Lucas love? I won't be a minute. Your aunt's nipped out to the baker's for some more bread. That lad you took in is eating us out of house and home.' But she smiled as she said that.

'I can wait for my food. It's a pleasure to see how well Joe is looking, how quickly he's growing now that he's not having to scavenge for food. And he thinks the world of you, Gwynna.'

'I'm fond of him, too, but it's you who rescued him from the streets.'

'Never mind Joe!' Lucas gave her a lingering kiss which had them both breathing more deeply, then sat down at the table watching her. 'It's not often you and I get time on our own.'

'I don't mind. I like living with your family. They're what a family should be like.' Her face clouded for a minute as she thought of her own parents, who spent as much time as they could afford drunk these days and who lived a hand-to-mouth existence. But Lucas had told them in no uncertain terms to stay away from her and they had done for the past few weeks, thank goodness. She pushed the thought of them away, not wanting to spoil this moment. 'Here, you look after Abigail for a minute and I'll cook you some ham. And how about an egg to go with it? I bought some lovely big ones at the market.'

'Sounds wonderful.'

There was a knock on the door and Joe poked his head in. 'Mr Forrett sent a piece of paper for you.' He held it out, looking across at the big stove.

Lucas took it from him. 'Thanks. Get back to work now,

Joe. We'll call you when dinner's ready.' He opened the folded paper.

About time we discussed the orphanage. Come to tea tomorrow
afternoon at four, you and Gwynna both.
   James Forrett

Lucas passed it to Gwynna, who read it and pulled a face.

'He loves to order people around. Shall we go?'

'Why not?'

'I'll feel a bit strange having tea with him when I used to be a servant in that house.'

'You're not a servant any more and you're as good as the next person when it comes to having tea. Don't put yourself down.'

Their eyes met and she smiled tremulously. It still brought tears to her eyes to think how far she had come from the lass who'd once had a stillborn child out of wedlock, who'd once had nothing but the clothes she stood up in until Nev Linney took her in and made her feel like one of the family.

Lucas squeezed her hand and she gripped his tightly for a minute, then shook her head as if shaking away bad memories.

'If Mr Forrett still intends to build an orphanage in memory of his daughter, then I'll help him every way I can.' Lucas looked into the distance for a moment or two. 'On my own I've been able to rescue Joe from a life on the streets. With Forrett's help we can rescue a lot of children. But you'll be the one who does most of the daily work if we go into this, so you have to be sure you want to do it.'

She went to link her arm in his. 'I do. I understand what they're going through. I had parents but I was brought up any old how. We often went hungry, were dressed in rags – but at least we had a roof over our heads. How much worse must it be for those who've nowhere to lay their heads?' Her voice died away. 'I've been meaning to ask – would you mind if I give my sisters a bite of food now and then, not to carry home or my parents would take it away from them, but to eat here? Just the leftovers.'

'Of course not. And more than the leftovers, I hope.' He put one arm round her and she leaned against him with a sigh of pleasure, this tall, strong man she'd married not so long ago. Each day that she woke beside him, saw him smile at her, she marvelled at how good life had been to her.

Carrie and Eli got back from London feeling tired but triumphant. Before they went back to Linney's, where they were staying temporarily, they went along Market Street with Jeremiah to look at the site where the Pride had once stood. The land had been cleared and fenced off since the accident, but the earth was still blackened in places, there was a pile of scorched bricks at the rear and the remaining chunks of wall bore testimony to the collapse of the new workings. The sight of it saddened everyone who had known the place in its prime, full of happy people enjoying the shows, with bright, flaring gas lights making a cheerful entrance against the darkness of the night.

'It looks a right old mess.' Eli scowled at it.

'It'll look worse before it looks better,' Jeremiah said. 'But I must say, I'm looking forward to getting started on it. It seems a long time since I did any real work.'

'I'm just looking forward to having my music hall back,' Eli said.

'Well, we can make a start as soon as we hire the men. Barton and I have agreed to keep the present cellar, but we'll need to rebuild the walls strong enough this time to support what's above them.'

When Jeremiah had walked on, Eli still lingered.

Carrie gave him a sharp nudge. 'You can't stand here all night dreaming of what you're going to build.'

He looked at her and gave a shamefaced laugh. 'You know me too well.'

'And you've been moving as if that arm's aching. Let's fetch Abigail, then you can have a rest. I'll carry the bag for the moment.' She knew she'd guessed right when he didn't protest about her taking it from him. But aching arm or not, he'd been looking really happy since they spoke to Mr Barton in London and saw the plans he had, which were quite easy to adapt for their new music hall.

Abigail crowed with joy at the sight of them and insisted on walking home, not being carried, which was a good thing for Eli even though it slowed them down.

Carrie smiled as they walked along the side passage into the kitchen at Linney's. Actually, it wasn't just Eli's happiness that was at stake here, but hers. She too was longing to have a music hall to run again, instead of the occasional Saturday concerts they were currently putting on in the church hall. He had been the Chairman, who conducted the show, but she had made sure everything was clean, that good food was available, that people were comfortable. She loved organising things.

Two days after her little son's funeral, Ishleen's neighbour ran into her house calling, 'Come quickly! The priest sent a message round that he has some food for us.'

They hurried down to the church and went inside to find other women gathered, sitting in the front pews and waiting patiently for Father Gregory to join them. All were gaunt and looked hungry, and Ishleen supposed she was the same.

When the priest came out of the vestry, he was smiling. 'I have some good news for you all. The Bishop has sent us some Indian meal, enough to feed those in need in our village for a whole week, by which time the potato crop should be advanced enough to let us lift some earlies. I've—'

A groan from the women interrupted him and he looked at them in surprise.

'It scours you out, that stuff and does more harm than good,' one complained.

'Brimstone, I call it,' another said. 'Yellow and nasty.'

He held up his hands for silence. 'This meal is of a good quality and has been properly ground, unlike the last lot. If you will only boil it thoroughly till it's soft, the nuns say you'll have no trouble eating it. What's more, the good sisters have collected enough money to buy each child a cup of milk every day, which I'll get from Mr Maltravers' cowman. If you send the children here at noon, I'll have it ready for them, and perhaps one or two of you can come each day to help.'

Voices muttered, 'Bless you, Father!' and women's eyes filled with tears, because even worse than going hungry themselves was seeing their children grow thin and pale with the hunger.

'There are several pounds of meal for each family, so—'

Ishleen knew, with a sickening certainty that if there were any food on her shelves Milo would take some of it to hand to his friend with the illegal still, without any thought of tomorrow, because getting drunk on poteen seemed to be all he cared about these days. She stood up and interrupted the kindly old man. 'Could you just give a day's worth at a time, Father? Otherwise, who knows what'll be done with it?'

There was silence, then one or two other women with feck-less husbands added their pleas to hers.

He nodded, his eyes full of sympathy and understanding. 'Yes, I'll do that. We've got better storage facilities here, haven't we?'

They all nodded, as if that was the reason.

The yellow Indian meal was still very coarse compared to real flour, so Ishleen made a stirabout with it and cooked it until it was thoroughly softened. She was thankful that at least they had enough peat from their own patch to cook it. For the first time in days the smell of food made her feel hungry, but she waited until she was sure it was well enough cooked before she even tasted it. Since she had a belief that green stuff was good for you, towards the end of the cooking, she put in some more nettles which she'd got from the landowner's woods again.

She was getting brazen about this foraging and early this morning, not knowing about the Indian meal, she'd crept round to the stable stores and taken two handfuls of oats from the horse feed, knowing they'd never miss that small amount. She'd tied it up in the corner of her apron and at home had tied it in another rag, stuffing it carelessly in a corner of a shelf in open sight. She doubted Milo would think to look inside a pile of rags.

On the way back she'd spotted some half-rotten turnips on the compost heap at the home farm and taken some of those too. You could easily cut off the bad bits.

When Milo came in, he sniffed the air and smiled. 'I heard about the food.'

There was nearly a stand-up fight when she only gave him a small serve, so she took out the sharp knife she'd slipped into her apron pocket, pleased that her hand was steady. 'I'll kill you before I'll let you take more than your share this time!'

He stared from her face to the knife. 'What sort of woman are you to deny your husband food when it's here?'

'A mother who's lost one child and wants the daughter she has left to stay alive – and this one too needs to take food through me.' She patted her belly. 'So you only get the same to eat as we do from now on. And don't think I'll hesitate to use this. I'm fighting for my life and Shanna's too.' Her words hung in the air as she glared at him. She saw the precise moment when he backed down.

'Give me my share, then.' He scowled at the small bowlful and looked at the food shelf. 'I thought the Bishop had sent a week's supply.'

'Father Gregory is giving it out in daily amounts.'

'Why? Doesn't he trust us with it?'

'He knows *some of us* are stupid enough to eat it all in two or three days.'

Again the words hung like daggers in the air between them and if looks could kill, she'd have been dead.

'There'll be enough left for us to have the same this evening,' she offered, trying to smooth things over. 'And it'll fill you better if you eat it slowly.' He ignored that and gobbled it down, shoving the bowl aside and leaving the house without so much as a word of thanks.

She looked at his bowl and knew with a sense of shame that she'd clear it out with her fingertip before she washed it. He might scorn those small blobs of food, but she didn't.

'Da shouts a lot,' Shanna observed.

'Oh, he's good at shouting all right,' Ishleen agreed. 'Now, eat your food slowly and chew it well. And when you've finished use your fingertip to clean your bowl out. We mustn't waste a crumb.'

The boiled meal and nettles didn't taste of anything much, but it filled the belly. And the thought that at noon Shanna would have a glass of milk, then tomorrow there would be more Indian meal, and that there were still oats in reserve, was a huge relief.

Gideon walked into the town the following day to redeem Granny Horne's furniture from the pawnshop. He must be getting old because the floor had felt so hard he hadn't been able to sleep properly last night.

The pawnbroker lent him a handcart for sixpence extra and he pushed the furniture back on it. He was puffing slightly as he went up the hill to her house. One of the neighbours helped him carry the things inside.

I'm still out of condition, he thought as he went back for the rest of the stuff. Got to do something about that, go for walks, toughen myself up. He'd been strong and fit once, glorying in his strength, and now look at him.

When he'd taken the handcart back, he watched Granny run her hands lovingly over the pieces, which were ordinary but well kept like everything else in her little house. One or two of them, however, bore the marks of rough usage, which surprised him.

When she saw him looking at the damaged pieces, she grimaced, 'We had a lodger who used to get drunk. I had to ask Declan to throw him out in the end.'

'Declan's been very kind to you. Is he a relative?'

'No. But his auntie is slow witted and she gets treated badly too sometimes, so he knows what it's like for me with our Barney. Not that Barney's slow witted, anything but.'

'What exactly does Declan do for a living?'

She cackled. 'Owt he can. That family's done well for theirsen in England because they're hard workers, Irish or not.' She began counting things off on her fingers. 'They've a tripe shop . . . an' a market stall . . . an' a donkey cart . . . all sorts of ways to turn a penny. The oldest brother sings on the stage now with his wife, beautiful voices they have, make you think you've gone to heaven when you hear them. They're addling a lot of brass, singing all over the country. Between you an' me, I reckon Declan's jealous of his brother getting rich and since Bram got famous, Declan's stopped boozing so much and has started trying to make money. And good luck to him, too.'

'I wonder what sort of job he wants me to do.'

'He'll work you hard if I know Declan.'

'I'm not afraid of hard work.' Gideon took a step towards the door. 'Well, I've some things to buy for myself so I'll be getting on. Do you need anything in town?'

'No, I'll be going to the market mysen. It's held one full day and two half days a week now an' they're talking of having an indoor market open all the time. That'd be grand, that would. I can't afford the prices at the Emporium an' some of them little corner shops sell poor stuff. Our Barney goes errands for me sometimes. It's all right if he goes afore the mills close and he does well enough if you don't rush him. He doesn't look clever but he is, only he can't speak properly so folk think he's a dummy!'

'I can see that.' Gideon made his escape at last.

Now that he had somewhere to live, he intended to start doing something about his auntie's cottages. The first thing, he reckoned, was to get a good look at the man who had stolen his name and inheritance, see if he recognised him. He walked up the hill again and kept an eye on the cottages from further up the slope, sitting in the lee of a rocky outcrop on some pieces of stone he shoved together. But there was no sign of any movement at Number One. After a couple of hours he was hungry so went back into town, taking a longer way round to help get himself stronger and coming back into town at the far end.

As he was walking towards Granny's, he passed a large house on Market Street and stopped to read the brass sign on the wall outside: Charles Hordle. That was the name of his auntie's lawyer, according to her neighbour. He didn't go inside, not yet. When he saw another lawyer's sign further along saying Jack Burtell, he decided to ask Declan about this one. He'd need to hire a lawyer of his own to get justice, he reckoned, even if that did eat into his money, because the Hordle chap would probably side with the impostor. But he wasn't going to rush into anything, furious as he was about being cheated – mustn't. Rash acts led only to trouble, especially when you had no proof of who you were.

He'd not been able to stop thinking about this problem. The impostor would have had to prove who he was to a lawyer's satisfaction, so it had to be someone from the ship, probably the same person who'd stolen his things. The rest of his regiment was still in India, but sometimes men were sent back to England for a variety of reasons, especially illness or injury.

The trouble was, he didn't even remember landing in England, let alone know who had cared for him, so he'd no idea who the thief could be, wouldn't recognise him if he walked right up to him. He'd spent some time in an infirmary near London used by the military, at first out of his senses, and they'd told him later that his life had been despaired of.

Yes, that'd be how it had happened. Some fellow would have taken advantage of his being ill, not expecting him to live. He'd mentioned his aunt to his fellow travellers now and then during the first part of the journey, as you do when you're chatting about your family. Someone must have gone to see her, to find out if there were any pickings to be had for her sole surviving relative, and they'd fallen lucky.

Well, whoever the sod was, he'd pay for it one day, Gideon would make sure of that.

But he wasn't doing anything about it until he saw his way clear. And the first thing was to get a look at the other person calling himself Gideon John Shaw. The second thing would be to wait for proof of who he was to come from the Army. Who knew how long that would take when letters had to go back and forth between regimental headquarters in Preston and India?

4

Gwynna twisted to and fro in front of the mirror then turned to Aunt Hilda, who had come upstairs to help her prepare for taking afternoon tea with the man who had been her employer not so long ago. 'Will I do?'

She was wearing the dress she'd been married in, a dark maroon outfit in fine wool. It had been part of her outfit when she was a nursery maid. She'd sewed some braid on it to make it smarter, making an upside-down V shape from the waist to the hem at the front, something she'd seen on the skirt of a well-to-do lady walking down the street. She was wearing an extra petticoat, too, to make the skirts look fuller. The neat, cream lace-trimmed collar matched the lace inside the brim of her modest straw bonnet, which she was holding, ready to put on.

'You look lovely, dear. Here, your hair's come adrift at the back. Let me fix it before you put that bonnet on. Lovely hair you've got, such a pretty shade of brown.' They both smiled at one another in the mirror as Gwynna tied the bonnet strings. 'Get off with you now.'

Downstairs Lucas was waiting impatiently for her, also clad in his Sunday best. 'You look good enough to eat,' he murmured in her ear.

Her husband's admiration gave her extra confidence, because she was a bit nervous about today.

As they went across the mill yard to the house, Gwynna slowed down. 'Front door or back?'

'Front,' Lucas said firmly. 'After all, we're here to take tea with Mr Forrett, not to deliver groceries.'

The housemaid she'd once worked with opened the door to

them, giving her a quick smile. It felt strange to be shown into
the front parlour, but when Mr Forrett came across the room
and shook her hand, keeping it between his big, gnarled hands
for a minute or two and patting it, Gwynna felt suddenly at ease
with him again.

'You look as if marriage suits you, lass.'

'It does, Mr Forrett. It suits me very well.'

He turned to Lucas and shook his hand too, then gestured to
the sofa. 'Sit down and we'll have a cup of tea and a bite to eat.'

She thought he seemed thinner, a sadness in his eyes still, his
grey hair brushed back from his face anyhow, a couple of areas
on his chin missed during the morning shave that had once been
so meticulous. Well, you would be sad if you'd lost your baby
daughter because of your wife's stupidity, wouldn't you? And
he'd been particularly fond of the child. 'How are you?' she asked
gently, forgetting to be nervous in her concern for him. 'You look
tired.'

He shrugged his shoulders. 'I'm all right. Keeping myself busy.
I had some news last week and don't know whether to be sad or
relieved. My wife died suddenly.'

'I'm sorry to hear that.'

'Well, I didn't wish her ill, in spite of what she did. It makes
you think, though, when someone your own age dies. She was a
bonny lass when I married her. I've been trying to work out why
she changed, grew so unhappy, started taking that damned
laudanum.' He sighed, then shook his head as if to clear the
unhappy thoughts. 'Well, death comes to us all eventually, doesn't
it? What's upset me most, though, is a letter from my elder
daughter. Alicia blames me for her mother's death and she said
some cruel things.'

'She'll have been upset. She won't have meant them.'

He looked at her sadly. 'I wish I could believe that, but she's
been angry ever since I put my wife in that place, even though
Dr Pipperday knows the owner and promised me they'd be kind
to her.'

There was silence for a moment or two, then he said briskly,

'Well, enough of that. About this orphanage . . . I want to get started on it as soon as I can. There's a warehouse for sale on River Walk that might do us, not too big and very soundly built. I'd like you to come with me to see it after we've finished our tea. We'd need to make some changes to the inside, of course, but that'd still be quicker than building a place from scratch.'

Gwynna poured the tea for the two men and coaxed her former employer into eating a second piece of cake. He would have eaten two pieces and several scones as well in the old days. No wonder he was thinner.

When they set off for the warehouse, he offered her his arm and after a moment's hesitation, she took it, though she was sure people would stare to see him treating her like a lady. Lucas walked beside them on her other side, telling Mr Forrett about how well Joe was doing.

The warehouse was an old-fashioned one, built of stone not brick. It was quite near the river and had a piece of land at the back where drays had loaded and unloaded their goods. It was, as he had said, soundly built, with no signs of the roof leaking, but to Gwynna it felt bleak and cheerless inside.

'The more I see it the more I think it'll suit our needs,' Mr Forrett said, not seeming to notice her hesitation. 'We'll make separate living quarters for you two at one end because you'll want your own place.'

'Not just for us,' she said at once. 'We'll need to employ a woman, perhaps two later on, to live in and help me, as well as scrubbing and washerwomen if we're looking after a lot of children. We could maybe get people from the workhouse.' It had already been decided that Lucas's aunt and uncle would stay in the house where they were presently living, which was attached to the workshop where Lucas would continue to work in the daytime.

Forrett nodded. 'All right. I expected you to need help. I'm setting up a trust to run the orphanage, one that'll bring in money regularly, even after I'm gone.'

'You're very generous.'

'I want my daughter to be remembered: the Libby Forrett Children's Home I want to call it now, not orphanage. It sounds so cold and cheerless, orphanage does. Home is a much nicer word.'

'That's a lovely idea,' Gwynna said softly. She patted his shoulder then walked up and down the big open space again, her footsteps echoing on the stone-flagged floor. It felt as though she was inside a prison because the windows were too high to see out of. When she turned round she was a bit nervous, but determined to say her piece. 'You've changed the name of this warehouse, but it's not enough. Do you want an institution where children feel uncomfortable or a homely place where they'll be happy?'

He looked at her in puzzlement. 'I don't rightly know what you mean.'

'It's a sound building but at the moment it feels like a prison. You can't see out and the ceiling is so high, it'll be impossible to heat the rooms in winter. There could be two floors in here, actually, which would give us a lot more room.'

He turned slowly round on the spot, studying it again. 'You're right. We could put proper windows in and build another floor upstairs, but we'll need to find an architect to sort all that out. Do you think this place will be all right if we do that? I do want to make a start on it as soon as possible.'

She went across to take his arm again, he looked so lonely standing there. 'When it's finished, I promise you it'll be the best orphanage there ever was and your daughter's name will be remembered with affection and blessed by all who come here.'

He pulled out an enormous handkerchief and blew his nose loudly. 'That's what I want. Eh, Gwynna lass, I've never seen anyone as good as you with children. Save them for me! I don't want other children to die like she did when they could live with a bit of help.'

As he buried himself in his handkerchief again, she walked back to Lucas to give the millowner time to pull himself together. 'What do you think, love? You're not saying much.'

'I don't need to. You're saying it for me. I agree with everything you've said. I do have one thing to add, though.' He raised
his voice, 'We should make a garden outside, Mr Forrett, bring
in some good soil for that piece of ground at the back, plant
some trees and flowers, vegetables as well. It lifts the spirits, a
garden does. The older children could help tend it.'

Mr Forrett walked across to the rear area where drays had
once unloaded and flung open one of the huge doors. 'Aye, good
idea.' In some surprise he added, '*I've* never had a garden, either.'
Then he drew a deep breath and shut the door again. 'Well then,
if we're agreed, I'll look round for an architect.'

'How about Mr Channon?' Lucas suggested. 'He's just setting
up in Hedderby and he seems a very practical fellow to me, one
who knows his job. I had some dealings with him when the new
Pride fell down because he hired me to get the site cleared and
the place fenced off properly. I enjoyed talking to him. He has
some sound modern ideas.'

'I'll send for him, then, see what he thinks. And you two must
talk to him as well about the practicalities. I know nowt about
kitchens and such.'

When they parted company with the millowner at the end of
River Walk, Gwynna turned to watch him go. 'He's so sad and
lonely. After we get the orphanage started, we must get him
involved. Children always cheer people up.'

'I doubt he'll want anything to do with the day-to-day running
of it.'

'I think he will if we can find a way to catch his interest. He
hardly ever sees those grown-up daughters of his, so all he has
is his work. Every evening he sits by himself in that dark, stuffy
parlour reading the newspapers. It'd make anyone feel down,
being alone like that would. You'd think the daughters would come
to visit him, wouldn't you, but they hardly ever do.'

'He can visit them.'

'He isn't invited because they've married above themselves and
are ashamed of a father who doesn't speak in a fancy way. I've
seen them and their husbands look down their noses at him and

wished I could give them a good shaking. That Alicia's the worst, the eldest one. The younger daughter's not as uppity, but she lives further away now.'

Lucas shook his head at her. 'The man's more than twice your age, and rich with it. You must leave him to sort all that out.'

'I can't help caring about people.'

His steps slowed down and they stopped walking to stand staring at the shallow water. 'It's a lot to take on, this responsibility for an orphanage. And I've been thinking: what shall we do when we have our own children? Shall we still continue to look after the others?'

'Yes. And we'll love them all,' she replied without hesitation.

He smiled down at her fondly. 'You can't mother the whole world, Gwynna.'

'I can mother those I meet, who need me.' She looked at him and her smile faded a little. 'I wish we could start our own baby.'

'It'll happen. And it'd not be the best time just now.'

'No, I suppose so.' But she sighed as she said that.

When they got home again, Aunt Hilda and Uncle Fred were full of questions about the old warehouse, but after a while they both fell silent, exchanging glances.

'What about us?' Hilda said hesitantly. 'What will happen to us if you go to live in the orphanage?'

'You'll still live here, I hope,' Lucas said. 'And keep an eye on the workshop for me.'

Gwynna smiled. 'You could both help out with the orphans too, if you want. You get on well with young lads, Uncle Fred. Look how Joe comes to ask you about things and tells you his troubles.' Inspiration struck her suddenly. 'And someone has to manage the money side of things. I'm a bit frightened of that, but you used to work in Mr Forrett's office, so you'd know how to do accounts. I don't think you could do your old job again, but this would be lighter work, just part time.'

His expression brightened and he blinked his eyes furiously. 'Do you think he'd hire me?'

'I'm sure he would.'

'You've got a good wife there, our Lucas,' Fred said as they were clearing up the workshop that night.

'I know.' He paused, a piece of wood in his hand. 'She surprised me today, though, the way she spoke out, the sensible ideas she had about the building.'

'Mebbe she's never had anyone as'd let her speak out afore,' Fred said, 'or anything to speak out about.'

'Mmm.' But Lucas was thoughtful as he sent Joe to get the broom and sweep up the shavings and sawdust. He hadn't expected Gwynna to be so independent, wasn't quite sure he liked it, wanted to be the one to cherish her, while she seemed not to need that, but to want to look after the whole world.

Don't be silly, he chided himself as he washed his hands ready for his evening meal. You should be glad she's got so much gumption. And he was, of course he was. But he wished sometimes she was a bit more dependent on him. He wanted to protect her, make her happy.

And he too wished they could have a child of their own.

Dora waited all day for Benting to make another move but he ignored her completely. He imposed a lot of extra fines, as always when he was in a bad mood, but he was fining others, not her. His scowl didn't lift as he went about his work with his usual meticulous care. You had to give him that, she thought. For all his faults, he knew his job when it came to keeping the mill running smoothly, and kept his Deputy Overlooker hard at it as well. Even the engineer who tended the steam engine as if it was a beloved child had respect for Benting's experience and skill. Only Mr Forrett knew more than he did about spinning cotton and running a mill.

At the end of the day she breathed a sigh of relief and left work in the middle of a cluster of other girls. She had to pass Benting because he was standing at the gate, and for the first time that day his eyes rested on her openly, with a cold, hostile gaze that made her steps falter for a moment. As he saw her looking at him he smiled slowly and she shivered. That smile promised – something nasty.

Her friends were silent until they were well out of earshot and even then they kept their voices down as they discussed it.

'Did you see how he looked at Dora,' one said at last.

'Best be careful, love,' another added.

'You should find a job somewhere else, leave Hedderby completely,' a third advised. 'He'll find a way to get at you, he always does.'

'How can I leave the town? My family live here.' But she would be very careful from now on, Dora promised herself. No more walking alone by the river, for a start.

She was glad to get home, to play with her puppy and do her chores, then sit with her younger brother and sisters in the front parlour while Raife played the piano to them and they sang all the old favourites, as they often did in the evenings.

When she looked down, Nippy seemed to be listening to the music too, holding his head on one side, so she took his front legs and began tapping them on her skirt in time to the music. He didn't seem to mind, was always hungry for cuddles or attention. When she stopped doing it, he batted her hand with his paw as if to say that he was still there, so absent-mindedly she continued to fondle him.

After a while, however, he got restless and tried to get down from her lap, scrabbling determinedly.

Raife noticed and stopped playing to say, 'Take him outside, love. He probably needs to do his business. Put him on that patch of bare earth at the very bottom of the yard and don't let him do it anywhere else. I need a break myself.' He flexed his fingers and stretched his arms.

So she took the puppy outside and when he started sniffing around near the house, she insisted he went with her to the far end of the yard, praising him extravagantly when he did a wee exactly where she wanted.

If only the rest of her life was as pleasant as the time she spent at home with her family, she thought. She was dreading going to work tomorrow and still didn't know whether to say anything about Benting to Nev.

As she turned to go back into the house, she saw a dark figure straddling the top of the wall and gasped in fright as it raised its hand threateningly.

Before she could run into the house, the world exploded in pain and darkness swept her away.

A few days after the funeral, Ishleen got up as soon as it was dawn because she didn't seem to need much sleep these days. She brought in more peat from the pile outside and found enough embers to get the fire burning, enjoying the fresh tangy smell of the new turfs. Milo seemed to have stopped doing anything around the house these days and either sat slumped in a chair, scowling at her, or disappeared with his friends, not telling her where they were going.

When she went outside again she stopped dead, one hand going up to press against her mouth to hold back a cry. In the clear grey light of early dawn the nearest edge of the potato field had a yellowish look to it. No! It couldn't happen again. It couldn't! It was just the light. Colours never looked right till the sun was fully risen. But though she blinked hard the yellow tinge didn't go away and her heart began to thump with fear.

It was a few moments before she could make herself go across to look more closely, by which time the light was brighter and the colours clearer. She didn't have to touch the plants or bend down, because there was no doubting what had happened. She let out a wail of pure anguish then stood there with her hands pressed flat against her cheeks.

Blight!

Impossible to hold back the tears. How could it have happened again? They'd been so careful to find clean seed potatoes, to turn and re-turn the soil to let the air and sunlight cleanse it.

She didn't know how long she stood there but eventually, moving like an old woman she walked back into the house and shook Milo awake.

He was sluggish and grumpy, as always in the mornings. 'What's the matter that you have to wake me so early? Can a man not get a proper night's sleep in this house now?'

'It's back.'

He stared at her as if she was speaking gibberish.

'The blight. It's back. Come and look at the plants.'

He was out of bed quickly enough then, pushing past her to go and stand by the corner of his field, looking down on it, only half-dressed, his bare feet leaving imprints in the soft soil.

'Dear God in Heaven!' he muttered, standing motionless by the corner plants.

She went across to lay one hand on his shoulder, because for all their differences recently, she knew how he was feeling – the same as her, sick to the depths of his soul.

When he shook off her hand and set off walking without a word, she let him go. She watched with tears in her eyes as he made his way slowly round the side of the potato field then back through the centre of it. When he came back he stared at her with eyes that seemed to have no life in them, his face grey, haggard, looking decades older than he had yesterday. 'We're done for. We might just as well kill ourselves now and get it over with quickly. I can't go through it again, Ishleen, I just can't.'

She could find no words of comfort to offer him, not one. Nothing she said or did would change things so he'd just have to go through it again, they all would.

'I'll go and see if others have got it too,' he muttered in the end and walked off into the early morning stillness.

As he vanished down the lane, a shaft of sunlight broke through the clouds and shone on the field as if mocking her. With another groan, she ran inside. She couldn't bear to look at it.

What were they going to do now? They'd sold everything they could last time, hadn't a penny in reserve, not even a change of clothes. And the priest had only enough meal promised to last them the week.

Perhaps richer people would be charitable and send them

food – or perhaps they'd just leave them to die. Sure, they were half-starved already.

Gideon dreamed of Lalika that night, not as he'd seen her the last time, wasted with cholera, but as she'd been before, smiling and pretty in her colourful saris, her stomach gently rounded with his child. She seemed to be trying to tell him something and when he couldn't understand, her expression grew sad and she reached one hand out to him before turning to walk away.

He wanted to call to her to come back, but couldn't frame a single word, could only watch helplessly as she turned and waved farewell, then vanished into the mist.

He woke with tears on his cheeks, as he'd woken so many times since her death. But this time the dream had felt different, as if she'd been saying a final goodbye, as if he'd never dream of her again. He couldn't bear the thought of that. It was the dreams of her and their happy times together that had kept him going over the past few months.

What would keep him going now?

His mind was sluggish and it took him a while to think of something that gave his life a purpose. Then he remembered the impostor and felt something stir in him, like a last ember glowing in the ashes of a dead fire. For a start he'd find out who had stolen his name and inheritance. Then he'd build some sort of a life, even if it could never be truly happy again.

Maybe he'd marry again some day, a sensible marriage this time, a widow, an older woman who would work alongside him. Younger women needed the sort of loving commitment he could never again offer.

You couldn't expect to find great love for a second time. Most people didn't even find it once.

As Dora dropped to the ground unconscious, the dog whined and nudged her, then turned to the man who had swung his other leg over the wall as if about to get down into the yard. Nippy began to bark hysterically and the man stopped moving to hurl another stone across the yard. But it missed the little dog, who was leaping about in a paroxysm of fury.

The back door opened and a voice called, 'What's the matter with Nippy, Dora?'

The puppy made a quick dash towards the door, then back to the still figure on the ground, barking and growling in the direction of the wall.

Raife gaped at the sight of a man, whose face was covered by a muffler, climbing back over the wall. He heard the intruder curse as he jumped down into the alley that ran along the back of the houses.

For a moment Raife couldn't move from shock, then he began yelling at the top of his voice for someone to come and help him. He ran down to where Dora was lying on the ground and in the light streaming from the kitchen windows saw the chunk of brick and the dark sticky patch on her temple. Falling to his knees beside her he muttered, 'Eh, no! Eh, no!' and touched the pulse at her throat to check that she was still alive, still breathing.

When the others came pouring out of the house in answer to his urgent calls, they stood in a shocked circle round the still body.

'She's not dead, is she?' Lily asked in a quavering voice.

'Nay, she's still breathing,' Raife said. 'Someone threw a brick at her and knocked her out. What a good thing I came out to check that Nippy was behaving hissen or who knows what the fellow as did it would have done to her? Nev, can you help me carry her inside?'

Ted pushed to the front. 'I'll help Nev carry her. You bring Nippy in, Raife.'

'I'll go and get some water ready to wash that wound,' Essie said.

'Someone pick up that brick and bring it in,' Nev called as an afterthought.

Lily bent and picked it up, then helped Raife to his feet, because he was a bit stiff these days. As they went inside she asked, 'Who would want to hurt our Dora?'

Raife shook his head. 'I don't know, lass, but I intend to find out.'

Dora groaned and tried to open her eyes but quickly shut them again.

'She's coming to,' a voice whispered.

'The light's shining in her eyes. Here, I'll move the lamp.'

When Dora moved her head it hurt. She heard a moan and it took a minute or two for her to realise it was herself who'd made the noise. Someone gripped her hand and she looked in that direction, relieved to see her eldest sister sitting next to her. She squeezed Carrie's hand, glad of the comfort it offered, then realised she was lying on her bed. 'How did I . . . I was out in the yard . . . what happened?'

'Someone threw a brick at you and it hit you on the forehead. It knocked you out,' Carrie said quietly. 'The intruder was climbing over the wall into the yard till he saw Raife come out, then he ran away. We carried you back into the house, so you're quite safe now. Ted and Nev have gone down the back lane to make sure no one's still lurking there.'

'Nippy?'

'He's in the kitchen. He gave warning by barking, probably saved you from worse.'

Dora smiled and let her heavy eyelids close. 'He's a good dog. Mmm. I feel sleepy.'

'You rest quietly,' Carrie said. 'I'll stay with you.'

'That's nice. Feel safe – with you.'

The rest of the family gathered in the kitchen, sitting round the big, scrubbed table as usual.

'What's the world coming to when you get attacked in your own back yard?' demanded Essie.

'Why would anyone attack our Dora?' Raife wondered. 'It can't have been for money, that's certain. And there's only one other reason a man attacks a pretty young lass.'

They exchanged worried glances. 'I thought that sort of trouble was done with in Hedderby after that nasty Stott fellow died,' Essie muttered. 'Who else would want to ravish young girls?'

Lily opened her mouth to ask what ravish meant, but Gracie

nudged her and touched a quick finger to her lips to keep her quiet.

Raife shook his head. 'I don't know who it can be. Maybe Dora will have some idea whether there's anyone who wishes her ill, but we won't ask her about that tonight.'

Nev and Ted came in. 'No sign of anyone.' Nev went to put an arm round his wife. 'Now, Essie love, don't look so upset. We'll make sure this sort of thing doesn't happen again.'

'How? You can't guard someone every minute of the day.'

He sighed. 'Well, we can make sure she's more careful in future, can't we? Any chance of a cup of tea and a piece of your cake?'

Ted went to sit quietly beside Raife. 'I'll go outside again in the morning as soon as it's light and see if I can find anything.'

'There's the chunk of brick,' Raife observed. 'It looks like it's come from the old Pride, because it's been burned. And if it has, someone may have seen the fellow lurking on the site. I'll ask around tomorrow.' He looked across at his daughter-in-law. 'Don't take on, Essie. Forewarned is forearmed.'

But for all his encouraging words, he didn't feel very hopeful of finding the culprit. And he too hated the thought of them being attacked in their own back yard. Bad times bred bad folk, he reckoned, and in some ways the past few years had been as bad as he'd ever seen in Hedderby.

5

Dora didn't go to work the following morning because Essie flatly refused to let her. She didn't even argue about it, because she didn't want to go into the mill ever again. There was only one person who could have done this and he'd have been smirking every time he saw her if she'd gone to work.

They sent Lily to tell Dora's friend to give a message to the overlooker that Dora had had an accident and been injured, so would be away for a day or two.

After everyone had gone to work or school, Essie went upstairs to see how her stepdaughter was feeling. 'You look pale and that's a nasty bruise.'

'Benting will sack me, I know he will,' Dora muttered, near to tears.

'Why should he do that?'

Dora looked at her, then the story came tumbling out. Essie listened in grim silence until it had ended. 'I'm fetching Nev and Raife up and you can tell them what you just told me. No, you're not getting up. You're staying in bed this morning and we'll see how you are later.'

She was back a short time later with the two men and Carrie. All of them listened to Dora's halting story, prompting her with questions, then Nev said firmly, 'That's it! You're not going back to that mill again.'

'But I have to work—'

'You don't have to work there. We can feed you until you find something else. We're not short of a bob or two.'

'There isn't much else in Hedderby for lasses like me but the mill, is there? And you've not got much money coming in at the moment, because there are no performers from the Pride staying here. So you need my wages.'

His face took on its stubborn expression. 'We can manage without your wages for years, if we have to.' He hesitated for a moment before confessing, as if it was something to be ashamed of, 'I've got plenty of money put by for a rainy day.'

They all looked at him in surprise.

He went a bit red. 'I've allus been good at making money and careful how I spent it. The pennies mount up and I've a fair bit in the new savings bank now, yes and in other places too. I don't keep all my eggs in one basket where money's concerned.'

Nippy crept into the room, though he was not supposed to be upstairs, and it was Essie who scooped him up and plonked him down on the bed. 'You have a rest, Dora love. You're not in a fit state to think about the future just now. You can keep Nippy up here, just this once.' She looked round and dared anyone to contradict her. 'It'll stop him getting under my feet.'

When she was alone Dora lay back with a sigh, admitting to herself that she was relieved not to have to work at the mill any more. All her previous confidence in herself seemed to have vanished and she couldn't help wondering what she had done to make Benting think he could have his way with her.

As if he knew she was upset, Nippy nestled against her and fell asleep. After a short time, she did too, her hand still resting on the dog's wiry coat.

Downstairs there was a council of war going on.

'Do you think it's Benting who threw that brick?' Carrie asked. 'I wouldn't put anything past that man.'

'I wouldn't be surprised,' Raife said. 'I'm going out to ask if anyone's seen folk on the site. That was definitely a brick from the old Pride. It's still got the scorch marks on it. There's plenty of 'em on that pile of rubble at the back still. They're going to use them to fill in behind the cellar walls.'

Essie sighed and started preparing a meal.

Carrie went along to the small room she and her husband were using as an office and sat down at the desk to check her lists.

They were planning to run several Saturday shows in the church hall now that Eli was his old self again, possibly even Friday and Saturday if things went well. They'd be able to find Dora a few hours' work helping out in the kitchens there, at least.

But it all took time. It seemed so long since they'd had a proper music saloon.

Declan sent a message to Gideon that he should start work at the market at six o'clock the following morning. He found the area in a state of chaos as farmers' wives set out their produce and other folk brought in goods of all sorts purchased from the many mills and manufactories of Lancashire. Every necessity of life was there for those with money to spare.

Declan was setting out a stall, together with a man who resembled him in a quieter sort of way. 'This is my brother Michael, who runs the main stall for us. I want you to take over from him so that he can get out and about more to buy goods for us. I'll give you a couple of weeks to learn, then if things work out all right, you're on your own. If not, no hard feelings on either side and we'll part company.'

Gideon looked at the goods for sale. 'There are a lot of different things here. I thought each stall specialised in something.'

'We sell whatever's going cheap, often things that have a small fault. They're household goods mainly, from pokers to lengths of sheeting to pots and pans, but we sell second-hand goods too if we can turn a penny on them. It's all thanks to the railways. We couldn't have got around buying stuff like we need to, or transported things back to Hedderby so easily in the old days.'

'Is there a good living to be made from such things?'

'If you know where to get stock and you have contacts. My uncle is thinking of starting a stall selling food at the markets now they're getting bigger. He's got a tripe shop, but he wants to earn more money providing food for people to eat on the spot.' He grinned. 'Us Heegans aren't proud. We'll do anything that brings in the money. Anyway, for today you just stay with

Michael and watch what he does, help him where you can. If you can talk the hind leg off a donkey, it helps.'

Gideon felt very dubious about that. He had been talkative as a lad, but had grown quieter as he got older, especially after his marriage to an Indian woman, which hadn't been approved of or recognised by his officers, and had been scorned by the other men in his regiment. And Lalika's family had disowned her, so there had been no one but the two of them.

It had been a foolhardy thing to do, marrying her, he could see that now, but he'd been head over heels in love with her and she with him. Only his skill with guns had saved him from retribution by his officers for disobeying orders and marrying her without permission. They'd valued his skills too highly to lose them, but even that hadn't been enough to get him married quarters in the barracks, as he'd hoped.

He looked down at his mangled hand and sighed. He suspected that someone had tampered with his rifle or ammunition, to make it explode like that. He'd upset one or two folk on his way up to sergeant, because he'd insisted on the highest standards at all times. But the explosion had been signed off as an accident due to faulty workmanship and . . . Ah, what was the use fretting about something that couldn't be changed? You just had to get on with it, whatever life brought you.

He stayed at the market the whole day, first helping to unload and set out items on the stall, and in the latter at least displaying a knack for making stuff look more attractive that won Declan's praise. After that, he followed Michael's instructions and began selling a few pieces, later minding the stall while Michael did other 'little jobs'. Declan's brother never stopped working and Gideon admired that. By the end of the day he'd begun to have more confidence about bantering with the customers, to enjoy it even.

The experience made him quite sure that this wasn't the sort of life for him, but it'd do for the time being. The main thing was for him to earn enough to pay his way, so that he'd have a visible reason for staying in Hedderby.

He intended to walk up past the cottages regularly, keep an eye on things. The walk would strengthen him and the impostor was bound to come back. He'd be waiting when the fellow did. In fact, he was itching to get a sight of the man who'd robbed him.

The markets didn't close until late and he was weary by the time he made his way home, which perhaps explained why he wasn't paying attention and allowed himself to be cornered in a quiet road just off Market Street by the same three young louts he'd had two encounters with before.

He gave a good account of himself, but they were three well-grown lads and quickly began to gain the upper hand, taunting him and shoving him from one to the other. He was planning how to break away and run for it, because he wasn't foolishly proud about how he saved his skin, when a man came pounding along the street, yelling at them to stop that at once. They ran away, melting into the darkness before the newcomer reached them.

'Thank goodness you turned up,' Gideon puffed, wiping the blood from his cut lip and moving towards a street lamp so that he could see what he was doing.

His rescuer walked with him. 'It's my job to keep the peace, sir.'

He blinked the sweat from his eyes and saw the uniform, the frock coat and top hat, with a well-polished leather belt. They'd polished things like that in the Army. 'You're a police constable?'

'Yes, sir. Could you tell me how this started?'

'Those three jumped out at me and started thumping me. They're the same ones I stopped from attacking young Barney Horne the day before yesterday – and I stopped them from torturing a puppy before that.'

'You know who they are, then?'

'I most certainly do.'

'Good. We've had a few attacks recently, money stolen from victims, but they've all insisted they didn't recognise their attackers. We don't believe that, we think they're afraid to say who they are, but we can't force them to tell us. So I'd be grateful if you'd come to the police station and report the incident.'

'I can find out the others' names, but I know for certain that the ringleader is called Huey.'

'Ah. We know that one and can make a good guess at who the other two are.'

But when Gideon went along to the police station the following afternoon, it was to find out that Huey's father had vouched for the fact that the lads had all been at his house at the time of the attack.

'Were they bruised about the face?' he asked the constable.

'Yes. But we can't prove they were your attackers because only you saw them. The father, Benting, is a respected figure in this town, though not well liked. He's the overlooker at Forrett's mill.'

'I see. Well, thank you for your help last night anyway. You saved me from a nasty beating.'

'I'd be careful how I went from now on, sir.'

'I shall. And they'd better be careful too.'

When he got back to his lodgings Gideon took out a walking stick he'd brought from India, one of his few possessions which hadn't vanished. It had a carved cobra's head handle which was weighted with lead, so it made a good weapon if you needed to defend yourself.

This wasn't how he'd expected his life in Hedderby to be.

Nothing was as he'd expected.

It was going to be a struggle to prove who he was and get what was owed to him, but he'd never been one to back away from a fight.

When Milo didn't come home that evening, Ishleen thought nothing of it. It wasn't the first time he'd stayed out late with his friends by any means. But when he stayed out all night, she couldn't settle to sleep, kept waking thinking she heard him and then realising she was still alone. By morning she was worried. This wasn't normal. He liked the comfort of a bed, Milo did.

Hearing a tap on her door, she called out, 'Come in!' thinking it was one of her neighbours, but when she turned she saw the landowner's agent standing just inside the door, hat in hand.

'Mr Keilan!'

'I'm afraid I have some sad news for you, Mrs Milane. Perhaps you'd like to sit down?'

Her first thought was that Milo had been taken up for poaching or thieving. She folded her arms, holding herself together. 'Just tell me.'

'I'm afraid one of our keepers found your husband in our woods this morning. He'd hung himself, was quite dead.'

The room lurched round her and he came across to help her sit down. It was a minute or two before she could control herself enough to ask, 'He's – dead? Milo's *dead*?'

'I'm afraid so.'

There were footsteps outside and Father Gregory came in without knocking.

The agent nodded. 'Thank you for coming, Father. I'll leave you with Mrs Milane now.' He turned back to Ishleen. 'We'll send the body across later.' He fumbled in his pocket. 'This is from Mr Maltravers, to help with the funeral.'

She looked at the table and saw half a guinea sitting there. Instinct made her snatch it up and slip it into her pocket the minute Keilan had left, then she looked at the priest. 'A suicide can't have a proper funeral, though, can he? Even though he was born and bred here, brought up a Catholic?'

'No, I'm afraid not.'

'I'd not spend a penny of this on Milo anyway. It'll all go on feeding Shanna.' She looked the priest steadily in the eye as she added, 'He was a fool and a drunkard, not even a good father to our children. He only deserves a pauper's funeral.'

'You're overwrought. You don't mean that.'

She shook her head. 'No, I'm not overwrought, Father. I'm angry. I've been angry with him for a while now.' She touched her stomach.

'That's God's will.'

'It's Milo's stupidity. He forced me.'

'It was your wifely duty to submit to him, and the child was the Lord's will.'

She didn't argue. They'd never agree about this. Men stuck together whether they were priests in long robes or starving smallholders in rags.

There was silence for a moment, then Father Gregory asked, 'What shall you do now?'

'I don't know yet. I'll have to think. The first thing is to bury him. My neighbours will help, I know. And the baby's due soon. I can't do anything much till after it's born.'

'You can bury Milo in that piece of land just outside the churchyard on the far side. Others have used it in such cases. It's the best I can do, I'm afraid. Will you be all right for a moment or two? I'll go and fetch help for you.'

'I'll be fine, thank you, Father.'

She watched him leave, sat there dry-eyed, holding tight to the anger to give her the strength to do what was necessary. She got through the rest of the day this way.

They buried Milo at nightfall, a furtive business, with a few of her friends coming along to support her, and her closest neighbour minding Shanna.

But when Ishleen got home, she put Shanna to bed and sat up by the table, alone in the darkness. She hadn't thought till after the burial was over that there could be nothing to mark Milo's grave. It was as if he'd never existed. Suddenly she remembered the lively young man who had caught her fancy, and for all her anger, she couldn't help weeping for what might have happened to them had he been stronger in character. They could have gone to her cousins in Lancashire. The Heegans always looked after their own. Or they could have gone to America. Milo had a brother there. But he'd refused even to consider leaving.

She fell asleep at the table, with her head on her folded arms and the tears drying on her cheeks.

Benting looked at his son in disgust, feeling so angry he gave him a clout over the ear. 'What did you think you were doing, attacking that fellow openly in the street?'

'Getting my own back on him like you allus do.'

'All the man did was save a puppy for a pretty young lass.'

'He interfered later as well.'

'Because you were stupid enough to attack Barney Horne. Why do you keep tormenting that one? He's not worth it.'

'He's a dummy,' Huey said sullenly. 'They should be killed at birth, fellows like that. I hate to see him walk with that arm flapping about.'

'Then close your eyes next time you pass him.' He clouted Huey again for good measure. 'And for that you risked being taken up by the police! I sometimes think you haven't the sense of a newborn babe. I have a position in this town and I'm not having you bringing the family's name down.' He turned round and went to stand by the window, looking out, getting his anger under control before he turned back.

Huey scowled at him, his lower lip jutting out stubbornly.

'I mean it. You're to stay away from trouble from now on.'

'*You* aren't staying away from that lass.'

Benting shot a quick glance towards the door, relieved to see it closed tight. 'What do you know about that?'

Huey smirked. 'I followed you an' I seen you chuck a brick at her. Didn't get what you wanted, though, did you?'

Benting let loose a punch that sent his son sprawling on the floor. 'That'll teach you to mind your own business in future, you stupid young sod.'

The noise of ornaments crashing off a table Huey had bumped into brought Benting's wife to the door. 'What are you *doing*?'

He rounded on her. 'Stay out of this, Sarah. If you don't want to see this idiot son of ours end up in prison, you'll leave me to teach him a lesson.' When she didn't move, he took a step forward and she backed hurriedly out of the room clutching her belly, because she was very near her time.

Benting turned round to his son and cuffed him about the head, punctuating his words with more blows. 'Just remember this – I'm not only older than you, I'm stronger *and* – I know more. Don't *ever* – meddle in my affairs again and *don't* – follow me around. And you're to leave that Potter fellow and the dummy alone from now on.' He took a step backwards, panting slightly.

Huey muttered something, rubbing his ear.

'I'll have no cheek from you, my lad.' Benting raised one fist again and his son cowered away from him. 'Now, get out of my sight!'

Once Huey was past him, Benting lashed out with his foot and sent the boy sprawling, then heaved him up by his collar and threw him out into the hall. Ignoring him, he then went into the back room and sent one of his other sons out for a jug of beer. Returning to the front room to wait for its arrival, he lit the fire, because he always seemed to be cold these days. He stood toasting his hands at it.

No one came near him and the children were all very quiet in the back room, which was wise of them. He had a lot to think about. Forrett had gone soft in his old age and Benting was getting increasingly worried about that. If his employer was going to start interfering in how the mill was run, it could mess up a lot of things, especially the fines paid, half of which went into Benting's own pocket, and his 'little extras' when he fancied a lass. As for spending good money on an orphanage, that was plain stupid. If he wanted to give money away, he should give it to the overlooker who'd helped him build up a thriving mill.

The beer arrived and Sarah brought it in, together with a clean glass. His wife was in her ugly phase, so swollen with child he hated even looking at her, let alone touching her, however desperate he was for his bed rations. She looked pale and ill, which annoyed him. He couldn't afford her to get sick. 'Get out, you fat ugly sow!' he said as soon as she'd poured his beer.

As he sipped, his thoughts went back to Forrett. His employer's son-in-law had had a word with him in the mill yard when they came over for the baby's funeral – what a fuss to make when so many young 'uns died! – and Gleason had suggested keeping in touch. He'd mentioned how unhappy he and his wife were about the orphanage plans and hinted at a reward for keeping them in touch with what was going on in Hedderby. They didn't want his wife's father doing anything silly. They were worried that he might be losing his wits in his old age, as sometimes happened.

It wasn't hard to guess what was on the son-in-law's mind. The mother had been locked away and there was nothing to stop them doing the same with the father, if it could be shown to be for his own good. Eh, there was nothing like money for stirring folk up.

Benting smiled grimly and took another sip of beer. For Forrett's own good! The only good the son-in-law was thinking about was his own. That young fellow didn't want Forrett frittering away his wife's inheritance on pauper brats. Well, who would?

So if his employer thought he had the whip hand, he might find out differently one day. It was a question of wait and see. Benting intended to work out where his own best interests lay and sod the rest of the world.

Even dealing with Dora Preston could wait. She knew who'd thrown the brick at her, which was a start, and since she was no longer working at the mill, she couldn't undermine him there.

He drained the glass and reached for the jug to pour himself another. Those Linneys and Prestons were an uppity bunch, thinking they were a cut above everyone else in the lanes near the mill. He'd not forgotten the sister Marjorie, either, the bitch. She'd defied him too.

He'd done well in life for a lad from the slums . . . but he'd not finished yet by a long chalk. He intended to have a secure old age and give up work when the time came with enough money to see him out in comfort, unlike his father, who'd died in the workhouse.

Forrett wasn't going to prevent that by bringing a thriving mill to ruin with his stupid charity, millowner or not.

At the Wednesday market, there were far fewer stalls than at the weekend and the place was only open in the morning, but still plenty of women came to buy fresh stuff.

Today Gideon found himself helping sell eggs, milk, cheese and poultry, which the Heegans sold mid-week for a small commission on behalf of several farmers' wives. Michael had set off in the donkey cart in the early dawn to visit the farms, taking Gideon with him so that he could do the collections on his own within a week or two.

To sell the fresh stuff Gideon was wearing an apron made of coarse, unbleached twill to protect his clothes and the thought of how he looked made him smile ruefully. He looked like a real stallholder today, not a smartly dressed sergeant!

But he didn't feel like a stallholder. He felt strange, unsettled, wanting to make something of his life. If only he knew what!

Towards the end of the morning he turned to see Dora standing at the next stall, talking animatedly to the old woman behind it. One of his wants surfaced immediately, making him stir uncomfortably. It had been a long time since he'd had a woman.

Then she turned round and he forgot himself, aghast to see a huge bruise on her forehead. She hesitated, looking at him uncertainly, and he went from behind the stall to join her. 'Whatever happened to you, lass?'

'Someone threw a brick at me while I was letting Nippy out in our back yard.'

'Do you know who?'

'I can guess.' She stared at his face. 'You look like you've been in the wars yourself.'

'The same three louts we met by the river, but someone called Benting, who's the father of their leader, swore that all three were at home with him at the time of the attack on me.'

'That man!' Her voice was burred with disgust and she pointed to her forehead. 'It was him as did this, I know it was, but his wife told the police he was at home when it happened.'

It wasn't his business, Gideon told himself firmly and nearly managed to turn away. But somehow he couldn't abandon her. 'Have you some other shopping to do?'

She nodded.

'If you wait till we've cleared up, I'll see you home.'

'Why?'

He sought for words to explain his offer, but he couldn't find any, not for himself, not for her, so he took refuge in, 'I don't know many people in Hedderby. I hope you and I can be friends. And I'd really like to see that little dog again.'

Her face lit up and in spite of the bruise she was so bonny that Gideon had to swallow hard.

'Nippy's ever so clever. He's learned what we want him to do and he even tried to protect me when I was attacked. Raife said he was barking and rushing at the intruder.' Her smile faded and she looked at him with a return to uncertainty. 'You're not married, are you, Gideon? Is that why you said you weren't for such as me? I'm sorry to be so personal, but I don't want people to think the wrong thing about me.'

He closed his eyes for a moment because it still hurt to say it. 'I was married. My wife died.' He felt a fleeting touch on his arm and opened his eyes to see her looking at him with warm concern on her face.

'I'm sorry, Gideon. You're still grieving for her, aren't you?'

He nodded. 'I'm over the worst, but I feel sad to think how young she was. I think you never stop missing those you've lost.'

'Then you'll need friends to cheer you up. I'll introduce you to my family and you'll meet plenty of other people if you're working at the market.' She smiled. 'There are a lot of us Prestons, I'm one of eleven children, not to mention the Linneys and Becketts. And we're related to the Heegans by marriage because Eli's cousin married Declan's brother.'

They might have been alone on top of a hill for all he noticed about what was happening around him. He couldn't find the strength to drive her away a second time. Just friends then, he warned himself. And thought he heard the tinkling sound of Lalika's gentle laughter somewhere in the distance.

'Are you serving here or not?' a woman's voice demanded right next to him.

Gideon swung round sharply. 'Sorry, missus.' He glanced back at Dora, who smiled at him.

'I'll come back later.'

The customer smiled at him too as he counted the eggs into

her bowl. 'I like to see young lovers talking. She's a nice lass, Dora Preston is. I hope you mean well by her.'

He blinked at this frank speech. 'We're just friends.'

'Oh, early days, is it?'

He didn't even try to argue, could see that the woman's mind was made up.

Dora came back half an hour later as he was finishing packing up the unsold bits and pieces from the stall.

'I forgot that I have to take this lot round to Declan's uncle's tripe shop. Michael had to leave early today.'

'Oh, I'll come with you. I like old Mr Heegan. Declan's uncle is always so cheerful. We buy his tripe and onions sometimes. Essie says it's cooked properly and his shop's clean or we'd not go near it.' She sighed. 'Anyway, I've nothing much else to do.'

'You're not working?'

'I've left the mill. Things were getting difficult – with the over-looker.' She blushed. 'Essie says I don't need to find a job yet, but I don't know what to do with myself all day. I do the shop-ping for her but that doesn't take me more than an hour or so. She's got the house so well organised she doesn't really need me there and has a woman come in mornings to scrub and keep the house clean. And to tell you the truth, I don't like looking after little children.'

'Don't you? I thought all young women loved babies.'

'Not me. And my sisters aren't too keen on them, either. There were always babies underfoot when my mother was alive and we older girls had to mind them. A puppy's much more fun and far less trouble, especially one as clever as my Nippy!'

They arrived at the shop and she exchanged cheerful greet-ings with Mr Heegan. Gideon envied her that sunny nature, but enjoyed it too. She was obviously popular from the way several people had greeted her as they walked. She'd had to explain about her bruised forehead no less than five times during the short walk to the shop.

When they got back to Linney's, she insisted he come inside for a cup of tea and he found himself sitting with a group of the older members of her family, all of whom made no bones about studying him and asking him about himself.

The little dog recognised him as soon as he went in and spent most of the visit sitting beside his feet, wagging hopefully every time he looked down at it.

When he left, he felt as if the day had suddenly grown cooler and wished he could rejoin them and go on enjoying the simple warmth of their companionship.

'He doesn't say much, that friend of yours,' Essie said when Dora came back after seeing Gideon out. 'Has he no family at all?'

'No, none. Isn't that sad?'

'I'd have thought a chap his age would be wed.'

'He was. His wife died. In India, he said. He was in the Army there till his accident and he's working for Declan Heegan now.'

'Oh, that's all right then. Declan wouldn't take on somebody shifty.'

'Gideon's not shifty!' Dora said indignantly.

Essie grinned. 'Like him, do you?'

'No! Not like that, anyway. He's just a friend. Will you *stop* trying to pair me off!'

But she wished Gideon was more than a friend. She admitted that to herself, though she didn't intend to let anyone else know.

He'd made it plain that he wasn't offering anything but friendship. He must have loved his wife very much.

When he left Dora and her family, Gideon walked along Market Street, ending up outside the lawyer's rooms. He'd casually mentioned this Mr Burtell to Declan, who'd said he was a good fellow, a true gentleman who treated his poorer customers civilly and had helped get justice for quite a few.

Gideon hesitated then walked inside, gave his name to the elderly clerk and asked to see Mr Burtell.

'You'll have to come back in an hour. He's busy now,' the clerk told him.

So Gideon went for a stroll up to the edge of the moors to

fill the time, taking the usual route. When he saw the front door of Number One standing open, he stopped and said, 'Aaaah' in a low voice, then moved further up the hill to the vantage point he'd found at the base of a rocky outcrop where he wouldn't be silhouetted against the sky.

His patience was rewarded about ten minutes later when a man came out of the door, locked it carefully behind him and began walking down the hill into town. Gideon could see him quite clearly and debated following him. No, not yet, he told himself, not till he knew where he stood. He didn't want to rouse the fellow's suspicions.

He frowned as he made his way more slowly down the hill. He hadn't recognised the impostor exactly, but something about the man had seemed familiar, as if he'd seen him a couple of times. No name sprang to mind, though there was something nudging him, something he ought to remember.

He racked his brain, but all he could recall of the second part of the voyage and his time at the infirmary were fever dreams and days that slid by in a blur, with faces coming and going around him as strangers tended him.

He strolled up and down the main street, relieved when the Town Hall clock struck the hour and it was time to return to Mr Burtell's.

As he began walking he suddenly remembered having a watch, a silver one which he had bought when he was promoted to sergeant. It had been engraved with his name. No doubt the impostor had it now. He'd been so proud of that watch. He'd get it back one day, by hell he would!

6

Carrie and Eli received a letter about the new music hall from the London architect that had them rushing round to see Jeremiah Channon. He lived in a recently built detached villa on some rising land leading up to the moors but he'd also opened up a place of business on Market Street, and that was surely where he'd be at this time of day.

'You know, we ought to be looking for a house for ourselves,' Eli said as they walked briskly along the busy thoroughfare. 'We shan't be able to live above the new theatre like we could above the old pub.'

'For the moment, it's very convenient living at Linney's. Essie and young Betsy often keep an eye on Abigail for us.'

'Most women would want their own house.'

'I'm not most women, as well you know. And what I really want is my old job back. I've not got any desire to go on the stage, like our Marjorie, but I did enjoy organising the daily life of the music saloon, the cleaning and refreshments. It was so *satisfying* to make everything nice and see people enjoying themselves. I miss that.'

He nodded but his thoughts had clearly moved on. 'I wish we didn't need to take Channon on as a partner.'

She shrugged. 'We don't have enough money to build the new place properly otherwise, so there's no use repining over that.'

He was silent for a few moments, then went off at a tangent. 'I'm glad I can't remember those months after the fire. I must have been mad to have given so much money in advance to that fake architect.'

She didn't say anything. It fretted him sometimes that he'd

wasted part of their capital, but she was too relieved to have the old Eli back to worry about that. *Worry about what you can change, not what's done and can't be altered,* she always told herself.

They were shown straight into Jeremiah's office and he greeted them with a smile, looking a very different man since his marriage, happy and relaxed.

'We can start work as soon as the plans have been approved by the Town Council,' he said after their discussion. 'I'm going to see if Lucas Kemp will work for me supervising the day-to-day practicalities of the work.'

'Can he afford to do that? He has his own business to run, after all. Needs to keep his customers happy.'

'I think he wants more stimulating work if he can get it. He worked for a friend of mine in London in the same capacity for a time and Reginald can't speak too highly of him. I should think Lucas will be able to find a carpenter to work in his own business without too much trouble. Even though times are better than a few years ago, there are still good men seeking work, especially those who've just finished their apprenticeships.'

'So we're all set to start work on building the new Pride, then?' Eli asked.

'Indeed we are.'

'And how long do you think it'll take to complete?'

'A year or so.'

Eli sighed.

Jeremiah looked at him severely. 'I'm not skimping on anything or rushing the work. I'm a partner as well as an architect and I want it all done to the highest standards.'

'You're right really. I'm just impatient.'

'So we'll begin.' Jeremiah held out his hand and shook Eli's, then surprised Carric by shaking hers too. She liked the way he treated her as an equal, in that serious, considered way of his.

As for Eli – she smiled – her husband treated her as an equal partner because she was one. If she'd been a helpless, dependent wife, he'd have treated her differently, but she'd played an important part in the old business and intended to do the same in the new one.

Actually, she thought with a smile, if a monkey came along which was able to help Eli set up the music hall he was so passionate about, he'd have treated it as an equal too. He had a wonderful way of accepting people for what they were.

Gideon sat in the lawyer's waiting room under the shrewd gaze of the elderly clerk. Eventually, ten minutes after the time of his appointment according to the clock on the wall, two gentlemen came out of the inner office and shook hands with one another. The taller one left and the smaller one turned to him.

'I do apologise for keeping you waiting, Mr Potter. Please come in.'

Inside the comfortable and slightly shabby office the lawyer indicated a chair at one side of the desk and sat down at the other side, easing his shoulders a little as if he was stiff and tired. 'Now, what can I do to help you?'

'It's advice I need at the moment.' Gideon explained the situation and had the satisfaction of seeing Mr Burtell lose his air of weariness and lean forward with an alert, interested expression on his face. 'Do you believe me?'

His head slightly on side, looking like a watchful bird, Jack studied Gideon for a moment, then nodded slowly a couple of times. 'Mmm. I'm inclined to.'

'Can I ask why?'

'Instinct. It doesn't usually let me down when it comes to judging people's characters. But I shall require you to prove it before we're through, since that's what you'll have to do in a court of law to regain what's rightfully yours.'

'How can I prove anything? My regiment is still in India and I have no family left in England, so who can vouch for me?'

'You were discharged from the infirmary recently. Surely there will be a doctor or someone else who knows you there?'

'The paperwork had been mislaid on the ship, so there was only my word for who I was when I arrived at the infirmary. I insisted on Gideon but for a time I couldn't remember my surname or much else, because I was still feverish. I didn't see much of the doctor anyway, for which I'm glad. I think I survived in spite of him not because of him. Infirmaries aren't comfortable places to be in and more people seemed to be carried out of mine feet first than walked away cured.'

Jack smiled. 'The day will come when we'll understand human bodies better, I'm sure. We have an excellent and very forward-thinking doctor in this town, thank goodness.'

'Dr Pipperday?'

'You've met him?'

'No, but I've certainly heard his praises sung. I'm lodging with Granny Horne and Dr Pipperday treated her grandson when he was ill.'

Jack nodded. 'He turns no one away. He's agitating about our water supply at the moment, says we need to get everyone on to piped water and close down these old wells, but he's not getting very far with the Town Council.' He looked at Gideon thoughtfully. 'I'd like to do a few specific things in connection with your claims, but they'll all take time, given the distance of your regiment in India. Have you a means of supporting yourself for a few months until we can resolve this matter?'

'Yes. And don't worry – I can afford your fees, too. I'm careful with my money.'

'I wasn't worrying about that. I'd have taken your case anyway, because it's an unusual one and I'll enjoy that. Now, this is what I suggest we do . . .'

Dora was delighted to be going to the concert Eli was putting on at the church hall on the Saturday night. She loved these shows and though today she would be working there, helping serve refreshments, that wouldn't stop her seeing something of the acts, or thinking about them for days afterwards.

Of course these shows weren't nearly as splendid as the ones at the Pride had been, because the top performers wouldn't come for just one or two nights in a mere church hall. But the shows still gave ordinary people from the town a lot of pleasure. And some of the performers stayed at Linney's, which brought in some money for Nev and Essie.

This time the act she most wanted to see was one featuring a performing dog, billed as the cleverest dog in England. She stood watching entranced as a large dog obediently performed tricks and did as its master wished. It was clever, but she didn't think it any cleverer than her Nippy and the act didn't grip you like some did. It needed more . . . more *something*, she couldn't work out what.

She made sure she was the one who took the cups of tea through to the performers and managed to have a word with the owner of the dog, a man who looked very ordinary without his fancy clothes.

'How did you get started?' she asked.

He cocked one eyebrow at her. 'Want to go on the stage, do you? Lasses usually go as singers or help fellows with their acts. I've never seen one with her own dog act.'

She tried but couldn't hide her eagerness and pride. 'Then I'd like to become the first. I've got a dog, you see, who's so clever. I'm sure he could do tricks like yours. So how *do* you get started?'

'Any way you can. Play a turn at markets and fairs, or go on in singing rooms, wherever you can find to practise till you're not nervous any more and till the dog gets used to crowds.'

She frowned as she took in his words.

He smiled at her. 'And another thing: you don't want to do the same tricks as someone else, or you'll get nowhere. You have to have an act that's different and if you can sing, then find a song of your own to finish off with. I can't sing, got a voice like a croaky old crow, and that's held me back. You're a pretty young girl. The audience would like to see you on the stage. But it'd still help to have a fellow playing with you. It's not only for on the stage, but for when you're travelling round the country. You'd be a lot safer if you had someone to look after you.'

'As long as you can trust the fellow,' she said darkly, remembering her sister Marjorie and how she'd been tricked and betrayed by a singer who was still performing with another woman helping him. The fellow would never be allowed to perform at the Pride again, though.

The dog act man seemed to be enjoying talking to her. 'You're a bit young to sound so bitter. Did someone betray you, then?'

'No. It happened to a friend of mine. But it makes you careful.'

'Well, I'd be even more careful if I was you. A pretty lass like you should find a fellow with a good trade and settle down, not go making a spectacle of herself on the stage.' He reached down to pat his dog. 'I'd not be doing it if I had any family left. Bandit here is my family now.' He sighed then shook his head as if annoyed at himself. 'What am I doing talking of such sad things to a young lass? Thank you for the tea, love. It's very welcome. They always treat you well at the Pride, even in this temporary place.'

She went back to help serve the refreshments to customers in the interval, because Eli and Carrie made extra money from selling all sorts of drinks and snacks, gooseberry cordial being a top favourite with the young women.

The following day she couldn't stop thinking about the dog act and at teatime was rash enough to say, 'Me and Nippy could do just as well as that dog last night if we went on the stage.'

There was dead silence, with Essie throwing a worried glance at Nev. He set his knife and fork neatly on his plate and frowned down the table at Dora. 'No one else from this family is going on the stage. It's a dangerous place for young lasses, as Marjorie found out to her cost. So you be sensible, my girl, and turn your thoughts to a safe, normal life. It's more than time you found yourself a fellow. You'll be twenty next year. You need to settle down, start a family of your own.'

She didn't even stop to think, just tossed her head and stared right back at him. 'I'm *never* settling down. I'd go mad from boredom shut up in a house all day doing the cooking and washing.'

There was another silence then Nev said firmly, 'Well, if you want to keep that dog of yours in *my* house, you'll stop such talk and set your mind on more sensible things. If it's him who's giving you ideas, I'll find him another home.'

Dora stared at him in horror. She couldn't imagine life without Nippy now. She closed her mouth on an angry response because she knew she'd pushed Nev far enough. Her stepfather was kind to them but he had some very definite views about life, and he cared greatly about being respectable and looked up to by people in the town.

But she wasn't going to change her mind. The more she thought about it, the more appealing a life on the stage seemed. She'd talk to her sister Marjorie about it next time she came to visit them.

She'd find a way to do it somehow.

For two days Ishleen did nothing except fetch the daily allowance of meal from the priest, cook it for her daughter, pick at it herself and sit around the house. Her friends and neighbours tried to comfort her, but there was no comfort to be found, because all she could see facing her was ruin.

Just outside her door was a stinking expanse of slime that had once been a field of potato plants. She tried to ignore it but the smell and sight intruded on her nostrils all the time. Some of her neighbours were in the same trouble and others seemed to have escaped the blight – though you never knew. Last time it hadn't struck everyone at once, allowing some to hope, then cruelly striking the plants down just as it seemed safe to harvest the crops.

She knew she should be making plans for the future if she was to avoid the workhouse, but somehow she couldn't think, couldn't do anything but sit. The long shadows slanting in through the open door reminded her that it was time to get the evening meal for Shanna. As she stood up, a pain shot through her and she bent over, clutching her belly and moaning. It was cruelly sharp, not like the birthing pains she'd felt before, for she'd had an easy time of it, or so the other women told her. It was a minute or two before she could pull herself together and tell Shanna, who was playing in a corner with her rag doll, to go and fetch the neighbour, tell her Mammy was sick.

When the child had run off, Ishleen went to get out the rags and baby clothes ready for the birth, and was about to fetch a bucket of water when the pain struck again.

The neighbour found her doubled up on the floor, moaning, and once again, Shanna was sent running for help.

It took Ishleen only an hour to lose the baby and it never breathed. Indeed, it looked so thin and waxy white that she turned her head away from it. The women cleaned her up and asked her if she wanted to see the priest.

She could only nod because she felt so weak.

When Father Gregory came in she was holding on to one idea. 'Will you write to tell my cousins in England that I'm dying? They'll take Shanna, I know they will. Promise me you'll write to them, Father.'

'Do you have their address?'

She knew it by heart because they'd had two or three letters and she'd kept them, proud of how well her relatives were doing across the water. The address came out in gasps and bursts, because she didn't seem able to think or speak clearly. The priest copied it down in his little book, spitting on the ink block he always carried with him. When he'd finished he gave her the final rites with fingers that were black-stained.

Neither of them had any doubt that she was dying.

The letter was addressed to Bram, but the postman brought it round to Declan, because everyone knew Bram was away singing on the stage in London. He stood on the doorstep staring down at it in surprise. The address of the priest who'd sent it and the word URGENT were written across the back of the folded piece of paper that was stuck together in the old-fashioned way with sealing wax.

I'm writing to seek your help, since you're a cousin of Ishleen Milane. She's grievously ill, will likely be dead by the time you receive this. We need someone to look after her daughter Shanna, who is four years old, because Ishleen's husband killed himself a few days ago. The blight is back in the potato crop and people here are like to starve again. No one can take in another child.

Please come quickly in God's name or Shanna will have to be sent to the workhouse.

- (Father) Gregory

Declan stared at the letter aghast and read it through again more slowly, trying to take in the news it had brought.

His wife's shrill voice interrupted his thoughts. 'What is it? Are those relatives of yours asking for money again?'

When he didn't answer, Ruth tried to take the letter from him though she wasn't a good reader.

He held her off impatiently. 'It's from Ishleen's priest.' He read it out to her. 'She's a sort of second cousin, a few years younger than me.' He vaguely remembered a dark-haired child, tall for her age. How sad that she was dying so young and leaving her daughter alone in the world!

'Huh! Well, let them look after their own, I say. *We* can't take the child. I've enough to do looking after our own sons, and you're so mean with money I'd have to stint our sons to feed another one. Any road, I'm not stupid enough to look after someone else's child. Declan! You're not listening. You never listen to me. But I mean it. I'm not having a pauper child here.'

He stared at her blankly, ignoring her usual lies and complaints, then went up the stairs in giant strides. He stared round the bedroom as if he'd never seen it before, because if truth be told he preferred to close his eyes to the mess inside his home and spent as little time there as possible. Most of his spare clothes were dirty because Ruth was a lazy, whining bitch. He'd have to get a washerwoman to take them again. He heard her coming up the stairs, puffing and panting because she'd got fat lately. 'I need some clean clothes to take with me.'

'*Take with you!*'

Her voice was a screech, painful on the ears and he closed his eyes for a minute until she came and stood in front of him, so close he could feel her breath on his face. She'd been drinking again. She drank most days now and nothing he said or did would stop her.

'You didn't hear a word I said. I'm *not* looking after that child, Declan.'

He glared at her. 'I'd not give a little lass to you. Even your own sons prefer to go round to Michael's. But understand one thing: I'm not having a Heegan put into the workhouse.'

'But she isn't a Heegan. Milane, her name is, so let the father's family look after the child.'

He looked at her with utter loathing. 'You're a lazy, selfish bitch, Ruth Heegan, and I rue the day I married you.' He'd never put it into such blunt words before and what he'd said hung in the air between them like the echo of a tolling bell.

Ruth blinked and took a step backwards, tears welling in her eyes.

She cried easily, used tears to get her own way all the time, so he ignored that. 'I'm after bringing the child back with me. I'll be gone for a few days.' He'd have to buy a change of clothes from the second-hand shop to take with him. He hoped they'd have some clean ones.

His mind busy now planning how to cover his absence, he ran out of the house, calling in at his brother's to ask Michael's wife Biddy to keep an eye on his sons. He borrowed a clean shirt of his brother's and underwear too, giving Biddy the money to buy new ones for Michael.

He pressed some more coins into his sister-in-law's hand. 'Tell Mam where I've gone. And get the washerwoman into our house while I'm away, will you, Biddy? Ruth's not done anything for a couple of weeks. And see if you can get her to wash herself too.'

'She'll not listen to me. But I'll do your washing for you.'

'No, love. You're expecting a child and shouldn't be doing heavy work. Pay someone else. I mean that.'

'Who'll look after the little girl on the journey back?' she asked. 'You need a woman with you.'

He'd been about to go to the market to give Michael instructions, but that stopped him in his tracks. 'Do you think so?'

'Yes, I do. What do you know about looking after four-year-old girls?'

He pulled a rueful face. 'Nothing. How will I find someone?'

She shook her head. 'Ask around at the market. Someone will know a widow who'll be glad to come with you and earn a bit of money.'

At the market he found Gideon talking to Dora, who had a puppy on a lead. 'Sorry to interrupt, but I have to go to Ireland suddenly and I need Gideon to do a few things for me.'

She stepped back as he explained. When he'd finished, he added, 'Michael's wife says I should take a woman with me to look after the child. Where the hell am I going to find someone who'll be ready to leave with me in an hour?'

Dora, who'd been listening in fascination, stepped forward. 'I could do it, Declan. I've given up my job in the mill so I've time on my hands.' She looked down at the little dog. 'And I'm sure Raife will look after Nippy here for me.'

'You're a bit young.'

She laughed. 'If there's one thing I know about, Declan Heegan, it's looking after children. And you're a sort of brother-in-law, so no one will worry about me going with you.'

He hesitated, then spread his hands helplessly. 'We'll go and ask Essie. You're only coming if she agrees.'

Dora hurried through the streets with him, excitement humming through her. She felt lost without a proper job, not knowing how to pass the day. And though she helped Essie as much as she could, her stepmother had to be the world's most efficient housekeeper and didn't really need her.

Essie listened in silence, nodded and said, 'You do need a woman with you, Declan. I'll help our Dora pack.'

With a sigh of relief, he went off to buy himself a travelling bag. He'd had one, but couldn't find it, suspected that Ruth had pawned it, as she'd pawned a few other items till he put a stop to it.

'Raife, you'll look after Nippy for me, won't you?' Dora asked.
'Of course I will, lass.'

She beamed at him, then followed Essie up the stairs. She'd
not been any further away from home than Manchester before
and was looking forward to seeing a bit of the world. Then she
felt guilty for being excited when some poor relative of Declan's
had just died.

If they hadn't been travelling for such a sad reason, Dora would
have loved the journey. Even on the ship going across to Ireland
she didn't experience a minute's seasickness, though Declan
became very quiet and his face took on a greenish tinge, then he
rushed to hang over the rail and vomit into the sea.

She also found it exciting to stay overnight in a strange boarding
house. Declan recovered enough to complain about the bumpy
roads because he'd expected to travel all the way by train. They
could get as far as Kinnegad, but after that they had to travel by
coach. The roads weren't very good and the overloaded vehicle
was slow, rocking about terribly, which made poor Declan turn
pale again and become grim-faced.

Dora thoroughly enjoyed both the train and the coach jour-
neys. She loved the green landscape, which was so much softer
and prettier than the moors near her home in Lancashire. The
final stage of the journey had to be in an open cart, because no
coaches ran to such a small village. That didn't upset her, though
rain was threatening.

'Where do you get all your energy?' Declan grumbled as the
cart jolted slowly along some deeply rutted country roads.

'Now that I'm not working in the mill, I seem full of it. I
don't know what to do with myself half the time and that's a
fact, because Essie has the house running so smoothly that
there are plenty of times when she doesn't need my help at
all. And Betsy looks after the children. We don't want to take
her job away from her because her family need the money.
Essie has been saying something would turn up for me and
now it has.'

'I can find you occasional work at the markets, if you want,' he said, still in a grumpy voice. 'Why didn't you ask me?'

'I was waiting till my forehead healed.'

He looked at her with more sympathy. 'And what about Benting?'

She hesitated. 'I can't prove it was him.'

'He's a nasty sod, that one, and so is his son.'

It began to rain just then and with a sigh, Declan hunched his shoulders underneath his overcoat and Dora wrapped herself more closely in her coat, pulling the collar up under her bonnet.

'This is the village, sir,' their driver said as they approached a few houses clustered round a very small church.

They stared round aghast at the fields of stinking, rotten vegetation. 'Is that the potato blight?' Dora whispered.

'It is so,' their driver said, his eyes sad. 'It's been the ruin of Ireland. I lost family and friends because of it myself.' He reined in his patient horse outside the church. 'There's the presbytery next door. You'll likely be finding the priest there.'

'I'll go inside, you stay here, Dora.' Declan got down from the cart without waiting for an answer.

She nodded, shivering because the rain was penetrating her coat and trickling down one side of her neck. It might be August but it wasn't very warm today.

He went to knock on the door of the house next to the church, which had a cross on its gable.

The priest answered the door himself. 'Can I help you?'

'I'm Declan Heegan. You wrote to my brother Bram, only he's away at the moment. Is our cousin Ishleen still alive?'

The priest nodded. 'She is, but only just. We thought we'd lose her quite quickly, but she's hanging on to life, poor woman. You'll be wanting to see her. The neighbours are taking it in turns to look after her and the woman next door has little Shanna. Will you be taking the child back with you?'

Declan nodded. 'And Ishleen – if she recovers.'

The priest pursed his lips. 'It's in God's hands, but I'm not feeling hopeful.'

'Is there somewhere in the village that can put us up for the night? I've brought a young relative with me to look after the child.'

The priest shook his head. 'There isn't anywhere at all suitable. The only pub is a hedge tavern and not fit for a decent woman.'

'I can pay for lodgings.'

'No one has any spare beds. And even if they had, they've sold all their bedding to buy food. They're starving, you see, nearly all of them. You'd be best going on to the next town after you've seen poor Ishleen.'

Declan dug in his pocket for some coins. 'Here. We're lucky. We've done well and I can earn more. Buy some food for the children.'

'Bless you, my son.'

'Can we go and see Ishleen now?'

'Yes. I'll show you where to go.'

When the priest joined them on the cart, Dora wasn't sure how to address him, since her family weren't Catholics. But he didn't seem to expect anything of her, just returned her nod of greeting and told the driver where to go.

The house at the end of a lane was very small and looked ready to fall down. Inside, it was damp and cold, reminding Dora of her childhood, because there was hardly a stick of furniture to be seen. But her mother had been feckless; these people had been forced to sell everything simply to buy food.

Ishleen was lying on a straw mattress on a beaten earth floor, with only a thin blanket over her. She was shivering and no wonder.

Without thinking, Dora took off her coat and flung it over the sick woman, rolling up her sleeves and looking at the fireplace. 'Is there no coal to be had to heat this place?'

'Peat,' the priest said. 'I'll show you where the pile is.'

As he and Declan vanished, Dora looked at the woman who'd been nursing her neighbour. 'Thank you for looking after her.'

'We were friends. But when Ishleen lost the new baby as well as the potato crop, she seemed to lose the will to live.' She looked down at the mattress with its still figure, her face sad.

She didn't seem to be thinking straight herself, Dora thought. Was that what hunger did to you, sapped your will to live, made you so listless you didn't even bother to put another turf on the fire? She shivered.

Declan returned with a pile of turfs and set about coaxing the embers into life. 'Is there anywhere we can buy some milk and maybe eggs?'

'From the landowner, if you have the money,' Father Gregory said. 'But he gives nothing away, that one.'

Declan looked at the neighbour. 'If I give you the money, missus, and a bit to spare for your trouble, will you go and buy me some food?'

The woman's face brightened. 'I will, yes.'

Declan looked at Dora, frowned then looked down at the bed. 'You'll need that coat yourself, love.'

'She's shivering.'

'She can have mine. Unless we can borrow or buy another blanket or two?' Again he looked at the priest.

'I've given all mine away, except for the one on my bed.'

'I've got some spare clothes in my bag. I'll put an extra layer on.' He gave Dora her coat back. 'Thank you, love. Have you any experience of nursing sick people?'

'A little. It sounds as if she's stopped eating, needs good food in her. If we beat up an egg in milk and give her half of it to start with, that may stay down.'

Just then the sick woman opened her eyes and stared at them as if she didn't believe what she was seeing. Declan went to kneel by her side. 'It's all right, Ishleen. I'm your cousin Declan and I'm here to look after you and Shanna.'

'You won't – let them take her – into the workhouse?'

'No, I promise I won't. And I'll make sure you get better too.'

She closed her eyes. 'I'm done for.'

He felt anger rise in him and shook her till her eyes opened. 'You're not done for. Shanna needs you. Don't you dare die on me!'

She looked at him in shock.

His voice grew more gentle. 'Ah, Ishleen, don't give up, lass. A child needs its mother. And you've family in Lancashire will be happy to take you in and find you work, too.'

A tear trickled out of one of her eyes, followed by another, then a whole flood of them. So he took her in his arms and held her wasted body close, feeling a tenderness rise in him at how much she had suffered.

'You're safe now,' he whispered. 'You and Shanna both. You've nothing to do but get better.'

They slept there that night, all four of them pressed close together for warmth on two straw mattresses pushed together. They put the coats over the top of them and Ishleen and her daughter in the middle. Dora lay awake for a long time. She'd not truly understood how lucky she had been in her life until now, because though they'd been poor, she'd always had her brothers and sisters, never been alone, and had usually had something to eat, most days anyway. How bad must it have been for the woman breathing softly near her to see her little daughter starving.

In the morning, there was the light of hope in Ishleen's eyes and a look of adoration too for Declan, who set about obtaining whatever was necessary for the invalid and her daughter.

'He makes me feel – I can live again,' she whispered to Dora once and fell into another long sleep with a smile on her lips.

It took two weeks before Ishleen was well enough to face a journey, two weeks during which Declan confronted the landowner and told him to his face he should be ashamed of letting his tenants starve, then went into the nearest town and purchased supplies with his own money that would give the people in the tiny village a meal each day for another month.

'The Lord will reward you for this, son,' Father Gregory said.

'It's reward enough to be able to help, to see the children eating,' Declan said sombrely. 'I'll send more money, Father, I promise, but I must keep back enough for the journey. Bram will give generously when he knows how bad it still is, and I'll make a collection among the other Irish in Hedderby.'

He didn't feel like talking that night and was relieved when Ishleen and Dora left him alone, murmuring to one another as they sat on the other side of the peat fire. What he'd seen here made him regret the years he'd wasted even more strongly, the stupid drinking and fooling around, and he vowed to do something worthwhile with the time he had left.

He'd been trying to make a lot of money out of jealousy of his older brother Bram, but now he'd seen the distress here and how money could bring life to so many people, well, he knew he'd never feel the same about it – or anything else either.

The next day they left for England, another long, complicated journey. He'd grumbled when coming here, because the station at which they arrived in Dublin was on one side of the city, with no rail connection to the station from which they left for Kinnegad. He felt guilty about that now because it seemed a small matter, hardly worth bothering about. What did such inconveniences matter compared to whole villages starving slowly and helplessly to death?

He would enlist Bram's help, he vowed, and they would save at least that one small village.

7

Gideon began walking home from the market, tired, not really looking where he was going. As he turned the corner, he nearly bumped into someone and was shocked to find himself nose to nose with the impostor. Drawing back, he muttered, 'Sorry!' and averted his head, trying to walk on without being noticed. But it was too late. The man had stopped dead and was staring at him in horror, clearly recognising him.

Gideon decided it would be no good pretending to be unaware of the other's stare. 'Why are you staring like that? Do you know me?'

'You – um – look like a friend of mine who's dead. Gave me a terrible shock to see you.' The man started to turn away.

Gideon put out a hand to hold him back as an idea occurred to him. 'Look, I'm sorry about shocking you. I was hoping you knew me because I don't rightly know who I am, apart from the fact that I was in the Army. I was brought back to England ill, out of my mind for weeks, and then there was a mix-up so they weren't sure who I was. I can't remember anything clearly, just my first name, Gideon. But this town was written on a scrap of paper, so I came to see if anyone knew me here. I've asked everywhere, but had no luck. If you can help in any way . . . ?'

The man took a hasty step backwards. 'No, no. I'm not – it was just – you looked so like my friend it shocked me. I've never seen *you* in my life before.'

As he hurried off, Gideon continued on his way, resisting the temptation to turn round and stare. He wondered if he'd been convincing, if he'd done the right thing. Mr Burtell said they needed several months for letters to go to and from India about him, because no court would take his word for it that he was Gideon John Shaw. The lawyer had had a quiet word with Mr Hordle and found out that the claimant had had plenty of proof to back up his story. Gideon's own possessions, it sounded like!

It was galling to think of someone else enjoying what should rightly be his, including his life savings. He wasn't going to give up till he got everything back.

Gideon was thoughtful as he made his way back to his lodgings. Perhaps if he could find out where the man went, it'd shed some light on this mystery. But how to follow him when he had a living to earn was more than he could figure at the moment.

After that he didn't bump into the impostor again, but sometimes he had the feeling that he was being watched. He still kept an eye on the cottage, but it stood empty for as many days as it was occupied. Where did the impostor go? Had he another home and family somewhere? And what did he plan to do with the things he'd stolen?

At least the lawyer's letters were on their way to India now. He hoped to hear a response to his own letter soon. There'd been plenty of time for it to reach his old regimental headquarters in Preston, though no one there would know him, as they'd been left behind to look after things in England, had never been to India.

James Forrett paced up and down the warehouse with the local architect Lucas had recommended. 'Well, Mr Channon? Do you think you can turn this warehouse into a place where children will feel safe and happy?'

'Yes. I'd love to. But I'll need some idea of what you're willing to spend before I start drawing up preliminary sketches.'

'I'll spend whatever it takes.' James sighed and stared at the light slanting in through one of the high windows. Its brightness seemed to mock the sadness that was lodged deep within him, a sadness that nothing seemed to shift. He'd found the joy of being a father only with his last, unexpected baby, and she'd died. 'Within reason, of course. I don't want anything fancy, just a homely place. It's the children who matter. I only realised that too late.'

'I lost a child, too, in a house fire. I know what it's like.'

James seized the architect's hand and wrung it, saying in a thickened voice, 'Then get to it, man. Make this place into a proper home.' He turned away, then swung back again. 'You'd better talk to Gwynna and Lucas before you start, though. They've got a few ideas of their own about what the place should be like, good ideas too.'

'I'll do that.'

'How soon can you begin work?'

'Since I've only recently moved to Hedderby, I have only one other project at the moment, supervising the building of the new Pride, so I can start on your project at once. I won't take on any other jobs until these two are completed because they're both going to be demanding.'

'Good, good.' His emotions threatened to overcome him, so James moved into a shadowy part of the big room. 'Can you show yourself out? I'd like a moment or two on my own.'

Jeremiah nodded.

When he'd gone the old man took out his handkerchief and blew his nose so loudly and defiantly that it echoed round the big, empty space. 'If I want to treat folk more gently, I can afford to do it,' he muttered, jutting his chin defiantly. 'It'll mebbe help make up for the years when I worked the mill lasses and their children too hard.' Another minute's frowning had him admitting in a tone of surprise, 'I worked myself too hard as well.'

Another prolonged blow of the nose, a squaring of the shoulders and he marched out into the sunlight.

Near the mill gate he met Benting and stopped, looking up to check that the windows were open, then studying the mill yard. 'I've been thinking. We should be giving the younger ones who work here better schooling than we are. The law says we should, too.'

His overlooker gaped at him. '*Give them better schooling?* What on earth for? They've just got theirsen shorter hours, thanks to that damned Act of Parliament. Let 'em be satisfied with that. If the Government asks us to do any more for the operatives, they'll ruin us.'

'Not they. We can well afford to treat our people better an' that's what I intend to do from now on.'

'Them children are too well treated as it is. They're there to tend the machines not scratch on bloody slates. And any road, who's to enforce the law? We get word when the inspector's coming, put on a show of schooling for him and he goes away happy. That's enough, it really is. If they get too much schooling, they'll never be satisfied to toil in the mill. They'll be wanting the boss's job.'

James poked a finger in the other man's chest to punctuate his words. 'If I want – to give 'em proper lessons – then I shall.'

'But we can't keep the machines running without the children!'

'Then employ more children and they can take it in turns to have lessons.'

'That'll cut the profits still further.'

'They're *my* profits and if I want to cut them, I shall. I can well afford it.'

Benting watched his employer saunter across the yard, still looking round thoughtfully. Before he got to the house he stopped and went across to pace out a square of ground in one corner, doing it not just once, but twice. The old man had definitely run mad. It had started when that baby of his died and it was going from bad to worse.

It was time to write a letter to young Mr Gleason, time to start making plans to safeguard Benting's income. But it'd have to be done carefully because Forrett was a wily old sod. Benting grinned. So was he. Just wait till he was the one running this mill. There'd be no more softness towards the lasses or children who worked here then. And the profits would double. He could safely promise that to the Gleasons.

On the journey back to Liverpool the sea was rougher than coming over and Declan was very seasick. So was the child. Dora and

Ishleen stayed on deck with Shanna, even though it was chilly, because she seemed much better in the fresh air. To their relief, she eventually fell asleep, lying on the bench with her head on Dora's lap.

'What's it like, this Hedderby of yours?' Ishleen asked, staring out across the dark, heaving sea.

Dora put her head on one side as she considered this. 'It's at least fifty, no a hundred times bigger than your village, a long thin town with rows of houses on the slopes at each side. There's a river runs through it and the moors are nearby.'

'Moors?'

She tried to find words but could only come up with, 'Hills'.

'Declan says he's taking me to stay with his mother. He doesn't talk of his wife much, does he?'

Even though no one was near them, Dora lowered her voice. 'That's because she's a shrew, always complaining and nagging. She drinks too. Everyone knows what she's like and feels sorry for him. You have to wonder why she does that because he's a really good provider and a loving father. I've seen him with his sons. It's a shame.'

Ishleen let out a soft scornful sound. 'I know what it's like to be married to someone who can't cope. My husband was a weak fool. He killed himself when we were needing him most, and I can't forgive him for that. It's sad that he died so young.' She sighed and added, 'I wish I could mourn for him but what I mainly feel is relieved to be rid of him. That's wicked, so it is, but I can't change how I feel.'

Dora didn't know what to say and as a big yawn overtook her just then, she sat in a companionable silence for a time. 'I think I'd better go and see how Declan is.' She tried to stifle another yawn.

Ishleen stood up. 'I'll go. You stay here with Shanna. You look tired out.'

'I didn't sleep much last night, I must admit. Are you sure you're up to it?'

'I'm feeling better every day.' With a smile, the other woman went below. She found Declan in their four-berth cabin, lying on a lower bunk. He groaned as she came in and looked ghostly white in the light of the lamp hung securely on the wall where it couldn't be knocked over. He'd been sick again, so she took the bucket and went to empty it, then coaxed a jug of water from the harassed steward.

When she returned to the cabin Declan opened his eyes and stared at her. 'You shouldn't be looking after me.'

'Why not? Haven't you looked after me?'

'You're not well enough.'

'I'm fine. Here, have a sip of water and let me wash your face for you.'

He let her minister to him, sighing in relief as she cleaned his skin and cooled his brow. 'My head spins if I lift it. I'm not a good sailor, am I?'

'No.'

'Haven't you been sick at all?'

'No. I'm feeling fine, though I'm thinking it's better in the fresh air than down here.'

'I was desperate to lie down, my head was spinning so much. How's Shanna?'

'Sleeping now. Dora's with her.' Ishleen sat down on the lower bunk opposite his. 'I don't think I've thanked you properly for all you've done for me, Declan.'

'You're family.'

'I'm only a distant relative. But I had no one else to turn to.' Her voice suddenly became fierce and determined. 'I'd speak to the Queen of England herself for my daughter.'

He smiled. She would too. He knew already how determined she could be, like the first time she'd stood up, wobbling furiously but refusing to give in to her weakness.

'Shall I be able to find work in Hedderby, do you think? I don't want to be a burden to you.'

'When you're better, I'll find you work.' Inspiration struck. 'My uncle wants to open a stall at the market, selling food. He'll need someone to run it. You could do that.'

'I could if someone showed me how.' She sat on without speaking, then smiled. 'It's good that you brought Dora with you. What a lovely person she is! She's been so kind to me and Shanna and there are some things that – need a woman.'

For the first time he realised that Ishleen had once been an attractive woman. She was gaunt now, with no curves or spare flesh, but her eyes were beautiful and her smile warm and tender. He'd lived with her for two weeks, thrown into an intimacy that had been difficult at times, living in that small cottage. He'd bought blankets in the nearby town and paid the neighbour to make them two more straw mattresses so that they could sleep separately, but there had still been long hours spent together, confidences exchanged, personal needs to tend to. He knew Ishleen better, in some ways, than he knew his own wife, liked her better, too. Which reminded him.

'I need to warn you. When we get to Hedderby, you'll meet my wife. Ruth's a sour, bitter woman and she'll be rude to you. She's rude to everyone. I can't stop her. Just – take no notice of her, whatever she says. She drinks sometimes and then she speaks wildly.'

The ship rolled about again as if they'd met some even bigger waves, and he clapped one hand to his mouth, ashamed of his weakness.

'Here.' Her voice was gentle as she held the bucket.

When he'd finished retching, though he'd little left in his stomach to cast up, he watched through his eyelashes as she wiped his face again, her expression serene and caring, showing no sign of distaste for the task. He closed his eyes fully and let her finish, but his thoughts wouldn't be closed off.

Why the hell hadn't he married someone like her? He'd been a wild lad in his youth and had married a wild, rough lass out of defiance because his Mam disapproved of her. But Ruth had been fun in those days. He'd never understood why she'd changed so much after their first son was born, losing that wild spark completely and turning into a bitter woman who used her tongue as a weapon and always looked on the dark side of life. She was unable to cope with a house and children, blaming others for everything that went wrong, when it was her own laziness and inability to organise anything that led to the chaos. He'd never beaten her, had always provided for her, couldn't understand why she seemed to hate him lately.

His eyes went back to Ishleen, now leaning her head against the wall and looking chalk white with weariness. He could feel his gaze softening. He mustn't think of her like that, mustn't show her any affection when they got back or Ruth would latch on to it and try to blacken Ishleen's name with everyone in the family.

'You'd better get back to Shanna,' he said as she jerked upright suddenly, having nearly fallen asleep. 'I'll be all right now. I've nothing left in my stomach.'

'If you're sure?'

'I'm sure.' His voice came out harshly because he didn't want her to leave and he saw her forehead crease in a slight frown. But he couldn't help it, needed to send her away before he said something he'd regret.

He couldn't stop himself thinking of her, though.

Gideon stepped back from the market stall and took a good long stretch. He'd been on his feet for several hours and could do with a sit down, not to mention a cup of tea. The widow who usually provided hot drinks for people at the market hadn't turned up today and they were all missing their cups of tea.

Michael came across, his expression as cheerful as ever. 'Do you want to take a break now?'

'It'll be the busiest time soon. You'll need me here. I'll just nip along to the conveniences, though. I'll just be a minute.'

On his way back one of the other stallkeepers stopped him.

'Have you heard?'

'Heard what?'

'About poor Jane. Dropped dead last night, didn't she, poor lass. We're going to miss her. She made a nice cup of tea. It puts heart into you, a hot drink does on a cold day.'

Gideon walked slowly back, thinking, not for the first time, how uncertain life was. Then suddenly he realised that here was an opportunity for him to gain some independence. They'd still need a hot drinks stall here. Declan's uncle was going to sell tripe and other cooked food, but Gideon could sell all sorts of drinks without interfering too much with the other man's trade, and perhaps sell cakes too. He'd ask Declan when he got back if that'd upset anyone. He'd rather work for himself, he'd found, though his friend was a good employer.

He was looking forward to Dora coming back, too. He'd missed her and so had the little dog, Raife said.

As if thinking about her had conjured her up, he saw Dora and Declan that very afternoon when he was on his way home from the market. They were accompanied by a woman who looked thin and exhausted and who was holding the hand of a tiny slip of a child. She and the little girl both looked white and bone tired.

He strode across and smiled. 'Hello. Welcome back.'

'It's good to be back. This is my cousin Ishleen Milane,' Declan said. 'Ishleen, this is my friend Gideon. He works with me at the market.'

Declan didn't look his usual self, in fact they all looked exhausted, so Gideon asked, 'Can I carry your little girl for you, Mrs Milane? She looks worn out.'

'That's kind of you. I haven't the energy to pick her up today and Declan and Dora have my luggage.'

Gideon bent to the child. 'Can I give you a piggyback, love?'

Her answer was to hold up her hands. He swung her up to sit on his shoulders and looked sympathetically at them all. They looked bedraggled and weary. 'Bad crossing, was it?'

'Aye.' Declan grimaced. 'And I'm a poor sailor, unlike Dora here.'

Gideon nodded briefly to her, but he'd sworn to keep away from her, from all women until he had his life sorted out, so he didn't even give himself the pleasure of walking beside her. 'When you've recovered, I've a business proposition for you, Declan.'

'I'll come and see you later after I've drunk of few cups of

Mam's tea and filled my belly. Sure, it's echoing like a bell in church.'

There it was again, Gideon thought. People loved drinking tea. He was sure he could make an adequate living from selling it until his life was sorted out. Maybe he could persuade the Town Council to let him open a stall every day, or better still a kiosk in the corner.

Ishleen forced herself to put one foot in front of the other as they began to walk uphill, though she was ready to collapse with weariness after such a disturbed night. She felt bewildered by all the people she encountered, every one of them a stranger, but the places she'd seen on the way here were even more frightening.

Dublin had been so big it'd take you hours to walk through it. In the centre there were great houses several storeys high and roads full of carriages, carts, men on horseback, so that you'd be afraid to cross the street. Though the pavements weren't much better, they were so full of people. Where were they all going?

Liverpool had been worse, to her mind, because even the voices sounded different, so harsh and clipped after the way Irish people spoke. She'd kept tight hold of Shanna's hand, terrified her daughter would get torn away from her and lost. By that time it was beyond her to understand anything about what was happening around her. She was relieved when they got on the train and into a small, safe space again, even though travelling so fast through the strange countryside made her head spin at first.

And now they were in Hedderby, which Declan and Dora said was a small town, but still seemed large to her after the village in Ireland. She was sure she'd get lost if she went out on her own. And more people . . . She stared from side to side, amazed. How did they all make a living or grow food when there wasn't enough land for them, only narrow streets and paved roads?

Declan's mother greeted her like a daughter and that was her undoing. She felt tears come into her eyes and overflow. 'I'm so grateful,' she managed in a choked whisper.

'Ah, she's worn out, Declan!' Mrs Heegan scolded. 'You should have looked after her better.'

'It was she who looked after me last night, Mam. I'm a poor sailor. That's what tired her out.'

Ishleen allowed them to settle her in a chair, pulled Shanna on to her knees and felt more secure, somehow, with the child in front of her. She accepted a cup of tea and a piece of cake. So much food she'd eaten in the past two weeks and yet she always felt hungry, as if she'd never manage to fill the great, echoing hole inside her. She ate her food slowly, enjoying the sight of Shanna cramming her mouth with cake more than the taste and feel of it on her own tongue.

When Declan's mother said the magic word 'bed' she nodded, too weary even to speak her agreement.

Carrie and Eli weren't going to make anything special of the day they started work on the new music hall, but somehow word got round.

When they were getting ready to go down to the site, Raife said suddenly, 'I'd like to come with you. It's a special day, this.'

'It's just an ordinary working day,' Eli protested.

'Not for the folk of Hedderby,' Raife said. 'They miss their music saloon.'

'I'd like to come too and wish the new place well,' Nev said. 'How about you, Essie?'

'I've cooking to do and children to look after.'

'You can leave them with Betsy for an hour, can't she, lass?'

The girl nodded.

So they all made their way down to Market Street, where they found the labourers who'd been hired to start the work waiting patiently. A group of spectators had assembled too, standing on the footpath next to the site, smiling and speaking quietly to one another as they waited for the work to begin, just as they'd waited beneath the big gas lanterns for the shows to start in the old days.

'Can you have it finished by the weekend, Mr Beckett?' one wag called. 'I'd like to bring my lass to a show.'

'I wish I could,' Eli called back. 'But we're putting on a show at the church hall next week. Bring her to that.'

'It's not the same without a pot of beer, though I suppose it's better than nowt.'

'Be patient. We'll get the Pride going again as soon as we can.'

Jeremiah came striding along the street with Maria on his arm and her two sons following them.

Eli went to pick up a shovel and gestured to Carrie and Jeremiah to join him. 'We'll give 'em a bit of a show, eh? Carrie love, you turn the first shovelful then me and Jeremiah will do the next ones. Tell her where to dig, Jeremiah lad. We want it to be a real hole.'

So Carrie took the shovel, moved to where Jeremiah had indicated and dug out a shovelful of earth.

'There, we've started!' Eli called in his great booming voice. 'You'll remember this day when you come here for your first show.'

There was a ragged cheer from the bystanders.

Carrie handed the tool to her husband, who also turned a shovelful of earth over, then Jeremiah followed suit before gesturing to his wife and Lucas to join them.

When they looked round, there was a line of people waiting and one by one they all turned over a small piece of the ground, cutting out an uneven line where proper foundations would be put in this time so that the walls wouldn't collapse.

'It's the heart of the town, this music saloon is,' one man said. 'Me and the wife miss it sorely.'

'The new one will be a proper music hall,' Eli corrected. 'Much fancier.'

'As long as it doesn't cost too much to get in.'

'It won't.'

'I met my sweetheart here,' another man said as he handed back the shovel. 'We're wed now, and it's all due to the Pride.'

Carrie listened to these and similar comments with enormous satisfaction, and felt tears in her eyes to see how many people wanted to be part of this impromptu ceremony.

The two labourers stood grinning and when everyone from the crowd had turned over some earth, however small a shovelful, they took over and showed people how it should be done, flexing their muscles and showing off a little by setting a pace they couldn't possibly maintain all day.

'We're opening in a year's time,' Eli said to his partner. 'I don't care how we do it, but we're going to have the Pride open again by this time next year.'

Jeremiah frowned. 'I'm not sure we can manage that.'

'We'll find a way,' Eli said confidently, his eyes filled with both dreams and determination. He turned to the crowd and shouted his news and they cheered loudly before starting to disperse.

He stood there on his own for a moment or two, as if seeing his music hall rising like a phoenix from the ashes. Then he let his wife tug him away.

'You haven't stopped smiling all morning,' she said.

'No. I feel like we're getting somewhere now.'

'Heart of the town, one man called it,' she murmured. 'Doesn't that make you feel proud?'

For answer he picked her up and spun her round. 'Not as proud as we're going to be the night we open.' Then he kissed her, right there in the street, to loud applause from the remaining bystanders.

PART TWO

March 1849

8

Dora hummed to herself as she got ready for work, wrapping up warmly because it was a cold day.

'Eh, I don't know how you cope with standing outside at the market all day,' Essie commented as she plonked first a bowl of porridge then a jam butty on the table in front of her. 'I'd be frozen.'

'I'm too busy to feel the cold and anyway, the urn and charcoal fire keep me warm. It is a nuisance when it rains, though, because even with the canvas cover to the stall, drips blow in.' Dora made short work of the food while Nippy cleaned out his bowl in the corner. She'd never had so much free time or energy to spare in her whole life. Instead of working six days in the steamy heat of the mill, she was working three days at the markets on the stall that Declan and Gideon had opened together to sell hot drinks and scones or small cakes. Nev and Essie said she was bringing in enough money and to enjoy herself while she could.

'Are you taking Nippy with you?'

'Of course I am. I've taught him to shake hands and the customers love it.'

Something in her tone of voice must have given her away, because Essie gave her a searching look and asked sharply, 'You're not still thinking about going on the stage with him?'

Across the table, Raife shook his head warningly at Dora.

She fumbled for words, not wanting to tell an outright lie. 'You and Nev said I couldn't. But it's fun to teach Nippy tricks and he loves it. Besides, it helps bring in the customers, because I only let him shake hands with folk who've bought something.'

As she walked to the market, Dora marvelled at how big the

town seemed to be growing. When she got to Market Street she stopped to look back along the road to the music hall, which was a proper building now, dominating the lower shops and pubs around it. She'd been with Gwynna the previous Sunday to see the warehouse, which was nearly ready for them to move in and open as an orphanage. She wouldn't want to spend her life looking after children, but Gwynna and Lucas seemed eager to do it.

As usual, Gideon was already at the market. He'd lit the charcoal burners under the two urns and the smaller one was already heated, with the big teapot standing ready beside it. He was a hard worker, that was sure.

She stopped for a moment to watch as he gave a free cup of tea to one of the old men who hung around the markets and slept where they could. He didn't like people to know about such small kindnesses, but she'd seen him do quite a few similar things during the cold winter months, seen the gratitude on the faces of those who were sleeping rough.

When she walked behind their stall Gideon gave her his usual nod of greeting and left her to get on with her morning tasks. She sighed, wishing he wasn't always so cool and distant with her, because she'd never met a man she liked so much, but she didn't seem able to make any headway with him. Of course Nippy went bounding up to him, tail wagging furiously, jumping around his feet until Gideon bent to pet him. The dog was a lot more successful at winning his affection than she was.

'One of these days, he'll go home with you instead of me,' she teased. 'I'm jealous.'

'He's a grand little chap. Never seen a smarter dog.'

'He is, isn't he? I mean, it's not just my imagination. He's a real little star.'

He frowned at her. 'You're not still thinking of going on the stage?'

'How do you know about that?'

'Raife told me.'

'I can't do anything till I'm twenty-one,' she said, trying to avoid a direct answer.

He wasn't fooled. 'So you *are* still thinking about it?'

She shrugged. 'Maybe. If I can get a start.'

'It's no life for a single lass, especially one as pretty as you. All that travelling round. How would you manage?'

'I'll have to find myself a fellow to look after me an' Nippy, won't I?' she answered flippantly.

Gideon turned abruptly and got on with his work, not saying anything else, but as the day passed, she could sense him watching her and when she sneaked a glance sideways she saw that his forehead was creased as if he was worrying about something.

Surely not about her going on the stage? She wished it was, wished it was him going on with her and Nippy.

When Dora got home that night she was a bit late because they'd had a rush of last-minute customers.

Essie greeted her with, 'Go up and change your clothes quick. Have you forgotten that Jim Sharples is coming to tea tonight?'

Dora sighed because of course she had forgotten. She trailed reluctantly upstairs to the bedroom she shared with her sisters. Ever since she'd turned twenty in January, Essie had made more effort to find her a lad.

Edith wasn't home from the shop yet, but Grace was combing her hair in front of the mirror, turning this way and that as she tried different styles. She greeted Dora with, 'Perhaps you'll like this fellow better than the last one.'

'I don't like any of these young men, and I wish Essie and Nev would stop inviting them to tea. Where do they find them all?'

'At church, or nephews of Essie's friends.' Grace giggled. 'This makes the sixth one this winter. They're determined to find you a lad.'

'Well, I don't want to get married and settle down. What if I'm like Mam, having one baby after another? I'd go mad.'

Grace looked at the door and lowered her voice to a whisper. 'Do you still want to go on the stage?'

'Shh! You know what Nev and Essie think of that.'

'Do you, though? You can tell me. I won't say anything.'

'There's nothing *to* say. I'm not twenty-one so I have to do as they want. And anyway, I don't have enough money saved to tide me over while I'm starting.' Footsteps on the stairs made her say hastily, 'Yes, I like your hair that way, Grace.'

Raife tapped on the door. 'Our visitor's arrived.'

Dora gave a little snort. 'I'll be a few minutes yet, Raife. I have to wash and change.'

She delayed as long as she could, then went to join the rest of the family in the front parlour, nodding a greeting to Jim, whom she'd already met at church. When it was time to eat, Essie managed to sit him next to Dora, so she couldn't ignore him completely, but she said as little as she could.

'You're very quiet tonight, love,' Nev said at one stage.

'Am I? I must be tired.'

They even sent her to see Jim out. At the door he hesitated. 'Will you come walking on the tops with me if it's fine on Sunday afternoon?'

'No, thank you.'

He looked at her in bewilderment. 'But Essie says you love it up there.'

'I like to go on my own.' Even in the darkness she could see him flush and felt guilty for treating him so abruptly, but she wasn't having him getting any ideas about her and she definitely wasn't going walking on the tops with him.

'Good night.' She shut the door and stormed back into the kitchen.

Essie looked up expectantly. 'He's a nice lad, isn't he?'

'No, he's a very dull sort of fellow. He bores me to tears.' Which was an exaggeration, but she had to make them understand she wasn't interested.

Essie's face fell, then her mouth went into a straight line as she got annoyed at Dora. 'You don't give them a chance and you look so fierce they're frightened to say anything. Jim's a lively young man when he's with other people.'

'Then let him stay with other people. I don't want him.'

'You'll wake up one day to find all your friends are married and there are no nice lads left, if you go on like this.'

'I keep telling you: I *don't* want to get married.'

'You're not going on the stage,' Nev said sharply. 'You can get that idea right out of your head.'

'You've made that plain. But it still doesn't mean I have to marry someone I don't even like.'

'What's wrong with that lad? Or with the last one, Trevor?'

'There's nothing wrong with them. I just don't find them interesting.'

'You didn't open your mouth much tonight, either. I was mortified.'

'Well, stop inviting them. It's not fair to raise their hopes. If I ever want a lad, I'll find one myself. I'm going to bed now. I'm tired.'

She wasn't, but she'd had enough of being nagged. She knew Essie and Nev meant well, that she was lucky to have such kind step-parents, but she just wished they'd leave her alone and stop bringing home all these lads.

There was only one man she fancied and he'd made it plain he wasn't interested in her.

Gideon watched Dora on the Saturday. She'd lost some of her usual sparkle and was less tolerant than usual with customers who couldn't decide what they wanted. 'What's wrong?' he asked during a lull in business.

'I don't know what you mean. Nothing's wrong.'

'Then why are you so brusque with everyone this morning?'

'I'm n—' She bit back more sharp words because he was only being kind. 'I'm sorry. I'm just a bit – annoyed.'

'What about? Anything I can help with?'

'No. It's my family. They keep inviting young men to tea, trying to set me up with one, and I'm fed up with it!'

'Most young lasses would be happy about that.'

'I'm not most young lasses. What do I have to do to persuade people that I've no intention of getting married for years yet?

My friend Lizzie isn't nineteen and she's expecting her second baby in August. My mam had thirteen children who lived and a few who died. What sort of life is that for a woman, having one child after another?'

'Is working on a market stall enough for you then?'

'It'll do for now.' She glanced down involuntarily at Nippy, who was sitting quietly behind the stall.

Gideon followed her glance. 'You're plotting something.'

She tossed her head at him. 'Nothing that need worry you. *You* aren't responsible for me.'

He didn't pursue the matter but he had a fair idea of what she intended, couldn't blame her for wanting more from life. He wanted more from it, himself. This market stall wouldn't hold his interest, but it made a decent profit, more than he'd expected. Before he could sort out a more interesting life for himself, though, he'd have to settle his problems and see where he stood financially. He was going to see Mr Burtell this afternoon to discuss progress about proving who he was – or rather the lack of progress. Only when that was settled could he work out what to do with his life.

The brightest spot on his horizon was Dora. The more he got to know her, saw her dealing with people, the more he liked her. She had a warm, generous nature and everyone thought well of her. He enjoyed her company and they rarely exchanged a cross word. But he'd nothing to offer her at the moment, so it wouldn't be right to raise false hopes in her. He'd been telling himself that all winter, but with less and less conviction.

What if he never proved who he was? What then? He'd still want her in his life, that was certain.

He felt a nudge on his ankle and looked down to see Nippy staring up at him. It was as if his little friend knew he was feeling a bit despondent. He bent to caress the dog's head and for a moment it leaned against him.

'He loves you,' Dora said from above his head.

He stood up. 'I'm fond of him, too.'

They stared at one another for a few moments, her eyes

searching his face as if looking for something there. Then the spell was broken by a customer.

'Where's that dog gone?' a woman said. 'I'm not buying a cup of tea until I've shook his hand. Hello, Nippy lad.' She offered him a piece of bread, but the dog wouldn't take it.

'I've taught him not to take food from anyone but me,' Dora reminded her.

'Poor little mite. Look at how he wants it.'

'If I let him take food from everyone who wants to give him a titbit, he'd get fat. But thank you for the thought.'

'I suppose you're right.' The woman bent to offer her hand to Nippy and he glanced at Dora, then when she made a certain hand movement, he put up his paw. 'Eh, he's that clever, better than a dog I saw at the Pride once.'

Dora couldn't help shooting a told-you-so glance at Gideon, who smiled but shook his head at her.

The trouble was, the woman was right. Nippy was a very special little dog, just as Dora was a special young woman.

Later that afternoon, after they'd packed up for the day, Gideon went along to see his lawyer.

'I've had a letter from the Army,' Jack Burtell said.

'Oh?'

'It's not good news, I'm afraid. They've investigated matters and are satisfied that you're not Gideon John Shaw, because they discharged a man by that name a few months ago who had all the correct paperwork.'

'*What?* But—'

Jack held up one hand. 'There's just one thing.' He held out the letter. 'Have a look at that and see if you notice anything.'

Gideon studied it. At first he didn't see anything wrong, then he sucked in his breath. 'There are two words spelled wrongly and the captain's signature – well, it doesn't look the same as the other one.'

'And yet, the same person is supposed to have sent it.' Jack pulled out another piece of paper and laid it next to the new letter. 'See.'

They both leaned over the desk.

'It can't be . . . Do you think it's possible that someone's intercepted my letter and is making up his own replies?'

'Could be. I've met corruption in all sorts of places, and I'm not surprised to find it in the Army as well. Maybe the impostor is paying someone to intercept our letters. I think I'll go down to London and have a confidential chat with a friend of mine about the best way to tackle this now.'

'You do still believe me, then?'

'Even more than I did at first.'

'When can we go to London?'

'I'd rather go on my own and find out how best to go about this. You still haven't got any real proof of who you are, you see.'

Gideon closed his eyes for a moment, bitterness washing through him. 'How long is this going to go on? I could wait patiently when I felt your letter was on its way to India, but now, well, I reckon it never went anywhere, nor did my earlier one. Maybe I should go to regimental headquarters in Preston myself and speak to the officer in charge.'

'Not yet. It's a delicate situation.' He patted Gideon's arm. 'The wheels of justice sometimes grind very slowly, I'm afraid. You're not – short of money or anything?'

'No, my market stall is doing well. But I wish I could . . .' He hesitated then said with a sigh, 'I've met a lass, you see, but how can I court anyone when I can't even prove who I really am?'

'If she loves you, she won't care what you're called.'

Gideon let out a snort of mocking laughter. 'No, but *I* care. I've lost everything, even my own name, it seems. I want things to be straightened out before I talk to her. And even then . . . well, she's younger than me and I wonder if I should let her find someone who's not been so *marked* by life.'

Jack was quiet for a moment, then said, 'I hesitated once to court a woman because I hadn't established myself as a lawyer, only I waited too long and she found someone else. Don't lose something valuable because of your foolish pride.'

His words kept coming back to Gideon as he walked back to

the market to finish clearing up. Was it foolish pride that was coming between him and Dora? Should he risk speaking out? It was agony not to respond to her overtures sometimes. Sheer, bloody agony.

On Sunday everyone at Linney's went to church, as usual. Dora avoided even looking at Jim Sharples as they settled down in their usual pew. She always found it hard to sit still for over an hour and was relieved that Nev didn't carry his insistence on church attendance over into what they did for the rest of the day. Some families had very miserable Sundays, not allowed to do anything.

'I think I'll take Nippy for a walk,' she said after they got back from the morning service. 'Mr Nopps has been preaching some very dull sermons lately.'

Essie smiled. 'I agree with you, but I still like to go to church. I like singing the hymns and stopping to chat to my friends afterwards.'

'Better not go too far, Dora love,' Nev said. 'I reckon it's going to rain by mid-afternoon.'

Dora went to the back door and studied the sky. 'I think it'll hold off for an hour or so yet. It's too cold to stay out for longer than that but Nippy does love his walks.' Even as she spoke the magic word, the dog began pawing at her and running to the door, making little whining noises in his throat.

'He understands English, our Nippy does,' Raife said with a smile.

They didn't realise how much that dog did understand, Dora thought as she set off towards the tops. She'd worked out a series of tricks with Nippy, but she was at a stage where she needed someone to watch them and tell her if they were interesting enough to be part of an act. She didn't think it was fair to ask Raife to do that because she didn't want to cause trouble between him and his son. She'd have asked Gideon, only he too seemed disapproving, and anyway, he avoided her after work.

She paused as she walked past the end of the lane that led to the four cottages, stopping for a moment as she always did, because they were so pretty she liked to imagine that she lived in one of them looking out over the town. So much nicer than a terraced house hemmed in by rows of other houses.

Nippy bustled to and fro as they walked, snuffling loudly and following scent trails only he could smell, but always staying within sight of her. When he felt she'd been standing still for long enough, he started to yip at her then run ahead for a few steps, as if to urge her to move on.

She went up to their special place, a level patch of land out of sight above the path, where no one could see what she was doing, and they began to practise the tricks. Nippy loved learning new ones and getting praised for them, not to mention eating the scraps of food she'd brought to reward him with.

It was when she spun round on the spot, arms stretched up to the sky, laughing with delight at how quickly he'd picked up a new trick, that it happened. Her foot turned over on a stone, which rolled from under her and she went tumbling down awkwardly, crying out in shock. She felt a stabbing pain in her ankle and lay for a minute, waiting for it to go away. Only it didn't. And when she tried to stand up, it hurt so much to put any weight on her left foot that she stayed where she was.

She sat still until the waves of pain abated then tried once again to stand up, but couldn't face the agony every time she jarred the ankle. How she was to get home again? Could she crawl?

She tried that and managed to go a few yards but it was slow work and she whimpered in pain a few times.

What was she going to do? She couldn't even call for help up here. Nippy came to press himself against her and for a moment she buried her face in his coat and gave way to tears.

Then a miracle occurred and she heard footsteps crunching along the rough stony surface of the path below them. She craned her neck to see who it was, but the person was hidden from her just as she was hidden from anyone on the path. Feeling foolish, she called out, 'Help! Please can you help me?'

The footsteps stopped and then a man's head came into view,

followed by the rest of his body as he climbed up the dozen or so yards from the path to this little level space.

Nippy growled at the stranger and Dora had to call him to her and shush him. 'I fell over and hurt my ankle,' she explained. 'I can't put any weight on it, so I don't know how I'm going to get back home. Can you go and tell my family for me, ask them to bring a handcart?'

He stared down at her in surprise before coming to kneel beside her. 'Let me see it.' He reached out for her skirt.

She pulled back, embarrassed to show a stranger her leg.

'I've had some experience with accidents,' he said. 'Used to nurse sick folk.'

'Oh. Well, all right. Just a minute till I get my stocking off.'

She fumbled for her garter and then rolled her stocking down past her knee. He took it the rest of the way, pulling it off as gently as he could. But it still hurt. Then he examined her ankle, which hurt even more. She couldn't help sucking in her breath and making a noise in her throat.

Nippy at once began to make little growling noises and she had to shush him again.

The man straightened her skirt and got to his feet, handing her the shoe and stocking. 'I won't try to put these on again. I think it's just a sprain, but from the swelling it's a bad one. It'd help to put it in cold water.'

'Can you go and let my family know? I don't know how I'm to get home without help.'

He looked up at the sky. 'It's going to rain soon. I think I'd better try to get you home myself, but I can't carry you all the way into town.' He stood frowning in thought then gave her a wry smile. 'I've got a wheelbarrow. It's not very elegant, but I could sit you in it and push you back down the hill.'

'I don't care how I get back as long as I don't have to walk. Would you mind? I live at Linney's. Do you know it?'

'Big house on the corner, takes in lodgers? Yes, I know it. I'll go and get the wheelbarrow.'

As he walked away, Nippy watched him suspiciously, still

rumbling in the back of his throat, which surprised her. Her dog didn't often react to people like that, though he still barked at Huey Benting every single time he saw him. Which just showed how intelligent Nippy was. Huey had never come near her again, but the way he looked at her made her feel uncomfortable, as if she wasn't wearing any clothes.

It seemed a long time until the man returned, and by then the dampness in the air had increased, showing that rain was coming shortly. 'I've got the wheelbarrow on the path below. I put a blanket on it. It'll be best if I carry you down to it. I can manage so far, I think. Can you put your arm round my neck and hold tight?'

She did so and he lifted her with a grunt, because like the rest of her family she was tall and sturdy. It felt strange to be held so close to a complete stranger, but he didn't try to take any liberties as he edged carefully down the slope, thank goodness. He took his time over the rough ground then settled her into place on the wheelbarrow, sitting up with her leg supported by a folded blanket.

Gratitude filled her and she smiled at him. 'Thank you. I don't know what I'd have done if you hadn't come along.'

As he stepped back he smiled back at her in a way that said he found her attractive and for the first time since she'd met Gideon, she found herself responding to another man's attention. And now she came to think of it, he looked a bit like Gideon, very upright with a sallow skin that looked as if it had seen the sun. But he was thinner and of course he had all his fingers.

It took some time to get back to Linney's because the wheelbarrow wasn't easy to push without it wobbling and threatening to tip over at corners and rough spots. Nippy trailed behind them, avoiding Dora's rescuer and letting out the occasional yip or growl of warning.

'He doesn't seem to like me,' the man commented. 'Must know I've never had much to do with dogs.'

'Don't you like them?'

'Haven't had the chance to find out.'

'You must live near here to have fetched the wheelbarrow so quickly.' She wanted to find out more about him.

He stopped for a breather and pointed to the left. 'I live in those cottages, at Number One.'

'Where Mrs Haskill used to live?'

'Yes. She was my aunt. She left the cottages to me.'

'I used to call in and see her sometimes when I was coming up to walk on the tops. She used to talk about her nephew in the Army. Fancy you being him! You were serving in India, weren't you?'

'Yes.'

'Do you know Gideon Potter? He was in India too. He runs a stall at the markets.'

'No, I don't know him.'

She frowned. 'Didn't Mrs Haskill say your name was Gideon too?'

'I was christened Gideon, yes, but in the Army they called me by my second name and I got used to that, so I think of myself as John Shaw now. What's your name?'

'Dora Preston. Nev Linney is my stepfather and I work for Gideon Potter at the markets.' She gasped as the wheelbarrow wobbled, hit a big rut and pain shot through her ankle again.

'Sorry. It's impossible to avoid all the bumps.'

'It's all right. I'm really grateful for your help.'

But by the time they got back she was feeling sick with pain from the jolting and had stopped trying to hold a conversation. John Shaw wasn't very talkative anyway. Or perhaps he was finding her heavy to push and was saving his breath for that.

Her rescuer knocked on the front door and when Raife opened it, Dora burst into tears.

'She's hurt her ankle. I'll carry her inside for you.' John lifted her up and at Essie's direction continued with her up the stairs to her bedroom.

He was a very strong man, Dora thought, leaning against his chest and enduring more bumping around. He gave her a sympathetic half-smile then went back down again. As Essie helped her undress and get into bed, she could hear snatches of his conversation with Raife in the kitchen below. He was introducing himself and explaining how he'd found her.

When Essie fetched a bucket of cold water and insisted she plunge her swollen ankle into it, that was so uncomfortable Dora forgot the stranger.

'It'll do the swelling good,' Essie insisted. 'Keep it there as long as you can.'

'Where's Nippy?'

'Raife's keeping him downstairs. Did you trip over him?'

'No, of course not. He'd never get under anyone's feet. I wasn't looking where I was going and stepped on a stone that rolled from under me.'

'I can't see why you're always going up there.'

'I like the fresh air and playing with Nippy. After all those years in the mill, it's wonderful to breathe so freely.'

'It's not natural, a girl your age going off on her own like that. Nev was saying to me only the other day that he'd rather you took someone with you.'

'Well, there isn't anyone to take. Raife can't walk so far and he can't walk fast. And most of the time my sisters are at school or work. Besides, they've other things to do. Nippy gets twitchy if he doesn't get his walks – and so do I.'

Essie shook her head. 'You're a strange girl.' She hesitated, then asked, 'What was wrong with that new young man at church? I could see he was interested in you.'

'He had a face like a sheep. And he was talking to me about Bible reading classes, going on and on about it!' she said indignantly. 'Imagine a lifetime of that! No, thank you very much.'

'You'll have to settle down some time, love.'

'Why? I can earn my own living.'

'You'll regret it when you're older if you don't have children.'

Dora looked at her, anger evaporating, knowing how much her stepmother regretted that. 'You've got us now, Essie,' she said gently. 'We're your family.'

Essie smiled and patted her shoulder. 'I know. But it came to me late and I want a better life for you girls than I had. Now, put that foot in the bucket again.'

It was a relief when Dora could pull her foot out of the cold water and lie down. The warmth of the blankets was so lovely she closed her eyes and immediately John Shaw's face came into her mind. She didn't know what would have happened if he hadn't come along. He didn't say a lot, but he'd been kind to her.

His face blurred and changed into Gideon's as the sound of rain beating against the windows lulled her to sleep.

9

When she went out shopping, Gwynna decided to call on Mr Forrett. He seemed so lonely, poor man, all by himself in Mill House with only two servants to keep him company.

She took young Joe with her because lately she didn't feel comfortable crossing the mill yard on her own. Benting always seemed to pop out of a doorway and stare at her in *that way* and he'd come into the mill house a couple of times, interrupting her chats with Mr Forrett and leering at her. What a horrible man he was! No wonder Dora was still nervous of him. When Gwynna had mentioned how she felt, Lucas suggested she never go to the mill on her own and she hadn't needed any persuading to agree to that.

The housemaid opened the door, looking harassed and worried, her hair untidy and her apron tied anyhow, which was not like her.

'Is something wrong?' Gwynna asked in surprise. 'You look – upset.'

Jen glanced quickly beyond her into the yard. 'No, there isn't. And you can just mind your own business about how I look. You might be all cosy with Mr Forrett, but that doesn't give you the right to pry into my affairs.'

Gwynna gasped in surprise. Whatever had got into Jen? When they'd both worked here as maids, Jen had always been a cheerful, willing worker. But this wasn't the first time she'd been grumpy lately. 'I've come to see Mr Forrett.'

'He's not expecting you, is he?'

'No. But he likes it when I call in.'

'Well, you can't see him today. He's tired and he's having a rest.'

'In the morning?'

'Yes.' She darted another anxious glance out across the yard as she spoke.

As Jen was about to close the door in the visitor's face, her employer came out of the front parlour into the hall. His clothes were awry, his hair was in a mess and he was staring round as if he didn't know where he was. Gwynna put her foot in the door and shoved it wide open again. Something was very wrong here and she wasn't going to be kept out.

'You can't come in, I said!'

Jen tried to push her out and the two young women had a brief tussle until Mr Forrett came up to them.

'Gwynna? Is that Gwynna? Come in, love. It's grand to see you.'

Jen stepped back, looking desperate.

Gwynna followed the other woman's glance and saw that Benting had moved across the yard and come to stand nearby, as if listening to what they were saying. Her puzzlement grew. Why would Jen and Benting be exchanging glances? And what business was it of his what anyone said to Mr Forrett's maid? His scowl was so fierce she felt suddenly afraid.

On a sudden impulse she beckoned Joe across and bent to whisper in his ear. As the lad nodded and ran off, she turned to Jen again. 'I'm staying for a chat with Mr Forrett. I've told Joe to come back for me later so that he can help carry my parcels from the shopping.' She spoke more loudly than usual to make sure Benting could hear her and then stood watching to make sure no one stopped her young messenger.

But it was her that Benting was watching, not the boy, and he was looking even angrier than before. She took a quick step backwards into the hall.

'You shouldn't be here, you really shouldn't,' Jen said. '*Please*, Gwynna, come back another day.'

'I'm staying.' On a sudden impulse she banged the front door shut so that Benting could neither see nor hear them. Mr Forrett was still standing nearby, looking bewildered, which really worried her because normally he'd have intervened and told Jen to get back to her work. She had to pull him to start him moving then guide him into the front parlour.

Jen tried to follow them inside, but Gwynna stood in the doorway.

'I need to clear away the master's morning tea things,' the maid insisted.

'You can do that later.'

'Cook will skin me alive if I leave dirty things lying around.'

'I need to talk to Mr Forrett privately, so you'll just have to wait.' Gwynna not only slammed the door in the maid's face, but some impulse made her turn the key in the lock. She watched as the door handle turned round and back, then was released, amazed at Jen's persistence. Then she forgot everything else as she went across to the millowner.

Mr Forrett only seemed half aware of what was going on around him. He looked so lost and helpless, she put an arm round his shoulders. 'What's wrong, Mr Forrett? You don't look at all well.'

He rubbed his forehead. 'I can't seem to think straight. I was all right this morning – well, I think I was – but after I had my morning cup of tea I started to feel dizzy. I think it was then it started. I can't rightly remember.'

She looked beyond him at the tray containing the tea things, a tray which Jen had been anxious to remove, and was suddenly reminded of what Mrs Forrett had been like when her former mistress had taken a dose of laudanum. She'd never forgotten because that befuddled state had led to little Libby's death. A horrible suspicion crept into her mind.

Someone banged on the door and Benting shouted out, 'I need to see Mr Forrett urgently.'

Gwynna took hold of the millowner's arm. 'Tell Benting to go away,' she urged.

He looked at her and muttered, 'Go away!'

His voice was too quiet and Benting was still hammering on the parlour door. 'Shout "Go away, Benting" as loudly as you can,' she told him.

'Go away, Benting.'

This time he roared the words at the top of his voice and there was no response from outside. But there was no sound of footsteps walking away, either.

'Come and sit down, Mr Forrett. I'll look after you till you feel better.' She guided him to a chair near the fire and left him sitting there to go and keep watch at the window. He didn't even turn his head to see what she was doing, just leaned his head back and closed his eyes with a sound that was half sigh, half groan.

What was wrong with him?

As she turned to check he was all right, her eyes lit on the tray and she went across to sniff the cake. It had a sickly odour that she recognised and hated. Her suspicions had been right. But why would anyone want to drug the millowner?

She had a quick word with Mr Forrett then went back to the window.

Ten minutes later a carriage drove into the mill yard. She'd seen it before and knew it belonged to Mrs Gleason, Mr Forrett's elder daughter. Why did *she* have to come here on such a day? Gwynna couldn't tell his daughter to go away. To her surprise, Mrs Gleason wasn't accompanied by her husband but by a severe looking man who was carrying the sort of bag Dr Pipperday carried. As usual she was fussing with her skirts and to Gwynna's surprise, Benting looked round in a way that could only be described as *furtive,* then went across to have a word with her. They moved to the other side of the carriage, leaving the stranger standing there, looking round.

The dreadful suspicion grew stronger. Why should Mrs Gleason bring a strange doctor to see her father? How could she possibly know he wasn't well? He normally enjoyed excellent health.

At that moment Lucas walked into the mill yard accompanied by Dr Pipperday, with Joe skipping along behind them. Gwynna let out a groan of relief and blessed the instinct that had made her send for the town's much-loved doctor after one glance at the millowner. She was relieved too that Mrs Gleason was still behind the carriage talking to Benting.

She went across to the man slumped by the fire. 'Your daughter's here. Mrs Gleason.'

His voice was slurred. 'What's she doin' here on a weekday?'

'I don't know, but I want you to see Dr Pipperday first. Will you do that for me? See your own doctor first?'

He nodded. 'Aye, lass. Alicia's no comfort to a sick man and I do feel strange.'

Gwynna hurried to open the front door and call, 'Come in quickly, Dr Pipperday. He's this way.'

As the two men hurried into the house, she grabbed her husband by the arm. 'Lucas, will you keep everyone out until Dr Pipperday's seen Mr Forrett? He isn't well. *Everyone*, including his daughter,' she added in a low voice. 'They're up to some mischief. I think they've drugged him.'

She tugged Dr Pipperday across the hall and let him into the front parlour just as Alicia Gleason's strident voice rang out and she began to hurry across the yard.

'Wait! You there! I want to see my father. Who is that man?'

Gwynna slammed the parlour door and saw Dr Pipperday stare in surprise as she locked them in.

'Is that necessary?'

'It is if we want to help him.'

At that he turned to Mr Forrett. 'What's wrong?'

Gwynna interrupted. 'He told me he was all right this morning, then he ate his mid-morning snack and afterwards he felt bad. I think someone's drugged him. I smelled the cake and it's got a funny smell to it.'

'Show me.'

She bent to pull the tray from under the sideboard and stopped in dismay. 'It was here a minute ago, just before I came to the front door to let you in. Jen must have nipped in and taken the tray.' She turned to Mr Forrett. 'Did Jen just come in?'

He looked at her, frowned then nodded. 'She took the tray.'

'Oh, no! I won't be able to prove anything now. But it smelled of laudanum, doctor, it really did. Most people wouldn't notice such a faint smell, but I've got a good sense of smell and anyway, I hate that stuff. It always reminds me of how Libby died.'

'But why would anyone dose Mr Forrett with laudanum?'

She put her horrendous suspicions into words. 'I think they're trying to say he's losing his wits so that they can lock him away. His daughters have never forgiven him for locking their mother away. But *she* was addicted to laudanum and she really had lost her wits. Mr Forrett hasn't. It's the orphanage, you see. He's spending a lot of money on it, money his daughters had expected to inherit. He told me and Lucas that they're angry with him about it.'

The doctor frowned at her then examined his patient, checking the pupils of his eyes and taking his pulse. His gentle questions elicited only slurred and hesitant answers. Mr Forrett did as he was told, but seemed half-asleep. Dr Pipperday stood up and came across to the window, speaking to Gwynna in a low voice. 'I was chatting to him only yesterday about the orphanage and he seemed as normal as the next man.'

'He is. I think Benting is involved in this. Jen kept looking at him when she tried to stop me coming into the house. I pushed past her and came in anyway, but a minute later Benting knocked on the door of this room, saying he needed to speak to Mr Forrett urgently. And why should Mrs Gleason arrive at exactly the right time to see her father looking so muddled? That man with her looks like a doctor to me.'

Dr Pipperday frowned at Gwynna. 'He could have been drugged, I suppose.'

The voice arguing in the hall suddenly grew louder and Mrs Gleason began shouting at them to open the door or she'd fetch the magistrate to them.

'We can't let her in,' Gwynna said desperately.

'We can't stop her for long,' the doctor said, watching as Mr Forrett closed his eyes, completely ignoring them. 'If Mrs Gleason does fetch the magistrate to get a ruling about her father, he'll give her the authority to look after him because the man does appear to be losing his wits and we've no way of proving that he's been drugged.'

The day after Dora's accident John Shaw called at Linney's to see how she was. She felt flattered that he would do that and glad to see him. He was quite goodlooking and tall – though not as good-looking as Gideon. She was feeling restless because she couldn't do anything but sit around the house and rest her ankle, and she wasn't the sort to laze around all day. She chatted to him in the front room, where she was installed on the sofa, offering to show him some of Nippy's tricks to prove how clever dogs could be.

To her dismay, however, Nippy wouldn't go near him or perform properly. He growled when Mr Shaw first came into the room, but she told him firmly to be quiet so then he'd lain by her side, head on his outstretched paws, keeping watch on the stranger.

Raife came in to join them. He didn't smile or chat as much as usual, though he was polite enough to Mr Shaw.

The visitor stayed only for a few minutes then took his leave.

'Wasn't that kind of him to come and see how I was?' Dora asked.

'Aye, I suppose so.'

She frowned at Raife. 'Why do you say it like that, as if you don't like him?'

'I found nothing to dislike about him.'

'But you do, don't you? It isn't fair to judge someone when you hardly know him. And after he saved me, too!'

Raife shrugged. 'It takes all sorts and we can't like everyone we meet. I think I'll play the piano for a bit, if you don't mind. We've a show coming up in two weeks and Eli's given me a list of songs. He was saying there's a dog act in it.'

This distracted her, as he'd hoped, and, as she sat half-listening to the music, she wondered what tricks they would perform in this dog act. No animal could be as clever as Nippy, she was certain, but she hadn't settled yet on what to do with him on the stage.

She insisted on hopping into the kitchen to have her midday meal at the table with the others. The three young children had a smaller table in a corner with special little chairs to sit on and Betsy to help them, while the rest sat at the big kitchen table. There was always a crowd at Linney's.

As they waited for Essie to serve them, Dora looked across the room and chuckled, putting one finger on her lips and pointing so that Raife and Nev turned to see what was amusing her.

Essie hated Nippy getting under her feet, so when the dog was particularly hopeful of titbits falling his way, he'd developed a trick of staying behind her as she worked. Whenever anything fell to the ground he would then dart round her to lick it up, even a splash of soup or gravy. Nothing was too small to attract his interest. As long as he didn't trip her up, Essie put up with this because, she said, it saved her bending to pick things up and they did mop that part of the floor clean every night, after all.

When Raife helped Dora back into the front parlour for a rest afterwards, he lowered his voice and said, 'You know, lass, if you really want to work up an act with Nippy, you'll need some sort of story to play out, like Marjorie and Hal do in their comedy act. Watch how this chap in the next show does it. I've seen him afore. He's got a lovely dog. His wife used to be in the act, but she died and his sons are working with him now. The whole family travels round together. It must be hard to raise lads like that.'

She hesitated, then asked, 'I hope Nev and Essie haven't guessed that I've not given up on my dream of going on the stage. Everyone else seems to know.'

'People believe what they want to believe. If Nev and Essie knew more about dogs they'd realise that Nippy knows far more tricks than other animals do. But you'd better keep quiet about your plans until you can do summat about 'em. You know Nev's dead set against any more of you going on the stage after the trouble your Marjorie got into afore she met Hal.'

'I'll find a way to do it, see if I don't.' But it would be ten months before Dora was twenty-one and free to do what she wanted. That seemed such a long time to wait. She felt so restless lately, as if she was marking time . . . no, *wasting* time.

Dr Pipperday looked at Gwynna then at his patient. 'I've met Mrs Gleason before. She can be very – officious with people. Even if he is losing his wits, I'd not willingly entrust him to her tender mercies.' He smiled and reached into his bag, pulling out a small blue bottle. 'Laudanum. I prescribe it for toothache sometimes. We'll say that Mr Forrett sent for me because he had toothache and I made him take some.'

She looked at him in relief. 'That's very clever.'

He looked back at her warningly. 'So far I've only your word for what you think is happening. From now on, I'll be observing him regularly to make sure he is all right.'

He poured a tiny amount of the liquid into a spoon, dipped a fingertip into it and smeared a little near Mr Forrett's mouth, then put the spoon down next to the bottle on a small table. 'Can you pretend you've got toothache, Mr Forrett, that I've just given you some laudanum to help with the pain?'

Even drugged, James remembered his wife's addiction to laudanum and grimaced. 'I'd never willingly have that damned stuff in the house.'

Gwynna went to crouch beside him. 'I hate it too, but if you just trust us for now, I'll explain what's been happening tomorrow when you're feeling more yourself. Your daughter's here and we need to pretend you have toothache.' Inspiration struck her. 'You can complain about Dr Pipperday giving you laudanum.'

For a moment Forrett stared at her, then he nodded. 'I do trust you, lass.' He took a deep breath and sat upright, muttering, 'It's like thinking through a fog.'

'You've had toothache all night,' she repeated. 'You're angry at Dr Pipperday for giving you laudanum.' Praying that he'd remember it, she went to open the door.

Lucas was standing there barring the way and he looked at her anxiously.

Benting pushed him aside and gestured to Mrs Gleason to come in. 'I don't know what you think you're doing, Kemp, keeping a daughter away from her poor, sick father!'

Forrett said without prompting, 'Get back to your job, Benting. Can't a man have toothache in peace now?'

The overlooker looked at him in shock, but only retreated as far as the hall, staying there listening to what was being said.

Dr Pipperday didn't move from his patient's side as Alicia Gleason rushed across to kneel by her father. 'Are you all right? They said you weren't well. I've brought my own doctor to see you.'

Gwynna held her breath.

Forrett scowled at his daughter. 'Don't need your doctor. Got my own.' He gestured to Dr Pipperday.

She stood up. 'My doctor is a Manchester man. He's very expert – in these cases.'

Dr Pipperday drew himself up indignantly at this insult. 'I've been Mr Forrett's doctor for several years now and I can assure you, Mrs Gleason, that I'm perfectly capable of dealing with toothache.'

'It's more than toothache, from what I've heard.'

The older man with her came to stare down at Mr Forrett and then look suspiciously at Dr Pipperday. 'I'm Paul Helton. I've been brought here especially to attend to this man, so you can leave him to me now.'

Forrett had been listening, a frown on his forehead as he strove to concentrate through the cloudiness in his brain. 'Don't need another doctor. Didn't send for you, don't want you. Pipperday has my full confidence. It's only toothache, dammit.'

'The man's speech is certainly slurred,' Helton said. 'You were right to be concerned, Mrs Gleason.'

'Of course his speech is slurred,' Dr Pipperday said. 'He's been given laudanum for the toothache.' He picked up the spoon and brandished it at them.

Dr Helton came across and took the spoon out of his hand, sniffing it. 'It *is* laudanum.'

Pipperday looked from Mrs Gleason to the doctor. 'Of course

it is. The man's been in severe pain all night. I'm going to recommend he has that tooth pulled.'

'I hate taking that damned stuff,' Forrett said. 'Shouldn't have let you p'suade me.'

'I'd prefer you to see my own doctor, Father.' Alicia scowled at Pipperday. 'Send this man away now.'

'What for? He's an excellent doctor and he's *my* doctor.' He clapped one hand to his cheek. 'Ow! Go away and leave me in peace.'

There was a moment's hesitation as she looked at Dr Helton. Gwynna noticed that Benting had reappeared in the doorway and wondered what would have happened if she hadn't come here today, if they'd perhaps have taken Mr Forrett away forcibly with them. She was relieved when she saw her husband step forward to stand close behind Benting. If there was any trouble, Lucas was as strong as the overlooker, probably stronger because he was twenty years younger.

The silence seemed full of dark undercurrents and for a few moments no one spoke.

It was Dr Pipperday who broke it in the end. 'My patient needs to rest now. I think you can safely leave him in my hands – as he just said.'

Dr Helton pursed his lips as if considering what to do, then looked at Mrs Gleason and shook his head slightly. 'If I'm not wanted, I'll wait for you in the carriage, my dear lady.'

She turned back to her father. 'Are you sure you'll be all right? Perhaps you should come and stay with us, then I'll be able to look after you properly? Yes, that's what we should do. I'll go and pack you some clothes.'

Forrett shook his head. 'I'm all right here.'

'But Father—'

'Did you hear what I said?' he roared.

'Well, at least promise to send for me if you're not feeling well another time.'

'The first person I'll send for will be Dr Pipperday,' he said with a flash of his old sharpness.

Making an angry little noise in her throat, Alicia turned and went out.

Gwynna slipped across to the window and saw Benting speaking to Mrs Gleason outside, while keeping an eye on the house. She was quite sure her suspicions were correct and he was part of this conspiracy.

She realised Dr Pipperday had come to stand beside her and confided her worries in him. 'I can't think why Benting would be talking so earnestly to her. Something is definitely going on here. And I'm a bit worried about leaving Mr Forrett alone until he's recovered.'

Across the room Forrett had leaned his head back. 'I can't think with that damned stuff clogging up my brain.'

Gwynna went across to him. 'We don't want to leave you alone, Mr Forrett. Someone in the house must have put laudanum in your food. What if they do it again? I'd better stay.'

Forrett smiled. 'You've got a husband to look after now, lass. Get Declan Heegan to send someone round to keep an eye on me, someone strong.'

'Oh, yes. He'll know someone. He always does. But I'll stay until you get help.'

He nodded and yawned. 'All right. You're a good lass.'

She looked at Dr Pipperday. 'Isn't there anything I can do to help him?'

He shook his head. 'Only time will help the effects to wear off.'

She sat down in a chair. 'The sooner you find Declan and send someone here, Lucas, the better.'

'Right, love. In the meantime, I'll leave Joe with you in case you need to send for help.'

'I'm going to lock the door again after you've gone.'

An hour later, Declan arrived at Mill House, accompanied by a sturdy looking man who was introduced as Kevin Reilly.

'Lucas explained what happened,' Declan said. 'You've had no further trouble?'

'No. No one's been near us.'

Mr Forrett was dozing, so she woke him up to introduce Kevin and explain why he was there.

'Good idea. Think I'll go up to my bedroom. Can't keep my damned eyes open.'

She and Declan went with Kevin to look at the millowner's room.

'There's a key here. See you use it till he's recovered.'

'There are spare keys in the kitchen,' Gwynna said.

'We'll take them before I leave.' Declan smiled at her. 'I hope I have you or someone like you on my side if I'm ever in trouble.'

'I only did what any friend would.'

He left with a final warning to Reilly. 'Make sure you sleep in Mr Forrett's room from now on.' He turned to Gwynna, saw her expression of surprise and added, 'You'd be surprised what can happen under the cover of darkness.'

She walked away, thinking that no one was completely safe, not even a rich man, and worrying that Alicia Gleason might try again to get control of Mr Forrett and his money. She'd often heard him say how stubborn his elder daughter was.

Gideon saw the impostor coming out of Linney's and stepped back to watch him without being seen. He'd heard how the fellow had rescued Dora and felt angry about that. Now the rogue was calling on her. Next thing you knew he'd be courting her.

Was the lawyer right and he shouldn't wait to start courting her? Mr Burtell had looked so sad as he said that. Dora had shown she was attracted to him and – his thoughts skidded to a halt. *Courting!* What was he thinking about? Hadn't he already decided that it wouldn't be fair to court a young lass like her? She deserved a fresh-faced lad, one who was unspoiled by life, not to mention whole in body, unlike him. He scowled down at his stupid claw of a hand.

Only, the impostor wasn't a lad either, he was about Gideon's age and a thief to boot. She shouldn't be getting mixed up with someone like him. He'd have to hope her family would realise what the fellow was like.

He watched the impostor stop, turn round and look thought-fully at Linney's, then walk away slowly. On a sudden impulse he followed him, keeping his distance, praying that he wouldn't turn round and see him.

But the other didn't seem to notice anything much. He pulled out a watch and consulted it, then strolled along to the railway station. Gideon followed at a distance, wondering if that had been *his* watch, itching to get his fingers on it and find out. He watched as the imposter bought a ticket, tempted to buy one too and see where the other went. But there was no way he'd be able to get on the train without being seen – and recognised! They'd passed in the street a few times and there was no doubt that the man recognised him, no doubt at all.

A train came in a few minutes later and when it had pulled out, Gideon waited for the passengers to disperse then walked across to check the times of trains on the notice board. This was a branch line and trains going in that direction only went to Manchester, but there were various villages along the route and trains stopped at them all. He was beginning to see a pattern in all this. The fellow often went away on a Monday morning and stayed away for a few days, usually coming back on Fridays to collect the rent money. Did he always go to the same place? Was it a village, or Manchester, or did he change trains in the city and travel on to some other town?

Lost in thought, Gideon bumped into someone and when he looked up saw he'd walked into Declan. 'Sorry.'

His friend fumbled in his pocket and presented him with a coin. 'Penny for your thoughts.'

Gideon stared down at the coin for a minute then took a sudden decision and gave the penny back. 'It won't cost you anything. I was thinking of telling you and asking your advice, but it's a long story. How about we meet for a drink tonight?'

The night following the attempt to drug him, James jerked suddenly awake as he heard a noise. He saw his bodyguard move across the room and pick up the lamp that had been left burning low.

'What's the matter?' he asked in a low voice.

'I heard a noise, sir. I'll go down and investigate. You stay here.'

'Nay, I'm coming with you.'

Kevin barred the doorway with one arm, speaking in a whisper. 'You'll stay behind me and keep back if there's trouble. I can't deal with anyone if I'm worrying about you, sir.'

'I'll do that. But I reckon I'm still able to give a good account of myself in a fight and it *is* my house. That stuff's mostly worn off now, thank goodness.'

They crept down the stairs and heard another sound coming from the kitchen. Kevin handed him the lamp, whispering, 'Turn it up!' and moved forward, opening the door at the rear of the hall suddenly.

A man with a muffler tied round the lower part of his face, who had been holding some burning rags turned with an oath and flung the flaming bundle at Kevin. By the time he'd brushed them off himself, the intruder had run out of the kitchen through the back door.

'I'll deal with this, you follow him!' James yelled and began to stamp on the burning rags, which must have been soaked in lamp oil to make them burn so fiercely.

Kevin ran out of the door, but came back a few minutes later panting. 'The sod can run too fast for me. Couldn't even see who he was in the dark, but he was a small man and fast.'

The two men looked at one another. 'Trying to burn us in our beds,' James said furiously. He didn't let himself think of who might have arranged this, not yet, not till he was alone and in full possession of his wits again.

By that time Cook and Jen had come down to see what was happening. At the sight of the charred rags and the scorch marks on her clean kitchen floor, Cook screamed and clutched Jen.

'Be quiet!' James told her sharply. 'No one was harmed and we put it out.'

'I'll not sleep a wink,' Cook declared, clutching her bosom

with one hand and Jen's arm with the other. 'What if they come back?'

'I'll stay down here and keep watch,' Kevin said. 'You'll be safe enough. I'll not go to sleep, I promise you.'

'Get back to bed now,' James ordered. When the two women had gone he looked at the bodyguard. 'You did well to hear him.'

'I'm a light sleeper. But I'm only one man. If you'll pardon me saying so, sir, you need a night-watchman in the yard.'

'I agree.'

IO

A few days later, after a stormy night, real April weather, Lucas went to the former warehouse early on the Monday morning to open up for the man who was to whitewash the kitchen walls. The place was nearly finished now, looking like a home because of the way Jeremiah had designed the inside. Lucas and Gwynna were making plans to move in before the end of the month. Once they were living there, they could start taking in children and . . . As he turned the corner, he stopped dead. 'What the hell . . . ?'

The front door of the orphanage was hanging loose on one hinge and some of the windows were smashed. When he ran inside, he exclaimed in outrage at the scene of destruction that met his eyes. The plastered and whitewashed walls of the entrance hall were gouged and in places daubed with bright red paint. More paint was splashed along both corridors leading away from it, splattered on the wooden floor as well as up the walls. The railing to the central stairs had been hacked, some of its wooden posts chopped right out and others leaning at drunken angles. And on the walls of one corridor, the words YOULL NEVER OPEN THIS PLACE were painted in huge red letters, with drops of paint dripping from the clumsy letters like blood.

A cold wind blowing along both corridors that led to the entrance hall made him guess that other windows must have been smashed in the building. Cursing under his breath he made his way along the left-hand corridor which looked to be the worse damaged, peering into one or two of the smaller rooms and finding broken windows and destruction in them all. As he walked into the big dining and day room at the rear, his feet crunched on the shards of glass littering the floor.

Tears came into his eyes and he clenched his fists, wishing he could smash them into the face of whoever had done this. Every window had been broken in this room, every single one! There were patches of damp on the plastered walls beneath them and an uneven line of puddles on the floor where the rain had got in during last night's storm.

He moved across the room and out of the far door to explore the second corridor which led back to the front entrance. There were smashed windows here and there, and some of the inner doors had been hacked with an axe. There was some destruction in his family's living quarters, but it wasn't as bad there and the villains seemed to have run out of paint by the time they got to this side of the building.

Why? Why would anyone want to destroy an orphanage? And do it so thoroughly? It simply didn't make sense. The only small mercy he could find was that they hadn't brought the new furniture over here yet! That was still stored at the mill.

As he began to walk slowly back to the front hall, he heard footsteps and stopped, setting his back against a wall and wondering if the villains had returned.

A man's voice called out uncertainly, 'Is anyone there?'

He sagged in relief. It was the carpenter he'd hired to help in his own business while he supervised the daily work on the two buildings for Mr Channon. Seb, a stolid, middle-aged man, was good at his trade but not so good at running a business of his own. He had come today to hang the rest of the new interior doors. 'I'm here,' Lucas called and hurried to join Seb in the front hall.

He found the carpenter gaping round, literally open-mouthed with shock.

'Eh, I've never seen owt like this in my life! Who could have done it, Mr Kemp? And why?'

'I don't know, but I mean to find out. Could you go and fetch Sergeant Hankin? I want him to see this before we try to clear up. Where's young Ted?'

'Fetching the door fittings and tools in the handcart. He'll be here in a few minutes. Not that we'll need them now.'

Lucas sighed. 'You go and get the sergeant, then.' He stayed in the entrance hall, unable to face investigating on his own what the damned vandals had done upstairs. He'd have to let Mr Forrett know what had happened, but hated the thought of doing that because the millowner had had enough to bear after the way his daughter had tried to trick him. Gwynna said Mr Forrett was his old self again and furious with his daughter, but they were all a bit worried about what else she and her greedy husband might try.

Lucas sucked in his breath sharply. *Maybe this was another attempt to stop Forrett?*

When Sergeant Hankin arrived, the three men went round the building together, studying the horrendous trail of destruction, muttering, cursing, exclaiming – all of them horrified at how much harm had been done.

'Someone's done this systematically,' the sergeant said as they returned to the front hall.

Lucas was too shocked by what he'd seen to answer him, not to mention saddened by what this did to the plans he and Gwynna had been making so happily for opening the orphanage.

Ted arrived with the handcart just as they were going up the stairs and stood goggling at what he saw.

'You wait here, lad,' the sergeant said. 'Don't let anyone in.' He turned to his companions. 'It must have taken whoever it was hours to do this. The storm would have hidden the noise they made and no one lives down this street anyway, there are just warehouses and workshops. You'd think that man of mine who was patrolling the town centre would have noticed lights here, though. They couldn't have done this in the dark. If I find he was sheltering somewhere from the rain, he'll be in serious trouble.' He frowned as he added slowly, 'He's in trouble anyway because he hasn't reported in yet. I hope he's all right.'

'Well, let's see what they've done upstairs,' Lucas said, forcing himself to start moving again. At the top he stopped. 'Listen!'

There was a faint sound coming from the far end of the corridor.

Sergeant Hankin set off at a run, flinging open the very last door. The police constable who'd been on night duty was lying on the floor, securely bound and gagged. He had a bloody wound to the back of his head but when they untied him, he was angry more than anything else.

'I saw the lights and came along to see what was happening. And then . . . well, I don't remember anything else till I woke up here, trussed like a damned fowl. I'm sorry, sir. I let you down.'

'Not you. There must have been several of them to do all this. One man wouldn't have stood a chance.'

They helped him up and made their way back towards the stairs, looking into rooms to find more destruction, though not on the scale of the ground floor.

'Never seen owt like it in my life,' Seb kept repeating. 'They must ha' run mad.'

The sergeant shook his head slowly and thoughtfully. 'No, it was done with a purpose, I'm sure. It's more than just destruction. It's as if someone has deliberately tried to destroy the whole place.' He looked sideways at Lucas as he added, 'Like they wrote on the wall, someone wants to stop it opening.'

'That's obvious,' Lucas agreed. 'But who?' He sighed and turned to Seb. 'Why don't you go down and wait in the hall?'

Only when the carpenter was out of earshot did the sergeant speak again. 'I mean to find out who did this. In confidence . . . you and your wife are friendly with Mr Forrett. Do *you* know of anyone who doesn't want this place to open?'

Lucas frowned, considering how much to reveal of what had been going on. 'Both Forrett's daughters are furious at what he's doing because quite a lot of the money they'd expected to inherit has been spent on the orphanage. At least, I know for certain the elder daughter is furious and I dare say the younger one is too.'

'You'd be surprised what folk will do when money's involved, gentry or not,' the sergeant said darkly. 'But don't they live in Manchester?'

Lucas nodded.

'Then they'd have had to get someone who lives here in Hedderby to do it for them.'

Lucas hesitated, then added, 'There's Benting too. He's furious about the changes Forrett is making at the mill, and scornful of this orphanage. Declan Heegan heard him in a pub, grumbling about lasses in the mill being treated too softly and good money being wasted by old fools.'

'I'll ask Heegan exactly what he heard.'

'And there's something else you should know . . .' Lucas explained about the attempt to drug and trick Mr Forrett.

The sergeant began to pace up and down, and it was a few moments before he spoke. 'I'll make a list of unsavoury characters I know in Hedderby, the ones who'd do owt for money, an' then I'll start talking to them one by one.'

'Do you think you'll catch the ones who did it?' Lucas asked.

'I'll do my best. I don't like this sort of thing happening in *my* town, and the Chief Constable won't like it, either. In the meantime, I'd suggest you get Mr Forrett to hire two night-watchmen for this place.' He frowned in thought then added, 'And it might be a good idea get a big, loud bell and hang it up for the watchmen to ring if anyone tries to break in. The police will come running if they hear it.' He grinned, a savage baring of the teeth. 'Only – if I were him, I'd bring the bell in here after dark and not warn anyone about it except my lads. We'll all come running if we hear it, including me. I only live just up the hill.'

'Good idea.'

The two men walked slowly down to the hall, where Seb was waiting patiently for them with Ted.

Lucas looked round, feeling disgust roil through him at the wanton destruction. 'Will you stay here, Seb, and keep an eye on things till I get back? You and Ted can start clearing up the broken glass.' He turned to the sergeant. 'I'd better go and tell our architect what's happened. I won't tell Mr Forrett till Mr Channon has assessed the damage and can come with me to make plans.'

'I'll walk along with you as far as the police station,' Sergeant Hankin said. 'I intend to bring the other two police officers to see this place. I think the Chief Constable will want to view the damage, too. Don't let anyone in, Seb lad.'

The two men strode off through the streets, but didn't say much because both were lost in their own thoughts.

As they parted company at Market Street, Lucas was already working out how to start repairing the damage. It'd put the opening back for weeks, though at least it was April and children living on the streets were less likely to freeze to death.

But if he ever got his hands on the villains who'd done this, he wouldn't be answerable for the consequences.

That same morning Jeremiah and Eli met as usual at the site of the new music hall to review the previous week's work and discuss progress. 'We shall get on more quickly once the roof's finished,' Jeremiah said, looking up at the men fixing the slates into place. 'We could have done without that heavy rain last night.'

'Aye, it's left ruddy great puddles all over the back part, where the roof isn't finished.' Even so, Eli looked with great satisfaction at the big space, which seemed more like a hall now that it had most of its roof in place. *Music hall*, he said to himself, loving the feel of those words, *my music hall*. Why stop at one music hall? Other men owned several theatres and so would he before he was through.

When he'd told Carrie about that idea, she'd just blinked and said, 'Wait till this one is finished and running first, love!' She was a wonderful woman. He was so lucky to have her. And he could do nothing else but wait, because he couldn't afford to do anything new until the Pride was bringing in money again. But it didn't hurt to think ahead. He might never get back his memory of the months after the fire, but he'd got all his old energy and ambition back again.

He'd never forget the old music saloon, though, his first. The place had been cobbled together out of some old stables next to his uncle's pub and even though it had been smaller than this one, it had been his pride and joy, and he'd never forget it. It had done well, proved he could make money from such a

venture. He intended to make this new one the pride of
Lancashire too.

He remembered suddenly the day they'd started work on this
place, when folk from the town had come to help dig out the
foundations. Heart of the town, someone had called it then. Well,
it was important for poor folk to have such places, the only decent
entertainment there was for women and families. They lived in
dark little houses, but he could give them a night in what was to
them a palace, full of bright lights and happiness. Not a bad thing
to do with your life, making people happy, eh?

This new place was going to make a lot more money than the
old one for the simple reason that it'd hold more people. It was
being built properly, in the modern way, with a stepped floor, so
that the seats at the back were higher than those at the front and
everyone could see the stage. The balcony was stepped too, though
there was only a skeleton of wood up there at the moment.

The only place that felt just about finished was the cellar. It
would provide plenty of storage space for scenery, backdrops,
props and costumes, because they always had to have such things
available. Performers usually brought their own costumes and
smaller props, of course, but accidents did happen, luggage go
astray, so you collected all sorts of stuff just in case.

Carrie had hired a couple of local seamstresses to make a start
on the stock of costumes already, and even his young sister-
in-law was taking an interest in them, making suggestions. He
grinned. He and Carrie knew why, of course. Nev might believe
Dora would obey him about not going on the stage, but Carrie
said her sister had been born stubborn – as stubborn as her two
older sisters. A dog act, too! He'd never heard of a woman running
one of those. Could be a good thing, if she did it well.

As he came up from the cellar, Eli's gaze strayed to where the
Chairman's smaller platform would be placed, at the right side
as you looked towards the front. *His platform*. His fingers twitched
to hold the new Chairman's gavel that Carrie had bought him
for his birthday, and give it a good thump on the wooden block
to get the audience's attention.

'Eli? Did you hear what I said?'

He jumped in shock and turned to Jeremiah. 'Sorry. I was day dreaming about when we open.'

'Well, you stay here and dream on. I was just saying that I've to go and check a few things at Forrett's orphanage. We're nearly finished there and it's looking really good.'

But even as they turned round, Lucas came striding into the half-finished building, looking grim . . .

After Jeremiah had inspected the damage himself, he went to Mill House with Lucas and they explained what had happened to the orphanage.

James Forrett stared at them in horror. 'Who the hell could have done that?'

'I – um – don't know.'

James stared at him then his breath caught in his throat as something occurred to him, something so dreadful that he couldn't at first voice it, could only stare down at the floor while he let the idea settle in his mind. And though it sickened him, he couldn't deny it was the most likely explanation.

After a minute or two he looked up and saw both men watching him, waiting for him to speak. 'I—' His voice cracked as he forced the words out, 'The only people who've been steadily against me building the orphanage are my daughters and their husbands. They've come to see me, both separately and together, during the past few months, and one of my sons-in-law said to my face that I was losing my wits to waste my living daughters' inheritance on such a wild scheme to honour a dead infant's name and . . .' He looked at them with pain etched on his face as he finished, 'Then there was Alicia's attempt to have me locked away. I don't know yet if Diana was involved in that, can't face asking her, to tell you the truth. Well, she'd only deny it and I'd be no further forward than I am now.'

He sighed and said in a voice made harsh by unhappiness, 'I'm just about certain that it was them, or one of them at least, who did this. And someone helped them.'

Getting up, he went to stand by the window with his back to them, outlined against the light streaming in through the panes, then turned slowly round to look at them. 'How could anyone do that, destroy things, waste so much money, when we're trying to help the poorest of children?'

'I don't know,' Lucas said with simple honesty. 'It's a terrible thing to happen, whoever did it.'

'It's an equally terrible thing for you to suspect your own children,' Jeremiah added in his quiet way. 'But I'm afraid you could be right. Who else would do it? The sergeant and I are both certain that this wasn't the work of lads on a spree, or an act of vengeance. It was a systematic attempt to destroy the orphanage and it will take us a month or two to set it to rights, if not longer.'

'I'd better go and see it,' James said.

'You don't need to,' Lucas said. 'You can leave it to us to start clearing up.'

Jeremiah shook his head. 'No. I think it's best that Mr Forrett does see it, best to face what evil can do and triumph over it. I shall not be charging you any more fees for my services during the period of repair, Mr Forrett.'

'Nay, I allus pay my way.'

'Consider it my contribution to a worthy cause.'

James had to bring out his handkerchief and blow his nose to hide his emotions at that.

'I wish I could make the same offer,' Lucas said as the handkerchief was put away, 'but I've my family depending on me. You can be sure I'll do everything in my power to get things repaired quickly, though. I'll work all the hours I can.'

James shook hands with Jeremiah and Lucas, saying in a voice thickened by emotion, 'It means a lot to know I'm not alone. When Libby died and my wife had to be locked away, things seemed very – bleak. But now, well, that orphanage has given me something to live for and I *will not* let anyone stop me opening it. But I shall employ watchmen both night and day from now on. No one will get a chance to damage it again, I can promise you.'

The three men walked through the streets, then the other two let Forrett lead the way round the interior at his own pace. When he'd finished, he was grim-faced but determination showed in every line of his body. 'Do whatever you need to and send the bills to me. And get some watchmen in, some of Declan Heegan's friends might be best. Yes, and do what the sergeant suggested. Buy a bell and install it secretly. Send the bills to me at the house, not the mill office.'

He went home to think about his situation carefully for a day or two before he took any further action. He was glad to have a strong fellow like Kevin Reilly around and he took on another of Declan's Irish friends as night-watchman, ostensibly to guard the mill, but the man was told to keep an eye on the owner's house above all.

It could only be Jen who had put that vile stuff into his food. He didn't believe Cook would have done it, because she'd been with him for years. But it baffled him why Jen would try to hurt him. She was a nice lass and from a decent family. Why, her married sisters both worked in the mill, had done for years.

That thought stopped him dead. *Her sisters were dependent on Benting for those jobs.* Yet another piece of evidence to suggest that his overlooker was working against him. Well, he needed the man until he found someone else to do the job, so Benting could stay on for the time being, but his days were numbered. He couldn't abide disloyalty.

He wasn't going to confront his daughters until he had solid evidence. Let them wonder what he was thinking. Let them think they'd fooled him.

An idea suddenly came to him, an idea so outrageous he stood utterly still as he considered it. Then a smile slowly creased his face.

Why not? It'd solve several problems for him.

Benting came storming across to the mill house to see James that evening. 'A fellow has turned up claiming he's the night-watchman.'

'Oh, sorry. I forgot to tell you.' He hadn't forgotten at all, but he'd wanted to see his overlooker's reaction.

'It's *my* job to hire and fire such people!'

'Well, since I own the mill and pay the wages here, I reckon I can do owt I want.'

'I could have found a dozen men for that job – though we've never needed a watchman before, so why you're even bothering . . . Any road, this one definitely won't do. I don't trust the Irish!'

'I trust this one. He comes well recommended.' James didn't intend to tell Benting about the second guard he'd hired as well. The man had been told to arrive later and leave early.

'Not to me he doesn't! I'll find you another one.'

'No, you won't.'

Benting glared at him with such animosity that James decided to speed up the process of finding a new overlooker.

'You're undermining my authority here, Mr Forrett. I can't let you do that. How will it look?'

'*Can't* let me do it? When you own your own mill, you can run it how you please. In *my* mill, I'm in charge, and if you don't like that, you can take yourself off and find another job.'

There was silence, then Benting left without a word, but James had seen the anger burning in his eyes and felt a strong urge to call him back and sack him on the spot. But if he did that without proof, his daughters might claim he was behaving irrationally, damn them! And his deputy overlooker, Thad, wasn't nearly as good at his job. He was a plodder with no special flair for keeping machinery running and lasses working. Besides, if Benting was here all day and every day, it'd be easier to keep an eye on him. And his damned son too, who had upset the carter again today, the lazy young devil.

But before James did anything definite about a new overlooker there was something else he intended to do in Manchester. It would be a rather drastic step but one which would protect him from his daughters like nothing else could. He planned his trip with Kevin Reilly and until his bodyguard carried his portmanteau down the stairs the following morning, James told no one else about his plans.

Only as he was leaving the house did he inform Cook and Jen that he was going away for two days. He didn't say where he was going and gave them strict orders not to let Benting or his daughters or *anyone else* set foot in the house while he was away, if they valued their jobs.

Then he set off with his bodyguard to walk briskly down to the station, amused to see Benting peering out of the mill door, with a look of surprise. On the way, Reilly pointed out an old fellow he knew, who was always standing around ready to run errands for folk, so James paid him to take notes to Lucas and Mr Channon to say he and Reilly would be out of town for a couple of days.

At the station James and his bodyguard watched carefully who got on the train with them and saw no one suspicious, so he felt pretty sure they'd got away without being followed. He hadn't even told Kevin what he intended to do, didn't intend anyone to know until it was done and could not be changed.

For some time Gideon had had the feeling that he was being followed. He'd tried all the ways he could think of to check whether this was so, but hadn't found anyone to suspect. No sooner did his suspicions settle on one person than that person would vanish. He seemed to bump into one of Huey's friends more often than he'd have expected, but there were plenty of times when none of them was around and he still felt that prickling feeling in his spine.

Was it the impostor? Or was it those young bullies wanting to catch him on his own and get their own back? He couldn't decide. Maybe it was both of them.

Barney looked at him as he got ready to go out one morning. 'What's the matter, Mr Potter?'

Gideon swung round. 'Why do you ask that?'

'Lately, when you're walking down the street, you keep – turning round – looking behind you. I've seen you a few times.'

Gideon knew by now that the frail body concealed a sharp brain. 'I keep feeling that I'm being followed, only I can't see any one person who's doing it. But I learned to trust that sort of feeling when I was in the Army.'

'I could – keep my eyes open.'

'I don't want you running into danger.'

Barney's eyes twinkled with amusement. 'Who would think – of bothering – about someone like me in the daytime? It's only at night they try to hurt me, when no one can see what they're doing.'

Gideon looked at him thoughtfully. 'Well, you could keep your eyes open when you're working at the market.'

The lad nodded.

Granny looked sharply from one to the other but made no objections. 'Have you two finished now?'

'Yes, thank you. You're a good cook, Granny.'

She nodded her head. 'When I have the food, I know what to do with it.'

He went off to work, whistling, forgetting his worries for a time – until he got that feeling again. This time when he turned round he saw Huey leaning against a wall, watching him openly. The lad stared back at him, then moved away with a nasty, over-confident smile on his face.

So – that was one enemy marked out, for certain.

Later that day he saw the impostor buying food at a nearby stall. The man turned round as if he'd felt Gideon's eyes on him and stared coldly across at him. He didn't speak or change his expression, but there was something in the grim set of his features that spoke of hostility.

Two enemies he had, but he didn't intend to let them get the better of him.

11

In Manchester Forrett summoned a cab and told it to take them to a quiet little hotel he used whenever he came into the city to meet his fellow millowners or attend cotton industry functions.

Kevin insisted on sharing his room at the hotel.

'No one knows where we are. There's no need for that.'

'Begging your pardon, sir, but you can't be certain. And how will I be looking after you, if I'm not within earshot? Declan told me to stay with you at all times, not let you out of my sight.'

James suddenly remembered how disoriented he'd felt when they'd drugged him and gave in. 'Oh, very well. But when we get to the house I'm visiting, I'm leaving you in the hall. Some things a man needs to do on his own and this is one of them.' He saw Kevin open his mouth to protest and said firmly, 'It's a private house and I'll only be in the next room.'

As he was shown inside the house James tried to hide the fact that he felt nervous. It was such a big step to take. This house had belonged to his old friend Jonas Grieves, who had committed suicide a month ago after his business failed, which had left a wife and daughter in serious financial trouble. James and a few colleagues had already helped the two women, but the house was up for sale and they would have to live very modestly from now on – unless they accepted his offer today.

He was shown into the small parlour at the rear of the house and found Mrs Grieves there, with her unmarried daughter Charis by her side. Charis was about thirty, plain-featured and sturdily built. She dressed dowdily and didn't put herself forward, but he'd got to know her better than most and when she was out of earshot of her mother, she relaxed a little, showing a dry wit and an intelligent understanding of the world that he always enjoyed.

He studied her and wondered yet again why she was unmarried. Plain she might be but until recently she'd been considered an heiress and a young woman with expectations could always find a husband if she wanted one. He'd have preferred to talk to her privately but knew Mrs Grieves would never allow that, so he'd have to say it to them both.

'Do sit down.' Mrs Grieves fluttered a black-edged handkerchief as if to wipe away tears from her eyes. 'I'll send for some tea, shall I?'

'Not for a minute or two, if you don't mind, Mrs Grieves.' He took a deep breath. 'I've a suggestion to make which would be to your advantage, given your present circumstances. I need help and I know you do too, so I thought we might help one another.'

They were both staring at him in puzzlement, so he stopped hedging. 'To put it bluntly, I need a wife and I thought of your daughter Charis.'

Mrs Grieves gaped at him, the handkerchief and affectation of grief quite forgotten. 'A wife! But I thought you already had one.'

Charis looked at James, her head on one side, a thoughtful look on her face. 'Let Mr Forrett explain, Mother.'

'My wife died recently and my daughters have taken it into their heads to interfere in my life, so I've decided to remarry.'

Mrs Grieves stared at him in amazement. 'I don't know what to say, I really don't. Isn't it a bit soon – if your wife has only just died. And you're so much older than Charis. Anyway I never thought she'd marry – and well, I need her to look after me, especially now – so . . .'

He watched Charis put her hand on her mother's arm and grip it tightly. The flow of exclamations stopped.

'Since this concerns me,' the younger woman said, 'I'd like to speak to Mr Forrett on my own, if you don't mind, Mother.'

Mrs Grieves forgot herself enough to hiss, 'You *can't* get married! I need you.'

'I might *want* to marry.'

'I won't allow it!'

'It'll be my decision, Mother. But I need to talk to Mr Forrett first.'

'Certainly not. It'd be very improper for you to be alone with him and anyway, we're in mourning and so should he be.' She cast a sour look in James's direction and said to him, 'It's not the time to talk of marriage, even if it is the right thing for you, though I'm sure it isn't, not at your age, and as for my daughter—'

Charis stood up. 'Please go and wait in the drawing room, Mother. I won't be long.'

'But—'

She pushed her mother out forcibly, though the older woman was still protesting.

James heard them arguing in low voices as they went along the hall and grinned. Selfish old biddy. He'd seen it before, mothers treating their youngest daughters like servants. He felt even more sorry for Charis after seeing her mother's refusal of what could only be an advantageous marriage for a young woman in such circumstances.

Charis returned a short time later. 'Shall we sit down again? I'm interested in your offer, Mr Forrett. Very interested. But would you mind my asking you a few questions about – about the practicalities?'

'Not at all. I'd think you stupid not to.'

'What has made you need a wife so urgently? The truth, if you please. I know that you and your wife didn't get on, so I'm surprised that you're rushing into a second marriage.'

He smiled, not in the least offended. 'You're right.' He explained what had happened over the past year and she listened quietly without interrupting. When he'd finished, he waited a few moments, studying the way her chest curved, hinting at a generous figure beneath that unflattering gown. Exactly the sort of woman he preferred. He hated scrawny females. She continued to stare down at her lap, a slight frown on her face as if she was considering what he'd said.

'So, what do you think?' he asked when he could bear the suspense no longer.

'I presume you'll make some sort of settlement on me so that if you die, I'll not be left penniless?'

'Not only that, but you'll inherit most of what I own when I die except for the trust I'm setting up for the orphanage. Though I have to tell you I've no intention of dying for a long time to come. I enjoy excellent health.'

She gasped in surprise. 'But what about your daughters?'

'Their husbands can look after them. They were generously dowered.'

'Is that wise? It'd cause a lot of trouble. And I don't need – so much.'

'After what they tried to do, I don't intend to leave my daughters a brass farthing. Wise or not, it's what's going to happen, to you or to someone else if *you* won't marry me. I'm quite determined about that.'

'I see.' She took a deep breath and asked in a voice which wobbled, 'It'll be a proper marriage, won't it? I – I'd love a child.'

He nodded, moved by that quaver in her voice. 'I'd like another child, too.'

She swallowed hard. 'Then I accept your proposal, Mr Forrett.'

'James.'

For the first time she flushed slightly. 'James.'

He beamed at her. 'I'm glad. I've a notion we'll deal comfortably together.'

'What would you have done if I'd refused you?'

'Gone out and asked the next woman on my list. But you were my first choice, the one I really wanted.'

Tears came into her eyes and she gave him a beaming smile. 'I'm pleased about that. I've always enjoyed your company because you never talked to me as if I was an idiot.'

'I always thought you a sensible woman. Now, let's discuss the practical arrangements. I want us to marry tomorrow by special license, so that I can present my daughters with a *fait accompli*. That should ensure that no dirty tricks are played to prevent us from getting wed. And after the wedding we'll need to go straight back to Hedderby. The day after that I'll change my will, you have my word on it. I'll let you read it, see for yourself that you'll be well looked after if anything happens to me.'

'Will you be able to get a special license so quickly – James?'

'I think so. Either for tomorrow or the day after, anyway.'

'Then we'd better call Mother in and tell her the news.' Charis hesitated. 'I think . . . I'd like to make one more condition.'

'Oh?'

'That you provide a separate home for Mother. I don't wish to live with her after I'm married.'

'Can I ask why not?'

She was silent for a moment then said quietly, 'Because unlike my sister I've been raised to be her slave, dressed in ugly clothes so that men won't want me – not that I ever was a beauty – and told never, ever to think of marriage. You saw for yourself what she was like when you said why you'd come. Looking after her has not been – the most pleasant of jobs, but I had nowhere else to go . . . until now.'

Pity flooded through him. What a way to treat a child! 'All right. It'll take a few weeks to arrange a home for her. It'd better be in Hedderby, then we can keep an eye on her. Unless she wants to live with your sister?'

'My sister wouldn't have her.' She gave him another grateful smile. 'Thank you. For everything. And I don't wish to sound as if I'm never satisfied, but I must be mistress in my own home during those weeks. My mother will try to take over, you see, to win you to her side, pretend I'm stupid. I'm not, but she's played that trick before and she does it cleverly, convinces people . . . You'll – support me against her, won't you?'

He liked Charis's honesty and practicality, and this hint of vulnerability made him feel protective towards her. 'I definitely will. The house needs bringing up to scratch again so I shall look forward to your taking charge.' Again a brilliant smile startled him, for it made her look attractive, something he hadn't expected.

'I'll start packing as soon as you leave. And I'll see if I can find something more flattering to wear for the wedding.'

When they called Mrs Grieves back to tell her what had been decided, she tried to forbid the marriage, then burst into loud, angry tears as it was made plain that she couldn't.

'I'm over twenty-one and can do as I please,' Charis said calmly. 'James, you have a lot to do today. Leave Mother to me now.'

He heard Mrs Grieves start screeching at her daughter even before the door had closed and smiled.

First he went to arrange for the wedding.

Then he went to spread the word that he wanted to hire a new overlooker.

After that he bought himself and Kevin a hearty meal, which he enjoyed more than anything he'd eaten for a long time.

Ishleen got up early, feeling happy because this was one of the days she worked at the markets. Declan's father had got permission to enclose a corner so that tables and benches could be set out, and was planning to open every day once the Council changed its rules.

She loved seeing the customers enjoy the food she served them. And during the slack times she could chat with the new friends she'd made in Hedderby, especially Dora Preston, who worked on a nearby stall.

Smiling, she shook Shanna awake and dropped a quick kiss on her daughter's soft cheek. 'Come on, sleepyhead! We don't want to be late for mass.'

'Don't want to go. It's cold in church.'

Ishleen hesitated. Shanna had looked heavy-eyed last night and it was icy cold in the church on days like this. There were charcoal heaters, but they did little to warm the air. She didn't dare take any risks with the only person she had left in the world, so tucked her daughter in again. 'You don't need to come today, then. Stay in bed until I get back.'

The little girl nodded and snuggled down with a soft, contented sound.

Just the rosiness of Shanna's cheeks filled Ishleen with deep satisfaction. Wrapping her shawl round herself, she walked through the chill morning to the small Catholic church, with its raw red brickwork, so different from the tiny stone-built church she'd attended in Ireland. Few people here went to mass as often as she did, but she felt so grateful for having been saved from starvation that she needed to keep saying her thanks for this second chance of life.

On the way Declan fell in beside her. 'I'm going to the same place.'

'You don't usually come to mass except on Sundays.'

'No.' He was unsmiling.

'Your wife won't like you to walk with me and someone will be bound to tell her.'

'Let them.' His steps slowed and hers did too. 'I enjoy your company, while Ruth and I hardly say a word to one another these days, let alone a civil word.'

Ishleen shook her head regretfully.

His tone softened, took on a pleading note. 'Can't two friends talk once in a while?'

She looked at him quickly, worried about what he meant. 'It isn't easy for a man and woman to be friends, Declan.'

'After what we've shared, how can we not be?' He caught her hand and dared to say it aloud, just once. 'I wish I'd met you before I met Ruth – only I was a wild lad in those days and you'd probably have turned up your sensible nose at me.'

For a moment she let him hold her hand, then pulled hers away and dared to admit she felt the same. 'I wish so, too. But we didn't.'

'Ah, what does it matter what Ruth thinks anyway?'

'It may not matter to you but your wife won't hesitate to confront me and accuse me of all sorts of things.'

'I'm sorry. She can be very spiteful.' He gave her one of his irrepressible grins. 'Do you want me to walk two paces behind you instead, then?'

She couldn't help chuckling. 'No, of course not. Why are you going to church on a weekday? Is today special to you?'

'No.' He felt his heart go out to her. She was so touchingly grateful for all they'd done for her, and yet it wasn't that much. She'd started work as soon as she was able, before she was fully recovered, in his opinion, and was proving such a tower of strength to his mother now that his father was ill that they'd asked her to make her home with them. 'I've family problems I need to talk to Father Timothy about. After mass seems a good time to catch him.'

'Is it your sons? Is there anything I can do to help?'

He shook his head. 'No, not the boys. It's Ruth.'

'Oh.' She didn't question him further. While the rest of the Heegan family had made her welcome and helped her in every way they could, at every family gathering his wife was like a barb in Ishleen's flesh, making pointed remarks about people who took advantage of others, commenting loudly on how much *that woman* was eating, or how much her new clothes must have cost the person stupid enough to buy them for her. Because her tormentor was Declan's wife, Ishleen had held her tongue, but when Ruth smacked Shanna, she'd cornered the woman and told her if she ever laid a finger on her daughter again, she'd beat her senseless. She'd meant it too.

Since then Ruth had completely ignored the child, but she'd sown enough poison about the mother that some of the family and neighbours now regarded the newcomer with suspicion.

'You look unhappy,' Declan said quietly. 'Is something wrong?'

'No. I was just thinking about something.'

'It wouldn't be my wife, would it? I overheard what she said about you last week and I apologise for her. It doesn't matter what I do or say, she won't stop being spiteful towards you.'

'Ah, don't be wasting your breath. It's best to ignore people like her.'

He couldn't keep the bitterness from his voice. 'I can't ignore her. She's picking on our sons now, hitting them, not caring for them properly . . .' He hesitated, then added in a harsher voice, 'And drinking more than ever, though she's so cunning I don't know exactly how much. I employ and control grown men, run businesses that make good money, but I'm at my wits' end how to cope with one vicious woman. So . . . I thought I'd ask Father Timothy to have a word with her, see if he can find out what's making her so sour.'

'Will she listen to him?'

'Who knows? She does go to church regularly.'

Ishleen frowned.

'What is it?'

'I go to Mass every morning and I've never seen her there.'

'She goes later, I think.'

Ishleen kept her mouth shut and her eyes on the ground, so that he couldn't read anything into her expression. She was fairly certain that Ruth didn't attend church. But she didn't want to come between husband and wife.

'I don't know if it'll do any good Father Timothy speaking to her, all I know is she won't listen to *me* any longer.' Except to ask for extra money. She was a pitiful housewife and kept a poor table, often presented her family with stale bread and dripping for tea, unless she could buy food already cooked. He'd taken the lads round to his uncle's tripe shop more than once for a meal, leaving Ruth at home with her damned bread and scrape.

He remembered with surprise how pretty she'd been when she was younger. He'd forgotten that, she looked such a mess now. That's what had attracted him to her, but once they'd married, she'd let herself go, not even keeping herself or her clothes clean. He'd been too stupid to realise what he was getting into, had been heedless of anyone's advice then, living for the moment, taking stupid risks and not always staying on the right side of the law. It was thanks to his older brother Bram that he'd not ended up in prison.

Nowadays he'd learned a bit more sense – at least he liked to think so – but he was still lumbered with Ruth, and she hadn't learned anything, still couldn't see beyond today. Put money into her hand and she spent it all. Feast or famine was her approach to life.

He sat beside Ishleen in mass, praying fervently for some solution to his problems, then nodded farewell to her and went to
see the priest.

'Trouble?' Father Timothy eyed him shrewdly.

'It's my wife. I'd welcome your advice and help.'

'Just let me change out of these vestments, then we'll go and
get my housekeeper to make us a nice pot of tea and you can
tell me exactly what's bothering you.'

Already Declan was wondering whether it was worth trying
to talk to the new priest about Ruth, because what could the man
do about her, after all? But Father Timothy was making a good
name for himself in the parish and it couldn't hurt to try.

He was so desperate he'd try anything.

Strange how hard he found it to bare his soul to the good
father, or to anyone, come to that. Except Ishleen. She'd suffered
through the worst of times and been strong enough to survive.
He found it all too easy to talk to her.

That was the one thing he didn't tell the priest – how attracted
he was to Ishleen.

When Eli took Carrie round to the orphanage to see if they could
help in any way, they found a man keeping watch at the front
entrance. But as he knew them by sight he let them in.

They followed the sound of voices and tracked down Lucas
and Jeremiah, who were going round room by room making lists.
The two men turned as they walked into the room.

'I can't believe anyone would do such a thing,' Carrie said.
'Lucas, I'm so sorry about this. If I can help in any way with the
clearing up, I'm happy to do so and I know one or two women
who used to clean for us at the Pride. They'd come like a shot
if you paid them.'

'That'd be very helpful.'

'Declan's aunt Bonnie is one of the best cleaners,' Carrie said.
'She's slow thinking, so you have to explain things carefully but
she's very thorough. I know she's missed working at the Pride.
Other people won't even give her a chance.'

'Thanks. I'll bear her in mind.'

'Any idea yet who did it?' Eli asked.

Lucas shrugged. 'Who's to say?' The sergeant had warned him not to name anyone, but the more he thought about it, the more he felt it had to have been organised by Mr Forrett's daughter or, more probably, her husband. He'd seen the anger on Alicia Gleason's face when they'd stopped her from taking her drugged father away – and had seen her talking to Benting, too. Perhaps the overlooker had organised it for her.

Why Forrett was keeping him on in the job puzzled Lucas.

John Shaw came to the markets on the Friday during a quiet time. He bought a hot drink from Dora and stayed to chat to her. He tried to stroke Nippy, who again would have nothing to do with him, so with a shrug he pulled his hand back. 'I don't seem to have the knack of making friends with dogs, do I?'

'No, you don't. Never mind.'

Gideon saw who was talking to Dora and watched as she gave the imposter one of her sunny smiles and continued chatting to him while she automatically cleared up and washed the cups from the last lot of customers. She was a hard worker, none better. But surely she wasn't attracted to that man now?

He was glad when the dog refused to have anything to do with the fellow, wished Dora had followed suit. He'd intended to go across and talk to her himself now that things were quieter, but perhaps he would wait now until *he* left. He didn't think he could bring himself to speak civilly to a thief.

Then Nippy sensed his presence and came trotting through the crowd, ignoring Dora's call to go back. Gideon bent to scoop up the little animal, which promptly licked his nose. 'Eh, you're a daft ha'porth, you are,' he chided softly. He changed his mind and with Nippy as an excuse, began walking towards her, still holding the dog and talking to it, till he got to the stall. Then he held the dog up and said with mock severity, 'Your mistress was calling out to you and you ignored her. What sort of manners is that?'

He set Nippy down and only then did he look up and meet the chill eyes of the so-called Gideon John Shaw. As the two men stared at one another the tension that sprang up between them was so marked that the dog began to growl and Dora scooped him up quickly, staring from one man to the other, wide-eyed.

Gideon stayed where he was. This was his stall, after all.

It was John who stepped back, saying, 'I'll see you again, Dora. Why don't you call in next time you're up on the tops of a Sunday? I enjoy a good walk myself.'

'I'll do that.'

Something about his accent, which had a southern sound to it, struck a chord in Gideon's memory and he stood still for a moment or two, desperately trying to pin down whatever it was that he knew. But the information slipped right away again, lost in the fever mists that clouded his memories of the last half of the voyage to England.

'Are you all right?'

He felt a touch on his arm and realised Dora was looking up at him in concern. 'What?'

'Are you all right? You looked strange for a minute or two.'

'I'm fine.' He looked round. 'Has that fellow gone?'

'He's got a name, as you well know. Why do you call him "that fellow" in such a tone? Don't you like him?'

'No, I don't. Me and Nippy are agreed on that.'

She tossed her head. 'Well, *I* find him very pleasant. What's more, I'm grateful to him. He was the one who found me when I sprained my ankle and if it hadn't been for him, I'd have been in real trouble that day.'

Gideon changed the subject, afraid of giving too much away if he said what he really thought of the imposter. 'How are things going today? Do we need some clean water before the midday rush?'

She looked at him for a moment, then stepped back. 'Yes, please.'

'Give me the buckets.' He went off to empty the bucket of slops and get clean water in the other bucket. Anyone who'd lived in India knew to keep water and food clean. Many of the female customers had noticed how fastidious he was and complimented him on both that and the good taste of his tea. That was because he didn't buy the cheap dusty stuff.

Dora watched him go. He wasn't whistling today, as he usually did. What was it between those men? It wasn't just Gideon who bristled when the two of them so much as saw one another across the street. John Shaw stiffened and looked hostile too. And yet each denied knowing the other.

Because he reminded her a bit of Gideon, she'd noticed John Shaw even before he'd rescued her. He too was tall and dark-haired, with that same upright bearing and sallow look to his skin. He usually turned up at the markets, bought what he needed and left immediately. Today was the first time he'd lingered to chat to anyone and his admiring looks had left her in no doubt why.

Hadn't he made any other friends in Hedderby? Surely people who'd known his auntie would have made it their business to get to know him?

She might call in on him next Sunday if she went out walking. Why not? Maybe he'd watch Nippy do his tricks and tell her what he thought. She looked down at the little dog, who wagged tentatively, sensing that she wasn't best pleased with him for running away. No, she couldn't show the tricks off because her dog wouldn't behave himself when Shaw was there.

It was all very strange. He seemed pleasant enough to her and it made a nice change to have someone interested in spending time with her instead of avoiding her or behaving like a polite stranger.

She forced her thoughts away from the two men and turned them to a more pleasant subject – the following evening's concert. She was especially looking forward to seeing the dog act. The whole family was going, except for the three tiny children, and Betsy was coming round to look after them. In fact, Essie was talking of having Betsy to live in, the girl was proving so willing to turn her hand to anything and was so good with the little 'uns, as everyone called the three infants.

Dora wished she could go into Manchester from time to time to see the shows there. She'd asked Raife to go with her but he said he was too old to go gallivanting. When she suggested to Nev that they all went, he said there was enough to see in Hedderby and she wasn't to go into the city on her own, or even with one of her sisters. He'd read in the newspaper that there were 300,000 people living in Manchester now. It just went to show what a crowded and dangerous place it was.

If she made a fuss it might give away why she wanted to go, which was to see other animal acts. Strange how the idea of going on stage with Nippy had caught her imagination. She was going to do it one day, whatever anyone said.

12

On the Friday evening James Forrett returned to Hedderby with his new wife on his arm and his mother-in-law trailing along behind them, scowling. He wasn't best pleased with Mrs Grieves, who had been in a grumpy mood ever since her daughter agreed to marry him, the selfish old biddy.

'Leave the luggage,' he told Kevin, looking at the big pile of trunks and boxes Charis had brought. She must have been up packing half the night, because he was sure her mother hadn't helped. 'I'll send a cart down for it. You give your arm to Mrs Grieves to help her up the hill. It's not far and we don't need to wait for a cab.'

The old woman bristled. 'I don't link arms with servants.'

'Well, the pavements are too narrow for us to walk three abreast,' James said with a wink at Charis. 'So if you don't hold on to Kevin, you'll have to walk on your own behind us.' He set off without waiting for her answer.

On the way up the hill they met the man he most wanted to see, his lawyer Jack Burtell. He stopped to introduce his wife, saw the surprise on Jack's face and grinned. He was going to enjoy the next few days.

'Excuse me a minute, my dear. I have a small matter of business to attend to.' He let go of Charis's arm and stepped aside to ask quietly, 'Can you write me up a new will, Jack? It's very simple. I want to leave everything to Charis.'

'*Everything?*'

'Yes. You'll maybe have heard of the trick my daughters tried to play on me? No? Well, they got someone to put laudanum in

my food and then turned up with a doctor, ready to lock me
away for being out of my wits.'

'Are you sure?'

'Ask Dr Pipperday and Lucas Kemp. They were there, fortu-
nately for me.' He glanced quickly over his shoulder and was
relieved to see that Charis was keeping her mother's attention
elsewhere, pointing to something along the main street. 'I want
to make sure my daughters never get their hands on my money.'

'They could contest the will. It might be better to leave them
something on condition they don't contest it.'

James pulled a face.

'Otherwise your wife might face years of litigation. I've seen
it happen.'

'You're sure of that?'

'Yes, unfortunately.'

'All right. Draw up the will quickly and leave them two thousand pounds each. I'll pop in to sign it tomorrow afternoon. I
want Charis protected.'

'Who will be your executors?'

'I thought of asking that Channon fellow and . . . I don't know.
How about Lucas Kemp? I trust those two, which is more than
I can say for my own family these days. Perhaps you could ask
them for me?'

'Very well.' Jack stepped back, tipped his hat to the new Mrs
Forrett and watched the small group walk off. Clever move of
Forrett's – if what he believed about his daughter was true. Could
it be? It wouldn't hurt to check that with Dr Pipperday. As a
lawyer, Jack had a responsibility to make sure that Forrett was
sound in mind when making this new will. In fact, he'd get the
doctor to sign a deposition about it. You couldn't be too careful
in situations like this.

At the front door of Mill House James stopped, put out his
hand to bar the way to his mother-in-law, who had pushed
ahead as if it was her right, and bowed to his wife. 'I'm too old
to offer to carry you over the threshold, Charis, but I do welcome
you most heartily to your new home.' He kissed her cheek and

led her inside, again leaving his mother-in-law to follow on her own.

Glaring at her daughter and her new son-in-law, Mrs Grieves looked round the hall scornfully. 'It's very shabby.'

Forrett turned round where he stood as if seeing it for the first time. 'Aye, it is. But Charis is going to do it up for me.'

'What does *she* know about doing up houses?' The older woman brightened. 'That's something *I* can do for you, dear James. I've had a great deal of experience in looking after houses and she has none.'

'Thank you, but it's my wife's job to do things like that.'

'But—'

'No buts. If Charis has no experience, then it's time she learned.' He turned to yell, 'Isn't anyone at home?'

Cook came out of the door at the rear of the hall, wiping her hands on a cloth and looking flustered. 'Sorry, sir! I didn't hear you come in.'

'Where's Jen? It's she who should be letting folk in.'

'She's in bed, poorly. Someone attacked her last night when she was on her way home from her sister's, hit her round the face, poor lass.'

James stared at her in consternation, then remembered to introduce his wife.

Cook gaped at her new mistress. 'Eh, you never said what you were doing, Mr Forrett or I'd have got things ready for you. Welcome to Mill House, ma'am. I'm that sorry you've caught us like this. Whatever must you think of us?' She looked ready to burst into tears.

James intervened. 'Can you find someone to help out till Jen's better, Cook? No doubt my wife will see about hiring some more servants in due course.'

'Oh yes, sir. My cousin will come in, the one who's helped out before.' She looked warily at her new mistress. 'She's a good worker, ma'am.'

Charis smiled at her new servant. 'Do send for her then. And I don't expect miracles, given the circumstances. Mr Forrett wanted to surprise everyone about our marriage so he couldn't tell you. If you'll just do the best you can for tonight, we can start sorting out the household tomorrow.'

As Cook bobbed a curtsey and left them, James turned to his wife, not sure what to do with her next.

Charis looked towards the stairs. 'I think I'd better go and see the maid who's been injured. We may have to call in the doctor if she's been badly hurt. Has she been with you for long?'

'Only a few months.'

'If you could just show my mother where to sit till we can get a bedroom ready for her . . . ?'

'A fine welcome this is!' Mrs Grieves snapped. 'Really, Charis, have you no sense? The maid can wait. You should— Oh!'

James took her by the arm and propelled her at a fast walk into the front parlour. 'You can sit in here till we have your room ready, Mrs Grieves, then you'll need to unpack, I'm sure. I want to see Jen too. I'll show you the way, Charis.'

On the first landing she stopped and clapped one hand over her mouth, trying to stifle a laugh. 'I'm sorry. It's just – my mother's expression when you hurried her into the front room!'

'She did look a bit surprised, didn't she?' His smile faded. 'You said she'd try to take over and I can see what you mean. I must tell Cook not to do anything your mother says without checking with you.'

She touched his arm shyly. 'Thank you, James.'

He nodded, pleased that she could laugh at the spiteful old biddy. He hadn't failed to notice how much happier Charis looked today, or how much nicer was the dress she was wearing, which wasn't as dowdy as the ones she'd always worn before. 'We'd better check on Jen.' He led the way up the next flight of stairs.

The maid's face was so badly bruised he stopped in the doorway to gape at her. 'What the hell happened to you, Jen?'

She burst into tears.

His voice grew gentler. 'Tell me who did it to you, lass?'

'I didn't see them.'

He saw the terror in her face and didn't press the point. 'Well, you'd better stay in bed for the rest of the day.'

'I want to give notice, sir. Only please don't tell – anyone. Just let me leave quietly. I don't want any more – trouble.'

He stopped pretending. 'You're going nowhere. But I'll make sure he doesn't get near you again. Or hurt your sisters.'

Jen gaped at him. 'Do you know who did it, sir?'

'I've my suspicions. But if you say one word to him about me knowing, you'll not only be out on your ear but I'll haul you up before the magistrate for conspiracy. Do you understand? And no more putting stuff in my food.'

She closed her eyes, whispering, 'Yes, sir. I mean, no, sir. I'm that sorry. I didn't want to do anything wrong, but I was frightened for my sisters, who work in the mill. The families would go hungry without their money.'

'I'd guessed that. You stay in bed today. Cook's cousin is coming in to help. And you'd better not leave the house till we get things sorted out, then he can't get to you. Think on! Don't even go out into the back yard on your own.' He turned to go then swung round again. 'I nearly forgot. This is my new wife, who'll be in charge of the house from now on.'

He ignored the shock on Jen's face and turned to Charis. 'We'll go down again now.' Outside he whispered, 'I'll explain everything later.' His overlooker was a worse man than he had realised if he could attack a lass so viciously.

It was a question now of finding proof and until he did, he wanted Benting where he could keep an eye on him.

He might have a word with sergeant Hankin about the situation, though. He'd a lot of respect for the police officer.

Benting saw the girls gossiping in the mill, mee-mawing at one another, lip reading because what they said couldn't be heard over the noise of the machinery. He'd learned to mee-maw as a lad so stopped to see what was causing so much 'chatter'. What he saw them saying sent him storming out into the yard, where he beckoned to his son.

Huey took one look at his face and approached hesitantly.

Grabbing his son by the front of his jacket, Benting hauled him into the office, shaking him like a rat. He might be shorter than Huey but he was well-muscled still, and there was something about him when he was angry that always terrified his family, and prevented Huey from retaliating now.

'What did you want to thump Jen for?' he demanded, letting go suddenly and pushing his son with the flat of one hand so that Huey staggered backwards. Benting followed him, jabbing one finger in his chest to emphasise his words. 'Have you – *no sense*? I told you to warn her to keep her mouth shut, and that's all I told you to do, you stupid fool!' He shoved hard with the flat of both hands and his son fell over.

Huey lay cowering on the floor, one arm raised to protect his face. 'You were mad at her, Dad. I thought you'd be *pleased* if I thumped her.'

'When I'm mad at somebody,' he turned and kicked his son hard in the side for good measure, 'I'll deal with it myself – like – this. You're too stupid to think straight, you are, so don't try doing anything in future without asking me first. Even here at the mill, you go at things like a bull at a gate. If you were working for anyone else but me, you'd have been sacked the first week. It's a good thing you've got a few muscles because there's nowt much in your hayloft!' He tapped his forehead.

Huey sighed in relief as his father turned and began to walk to and fro, but he didn't try to get up, not wanting to draw any more attention to himself.

'If Jen tells Forrett who hit her, we're in trouble.' He stopped to clench his fists and groan aloud. 'What did I ever do to be lumbered with a son like you?'

There was the sound of clogged feet clattering across the cobbled yard and the lad who acted as general dogsbody came panting in. 'Have you heard, Mr Benting? The drayman said I was to tell you.'

'Have I heard what?'

'About Mr Forrett. He's gotten wed, just brought his new wife home with him.'

Benting froze. 'I don't believe you.'

'I'm not making it up, honest. I seed her mysen going into th'house with him, her and her mother. Then the master sent word we were to pick up their baggage from the station. Only the drayman said I was to tell you first, then run back to help him.' He turned and left at top speed.

'The cunning old devil!' Benting forgot his son and went across to the window, but there was nothing to be seen now across at the house. 'Who the hell has he married?'

He forgot Huey as he went to a vantage point from where he could keep an eye on the house, forgetting everything but the need to find out who the woman was. He'd send off a letter to Mr and Mrs Gleason as soon as he knew. Eh, they'd be furious about this. Maybe he should let them find out for themselves? No. If he wanted to keep in well with them, he'd need to be the one who told them.

He just hoped to hell that Forrett hadn't put two and two together, and worked out what part his overlooker had played in the trouble the other day. No, he couldn't have. His employer would have sacked him on the spot if he'd suspected anything, and though he'd been a bit sharp with him lately, Forrett had been snapping at everyone else as well.

Eyes narrowed in thought, Benting watched the house for some time, but saw no sign of either Forrett or the new wife.

Hell and damnation! What a mess this was turning into! He looked at the clock on the mantelpiece. Nearly time for the final whistle to go. And tomorrow was Saturday, a shorter working day, which always annoyed him and reduced production. The Government had gone mad, passing that Ten Hours Bill two years ago. And he didn't care what Mr Forrett said about experiments in Preston by some millowner that showed shorter hours wouldn't lower production. All Benting could say was if he'd been Gardner's overlooker in Preston, he'd have showed them how to keep production up till the very end of the working day. Operatives shouldn't be treated softly; they should be worked to the limits of their endurance.

And Forrett had compounded the problem by refusing to allow Benting to work women and children in relays, so that the mill could still be run for the longer hours. The man had definitely gone soft in the head.

It should be up to the owners how long operatives worked, not up to members of bloody Parliament who knew less than nowt about cotton spinning.

Tea at Mill House was a makeshift affair that evening, but James had more appetite than for a while. His mother-in-law tried to sour the meal by making a couple of spiteful comments, so he set down his knife and fork and pointed his forefinger at her.

'Stop carping, woman! I should think shame to speak like that about my daughter! If you can't be kinder to my wife, you can eat your meals in your own room from now on.'

Mrs Grieves gasped and bright spots of colour flared in her cheeks.

'What's more, you'd do well to remember that you're dependent on me from now on. If you upset my wife, you upset me too.'

He then concentrated on his stewed lamb and potatoes, eating two slices of the apple tart that followed. He noticed that Charis didn't say much but he didn't comment on that. He wanted to draw her out of her shell, but that'd be easier without his mother-in-law sitting picking at her food with that sulky expression on her face. In fact, he'd make it a priority to find the old sourpuss somewhere to live. Jack Burtell might know of somewhere to let. His own mill cottages weren't good enough for the woman, unfortunately.

After the meal, James led the way into the parlour, where a fire was burning brightly and two lamps were shedding a clear light on the room.

'Oh, you've got a piano!' Charis exclaimed. 'I didn't notice it before.'

'Can you play?'

'A little. I do enjoy music.'

There was a muffled snort from the armchair. James saw his wife flinch and turned to his mother-in-law. 'I'll see you up to bed now, Mrs Grieves. A man likes some time alone with his wife on their wedding night.'

As he went across and offered her his arm, Charis stood up. 'I'll need to help mother unbutton her clothes, James. I shan't be long.'

He looked at them both with narrowed eyes. He was quite sure the old woman would be nasty to his wife even when she was helping her. 'If you can't dress and undress yourself, we must get you a maid, Mrs Grieves, mustn't we? Charis can see to it.'

Once the two women were alone in the bedroom, Mrs Grieves said in a low voice, 'Did you tell him to send me to bed early like this?'

'No, Mother. I doubt anyone could tell James what to do.'

'I suppose you think you're better than me now you've got a husband, though why he wants *you* is more than I can work out. A woman as ugly as you would never tempt a normal man into bed. Well, you're in for a painful night and it serves you right for being wilful. The marriage bed isn't a pleasant place for a woman.'

Charis could feel herself flushing but said nothing because arguing made her mother worse. 'Let me help you.'

'I'm not *ready* to go to bed yet.'

'He'll be expecting me down soon. I'll look at getting you a maid as soon as we can find one.'

'See that you do. And do something about this bedroom while you're at it. I'm not spending the rest of my life in a hovel like this.'

'James was talking about setting you up in a house of your own. I'm sure you'll be happier there.'

'On my own? In a town where I know no one? Oh, I'm sure you'd like that! But I won't go.'

Charis didn't even attempt to respond to that, just began to help her undress. But it took far longer than usual, because her mother was being deliberately awkward. Before they had finished there was a knock on the door.

'Charis? Are you going to take all night?'

With an angry sob, Mrs Grieves pushed her daughter away. 'Go to him! Never mind about me. I can finish the rest on my own.'

Charis went out on to the landing to find James waiting there. When she would have said something, he put one finger to his lips and they went quietly down the stairs.

'I was listening at the door. How the hell have you put up with her carping ways for all these years?'

'Because I had no choice.'

'You do now, lass.'

Tears came into her eyes and it seemed natural for him to pull her into his arms and give her a big hug. Then she began to cry in earnest.

'What's the matter now?'

'I'm so grateful to you.'

'Nay, I don't want your gratitude.'

'What do you want?'

'What I said. A child if we can. And a friend to keep me company of an evening.'

She sniffed and accepted the handkerchief he proffered. 'Thank you.'

'The sooner we find *her* somewhere to live, the better, though.'

She opened her mouth, then closed it again.

'What did you nearly say?'

'She'll need a companion. She can't entertain herself, needs someone to talk to her, suggest things to do and help her with her clothes. She has rheumatism, though she tries to hide it, and the pain is bad sometimes.'

'You're more generous than she deserves. But we'll get her whatever you consider right. Now, come and sit with me for a while and we'll have a glass of port. Or there's brandy if you prefer it.'

'I don't usually—'

'Try it. I'm sure you'll enjoy a glass of port at the end of the day, just one. I'm not a tippler.'

By the time they went upstairs, Charis had relaxed. To her amazement, James really did want to hear what she had to say, as well as to share with her some of the details of his own life and business. She had never known an evening at home pass so pleasantly. Her father hadn't been nearly as interesting to talk to.

And even in the bedroom James made it easy for her, gentling her as kindly as you would a nervous animal so that she found the experience of being bedded by a man not nearly as frightening as she'd expected.

'I'll make sure you enjoy it next time,' he said when they'd finished.

'*Enjoy it?*'

'You sound surprised.'

'My mother said it would hurt.'

'Your mother knows nowt and the sooner we get rid of the spiteful old besom the better.'

Within minutes he was asleep, but Charis lay awake for some time, marvelling at how much her life had changed for the better in two short days.

And she'd been his first choice as a wife. Oh, the confidence that gave her!

13

When Lucas sat down to glance over the plans he'd made for clearing up the mess in the orphanage, he groaned and rested his forehead on his hands. So much would have to be redone! The destruction had set back their plans to open the orphanage by months. Whoever had done this had made a very thorough job of it all.

Leaving Seb to mind the workshop, he took Ted and Joe with him to continue getting rid of the broken glass. The night-watchmen he'd hired were waiting for him at the orphanage, looking chilled to the marrow.

'Anything happen last night?' he asked at once.

'No, Mr Kemp. By, it were cold wi' all them brokken windows.'

'It'll be more comfortable once we have them reglazed. You'll be back tonight?'

'Yes, sir.'

He paid them the money agreed and expected them to walk off, but one of them shuffled his feet and the other cleared his throat.

'Is something wrong?'

'We thought we'd give you an hour or so before you leave, just to help you make a start. Well, we began clearing up the glass last night. Thought we might as well, since we were here wi' nowt to do but walk round.'

'That's – very kind of you.' He was so touched by this offer that his voice came out husky.

'I don't like to see childer living on the streets,' one of them said gruffly. 'I reckon what you and Mr Forrett are doing will be good for the whole town. We should look after our own in

Hedderby. So me an' my friend will do what we can during the night and we'll help you a bit each morning. Just an hour or so, because we need our sleep, but every bit helps, eh?'

Lucas set them to work shovelling up more broken glass – there seemed to be acres of it – and taking the pieces out to the handcart in a wheelbarrow.

The two worked for an hour or so, yawning from time to time, then left for home.

As they went out, Gideon walked in. 'I can spare you half a day.'

Lucas looked at him in puzzlement.

'I'm disgusted at what's happened here. I thought you could maybe use a hand.'

'I'll pay you the—'

'No, I don't need paying. I'm doing it for the children.'

As the day progressed other people, both men and women, turned up to offer an hour or two of their time. Lucas's spirits rose with each offer.

When Gwynna came in to bring his midday meal and discovered what was going on, she looked at him with tears in her eyes. 'Isn't it wonderful? Nothing will stop us now.'

So he had to pick her up and swing her round and round, while Joe and Ted laughed at them.

James Forrett decided to call in at the orphanage later that day on the way to his lawyer's rooms. He wasn't looking forward to seeing the destruction again, grew angry each time he thought of it, but wanted to show his support. To his surprise he saw two women in the front part of the building, kerchiefs round their heads, rubbing at what remained of the paint stains on the stairs with sandpaper.

He went to find Lucas and when he discovered what was happening, how people were coming in and volunteering their help, he couldn't speak for a minute or two. 'They're doing this without asking for pay?'

'Without asking for a penny. The idea of an orphanage has touched folk's hearts, it seems.'

Pulling out a large white handkerchief, James blew his nose, then blew it again, ashamed of his weakness but unable to control his feelings completely. 'I never realised how . . . Eh, I've been so wrong about ordinary folk, so very wrong . . . We must find some way to repay them.'

'They don't want repaying, but we could brew some tea and maybe set a woman to watch over it – it'd be a perfect job for an older woman who can't do heavy work. A hot drink is very welcome in weather like this.'

'If you arrange it, I'll pay.' Then James remembered why he'd popped in on the way to the lawyer's. 'Oh, I came to tell you that I've got myself a new wife. It seemed the best way to stop those daughters of mine trying their tricks again.' He couldn't stop himself smiling as he thought of Charis. 'And anyway, it's grand to have a bit of company in the house.'

'Congratulations, sir. I had heard rumours about it. I wish you and Mrs Forrett every happiness.'

'I dare say we shall rub along comfortably. She's got a bit of sense in her head, my Charis has. I'll bring her along to see this place later. I've told her what we're doing.' He took his watch out of his waistcoat pocket and held it at arm's length, squinting at it. 'I'd better get going. I've an appointment with my lawyer. Which reminds me, I wonder if you'd act as Executor for me. I'm making a new will, you see.'

'Me?'

'Yes. I need folk I can trust to see that my wishes are carried out if anything happens to me.' He couldn't stop himself grinning. 'Not that I'm expecting anything to happen. I intend to live to a ripe old age, if only to confound my damned family.'

'I'd be honoured.'

'Good. I'm asking Jeremiah Channon as well. If you'll pop into Mr Burtell's rooms, he'll sort it all out with you.'

James took his leave, passing yet another volunteer as he went out. The place was a hive of activity now. It took away the sour feeling you got from having been the butt of such furious destruction. His thoughts shifted to his daughters and sadness filled him.

That it should come to this! He shook his head to clear away the unwelcome thoughts and began to stride along the street.

But here again he met with a few surprises, because as he walked, people called out greetings and wished him well in his marriage. Others said how sorry they were to hear about the orphanage being damaged. In the end he was late for his appointment.

Jack Burtell waved away his apologies and listened to his explanation of what was happening at the orphanage. 'It's good to hear that such things can happen. Makes you proud of our Hedderby folk, doesn't it? I sometimes see the worst side of people in my job, but I try not to forget how decent most folk are, given half a chance.'

'I'd forgotten it completely,' James admitted. 'For years I'd forgotten, despised the lasses who worked in my mill, worked them as hard as I could – too hard. It took Libby's death to start me thinking straight again.' There was silence for a moment or two and when he looked up, Jack was smiling at him, so he smiled back, feeling a bit embarrassed by what he had revealed. 'Well, I suppose we'd better get this will signed. It is ready, isn't it?'

'It is indeed. It's a very simple affair and I'd prefer to draw up a more comprehensive will for you later, but this one will do what you want, which is to ensure that most of what you own goes to your new wife in case of trouble. You *are* still sure about that?'

'More sure every hour. She's a grand lass. Been badly treated by her family, but I know how to appreciate her.'

The will was brought in by the clerk and Mr Hordle was summoned from his rooms along the road to act as the other witness.

'Do we need to get him in?' James asked. 'Surely anyone would have done as a witness?'

'It's better to be sure. Mr Hordle is beyond suspicion as a witness – just in case. And together with Dr Pipperday's deposition, this makes you more secure.'

The other lawyer chatted to them both for a while, then the deed was done. James signed his name with a flourish, relieved that his wife was now safe.

Afterwards, when Mr Hordle had gone back to his rooms, James asked Mr Burtell to help him find a small house for his mother-in-law as quickly as possible.

'I've a couple on my books that people are wanting to let out to the better class of people.'

James listened to details. 'I'd better bring my wife round to look at them. How about tomorrow?'

As he walked home he realised suddenly that he was feeling happy, in spite of what had happened to the orphanage, happier than he had for years. And was particularly looking forward to sharing the tale of this day's doings with Charis.

The show Eli was putting on at the church hall on Saturday was to be performed twice, once at six o'clock and then again at half-past eight. He spent the day there, making sure the chairs were set out properly at the front, with the rough benches Lucas had knocked up for him ranged behind, and a cord stretched across the rear of the hall to keep the standing area separate. You could fit quite a lot of extra people in if they stood up.

Carrie was in and out all Friday supervising preparations to feed the audience. There was only a small kitchen from which to dispense the hot and cold drinks and special little pies and cakes ordered from two local bakers. She wished they could sell beer and wine, which brought in a bigger profit. Unfortunately the church committee, pleased as they were with the extra money paid for the use of the hall, had refused point-blank to allow alcoholic beverages to be served. The minister was very much in favour of abstention, it seemed. As if you could stop people drinking! She'd explained that they never let people get drunk at their shows because that led to interruptions to the acts, but the committee members were adamant: no alcoholic beverages were allowed on church premises.

In the late afternoon, the performers gathered in the small room to one side, pulling wry faces at the conditions in which they had to change and sit between acts. Eli knew they were all used to the occasional 'rough venue' as one called it, so he didn't worry. And as before, most of them settled down without too much fuss, their mood sweeter because Carrie sent a lass to serve them cups of tea or her popular gooseberry cordial.

The performing dogs were the best behaved of anyone, Eli thought later as he checked to make sure everything was all right. The two animals simply lay in a corner, followed their owner outside to relieve themselves just before their turn and then trotted on stage after him and his two sons.

Dora was helping in the kitchen but had begged Carrie to let her watch the dog act, which she did at each performance. The two animals went through a series of tricks which formed a vague story. They tracked a kidnapped 'princess' (a beautiful doll). A member of the audience was called up to 'walk' the doll across the stage and hide it. During the second performance, when a different place was chosen by the audience member, she guessed there must be some scent on the doll's shoes that the dogs followed and wondered what it was.

After the doll was in place, the man set up various obstacles and during their hunt the animals jumped over these and finally crawled through a tunnel of hoops. Then they went to fetch the hero who was hiding in the audience (the owner's young son, dressed in a blue satin stage suit and cloak, and wearing a sword) and guided him to where the princess was locked away, after which the dogs drove off the villain (the owner's other son, skulking behind a piece of scenery dressed all in black). The audience entered lustily into this adventure, encouraging the dogs with shouts, applauding when the two animals achieved anything, booing the villain and cheering loudly as the princess was restored to her prince.

It was a silly little tale, really, but it had pleased folk to see the dogs performing in it and that was what mattered. But if Dora had been doing any sort of act she'd have finished it with a little song and taught the dogs to bark at the chorus.

She went back to work, not caring nearly as much about the other acts. She was still lost in thought as she made her way home just before midnight, walking along silently with

Carrie, Eli and Raife, all of them weary after helping clear up the hall.

Gideon saw Dora at the Saturday concert, but he was sitting with Granny and Barney, so contented himself with a nod across the hall at her. She gave him a quick smile but didn't look his way again. It was what he wanted – wasn't it – for her to keep her distance? Only it didn't feel right. And he couldn't help watching her, knowing that the longer he'd worked with her the fonder of her he'd grown. She was always so lively and cheerful.

He was very disappointed by the dog act, which he thought silly. If *he* had been doing it, he'd have done something more clever, which didn't involve dolls and children. He'd have had a dog with a cheeky face and taught it to look at the audience and bark, as if asking them for help. Nippy came instantly into his mind. The dog loved doing its tricks and winning praise and pats from people. Gideon had become too fond of that little rascal, but it really was the cleverest dog he'd ever met.

And an owner as pretty as Dora would be perfect on the stage, much nicer to look at than a lumpy-faced man and two scrawny little lads. There he went again! Thinking about her. He turned his attention to the other performers, especially enjoying a singing act, two women who had beautiful voices and sang in harmony. He'd spent a good few evenings in the regiment singing all the old songs that everyone seemed to know. They'd been lucky to have a couple of good singers and he wasn't too bad himself, come to that, though he hadn't tried to sing since he'd arrived in Hedderby.

He was delighted when a later act consisted of a man and wife who encouraged the audience to join in the choruses and he sang along with them lustily.

'Eh, Gideon, you didn't say you had a nice voice!' Granny said as they waited for the final act. 'You're good enough to go on the stage yoursen.'

He chuckled. 'Hardly. I can hold a tune, but I've not got a good enough voice to be a singer up there.'

'Well, *I* enjoyed hearing you,' she said. 'Eh, I've not had such a good time for years. It's good of you to give us this treat, Gideon lad, right good it is.'

Barney nodded agreement from beyond her. From his beaming face, he too was enjoying himself.

But as the three of them walked home, Gideon heard footsteps behind them and swung round. Someone ducked into a doorway and he debated going to find out who it was, but decided not to leave his companions unprotected. After that he walked more quietly, speaking less and when he looked at Barney, he could see that the lad had also heard something.

The attackers came in a rush just before they got home and Gideon had swung round to face them even before Barney called a warning. Two figures rushed at him and he raised his special weighted walking stick to clout the nearest one hard on the arm, making him drop his cudgel and sending him staggering backwards.

'Shout for help, Barney!' he yelled, and at once both his companions started yelling at the top of their voices.

The other fellow was holding a cudgel and swung it at Gideon even as he turned, nearly catching him with it. But his years in the Army paid off and he ducked quickly, so that it just missed.

Behind him Granny and Barney were still shouting. His main concern was to protect them, so he wasn't free to use any tactics that took him away from them in this struggle. Once, he'd have despatched the two villains without any trouble, but his grip wasn't as secure on the walking stick without his main fingers.

So it was with relief that he heard something as Granny paused for breath. A shout rang out from down the street, then the sound of a policeman's rattle and footsteps came running towards them.

Both attackers had turned at the sound of the rattle and then vanished into the darkness. Was it his imagination or was there a third man hovering nearby in the shadows? If so, why hadn't he joined in the attack?

A policeman ran up to them. 'Heard you shouting for help,' he panted.

He'd have been no use if it had come to an out-and-out fight, Gideon thought. Plump and out of condition, panting from even a short run. I'd have trained him better than that. 'We were attacked by two men. They ran off when they heard you coming, so I'm grateful for your help.'

'Did you recognise them?'

'No. They were well muffled up. I'll report it at the station tomorrow, but I'd be grateful if you'd escort us home. I've an old lady and a crippled lad to look after.'

'I'll come with you, sir.'

The policeman walked beside them in silence then nodded farewell.

Gideon locked up carefully then lay awake for a while, wondering if the impostor had arranged this and wishing his problems with the fellow could be sorted out. The business was hanging on for too long. Why had no one answered Mr Burtell's latest letter of enquiry, the one he'd sent via London?

Even the Army didn't usually take this long to reply.

On the Saturday morning James breakfasted with his wife, relieved that the old lady didn't usually get up until later. As soon as they'd finished eating he whisked Charis off to see the two houses, enjoying having her on his arm as they walked along the street.

'I hope one of the places is suitable,' he said. 'I can't wait to get your mother out of our house. What was all that fuss about this morning just before we left?'

'She wanted me to help her dress. I usually do.'

'You'd think by her age she could dress herself. Anyway, Jen can help her from now on. We'll get another housemaid, eh?'

'We definitely need at least one more. How do you usually find your maids?'

'Cook usually knows someone. There's allus a lass or two as can't stand the heat and fluff in the mill. Makes some of them cough themselves sick it does in there. Benting keeps it too hot because that's how *he* likes it. I have to make sure he opens the windows. I shan't bother to introduce you to him. He's a disloyal devil and I'm sacking him as soon as I find another overlooker. Actually, I may have found one, though I'll have to go into Manchester to meet him.'

'What did Benting do to upset you?'

'Worked with my daughter against me.'

She made a sympathetic sound but didn't comment further. He liked the way she didn't gab on for no reason.

'The first house is along here, a nice level street, see, and just off the main road. The places were only built ten years ago. They call them villas.' At Number Seven he pulled out the key and flourished it at her. 'Here we go.'

They inspected the interior, which seemed all right to him but Charis was frowning.

'What's up?'

'It's a bit small.'

'Eight rooms and two attics for one woman? It seems plenty big enough to me.'

'It is, but she'll still complain, perhaps refuse to move.'

'Let her. I'll carry her out of my house and into this one if I have to.'

His wife was betrayed into a gurgle of laughter. 'I'd like to see that.'

'Don't think I wouldn't.' He looked round. 'The other house is further up the hill.'

The second house was bigger with views across the smokey valley.

'Well? What do you think?'

'I think the first one would be better. As you said, the street is level and she can easily walk to the shops. But the parlour will need redecorating.'

'Right, we'll take that one. Let's go.' He marched her smartly to the door of Mill House. 'I'll tell the old lady tonight, then we'll send for what's left of your furniture and move her in by the middle of the week.'

'We'll need to find her a cook and maid, as well as a companion.'

He looked at her challengingly. 'Don't tell me you can't do

that if you set your mind to it, Charis lass. Money's no object, you know. I just want your mother out of my home.'

'Maybe by next week then, if we can find the staff and someone to stay with her. No, James, Mother really can't manage on her own. I've got an idea about a companion, if you agree. I have a second cousin who was also left without money. We used to help Helen financially but she also takes in sewing. I didn't know what to do about her when we lost our money. Sewing doesn't bring in nearly enough, but she's very proud and doesn't like having to accept charity. She has to work dreadfully long hours and I'm sure she'd prefer to look after Mother to that.'

'Write to her at once, or go and see her, whatever you think best. I just want peace in my own home.'

As he'd expected Mrs Grieves burst into loud, angry sobs when told about her new home that night, but when she showed no signs of abating her hysterics, he thumped on the table and roared at her. 'Stop that! You can either find yourself a new home and pay for it too, or you can move into that one and I'll pay. I want the pleasure of my wife's company to myself. Charis can take you to see the house tomorrow and you can start making plans.'

He winked at his wife as he added, 'Charis says the parlour will need redecorating, but she won't have time to deal with it, so you'd better sort that out. I'll pay for it within reason.'

The old lady's tears had dried up but she flourished her handkerchief anyway. 'I never thought to end my days on my own.'

'I know that,' Charis said soothingly. She hesitated and pretended to think. 'We need to find someone to be a companion to you. Do we have any relatives or acquaintances who would welcome a comfortable home and money?' She avoided James's eyes as she paused and waited.

'I suppose we could ask your Cousin Helen,' Mrs Grieves said grudgingly. 'It should be you looking after me, you're the youngest, but at least she's a relative.'

Charis hid her relief. 'Oh, what a good idea! I'd forgotten about her. You always said her mother was a good friend of yours. I'll write to her straight away.'

'You can't wait to get rid of me, I see.'

'Well,' James said cheerfully, 'newly-weds need time together, don't they?'

She scowled across at him, but said nothing else, hunching her shoulders and picking at her food.

Sunday was fine, to Dora's relief, and after church she went for her usual walk, relieved that none of her sisters wanted to come with her.

'I don't like you going off on your own,' Essie worried, 'not after you hurt your ankle last time.'

'I'll only go up to just past those four cottages. That'll be far enough. But I do like to get out and about, breathe the fresh air. Do you want to go for a walk, Nippy?'

His excitement at this prospect made the dog leap around so much that even Essie had to smile.

Dora hesitated at the end of the lane leading to the cottages. Did she really want to get more friendly with John Shaw? An image of Gideon rose before her and she dismissed it with a wistful sigh, then grew angry with herself for thinking about him *again*, so marched along the lane. There were other men in the world and it was time she paid them some attention, Essie was right about that.

Even before she got to the cottages she was regretting her decision but the door of Number One opened while she was still a few yards away and John Shaw came out.

'I was hoping you'd come for a walk today, Dora.'

'Were you?'

He nodded but didn't smile, which surprised her. Gideon had a lovely smile. There she went again, thinking of him! 'I just wondered if you were feeling like joining us on the tops. Me and Nippy love it up there.'

But although the dog wasn't growling at him this time, he still refused to have anything to do with John.

They walked up the sloping path side by side and now, perversely, Dora was feeling shy, something unusual for her.

Essie always said she'd been born cheeky. 'Did you serve in India?'

'Yes. But I'm glad to be back in England and out of the Army.'

'Tell me about India.'

He pulled a face. 'It's a dirty country, full of fevers and illnesses and so hot it fair fries your skin. The people there are darkies and I didn't like dealing with them. Some of the other men liked the heat, but I didn't. And it was hell keeping your uniform smart when you sweated so much.'

She wished she hadn't asked him, since he had nothing good to say about India. And what did it matter if people's skins were dark or light? What mattered was whether they were friendly. 'Why did you leave the Army? Gideon says soldiers have to enlist for life, unless they're invalided out like he was.'

He didn't answer straight away, but perhaps that was because they were climbing up a steep bit.

Just as she was about to ask him again, he said, 'I left because I kept getting ill with fevers. I still get them sometimes. I was no use to the Army any more so they chucked me out.'

'Like Gideon. He lost some fingers and couldn't fire a rifle so they didn't want him. Do you miss the Army?'

'No, I don't. Nor I don't like to talk about it so don't keep going on. I've a new life now, a much better life, thanks to my aunt.'

He sounded so sharp she didn't say anything for a while. It wasn't proving very easy to talk to him and truth to tell, she didn't feel at ease with him. The looks he kept giving her were – assessing. There was no other word for it. This had been a mistake and the sooner she ended it the better. 'My ankle's starting to hurt. You go on if you want to walk further, but I think I'll go back. I shouldn't have come so far the first time after the accident.'

He looked at her as if he suspected that she was making it up. 'No, I'll walk back with you. I only came to keep you company. There's no fun in walking on your own. And I like a bit of fun. Don't you?'

She didn't answer that one and felt even more uncomfortable as they walked down because the way he was looking at her made her feel as if she had no clothes on. She hated it when men looked at you like that. Benting had been the same. When Shaw offered to walk her all the way home, she refused without hesitation. 'No, thank you. If people saw us out walking together on a Sunday, they might get the wrong idea.'

'Maybe I'd like them to get that sort of idea,' he said, stopping.

She stopped too, just out of politeness. 'Well, I wouldn't.' She saw that he didn't like this blunt speaking, so added hastily, 'It's not you, but I don't walk out with lads in that way, because I'm not interested in getting wed for years yet.'

'You *have* been walking out with me today, though. You shouldn't have led me on if you weren't interested.'

'I'm sorry if I gave you the wrong idea. I really do have to go now.' But when she tried to leave he took hold of her arm and pulled her towards him. She pushed him away, knowing he intended to kiss her. To her surprise the mere thought of him touching her in that way made her feel sick, yet he wasn't a bad-looking man.

But he didn't let go of her. She could feel how much stronger he was and began to feel frightened. 'Don't!' she pleaded breathlessly.

But he laughed and pulled her so close her body was pressed against his. Her heart began to pound with fear because there was no one nearby to help her. Why had she got herself into this? 'Please let go of me,' she begged.

Nippy suddenly began to bark hysterically, jumping up at John's legs. And when Dora continued to struggle and protest, the dog bit him on the calf.

He yelled and shoved her away roughly, trying to kick the dog. His angry expression made her so afraid she turned and ran off down the hill, calling to Nippy to follow. She was relieved when he scampered along beside her. She listened for signs of pursuit, but heard nothing, so stopped for a quick look back.

John was standing watching her, hands on hips, scowling. When he saw her stop, he started running after her as if he thought she was encouraging him. She cried out in fear and began running faster, calling, 'Come on, Nippy!'

As she turned a corner by a high wall, she bumped into someone who caught hold of her and she screamed in sudden terror.

'Hey up, lass! It's only me. And you'll fall if you don't look where you're going,' a deep voice said.

She realised who it was and sagged against him with a groan of relief. 'Gideon. Oh, thank goodness!'

'What's upset you? Who were you running from?'

'Nothing. I'm just a bit late.' But she couldn't help glancing back and even though she couldn't see John, she tried to walk on. Gideon kept hold of her arm and it occurred to her suddenly that she didn't feel afraid of this man because she knew instinctively he wouldn't hurt her.

'It's not like you to lie to me, Dora.'

She could feel her cheeks going hot and couldn't look him in the eye.

Nippy was pestering him for attention but he looked down and said, 'Sit!' in a tone that brooked no disobedience. The dog sat, head on one side, the very tip of his tail still quivering.

'The ground's too damp but there's a sheltered bit of wall in the hollow there. We'll go and sit on it and you can tell me what's upset you.'

She walked across with him and sat looking down at her tightly clasped hands, not knowing whether to admit what had happened.

'Dora?'

'It was that John Shaw I was running from. He came for a walk with me on the tops. I thought he was a nice enough fellow, but I should have trusted Nippy. You never liked him, did you, Nippy?'

The dog wagged and tossed his head, giving her a doggy smile.

'Go on,' Gideon encouraged.

'Well, when we were coming back, John grabbed me and wouldn't let go. I thought he was going to kiss me – or – or something worse.' She couldn't hold back a shudder as she added, 'And I didn't want him even to touch me. But luckily for me, Nippy bit his leg and that made him let go of me. I ran away but he started running after me. Didn't you see him?'

'I was watching you, afraid you'd fall because you weren't looking where you were going. Are you sure he didn't – hurt you?'

His hand covered hers, all warm and strong and she couldn't, she just couldn't pull away from him. She looked up to see an expression of genuine concern on his face and her voice came out breathless because of how it made her feel to be so close to him. 'No, he didn't hurt me.'

'If he had, I'd have made him sorry.'

She'd never seen that sort of expression on Gideon's face. Even that didn't make her afraid for herself, but she would not, she decided, like to get on the wrong side of him. 'The worst of it is, I'll have to find somewhere else to take Nippy for walks now, unless I've got someone else with me. That'll be a bit of a nuisance because this part of the moors is so convenient – but I'll manage.'

'You can take him for walks anywhere. You'd be safer staying in the town, where there are people nearby.'

'I know but—' She broke off.

'But what?'

'I've been teaching Nippy some more tricks and I don't want people to see what I'm doing. There's a flat bit of land that's sheltered, just up from those four cottages, and we go there to practise. Nippy's so clever, you should just see him. One day I'm going on the stage with him, and I don't care what anyone says, I'll find a way to do it.'

'It's a hard life for a lass.'

'I know, but it wasn't easy in the mill, either. And our Marjorie has managed to go on the stage, so I don't see why I shouldn't do it too. Nev's not going to stop me.'

'What sort of an act shall you have?'

'I'm not quite sure yet, but the ones with dogs that I've seen aren't quite . . .' She wrinkled her nose and shrugged. To her surprise he nodded.

'I know what you mean. They're not quite good enough. Well, they wouldn't be. You'll only get second-rate acts coming to a church hall.'

'I know. I wanted to go into Manchester to see the better ones, but Raife wouldn't take me and Nev says I can't go with one of my sisters because they're too young and giddy.'

It was out before he could stop himself. 'I'll take you, if you like.'

She turned to gape at him in surprise. 'You will?'

He nodded.

'But – you usually avoid me after work.' He was silent for so long she was afraid she'd said the wrong thing. Then he took her hand, looked at it and set it back down on her lap.

'I'm too old for you, that's why, and I'm not even whole in body.'

Her heart began to race wildly in her breast and she reached out instinctively to take that injured hand back in hers, lifting it against her cheek. 'As if a little thing like this matters to anyone worth their salt.'

He closed his eyes but didn't tug his hand away. 'It's not just that. There's something else I need to sort out before I – settle down, something I can't tell you about yet. And if it can't be sorted out, I'm not sure what I'd have to offer anyone.'

She looked at him in a daze, unable to believe what he was saying. 'Oh, Gideon, you'd be more than enough for me just as you are.'

Time seemed to stand still, then he asked, 'Are you sure?' in a voice that shook.

'Of course I am, you daft ha'porth.'

He chuckled and pulled her into his arms, kissing her gently, sweetly, with passion held in check by the feeling he'd been denying for months – love.

Only when they pulled apart did she say, 'I'm still going on the stage, though, whatever else I do in my life.'

He stared at her, his smile fading. He hadn't expected that.

★   ★   ★

John, who'd been following Dora along the other side of a dry-stone wall, stayed where he was watching them kiss, scowling darkly, not moving again until they'd walked away. She'd led him on, the bitch, and all to make another fellow jealous. And it had to be *that fellow*, of all others, the one whose mere existence threatened his present comfortable life!

Well, he wasn't going to let anyone spoil things for him. He'd had the wit to seize a golden opportunity and he'd use his wits now to keep hold of what he'd gained. He'd do whatever was necessary to make sure of that.

Those idiots he'd hired had failed in their task, but he'd get better help next time, bring someone in from Manchester, perhaps.

He should kill Gideon Shaw himself – only he'd never been any good at killing. The mere sight of blood turned his stomach.

But he'd find a way to get it done for him. He had to.

Gideon was very quiet as they walked into town. Before they went into Linney's, he stopped to ask, 'What are we going to do about your family?'

Dora looked at him uncertainly then told him what was worrying her. 'Never mind them. You didn't say anything when I said I wanted to go on the stage and you've hardly spoken a word since.'

'I need to think about it.'

'What does that mean? Does it – make a difference to us?'

'I don't know. I hadn't expected it. Women usually settle down once they're wed.'

'I can't, Gideon. I just can't. I don't love you any the less, but I want more from life.'

He sighed.

She screwed up her courage. Better to end it now than go on hoping for something that could never happen. 'If we start walking out, my family will hear about it, so if what I said has made you change your mind about me, you'd better tell me now.' He was silent a long time and in the end, just as she thought she could bear the silence no longer he smiled at her, a slow smile that had a wry look to it. Her heart did a little flip at his words.

'We'd better go and see them, then, hadn't we, Dora? We'll work the rest out somehow.'

She couldn't speak or move for a moment out of sheer relief, then she beamed at him and took his arm.

Inside Linney's they found the little ones playing in their usual corner of the kitchen, with Grace and Lily keeping an eye on them.

As they stood in the doorway, Dora muttered, 'We've all grown up surrounded by babies. Mam kept on having them, one after the other, and she was useless at looking after them.' But in spite of her grumble, when little Leah held up her arms for a cuddle, Dora obliged for a few minutes, then put the child down determinedly. 'Are Nev and Essie in the parlour?'

Lily lifted her eyes briefly from a book. 'Yes.'

Dora took a deep breath and gave Gideon a wry smile. 'Are you ready?'

He nodded.

She led the way into the front room, where Essie, Nev, Raife, Carrie and Eli all stopped talking to stare at them.

'We've been walking on the moors, so I brought Gideon back for a cup of tea,' Dora announced.

There was dead silence for a moment or two, then Nev stood up and shook hands with the visitor. Gideon nodded to the women, then somehow found himself sitting on a small sofa wedged up close to Dora.

Essie, who had brightened up at her stepdaughter's announcement, said, 'I was just about to serve some refreshments. I'll go and get them.'

'Our Grace and Lily can do that,' Carrie said. 'I'll go and tell them.'

'No, I'd rather do it myself.'

Essie vanished into the kitchen and Raife filled in the silence with a tranquil question about the weather up on the moors, then gradually the conversation veered round to the members of the family who weren't here today.

Gideon had never been part of a large family before and listened bemused as they talked about first one person then another, all relatives or as good as. Inevitably they talked about the destruction at the orphanage, and it seemed that they'd adopted Gwynna into the family too, because they referred to her as 'our Gwynna'. Would he one day become 'our Gideon'? He'd like that. He'd like it very much.

He was brought into the conversation by a question from Eli about India.

'I loved it there. It was a bit hot, but there was something special about the country. The women wore the most beautifully coloured clothes, saris they called them.' He hesitated, then added, 'I was married to an Indian woman, but she died.'

There was complete silence at this.

Dora stepped in hastily. 'You said she was called Lalika. It's a beautiful name. Was she beautiful?'

'Yes. I kept some of her saris but they were stolen from me on the boat coming back when I was ill. I was sad about that. You'd have looked good in one, Dora, with your dark hair. There was one in cherry red with gold edging that I'd bought for a present, only I never got to give it to her because she died suddenly.'

'Poor thing,' Dora said softly. 'And then you got injured.'

He looked down at his hand. 'Yes.'

There was another awkward silence, but luckily Essie came back just then carrying a tray. 'Could you fetch the other tray, please, Eli?'

When Gideon had left, they all looked at Dora with knowing smiles.

'Well, you're a dark horse,' Nev said. 'You didn't tell us you were walking out with him.'

'I wasn't – till today. But I always fancied him.'

'I don't like to think of him being married before and he's a lot older than you,' Essie said with a frown. Then she shrugged, 'But you always go your own way, you do. Just be careful until you know him a bit better.'

Dora flushed. She understood perfectly well what Essie meant by that. Babies. As if she'd take the risk. As soon as she could, she escaped, making the excuse that Nippy needed to go out the back.

Her sister Carrie joined her in the yard. 'Are you sure about this? Gideon is so different from you and older too.'

'I'm sure that I'm interested, but it's early days. We have a lot of things to sort out before we – get really steady.' She wasn't sure whether he'd want to join her on the stage, but she'd heard Granny Horne complimenting him on his singing and Nippy adored him, so maybe . . . it might just be possible.

Or would he only be interested in a woman who was prepared to stay meekly at home and look after him? Did he think she'd be the one to change?

She wouldn't, couldn't – even for Gideon. She'd never been a placid person, even when she was young, and had always liked trying new things. 'Our Dora's the cheeky one,' her mother used to say, just as Essie called her cheeky now.

But surely she hadn't mistaken Gideon? There was such a sparkle of life in his eyes when he was talking to people and though he'd tried to hide it, she'd seen how bored he got sometimes with the job at the market.

Surely he too wanted more than to settle down in Hedderby?

That made her stop and think. Why had he come here anyway? Why Hedderby when he didn't know anyone in the town? He'd never really explained that.

He'd said there was something he had to settle. She wished he'd told her what it was.

14

When the mill siren sounded on the Monday morning James woke with a start. He was a little later than usual waking up. As he turned over, his hand touched the soft figure lying next to him and he smiled, remembering that he was married once again. It was wonderful to have someone to snuggle up to during the chilly night hours, especially someone who smelled of newly washed skin with just a hint of lavender.

He tried to get up without waking Charis, but her sleepy voice stopped him.

'What time is it?'

'Ten minutes to six. Did the siren wake you?'

'Yes.'

'I'm usually dressed and ready by this time.' He went outside and brought the night lamp in from the landing, turning up the wick until its soft light filled the room. 'There's no need for you to get up.'

'I like getting up early. And anyway, there's a lot for me to do if I'm to arrange things for my mother's new home.'

'Very well then. I'm not denying I'll enjoy your company.' He rang the bell to let Jen know he wanted his hot water bringing up. 'I think we should fit up another room to wash and dress in. Can you arrange that? I'll just – um – nip next door.' He needed urgently to use the commode. That was the trouble with getting older. You couldn't hold on for as long if you needed to go.

When he got back Charis had her dressing gown on, an ugly grey garment.

He felt comfortable enough with her now to say, 'Are all your clothes so – um—'

'Ugly? Yes. My mother chose them like this on purpose.'

'There's a dressmaker in Hedderby that the better-off ladies use. Get her to make you some new clothes, the sort *you* like. I'll enjoy seeing you properly dressed. Get whatever you need, I'm not short of money.'

'Thank you, James. I'll do that.'

He reached out without thinking and stroked her cheek. 'You've got pretty skin and your hair could be nice too if you did it in a softer style. It's a lovely colour.'

She blushed bright pink. 'Do you really think so?'

He understood by now how her mother had crushed her spirit, how much she needed compliments and praise. 'I don't tell you lies, lass. Your hair *is* a lovely colour.'

'Don't lie to me, James. It's just an ordinary brown.'

'It may be brown but it has red and gold glints in it when the sun catches it.'

She looked at him uncertainly.

'I mean that. Now, what do you want to do first today?'

Charis hesitated. 'I want to see if Helen will come and act as companion to Mother. I'll write to her as soon as I'm dressed and take the letter straight to the post office. If I get it in the box before eight, it may get to her by second post.'

'Send Jen down with it.'

'Jen's got enough to do and anyway, I'll enjoy a walk.'

'All right. But don't let your mother put on you today. It's *you* who's mistress here.' He looked at her. 'Eh, what are you crying for, Charis?'

'It's just happy tears because you're so good to me.' She sniffed and mopped her eyes with a corner of the sheet. 'I'll wait for my wash till you've had yours.'

'Come downstairs in that damned dressing gown and share a bite with me, then wash later. On working days I generally have a proper breakfast about nine o'clock, but I need to eat something when I get up, to put me on till then.' He grinned. 'There's only Jen and me to see you. Your mother won't be up for hours.'

They shared a pot of tea and some fruit cake then he fumbled in his pocket. 'I nearly forgot to give you this.' He passed across a chinking purse of coins and a roll of banknotes.

She stared at it in shock. 'That's far more than I need.'

'Nonsense. You've a lot of things to buy for yourself, I'm sure, and bits for the house, too. Can't have you short of money. I'll settle the big bills, though. We've accounts with most shops in town, but if you buy anything at the market, you'll need this, or – I don't know. I just don't want you going short. You can leave Cook to buy the food, of course, but you tell her what you want to eat. Just get anything you fancy.' He waved one hand permissively. 'We've got a few nice shops in Hedderby, though they're nothing like the ones in Manchester, of course. Oh, and there's paper and pen in my desk for that letter to your cousin.'

'I can't go searching through your desk!'

He chuckled. 'There's nowt important in there, nowt secret either. All the accounts are over at the mill office. I'll send off for the furniture from your old home for your mother to use. Offer to pay your cousin whatever you think fit and tell her she's to put up with no nonsense from the old bid— I mean, old lady.'

When he'd gone to the mill, Charis sat for a moment, tears welling in her eyes at the thought of how kind he was, how wonderfully her life had turned round in the past few days. Then she smiled at herself in the mirror, dowdy grey dressing gown and all, and went upstairs to dress.

She'd have that letter in the post before her mother got up. Surely Helen would agree to come?

Quite early on Monday morning Kevin Reilly strolled down to the railway station and cast a quick glance along the platform to check who was waiting for the train. Whistling softly, he went outside again to sit on a bench in front of the Town Hall and wait until he saw the man he wanted approaching. He let his quarry go into the station and buy a ticket, then followed him.

Since the man at the ticket window was a friend, Kevin didn't scruple to ask, 'Where did that last fellow buy a ticket to?'

'Manchester. He allus does. Return. Comes back a few days later. Not a talker, so I don't know owt else about him.'

'Then I'd better have a return to Manchester too.'

His friend cocked an eye at him. 'What are you up to now, lad?'

'I'm on Declan's business. You'll not be saying anything about that.'

'Of course not. I owe Declan a favour or two mysen, so I'll help you if I can. I see people coming and going all the time, and I know all the regulars. They never think twice about me, though.'

'I'll mention your offer to Declan.'

His friend nodded and gave him his ticket and change.

When the train pulled in, Kevin got into the next compartment to John Shaw and sat down by the window, smiling. Using your wits or guarding folk was easy work compared to labouring and he was enjoying his new life.

Easy work or not, he nearly missed John Shaw getting out at a small village a few miles before Manchester, and only after the cloud of steam from the engine thinned did he see someone heading towards the exit. He strained his eyes, realised it was Shaw and started to get up. But his quarry turned at the exit and took a good look back at the train, so he could do nothing until the other man had walked out of the station. By that time the train was moving, but Kevin scrambled out anyway, ignoring the indignant exclamations of his fellow passengers and failing to slam the door behind him. He stumbled and fell, but stood up quickly and dusted his clothing down, then hurried towards the exit.

When he got there, the station master accosted him. 'Ticket, please.' As Kevin fumbled in his waistcoat pocket, he added, 'And what do you mean by jumping out of a moving train like that?'

'Sorry. I'd dozed off and didn't realise we were here.'

'Don't you ever do that again. You left the door of your compartment swinging wide open, which is against regulations, and you could have been killed. Think of the trouble that'd cause for me.'

'I won't do it again.' He went out of the station, staying back in the shadow of the doorway to check what was happening. To his relief he saw his quarry in the distance striding down the street. Shaw swerved round an old man who was limping along with a walking stick, then about twenty yards later he turned down a garden path on the left and went into a cottage. He didn't knock, just went inside as if he had the right.

Only when the front door of the cottage closed did Kevin walk briskly down the village street and overtake the old man, who had stopped to look regretfully across at the pub. He stopped next to him. 'Cold day for April, isn't it?'

The oldster nodded. 'Sort of day when a man needs a drink or two to loosen up his joints.' He looked at the stranger hopefully.

Kevin grinned. 'I'm a bit thirsty myself, so I am. Look, I'll buy you a pint in return for some information, granddad, and another pint if you'll keep your mouth shut about what I'm asking.'

'Good lad. And the answer's yes to both offers.' He held out his hand, so they could shake on the bargain, then led the way into the pub, calling, 'Hoy! You've two customers dying of thirst out here.'

A minute later a ruddy-faced man came out of the back. 'I thought I recognised that voice. What can I get for you, Bart?'

'A pint for each of us. My nephew's friend has called in with a message and has kindly invited me to have a drink with him.'

The landlord shook his head and turned to Kevin. 'Bart's daughter won't be best pleased if he goes home drunk.'

'Ah, it's just a couple of pints. He won't be getting drunk on that.'

With a shrug, the landlord turned to draw their beer from a barrel on a wooden stand behind the bar.

Kevin paid and took a sip, nodded approval and took a big swallow. 'Good beer, that.' He followed the old man to a table in the corner and watched him drink deep, then wipe the froth from his lips with a murmur of appreciation.

'What do you want to know, young fellow?'

'I saw a man pass you in the street and go into a cottage. I want to know his name and who lives in the cottage.'

'That's easy enough. His name's John Tolson. Don't know where he's from, though. No one does. He turned up here a few months ago.' He made as if to spit to show his disapproval, but stopped and swallowed hard instead, with a guilty look towards the bar. Taking another long pull of beer he leaned back to savour it, smacking his lips.

'Who lives in the cottage?' Kevin prompted.

'Kath Capley. Widow. Husband was a local fellow. He got hissen killed a few months ago.'

'How did he die?'

'He was attacked and left for dead in Manchester. Police come to tell her. His brother had to pay for the funeral. *She* wouldn't, said all he deserved was a pauper's funeral. Well, they were allus at each other's throats an' he used to beat her about a bit, so you can't blame her.'

'And now this Tolson's visiting regularly?'

The old man nodded. 'Has been doing since a month after the funeral. Her family isn't best pleased about her losing her good name, but she don't listen to them. Tolson must be keeping her because she's give up working at the farm an' she doesn't seem short of money. She's getten hersen some nice new clothes too. She doesn't look after them childer of hers properly, though, poor little things! Never was a good mother, Kath wasn't.'

Kevin let the old man ramble on, bought him another drink then looked at the clock on the mantelpiece. 'What time's the next train out of Manchester?'

'Stops here in fifteen minutes.'

'I'd better catch it. You'll not say anything about what I asked? I'll maybe be back this way again and if so, I'll be happy to buy you another drink.'

The old man tapped the side of his nose and lifted the second tankard to his lips.

Kevin didn't even glance at the cottage as he walked past it and kept his cap pulled down low. He reckoned he had enough information for the time being and didn't want Tolson – or Shaw – or whatever he was called – suspecting he'd been followed.

He was pleased with how much he'd found out.

Declan was going off on one of his buying trips, intending to set out early on Monday morning to visit some of the smaller mills and manufactories in towns and villages along the train line and see what he could pick up. Michael did this job sometimes, Declan others. It made a pleasant change from standing in the market all day.

Ruth hung around as he got ready, complaining as usual.

'It's all right for men. You can go off any time you want and who's to know what you get up to while you're away. For all I know, you could have another woman in one of those towns.'

He turned his back on her and continued to squint in the mirror as he shaved carefully.

'Don't even answer me these days, you don't.'

'What's to answer? You haven't asked me any questions.'

'Why don't you ever take me with you?'

He looked her up and down. 'Because you're dirty in body and clothes, and I'm ashamed to be seen in the street with you, even. Why do you never wash yourself or our clothes, Ruth?'

She blinked and for a moment a hurt look flickered on her face, then she tossed her hair back and scowled at him. 'Because it's back-breaking work, washing is, and a right waste of time. Clothes only get dirty again. And it's bad for people to wash theirsen too often, takes the oils out of your skin, it does. Not everyone's as fussy as you, with your clean shirts and shaving all the time.'

He continued to wield the razor, watching her carefully in case she attacked him or threw something at him and made him cut himself. She'd been irrational lately, her moods swinging wildly.

'Ah, who'd want to go out with you anyway?' she yelled suddenly. 'You've turned into a sobersides like your stupid brothers. You're no *fun* any more. Well, I've got friends who do care about me and I'd *rather* spend my time with them, whatever you say.'

She lurched towards the front door as if going out, but he pulled her back. 'I told you: Father Timothy is coming to talk to you today so I want you to stay home.'

'Well, I don't want to talk to him.' She suddenly began to struggle against him and as she fell against the table, she snatched up a pan and clouted him with it.

He fell back, his head ringing, saw the next blow coming and dodged it. 'Watch what you're doing, you fool! You've dirtied my clean shirt now. Just look at it.'

'*Dirtied my shirt*,' she mocked. 'Oh, my, we can't have that, can we? Your Irish lady friend wouldn't like that.' She picked up a cup and flung the dregs of tea from it over him, laughing loudly as the brown liquid made more splash marks on the front of his white shirt.

Furious, he clouted her about the ears, knocking her across the room. His hand was raised to hit her again when the door knocker went. He jerked back, glad of the interruption. He hadn't meant to hit her, didn't like himself when he did that, but she could drive a man to desperation in five minutes flat.

Taking a deep breath he swung round and went through the front room to answer the door. 'Father Timothy. It's good of you to come.'

When they went back into the kitchen the sight of the priest spurred Ruth on to a screaming fit, during which she hurled things at them until Declan got between her and the table to prevent her breaking any more cups and plates.

Bursting into noisy sobs, she plumped down on the nearest chair, howling like a child, her mouth open and moisture dribbling from it to join the tears making trails in the dirt of her cheeks and chin.

'I'm at my wits' end as to how to deal with her, Father,' Declan said slowly, knowing that the hard-won control over his temper wasn't fooling the priest. 'She accuses me of having other women, though how she thinks I'd find the time, I don't know. She screams and throws things like a lunatic – see what she just did to my clean shirt – and will you look at this place.' A sweep of his hand indicated the filthy kitchen with shards from the crockery she had thrown lying in piles and the tea dregs splattered on walls and floor. 'It's a pigsty.'

The priest nodded, but his eyes returned to the sobbing woman and he gave a little shake of the head. 'I think it might be best if you went out and left me to talk to your wife on my own.'

'You'll have to give me a few minutes to change. I can't go out like this.' Declan looked down at himself, anger rising again at how she'd dirtied his clothes.

She'd stopped crying to listen to him and now she burst into raucous laughter. 'Finicky devil, isn't he, Father? What's wrong with a bit of honest dirt, eh? Tell me that. Or are you a finicky devil, too? In which case you can bugger off.'

'I'm here on the Lord's business, Ruth,' he said quietly.

She stared at him uneasily, opened her mouth then shut it again, but the look she threw at her husband promised more quarrelling later.

When he left the house, Declan stood for a moment outside the front door, eyes closed, hands fisted by his sides, sick with disgust at her. It was a credit to his self-control that he hadn't killed her or at least, beaten her senseless.

'I heard the noise. In one of her moods, is she?' the woman next door asked sympathetically from her doorstep.

Declan opened his eyes and tried to speak normally. 'Good morning, Mrs Calden. And yes, Ruth is – a bit upset.'

'She needs locking up, that one does, and I don't care if she is your wife, it's the truth. She came into my house the other day and pinched half a loaf of bread. Swore she hadn't taken it but it could only have been her – and anyway, she left both our back gates open and wet footprints led into your place from ours because she'd walked through that big puddle in the back lane that someone ought to fill in.'

'I'll pay you for the loaf,' he said automatically. It had happened before and Mrs Calden knew he'd make good whatever Ruth had taken.

She came across to pat his arm. 'Eh, I know you will, lad. But I feel sorry for you and those little lads lately, I do that.'

He shrugged. The neighbours were all well aware of Ruth's furious outbursts and slovenly ways. How could they not be with a shrill voice screaming abuse day after day?

'The lads come into my house sometimes to hide,' Mrs Calden went on. 'I didn't tell you when it was only now and then, but it's every day or two now.' She shook her head sadly. 'Your wife definitely ought to be locked away, Declan. I'm old enough to be your mother and I'm telling you straight. Lock her away. The drink does that to some folk, turns their brains.'

'I know she drinks sometimes but—'

Mrs Calden burst out laughing. '*Sometimes?* She drinks *all* the time. Those friends of hers get it for her with *your* money and come round to help her drink it. She only has them in when you're at the market or out of town, but I've seen them creeping along the back alley with bottles of gin, even in the mornings.'

The pieces of the puzzle fell into place neatly. How the hell had he missed that? Because Ruth was cunning, that's why. She hadn't hidden the fact that she did some drinking, but he hadn't realised it was happening all the time. 'Why has no one told me before how bad it was? You must have known about it for a while.'

She shrugged. 'I don't like to come between husband and wife. I'm surprised one of your men friends hasn't told you, though.'

He wasn't. The ones he employed would be afraid to, and like Mrs Calden, most folk thought it better to stay clear of trouble between a man and wife.

'Thank you for telling me now. I wonder, could you add to your kindness by continuing to shelter the boys till I can sort this out?'

'Of course I will. They're nice lads – or they would be with a bit of discipline.'

When Declan walked on down the street it was with a feeling of despair. He was paying dearly for the wildness of his youth, far too dearly. And he could see no way out, for him or the boys. You couldn't just kick your wife out of the house, much as your toe itched to do just that. You were wed to a woman until death took one of you. It wasn't fair. How could you know when you were young whether things would turn out all right?

They hadn't for him, successful as he was in other areas. And he knew other men who regretted improvident youthful marriages.

Ishleen heard Mrs Heegan call out for help, so ran up the stairs to the front bedroom. She knocked on the door then walked straight inside. One glance told her that Declan's father had had a seizure. His face was drooping at one side and he had a panicked look in his eyes.

She went to put her arms round the older woman and pull her to her feet. 'Shh, now. You'll not do any good crying.' She bent over Mr Heegan. 'You've had a seizure, as I'm sure you realise. Remember, a lot of people recover from a seizure, so just rest yourself till I can fetch the doctor.'

She grabbed her shawl from the chair in the kitchen, looked at her daughter and hesitated, because she was worried about leaving a small child alone. But there was no help for it. She couldn't run and carry Shanna. 'Will you stay here and be a good girl for me? Mr Heegan's not well. I have to fetch the doctor. I won't be long.'

Running through the streets in a way that made people stare, she made her way to Dr Pipperday's house and rang the bell. The doctor's wife opened the door and when Ishleen explained, she nodded. 'My husband is just seeing a patient. I'll send him round the minute he's finished.'

So Ishleen hurried back, stopping at Declan's house to tell him the news, but finding only Ruth there.

His wife scowled at her. 'What do *you* want?'

'Declan's father has had a seizure. I wanted to let him know. I've just been for the doctor.'

'Serve the old sod right.' Ruth's voice was slurred and she had to support herself against the wall as she slammed the door in Ishleen's face.

The woman next door poked her head out. 'Did I hear you

asking for Declan? He's gone off round the nearby towns buying stock from the mills.' She beckoned and whispered, 'His wife's drunk. You'll get no sense from her.'

'His father's had a seizure. Will you tell him when he comes back? I'll go for Michael.'

Ishleen ran off again, finding the youngest Heegan son and his wife at home sorting out stock in the front room. When she told them what had happened they left what they were doing at once and came with her.

Dr Pipperday arrived soon after them and they all waited downstairs for him to see Mr Heegan. Before he'd finished, Ruth came in, smelling of gin and staggering a little.

'What's *she* doing here?' she demanded, pointing at Ishleen. 'She's not family.'

'She is so family,' Biddy snapped. 'And has been a great help to poor Mam, unlike some.'

Ruth plumped down on a chair, scowling at Ishleen. When Shanna walked past, she muttered, 'Pauper brat!'

And when Auntie Bonnie went across to put more coal on the stove, Ruth muttered, 'Dummy.'

The other two women looked at one another and shook their heads. This was not the time for a confrontation and it was never any use trying to reason with Ruth when she was drunk.

The doctor came down, smiling at Michael, who had jumped to his feet at the mere sound of footsteps on the stairs. 'It's not a bad seizure. If he survives for the next few days, there's every chance your father will recover. Your mother's a bit upset, though.'

'I'll go up to her,' Biddy went clattering up the stairs.

Dr Pipperday looked at Michael. 'I've written a note for the chemist. If someone can take it to him, he'll mix you up something to calm your father down. They panic, you see, when they can't move properly.'

Michael paid the doctor then turned to Ishleen. 'I'm so glad Mam's got you. She's been worried about Da for a while now.'

'I know. Will I go to the chemist's for you?'

He fumbled in his pocket. 'Yes. I'll give you the money.'

'I'll do that!' Ruth lurched across the room and snatched the money from him. 'That Irish bitch will only spend the money on herself.'

Michael looked helplessly at her and Ishleen bit her tongue for Mr Heegan's sake. She wished Declan was there, because he'd stand no nonsense from Ruth, but Michael was too soft for his own good sometimes.

'The doctor left this note,' Michael told Ruth. 'Could you wait for the chemist to mix up some medicine for Da and bring it straight back?'

'I'll do that.' She turned and left the house, bumping into the door frame on the way out.

'Should you perhaps go with her?' Ishleen asked. If it had been left to her, she'd have wrested the money and note from Ruth, not trusting anyone so far gone in drink.

Michael shook his head. 'It'll make her worse if I do and then she'll have a screaming fit, which will upset Da. Ruth will never listen to anyone when she's in this state. And she only has to give the chemist the note and pay for the medicine, after all. Even she should be able to manage that.'

'I suppose so.'

He looked at the clock on the mantelpiece. 'I'd better get back to work. Biddy will stay with you. Send for me if – well, if you need me.'

An hour passed, then another and Ruth didn't return.

Ishleen looked at Biddy. 'I'm going to find out what's happened to her.'

'Be careful. She's been known to attack people when she's in this mood.'

'She'd better not attack me or she'll be getting more than she expects. Can you keep an eye on Shanna for me? I don't want her involved if there's trouble.'

'Of course. She's never any trouble, are you, darlin'?'

Putting her shawl over her head and shoulders, Ishleen took some of her own money from the pot in the scullery and went out, hurrying down to the chemist's on Market Street.

'Did someone come in for Mr Heegan's medicine?' she asked. 'Dr Pipperday gave us a note two hours ago.'

'There's been no one asking for medicine for Mr Heegan,' the owner told her. 'Are you sure about that?'

She stared at him in shock. 'But—' Only it wasn't his fault, so she said she'd be back with the note and ran round to the doctor's house.

Dr Pipperday frowned when she explained that the note seemed to have gone astray and looked at her severely. 'How can that have happened?'

Ishleen was tired of people making excuses for Declan's wife. 'Ruth Heegan insisted on taking the note and she was already drunk. We thought she couldn't make a mistake going to and from the chemist's, but sure, she must have done.'

'It was foolish to entrust it to her. I've seen her about the streets and she's never sober.'

'It wasn't my place to stop her. Michael Heegan was there, but he said she'd be all right. Her husband's away buying today.'

His expression softened and he nodded. 'It can be difficult when they're drunk. I'll give you another note for the chemist. Make sure this one doesn't go astray.'

'I'll take it myself.' She took it to the chemist's and was back at the house within the half-hour.

Michael's wife was sitting in the kitchen, weeping, and Auntie Bonnie was with her, patting her shoulder and looking distressed. There was the sound of someone keening from the upstairs bedroom. Shanna was sitting quietly in the corner, cuddling her rag doll, looking scared.

Ishleen looked at Biddy. 'Is he . . .'

'He had another seizure a few minutes ago. I was there. It happened so quickly there was nothing we could do. What took you so long?'

Ishleen put the bottle on the table. 'I had to get another note from the doctor. Ruth hadn't even been to the chemist's. Maybe if he'd had the medicine earlier . . .' She sighed and pushed the thought away. No use thinking about that now.

There was a knock on the door and Father Timothy came in.

'He's upstairs, Father,' Biddy said. When the priest had gone, she looked at Ishleen. 'What are we going to tell Declan?'

'The truth. We don't want any other mistakes making about things that are important.'

'I don't like to speak ill of people.'

'I'll tell him. He needs to know.' But though Ishleen knew it was the right thing to do, it worried her that she had to be the one doing it. When you gave people bad news, they sometimes blamed you for it. But if she didn't tell him, who knew what harm Ruth would do next time?

Crossing herself, she began to pray quietly and fervently for the soul of Mr Heegan, who had been a lovely man, then got everything ready to lay out the body. She'd had all too much experience of doing that in the past year or two.

15

Ishleen went to meet Declan at the station, hoping he'd be on the five o'clock train from Manchester. He wasn't, so with a sigh for her aching feet, she went home for half an hour, then trudged back into town to meet the next train.

To her relief, he got off it, but he didn't see her and went straight to the luggage van at the rear to supervise the unloading of his boxes of goods. She decided to tell him after he'd done this necessary task, watching him share a joke with the porter who helped him, admiring how tall and vibrant he was in comparison to other men. He wasn't exactly good-looking, his features were too heavy for that, but there was something very attractive about his energy and vigour, the way his eyes crinkled at the corners when he laughed. *Stop that!* she told herself, as she had so many times before. *He's a married man.*

When all the boxes were off the train Declan turned to leave the station and fetch the handcart from Michael's, as usual, but saw her standing there. His smile faded and he hurried towards her. 'Is something wrong?'

She nodded. 'I'm afraid so. Let's go somewhere quieter than this.'

'No, just tell me straight away. Are my boys all right?'

'Yes. It's not them, it's your father. I'm sorry, Declan, but he died today.'

He crossed himself instinctively. 'How?'

'A seizure.'

He nodded, accepting that. It was a common enough way for an older man to die.

'There's more, I'm afraid.' She told him what Ruth had done

and watched his face lose its colour and life, his features setting into a grim expression like the statue of a martyred saint she'd once seen in a church.

'Thank you for coming to tell me. It can't have been easy for you. But I did need to know about Ruth.' He closed his eyes for a moment or two, then opened them and looked at her as if she was a stranger. 'I must go to Mam first. Let me ask the station master to keep an eye on my boxes. I'll deal with the problem of Ruth later.'

When he rejoined her, he didn't say a word, just set off walking along Market Street. Was he angry at her, too? She looked at him sideways and he turned his head just then and caught her staring. His expression softened for a moment.

'It's not you I'm angry with, Ishleen. It's Ruth. I have to do something about her, but I don't know what.'

She kept quiet. Not for her to tell a man what to do about his drunken wife. Especially this man.

When they got to the house, Declan put one arm across the doorway to delay her going inside. 'You'll stay on here with Mam, help her through it all?'

'Of course.'

His eyes searched her face as if trying to read something there. 'It was a lucky day for us Heegans when we fetched you from Ireland. I wish—'

His mouth snapped shut on whatever he wished and his expression grew cool again as he removed his arm and opened the door for her. She went inside and led him to the kitchen, standing to one side as his mother burst into tears and flung herself into his arms.

Shanna came to her and Ishleen picked up her daughter, hugging the child and whispering to her. No need to explain what was happening. Shanna understood only too well about people dying.

After spending some time with his mother and promising to arrange the funeral, Declan walked home. He met Kevin on the way and though the other was obviously bursting to tell him something, Declan shook his head. 'My father's just died and I've things to do.'

Kevin stepped back. 'I'll tell you later then.'

'I'll come to you when I've got things started. Go and stay with Mr Forrett again. I don't want to leave him unprotected for too long.' He had a bad feeling about the situation at the mill, had seen how that overlooker scowled at his employer when he thought no one was looking.

But Declan forgot about that, forgot about everything when he went into his house and found his two sons sitting huddled together in the front room, which was icy cold. From the kitchen came the sound of voices. Ruth was laughing with someone. He went back to the boys and said in a low voice, 'Go next door to Mrs Calden and ask her to give you some food. Wait there till I come for you.' He felt in his pocket for a shilling. 'Give her this.'

'Mam don't do nowt else but drink,' the younger boy muttered. 'It's not fair.'

The older one jabbed an elbow into his brother's ribs. 'Shh.'

Declan waited till they'd left then walked quietly to the door to the kitchen, pushing it wide open and standing watching as Ruth and two friends passed a bottle from one to the other. She was so drunk she could hardly sit upright, but she could still put the bottle to her lips and take greedy gulps of its contents.

No one noticed him until he took a step into the room, then all hell broke loose as Ruth screeched in shock and tried to stand up. Her friends took one look at Declan's face and ran out of the house the back way. He made no attempt to follow them.

'It were cold today,' she said. 'There's nowt so warming as gin. I *needed* a drink.'

He seemed to be seeing her tonight as a stranger would: a pitiful wreck of a woman brought low by booze. It came to him that he must end it between them for the sake of the boys, and make a better life for them. 'My father died a few hours ago,' he said quietly.

It took a minute or two for the news to sink in, then panic

made her clutch her throat with one hand, sketch a sign of the cross with the other as she stumbled backwards as far as she could go from him.

His words followed her, chill and measured, but he stayed where he was. 'The medicine you were fetching might have helped him, but we'll never know now, shall we?'

'I were goin' t'go an' get it later.'

'Do you have any money left at all?'

Her glance flickered towards the table and he saw a few coins flung there carelessly, not enough to buy medicine.

'Did you not talk to the priest this morning about your problem, Ruth?'

'Him! What does *he* know about how hard a woman's life is? I soon sent him packing and don't you bring him back again, neither.'

'Nothing seems to matter to you these days except the drink.' He looked at the nearly empty bottle in disgust.

'I've had a hard life. I need my bit of comfort. An' you're a mean devil, you are, never have any fun these days, you don't. I wish I'd never wed you.'

'You can't wish that any more than I do.'

They looked at one another in silence for a few moments, then she tossed her head and lifted the bottle to her lips, her eyes defying him.

'I don't care any more whether you drink or not, I only want to make sure that you don't harm the boys.' He glanced round the filthy room in disgust. 'It's over between us, Ruth. You can keep this pigsty of a house. I'll pay the rent and give you ten shillings a week to live on, not a penny more. The boys and I will find somewhere else to live.'

It took a minute for his meaning to sink in, then she yelled, 'I'm your *wife*! It can't ever be over. Till death, they said in church. Till *death*!'

'I'm not waiting that long. I'm leaving you now.'

'You rotten sod!' Suddenly she started hurling things at him. 'You're going to live with *her*, aren't you? That Irish woman. I've seen you looking at her, and the way she looks back at you is a shame. Well, I'll tell people, I will! They'll all know who you're sleeping with, I'll make sure of that. Decent folk won't even give her the time of day when I'm done.'

He had been going to move in with his mother, though not into Ishleen's bed, but now he realised how that would look and changed his mind. He'd move in with Michael till they sorted out somewhere else for Ishleen and Shanna to live, then move in with his mother and his aunt Bonnie. Ishleen could look after her daughter, but his lads needed a woman to care for them and his mother needed someone to look after, because she was that sort of woman, caring, loving. He couldn't look after his sons because he didn't know how to do half the things women did, and anyway he had his work to attend to. He'd been keeping his parents for a while now, though Bram sent them money regularly too.

Hell, he had to send a telegram to Bram, as well. His brother would want to come home for the funeral, but might not be able to manage it because of his singing engagements.

'I will. I'll tell everyone,' Ruth repeated.

Declan forced himself to concentrate on her. 'You can tell people what you like, but they'll soon see what a fool you are. Ishleen will be moving out of my mother's before the boys and I move in.'

As he went across the room, a plate hit him on the shoulder and smashed on the ground. He spun round and as she picked up a cup, he went across to snatch it out of her hand and shake her hard. 'Stop that! I'm not replacing the things you smash, so if you want any plates and cups left, you'd better stop.' He waited a moment, holding her at arm's length till he saw her sag, then he flung her down on the chair and walked up the stairs.

Behind him he heard the sound of weeping but it didn't soften his heart in the slightest. He knew how easily she could cry, how little genuine affection or feeling there was behind those easy tears.

He put together a few clothes for himself and the boys, gathered together their blankets, then tiptoed downstairs again with his bundles, setting them down near the front door. Ruth had slumped forward so that her head was pillowed on her arms on the filthy kitchen table. She was snoring gently, wouldn't stir till morning unless someone woke her.

If he came back before she woke from her drunken stupor, his other possessions should still be safe. He locked the back door, took the key and went out the front way, locking that door behind him too. He didn't want her drunken friends coming in until he'd cleared everything he needed out of the house.

His main feeling was of relief. The law might tie him to her legally for the rest of their lives, prevent him from marrying anyone else, but it couldn't force him to live with her.

In Manchester James leaned back in his chair and studied the man in front of him. He liked the looks and sound of Samuel Newbold, who was a bit young at thirty, but came well recommended. You couldn't blame a fellow for trying to better himself by getting a job as overlooker of a bigger mill. Even Newbold's present employer wished him well and said he was good at his job.

'All right,' he said suddenly. 'The job's yours. How soon can you start?'

'I'll need to give my present employer a couple of weeks' notice that I'm leaving. I don't want to let him down. Though he couldn't do better than give the job to my deputy, who's a capable chap, in which case I can come earlier. Shall I ask him to do that?'

'Yes. The sooner you can come the better as far as I'm concerned. My present overlooker has been disloyal and I want him out.'

'What about a house? I've a wife and four children.'

'I've a decent house for my overlooker, just got to get the other fellow out of it.' He grimaced at the thought of the trouble that would cause. Benting was going to be very unhappy. Well, let him. Once James had realised that his overlooker had conspired with his daughter, Benting's days at the mill had been numbered. And that son of his could leave with him. Lazy young devil, Huey was. He'd not have kept the yard job if it hadn't been for his father.

After leaving the hotel where the interview had taken place, James hired a cab and went to pick up Charis's cousin, who had written back by return of post to accept the job.

Helen Seylor looked as if she'd not eaten a hearty meal in years and was what he'd call a plain Jane of a woman, with a lumpy nose too big for her face.

'The old lady isn't happy about this, so it won't be a bed of roses for you,' he warned her on the train.

'Anything will be better than taking in sewing and living in one attic room,' she said.

'Well, whatever your aunt says, she doesn't have the power to sack you because it's me who's hiring you and paying your wages. So you don't need to take any rudeness from her. She's got a venomous tongue on her and has used it for years to keep my Charis submissive. You just answer her back if she starts on you.'

His companion blinked in shock. *'Answer her back?'*

'Yes. And what's more, if you put up with her till she dies, I'll make sure you never want again.' He watched tears fill her eyes and realised suddenly that she had beautiful eyes.

'Thank you, Mr Forrett.'

'It's a poisoned chalice I'm handing you.'

'No. It's a chance of a far better life.'

'Well, I'm your cousin by marriage now, so you'd better call me James.'

Of course the old lady kicked up another of her fusses at the sight of her niece, weeping and saying she wanted her daughter to look after her. She clearly hadn't expected them to act so quickly.

James watched with interest as Helen pointed out calmly that it was surely better for her aunt to have a relative helping her than to be on her own. He didn't speak again until the calmly spoken words sank in and the old lady subsided, still scowling. 'We'll move you into the new house next week, Mrs Grieves, so you'd better start thinking of how you want the parlour decorating. It's looking shabby.'

'How can you ask me to think of parlours when my own daughter is throwing me out?'

'You don't need to do it if you don't want. I'm sure Cousin Helen will see to all that for you.'

Mrs Grieves drew herself up. 'I think I'm still capable of choosing the colours and wallpaper. *She* is a hired companion and has no say in such things.' She scowled at Helen as she spoke.

James hid a smile. That was one problem solved.

As soon as he heard from Samuel Newbold, he'd have a much bigger one to deal with.

The day after his father's death Declan sent to find Kevin at the mill, listening as he explained what he'd discovered.

'You're sure of what the old man told you about Tolson?'

'He had all his wits still and why should he lie to me?'

'You did well. Can you find Gideon and tell him what you discovered. I'm going to be a bit busy today.'

'I'm sorry about your father. He was well liked.' Kevin hesitated. 'They're saying you've left your wife for that cousin of yours.'

'I've left my wife, yes, but not for my cousin Ishleen. How did you hear that?'

'Ruth's telling everyone.'

'Then I'd better tell everyone different, hadn't I? And I'd be grateful if you'd do what you can to stop the rumours too. The plain truth is, I'm leaving Ruth because she's a drunkard, dirty in her ways and a poor mother. I'm staying with my brother Michael until Ishleen finds herself somewhere else to live, then I'm moving back to Mam's with the lads.'

'Granny Horne has a room to spare. She's got Gideon Potter downstairs, but I heard the other day that she wants to let out her front bedroom as well. She's wanting to save money for her grandson. She's worried about what'll happen to him when she dies.'

'Is she ill?'

Kevin grinned. 'Not her. She's just got the taste for money, like you have.'

For the first time that day Declan smiled. 'Well, good luck to her!'

He went back to his mother's and offered to take Ishleen to meet Granny Horne.

'She could have shared the bedroom with me now your father's gone,' his mother protested.

He took a deep breath and explained the mischief Ruth was making already.

'We'll go and see Granny Horne then,' Ishleen said quietly. 'I'll get my shawl.' She saw the look on his face and added, 'It's for the best, you know it is.'

He stared at her and nodded. 'I suppose so. It doesn't feel to be for the best, though.' His eyes met hers for a moment, then she gave a slight shake of her head and turned to get Shanna ready for their outing.

They didn't speak as they walked through the streets together. What was there to say? They both knew the other was attracted, just as they both knew that nothing could come of it with a decent woman like Ishleen.

He introduced her to Granny, explained the situation and when terms had been agreed, turned to Ishleen. 'I'll find you some furniture.'

She nodded. 'I'd be grateful.'

He left her to chat to Granny and heard her making arrangements to move in the following day.

Granny looked at her. 'He's a fine man, Declan is.'

'He is, yes. But he's married.'

'Pity. Now, if you want me to look after the little lass as well while you're at work, I'm happy to do that for a shilling or two more . . . She'll be old enough to go to school next year. It's marvellous how they teach even poor children their letters these days, isn't it? I call that real progress.'

Ishleen nodded and chatted for a while then left to start packing.

She'd miss living at the Heegans', being in the centre of the family, but she wasn't going to give anyone a chance to blacken her name.

But she sighed as she walked back, thinking of Declan.

Benting knew something was wrong from the curt way Forrett spoke and the unsmiling way he looked at him, but he couldn't work out exactly what. Surely, if Forrett had suspected him of working with his daughter against him, he'd have sacked him on the spot? For the next few days he trod very carefully, didn't even look at the lasses, just carried out his duties at the mill as efficiently as ever. He'd written to Forrett's daughter about her father getting married though he hadn't received a reply, but he supposed by now Forrett himself would have told his daughters about his new wife.

He kept his eye on the master's house, watching sourly as the new Mrs Forrett began to transform it. Shopkeepers from the town kept turning up with bits and pieces she'd bought, or to measure up for new curtains, or to take away some of the old stuff.

To his surprise the plain, badly dressed woman who had come here blossomed into a comely woman in only a few days.

In the middle of all this Benting's wife had the new baby with as little fuss as always, another damned daughter though. Only this time she was so weak after the birth he had to pay someone to come in and help her. What was a man to do with so many lasses? It was sons you worked for, sons to carry on your name, though preferably not sons as stupid as his eldest.

Huey was now coming home drunk of an evening, though where he got the money from, Benting didn't know. He'd find out, though, he always did. But just at the moment it wasn't the most important thing. Just now, he didn't want to upset his wife so that she'd get better and his life could be comfortable again.

The new Mrs Forrett's mother was angry about something, though, and everyone working in the yard had heard the old woman's shrieks and complaints. He told Huey to listen in whenever they quarrelled and tell him what was going on. The lad didn't even have the wit to do that off his own bat.

'It seems they're moving the old woman out to live on her own down in the town,' his son reported that evening. 'Only she doesn't want to go. That's why she's kicking up such a fuss. Did you ever hear such a shrill voice?' He grinned.

'Right. Keep listening. Get on with your work now.' Benting stood there lost in thought for a moment or two. Why did Forrett want her out of the house when there was plenty of room? Surely his employer didn't intend to start another family at his age? But it wasn't all that long since the millowner had fathered that baby who'd died, so it was possible. His toffee-nosed daughters would be even more furious about that.

And where was Forrett today? He'd gone out very early this morning with that Kevin Reilly, who never seemed to leave his side, and the two of them still hadn't come back.

His master was up to something, but what?

Dora felt shy when she went back to work at the market with Gideon. But he was looking sad, so she forgot her own feelings and asked hesitantly, 'Is something wrong?'

'Declan's father died yesterday.'

'Oh, no. Mr Heegan was such a lovely man.'

'Yes, he was. It makes you think, doesn't it, and wonder how long you've got? I've had some close calls myself.' He looked down involuntarily at his damaged hand and then got on with the work of setting up the stall.

She'd expected Gideon to say something more personal today, something about them, but he seemed lost in thought and hardly spoke to her at all. Was he regretting walking out with her? That worry niggled at her for the rest of the day.

As they finished clearing up he said abruptly, 'I may have to go to Preston, perhaps as early as tomorrow. If so, can you run the stall for me? We can bring someone in to help you.'

'I think I can manage.' Well, she knew she could but didn't want to sound conceited.

He gave her another of those quick smiles. 'I think so too, Dora love. You've got your head screwed on all right and it's not difficult work.'

'You're bored with it, aren't you?'

He looked at her in surprise. 'Does it show?'

'It does to me.'

'Well, don't tell anyone.'

'It'd be more fun being on the stage and travelling round.'

'We'll talk about that later once I've sorted the rest of my life out.'

She didn't press the point, but he hadn't said he'd not go on the stage, had he? That was a hopeful sign – wasn't it?

With a final look round he picked up the handles of his little cart. 'Now, I'll just put these away then walk you and Nippy home. If I'm going to be away tomorrow, I'll call in and let you know.'

After he'd left her at Linney's he strode back along Market Street and to his relief, Mr Burtell's rooms were still open. He went inside to find the elderly clerk clearing up for the day. 'Am I too late to see him?'

The clerk frowned at him. 'It's very late. Can't it wait till tomorrow?'

'It's important.'

'I'll see if he's available.'

Gideon paced up and down the outer office, hearing the murmur of voices from the big front room in which Mr Burtell worked. When the door opened he swung round expectantly and the clerk gestured him inside.

Mr Burtell looked up from his desk with that easy smile of his. 'Do sit down. I won't be a minute.' He stacked the rest of the papers into two neat piles then leaned back in his chair. 'What can I do for you?'

'Have you heard anything from the regiment since you sent an enquiry via London? I can't understand why no one's written back yet.'

'I agree. I've been wondering whether to write to them again.'

'I've racked my brain about this and I can only think there's someone at regimental headquarters who's helping the impostor. He must have destroyed my other letters. So I thought we should maybe go across to Preston and make enquiries in person.'

Jack looked thoughtful. 'Would we get to see someone if we just turned up?'

'*You* might, being a lawyer and talking fancy. I definitely wouldn't.'

'Well, if your suspicions are correct, we can't write first because that letter would also go astray, so I don't think we have much choice.' The lawyer stared into space for a minute or two then nodded. 'All right. We'll do it. I've nothing really pressing on at the moment. We can leave tomorrow on the early train if that's all right with you. It is? Good. I'll meet you at the station. As you go out, would you just ask my clerk to step in here, please? I'll need to write a few notes of apology for cancelling my appointments and he can send them out in the morning. It really is a most unusual situation you're in, intriguing even.'

It was a damned annoying situation, Gideon thought, not intriguing. And if he hadn't started up the stall at the market he'd have run out of money by now, because the impostor had even been paid his gratuity for the years he'd served, damn him!

Gideon went from there to Linney's to explain the situation to Dora and her family. They immediately began planning how to run his stall for him while he was away, treating him like one of the family, so caring about his needs that it brought a lump to his throat.

It was Raife who understood his feelings and said quietly, 'You'll never call your soul your own again, lad. Once you're in with the Prestons and Linneys you're trapped and can never escape.'

'I don't want to escape. I've been in the Army since I was fifteen. I was mad for it in those days, though it wasn't what I expected by a long chalk. But I made the best of it and the regiment was like a family in some ways. I still miss that because I don't have any relatives of my own left now. So I'm enjoying having folk who care about me.'

When Dora came to see him out, she apologised for the way her family had behaved. 'You can't stop them. They just – take over.'

He gave her a hug then put his hands on her shoulders to hold her at arm's length. 'Your family are wonderful, Dora. Never apologise for them. You're lucky to have them. And about the other thing, going on the stage and all that – we'll think about it after I've solved my other problem, eh? You were right in what you said earlier today, though. I am getting bored with the market, even though I'm doing well enough out of it.'

Her face lit up and she flung her arms round him, giving him a kiss that started off as a quick one and somehow led to a longer embrace, with them both breathing very deeply as they drew apart. It was an effort to break away but he had too much respect for her to fumble at her body in the hall where anyone might see them. He didn't want to lose the respect of her family.

He carried the memory of that kiss with him to his lodgings and woke up the following morning full of need for her. His body had recovered those sorts of urges at last, thank goodness.

But he had one serious worry: could he go on the stage? It was one thing to sing with the lads, quite another to perform in public and do it well enough to get paid for it. He wasn't sure he'd be any good at it and the thought of getting up in front of a crowd of people made him shiver. Yet if he wanted Dora, he'd have to try. And he did want her. Very much.

The carriage turned into the mill yard and stopped in front of the house. Alicia got out, shook her full skirts to straighten the flounces and smoothed her gloves.

She waited for the front door to be opened, then walked straight in with only a curt, 'I wish to see my father.'

Jen bobbed a curtsey. 'He's out, Mrs Gleason. I'll show you through to the mistress, shall I?'

'So it's true!' She breathed deeply for a minute, then said in a tight voice, 'I suppose I'd better. Don't announce me. I'll introduce myself.' She waved a hand dismissively towards the door at the back of the hall.

Jen took a deep breath and stood her ground. 'I think I'd better announce you properly, Mrs Gleason. The mistress wouldn't like it if I didn't do my job.' Before the visitor could reply she hurried across to the parlour door and knocked on it, popping her head inside to say, 'Mr Forrett's daughter is here, ma'am – Mrs Gleason, that is.'

Charis put down the list she was studying, shot a quick glance at the mirror and took comfort from her new appearance. She went forward to greet her visitor, shaking hands and pretending she was glad to see her. She wasn't. Not without James at her side. 'Would you like to sit down?' She turned to the maid. 'Perhaps you'd let Mr Forrett know we have a visitor, Jen?'

Alicia stayed where she was as the door closed, studying the woman her father had married. 'How did you persuade him to do it?'

'I beg your pardon?'

'Marry you.'

Charis drew herself up. 'I think it would be better for everyone if you remembered your manners.'

Alicia shrugged and sat down, easing off her gloves. 'Do I have to ring for refreshments myself?'

'I've no intention of offering you anything if you intend to continue being offensive.'

The two women stared at one another, then Alicia shrugged. 'I really wanted to see my father.'

Charis went back to her lists. Two could play at that game and if Alicia thought rudeness could intimidate someone who'd lived with it for years, she had another thing coming.

Jen rushed through the kitchen, saying, 'It's Mrs Gleason and she's in a right old temper, so I've to fetch Mr Forrett.'

'Do they want refreshments?' Cook asked.

'I should wait till the mistress rings, if I were you. I'd not go in there unless I was sent for.'

Jen ran across the mill yard and out down the street, knowing her master would want to be told about his daughter's arrival. She found him just coming out of the Town Hall and gasped out what had happened, ending, '. . . so I came to fetch you straight away, sir.'

'You did right.' He set off at a rapid pace, hoping Alicia wasn't being too rude to Charis.

When he got to the house, he went straight into the front parlour, finding Charis looking serene and busy with her lists while Alicia sat near the fire with an expression like thunder. He went across to his wife first, kissing her on the cheek. 'Sorry I was out, love.'

'That's all right, James. Your daughter didn't want to observe the niceties and converse with me, so I just got on with my work.'

He grinned. 'Good lass.' When he turned to his daughter, his smile faded. 'If you've come to cause trouble again, you can go away.'

'I need to talk to you alone, Father.'

He studied her then turned to Charis. 'Will you excuse us, love? I'll take Alicia into the dining room.'

'Of course, James.'

He ushered his daughter through, then she burst out with, 'Have you run mad, Father? Who is that woman and how did she persuade you to marry her?'

'She's Jonas Grieves' daughter and I've known her for years. I always did like her, but I'd not have thought of marrying her if you hadn't put the idea into my head.'

'*Me!* I never did any such thing.'

'Oh, but you did. You made me realise that I needed someone with a better legal right than you to look after me if I really lost my wits.'

'You *have* lost your wits.'

'I don't think so. I've not been as happy in years.'

He smiled and something about his smile made his daughter snap her mouth closed on what she had been going to say and stare at him.

'With a bit of luck,' he went on, 'I'll father another child or two to comfort me in my old age.' He looked at her sadly. 'Can you not reconcile yourself to what's happened, be glad to see me happy?'

'I'm too disgusted.' She rose. 'But I can see that it's no use talking to a man as besotted as you, so I shall leave.'

He walked to the door with her, watching as she walked straight out without a word of farewell or even a look back at him. Her coachman hurried to open the door and take the nosebags off the horses.

James stayed there until she was gone, but she didn't even look out of the window. As he turned back into the house, he shook his head, feeling sad, remembering Alicia as a pretty little girl who loudly proclaimed her love for her daddy. Now, she was a sharp-featured shrew who cared only about his money. And he still didn't know whether Diana held the same feelings towards him. She lived further away, so he saw her very rarely. It might be worth writing her a note, explaining who Charis was, inviting her to come and meet his new wife.

He looked across at the office window and saw the outline of his overlooker. Benting spent far too much time spying on the comings and goings at Mill House. Well, let him look his fill. He'd not be there much longer.

16

The letter was very short and to the point.

Meet me Manchester midday Tues usual place. Can't stall them much longer. Bring more money.

No signature and the handwriting was an untidy scrawl, deliberately disguised, difficult to read. But John knew who'd sent it and how much it would cost to keep the clerk on his side. He swore under his breath. What the hell had happened now to cause this?

He travelled into Manchester dressed smartly, as he always was these days, but with rougher clothes and a cap he could pull down to hide as much of his face as possible hidden in a carpet bag. He changed in the third-class waiting room at the station, waiting in the cubicle to make sure no one was around who'd seen him come in before he left, then leaving the bag at the left luggage office.

Anger was simmering inside him, had been for months. It had started when he first saw the real Gideon Shaw – still alive damn him! – and had continued to hum through him as he tried to work out what to do. The anger had grown much stronger after his encounter with Dora on the moors, though. The bitch had been leading him on just to make the other man jealous. Well, John wasn't going to let a slip of a lass use him like that and he'd make sure she regretted it before he was through with her, by hell he would!

But she wasn't his main worry, so she could wait her turn. If he didn't deal with the real owner of the cottages quickly, he might lose everything – or worse, his crime might be discovered by the Army authorities. Who'd have thought Shaw would cheat death after being so ill on the ship coming back to England? No one had reckoned he had any chance of surviving.

John had read the letter sent to Shaw in India to say he had an inheritance coming to him when he checked through the dying patient's possessions to see if there was anything he could steal, though he didn't regard it as stealing, because those he took from had no further use for the stuff. The poor sod had been too delirious to take in the news when the attendant read it to him and had gone downhill since then.

John had quickly realised how easy it would be to take the dying man's place – why, they even looked a bit alike, both being tall and dark. It was a way to get hold of some money and leave the Army in one fell swoop, because once Shaw was dead, no one else would know about his aunt if the lawyer's letter went missing.

He realised he'd nearly walked past his destination and forced himself to stop thinking of Shaw. He went into the dirty, one-room pub on the outskirts of Little Ireland, bought himself a glass of beer and sat in a corner from where he could watch the door. Bob was late as usual, damn him!

John was halfway through his second beer when the regimental clerk at last turned up. 'Where have you been? Don't you know how risky this is for me?'

'For me too.' Bob sat down. 'Well, aren't you going to buy me a beer?'

John raised one finger and the tapman came over. 'Another beer.' He waited until it arrived and watched his companion sip it appreciatively. When the other still didn't speak, he could bear the waiting no longer. 'Well? What's happened?'

'That lawyer's written again.' He felt in his pocket and passed across a piece of paper. 'This is a copy of it.'

John read it, mouthing some of the words, which were long enough to crack your jaw in half, and not always understanding them, though the gist of the letter was clear enough. He groaned and looked at the top of the page. 'It's dated two weeks ago. You should have destroyed it when it came in.'

'I thought of doing that, but this came from London, so they'll have a record of it and be waiting for a reply. No one minds if we're slow replying, but they do keep records, you know. Eventually they'll ask what happened to the other letters and I'll be in trouble. So unless you do something about Gideon bloody Shaw, and do it quickly, I'm going to discover this and the last letter, and a few others I've been saving as well, fallen down the back of the spare desk. I'll pass them on to the Captain and he'll believe me because he doesn't like to bother too much about details, that one.' He grinned. 'Never had such an easy officer to deal with.'

John scowled into his beer. He'd tried to get rid of Shaw, wasted good money hiring men to do the job for him in Hedderby – and they'd failed him both times. It wasn't easy to find men willing to kill someone for you. He'd no choice now but to do the job himself, though he wasn't keen on violence, never had been. But he was even less keen on losing his comfortable new life, or being dragged back to his regiment and facing a flogging, not to mention being branded on the arm with a D for deserter.

He'd received ten lashes once for a minor offence and had never forgotten the humiliation of being flogged in front of the regiment. The damned sergeant had it in for him and had really laid it on. He'd pissed himself with the pain. Hard to live something like that down. And you'd get more than ten lashes for deserting, he was sure. How men had survived in the old days when they got hundreds of lashes, he didn't know.

It had fair turned his stomach to kill Kath's husband, but he'd been furious about how badly she'd been beaten up and that had got him through it. When he arrived in England he'd gone to find her out of sheer curiosity, because he'd been fond of her once and anyway, he had no one else to go to when he deserted. He'd soon discovered how unhappily married she was and had been shocked by the bruises on her body. All over her, they were, new dark ones and old yellow ones. What sort of man beat a woman like that? One who *deserved* to die, that's what.

But Shaw didn't deserve to die, not really. He just – couldn't be allowed to live.

His companion jabbed an elbow into his ribs. 'Have you gone to sleep there?'

'I'm thinking.'

'Well, I've only got half an hour to spare, so think quickly. The Captain's got me running all over Manchester today.'

John scowled at him. 'Leave it to me. I'll get rid of Shaw then the lawyer will stop writing.'

'Two weeks. That's all I dare leave it for. There'll be some men coming back early from India to help get ready for the rest of the regiment to return.'

'The regiment's coming back to England?'

'Didn't I just say so?'

John cursed long and fluently. This raised a whole series of other risks for him. It only needed one fellow from his old regiment to see him and his goose was cooked. 'I'll send you a letter when I've got rid of him,' he said at last. 'I'll just put three crosses inside it and you'll know he's been disposed of.'

'Two weeks,' Bob repeated, drained his glass and held out one hand, palm upwards. 'I reckon what I've done for you is worth another five guineas.'

'*Five guineas?* Do you think I'm made of money?'

'You won't miss a guinea here and there, and I'm not taking these risks for nothing. If I hadn't had to come into Manchester on business, you'd have been paying my fares too. But I'm an honest man in my own way, so I didn't charge you for that.' He thrust his hand even closer.

John had come prepared so he fumbled in his pocket and slapped the coins down into the outstretched hand. If it'd been him, he'd have been asking for ten.

He set off back to the station, where he retrieved his bag, changed his clothes and caught a train. He got off it at Kath's village. She was all over him as usual. Well, she knew how much she owed him. But somehow, even as he was lifting Kath's skirts, he kept thinking of Dora, who was fresh and unspoiled, and who didn't smell of cheap gin. He swore to himself that before he left the country he'd have her slender young body under him and make her rue the day she'd used him to make another man jealous.

He went back to Hedderby the next morning, knowing he couldn't afford to wait much longer to get rid of the real Gideon Shaw. After that was done, he'd sell the cottages and leave the country. He didn't *want* to live overseas, he'd had his fill of that, but if the regiment was on its way back to Lancashire, that was the only way to keep himself safe. He'd go to America, perhaps. No one would know him there. Australia was too damned far away, even further than India.

James opened the letter eagerly and let out a satisfied, 'Aha!' as he read it.

'Good news?' Charis asked.

'Very good. Newbold can start work next week. I'll tell Benting this morning that he's sacked and is to get out of the house within two days. I'm looking forward to that.'

'You said his wife has just had a baby. Do you have to put them out of their house at once?'

He looked at her. 'Aye, I do. He's in the overlooker's house just across the way and he's not going to be the overlooker any more, so I don't want him anywhere near my mill.' He saw the disappointment on her face at his answer, though she tried to hide it. 'Oh, very well. I'll tell him he can have one of the cottages up the back end of the lanes till he gets himself sorted out. For the wife and children's sake.'

Her face brightened and he looked at her fondly. He liked a woman who cared about others.

Then he picked up the other letter. 'From my younger daughter, Diana.' He didn't want to open it, but forced himself to do so, frowning.

'What does she say?'

He grimaced and passed it to her. 'Read it for yourself. I never thought I'd be glad she married a prosy stick of a fellow. If he didn't keep begetting children I'd think he had no emotions whatsoever, that one.'

Dear Father,

Thank you for your letter informing me of your marriage and inviting us to come and meet your new wife. Unfortunately, I'm expecting a child in a few weeks' time and cannot risk a long journey at this stage.

I heard from Alicia by the same post, and she's very upset about your marriage. But Ogden says she sounds hysterical and immoderate. He feels I shouldn't let her dictate how I behave and, as always, I shall rely on his judgement.

Perhaps after the new baby is born you could come over to visit us instead and bring your new wife?

Your respectful daughter,

Diana

He smiled as his wife looked up again. 'Better than I'd expected, really. At least I still have one daughter speaking to me.'

'I'm so glad, James.'

'Hmm. Well, you won't be when you meet them, for a more starchy pair, I've never come across. They look down their noses at me, and they will at you too.'

'That doesn't matter. I don't like being the reason for you being estranged from your daughters.'

'You never were. It's the money Alicia cares about.'

When he'd gone across to the mill, Charis returned to her domestic duties, continuing to go through the house, room by room, cupboard by cupboard, and make it more comfortable. Cook knew of a girl seeking a position as a maid – untrained but willing – so they were seeing her this afternoon.

With her mother living elsewhere, this now seemed most truly Charis's home and even with one stepdaughter's hostility and the shadow of Benting's dismissal, which she was sure would cause trouble for her husband, she felt happier than she had for years.

* * *

James asked his burly bodyguard to accompany him across to the mill office. 'I'm going to sack Benting and there's bound to be trouble, so I want you to be there.'

Kevin was sufficiently relaxed with the millowner now to let out a long, low whistle.

James scowled as they walked across the yard, muttering, 'When I was younger I could have sorted this out on my own, but there's no denying I'm getting a bit long in the tooth for fighting.' He looked sideways. 'You're a sensible fellow, Reilly. If you want a job in the mill when all this fuss is over, I can always use a capable fellow.'

'I know nothing about spinning.'

'I can teach you what you need to know. I'm not talking about an ordinary job, but one helping me run the place.'

'Then I'd be interested, sir, I would indeed.'

As they went into the inner office James beckoned to the lad who was filling the inkwell in the outer office. 'Fetch Benting.' Then he went and sat behind his desk to wait, fingers drumming on the polished wooden surface.

The lad came hurrying back. 'He says to give him an hour. There's trouble with one of the machines on the second floor.'

'Tell him to leave the damned machine to his deputy. I want to see him now.'

Kevin went to stand to one side of the door, arms hanging loosely, looking alert and ready for trouble.

There was the sound of footsteps stamping along the corridor and Benting entered, wiping his hands on a piece of cotton waste. 'What's up?'

'You're fired.'

'*What?*'

'You heard me. Get your things out of your office – Kevin here will help you – and be out of my mill within the hour.'

'But why?'

James raised one eyebrow. 'Did you think I hadn't noticed that you were helping my daughter *against* me? Or that some of the fines money has been going into your own pocket?'

Benting opened his mouth as if to protest, then shut it again, looking dumbstruck.

'I need you out of the overlooker's house within two days so that the new man can move in. You've Mrs Forrett to thank for reminding me that your wife has recently had a baby, so I'll let you have one of those empty cottages up the back end of the lanes till you've had a chance to find yourself a new job.' He leaned forward. 'I'm hoping that job will be somewhere else than Hedderby. If it is, I'll give you a reference about your work. You've been a damn good overlooker in your time. A pity you didn't stick to your work.'

The look on Benting's face made Kevin take a step forward. For a minute the two men measured one another up, the air around them almost crackling with tension, then Benting let out a long, low growl of breath and turned to leave.

'Oh, and you can take that son of yours with you, too. Worst yard lad I ever employed, that one is.'

Benting's fists clenched then slowly unclenched and he turned to look once more at his former employer, needing no words because his expression said exactly how he was feeling.

As he left the room Kevin followed him.

James leaned back in his comfortable chair, frowning. 'Unless I miss my mark, I've not heard the last of that bugger.' He got up and went to the window to watch as Benting yelled to his son, beckoned, then disappeared inside the mill.

'I'd better send for the deputy overlooker,' James muttered and sent the office lad running again. A couple of minutes later someone tapped on the door then Thad peered round it.

'Did you want to see me, Mester Forrett?'

'Aye, lad. Come and sit down.' He waited until Thad was seated then told him what had happened.

The ageing man goggled at him. 'Eh, mester, I'd not have believed it if I hadn't heard it from thee!'

'Aye, well, there you are. There's nowt so queer as folk, is there? Any road, you'll be in charge till Samuel Newbold arrives.'

'All reet. I'll get young Peter to take over my jobs. He's a good lad, that one.' He left the office, shaking his head and muttering under his breath.

James smiled. He'd known he'd have no trouble with Thad, who was a stolid fellow without the skills to take over long term from Benting and without any ambition to rise higher in the world.

Over an hour later there was the sound of doors banging and James went to stand by the window and watch as Kevin followed Benting and Huey to the gates, standing there with arms folded until they were both out of sight.

He should have felt a sense of relief, but he didn't. Instead he felt a sense of apprehension. Benting was a tricky devil. He'd been behind the wrecking of the orphanage, James was sure. Who else had been involved? Was it his son? There must have been several men involved to cause so much destruction, but the sergeant hadn't found out who they were.

He'd keep the watchmen there at night, and maybe set on another at the mill. He nodded slowly. Yes, he'd definitely do that. And not old men, but ones young enough to give a good accounting for themselves in a fight. Declan would know some suitable fellows, no doubt.

Benting stormed across the street to the large house that had been his home for several years, glaring so fiercely at anyone who got in his path that they stepped aside quickly to let him pass. His son walked slightly behind him, not daring to say a word.

At the house Benting kicked the door open and roared for his wife. When she appeared in the kitchen doorway, the new baby in her arms, he shoved her back into the room.

'Forrett's just sacked me!'

She let out a shrill cry and took a quick step backwards, cringing as if she expected him to hit her. 'But how will he manage without you?'

'He's got someone else coming in. I don't know who, but when I find out I'll chase him out of town, see if I don't.' He looked round, fighting back pain as well as anger at the sight of the large comfortable kitchen which was no longer his. 'We've to get out of the house in two days.'

She fumbled for a chair and fell into it as if her legs wouldn't hold her. 'But where will we go?'

'He says we can have one of them empty cottages up the back end of the lanes. Aye, you might well wince. How we'll all fit in I don't know, you've bought that many bits and pieces.'

'It's ungrateful of him after all you've done for him.'

'Aye, an' he'll regret it. No one understands them machines like I do.'

She looked at him and tears filled her eyes. 'We'll need help with the packing, Jack. I'm not myself yet. I fainted again this morning.'

He glared at her. 'Just when I need you! Do you know someone?'

She nodded. 'I know a couple of women.'

He opened his mouth to complain, then saw how white she was and shut his mouth again. She looked ill, hadn't recovered from her lying-in. Dr Pipperday was right. She wasn't fit to bear any more children. But how would he manage without her in bed? He muttered something, didn't let himself give in to his anger, just said, 'Give me their names and I'll go and arrange it. I'll go and look at the cottages, see which will be best for us.'

She put her hand out to touch him. 'I'm sorry, love.'

He looked down, shocked at how thin her hand was. 'Not your fault. It's Forrett who's going to be sorry afore I've done with him.'

'Jack, no! Can't we just go somewhere else? You'll find a job easy and—'

'Shut your gob and as soon as them women arrive, start 'em packing. And don't go gossiping about this to the neighbours, neither.' He looked at her and for a moment, but only a moment, his expression softened. 'Don't look so worried. I've money saved. We'll not go hungry.'

'We should leave Hedderby.'

'No. I'm not giving in. I've helped build up that mill, worked in it nearly all my life, and by hell, I'm not letting him take it away from me.'

'But how can you—' The wild look in his eyes made her forget the rest of what she'd been going to say. 'Oh, Jack,' she said instead. But he wasn't looking at her, let alone listening to her.

She picked up the baby and put it to her breast, letting her tears fall silently on its little bonnet. When she looked up, Huey was watching her with a puzzled expression on his face. 'I'll get you something to eat in a minute, love,' she said. She should have talked to them, explained how ill she was, but she couldn't summon up the energy.

Huey nodded and continued watching her.

Benting sat still for a few minutes, staring into the fire, then muttered something and went out.

Gideon and his lawyer took a cab from Preston railway station to regimental headquarters. He stood outside for a moment or two, memories flooding back from so long ago, when he'd been a gangling youth struggling to cope with a new life. He'd not been back here since India, had been discharged from the Army in London, because they insisted they couldn't spend money sending a nameless man round the regiments in case anyone recognised him. It wasn't as if anyone would want him back, was it?

It had been no good telling them he had a perfectly good name and knew exactly who he was. They'd already discharged one Gideon John Shaw, who'd had all the papers to prove who he was, so this second Gideon Shaw must be making up this story as far as they were concerned. They'd threatened to punish him by withholding the discharge money due to him if he persisted, and he'd not dared risk that.

He felt a nudge, saw Mr Burtell looking at him sympathetically, squared his shoulders and led the way inside.

The last time he'd been here, it'd been all bustle, with men moving to and fro on a multitude of errands as they prepared to embark for India. Now the place was deserted and dusty, their footsteps echoing in the hall.

The office was unattended and a sign said: *Away all day, come back tomorrow.*

'Does this often happen?' Burtell asked.

Gideon shook his head. 'I've never seen it before, but then I've never been here when the regiment was away.'

Just then they heard footsteps and swung round as an officer came into the room, a man whom Gideon had seen before. 'Captain Darrow!'

The officer stopped dead, stared at him then put two fingers to his temple and half-closed his eyes, saying slowly, 'Sergeant – no, don't tell me, it'll come to me in a minute.' He clicked his fingers triumphantly, 'Shaw! Gideon Shaw.'

Gideon closed his eyes, feeling the room spin as waves of relief washed dizzily through him.

'Aaah,' said Mr Burtell softly.

'I heard you'd been invalided out with recurrent fevers, Shaw. Indeed, I signed some papers in connection with your discharge last year. I must say, you look hale and hearty enough to me now. You wouldn't care to sign up again, would you? After all, there's no chance of us doing another tour of India in your lifetime.' He smiled at the lawyer. 'Best sharpshooter I ever saw, the sergeant here.'

It was a moment before Gideon could speak coherently, then he exclaimed, '*Fevers!* I was invalided out because of this.' He held up his maimed right hand.

'What? But—' Darrow broke off and stared at him for a minute. 'Thank God you came today, when Sergeant Payne is away! A few things are beginning to fit together and . . .' He looked questioningly at Jack Burtell.

'This is my lawyer, sir, Mr Burtell.'

'Pleased to meet you, sir.' He glanced up at the clock. 'Look, just in case Payne gets back early, would you mind if we had a little talk elsewhere? I know a good chop house in town. Let me buy you a meal and we'll talk there.'

He bustled them out, locking the door behind him with a cheerful, 'If anyone wants to see me they'll have to come back another time.' Hailing a cab he whisked them into town and led the way into an eating house of the sort usually patronised by the better sort of person. The proprietor himself came forward to greet him by name. 'Do you have a private room? We've got something rather delicate to discuss.'

'If you don't mind using my family's dining room, sir?'

'Be very grateful for the privacy.'

They were soon ensconced at a polished wooden table and the proprietor's wife herself waited on them, bringing their meals then leaving them alone.

'We'll eat quickly, then you can tell me what happened to you,' the captain said.

When they'd cleared their plates, Gideon explained.

'And you say you've had no reply?'

'I had a reply to my first letter,' the lawyer said. 'It said it'd take a few months to send a message to India. I've had no reply to a letter I sent two weeks ago via London.' He fumbled in his briefcase. 'These are copies of them.'

The captain read them quickly. 'I wasn't here when the first one arrived, but I definitely didn't see the second one. Payne again. There are some – irregularities in his work and conduct which I'm currently investigating. I wonder if you could leave this matter with me until reinforcements arrive. I don't want to upset the apple cart just now, because I also suspect he's been making some major money out of the purchases needed to get the barracks running properly again. I don't want him to get away with *anything*.'

'What about Tolson. Do you recognise the name?'

'Yes. Used to be in the regiment, a surly fellow, but kept out of trouble after one taste of the whip. Payne told me he'd died on the way back.'

Jack looked at Gideon. 'How do you feel about waiting a little longer?'

'As long as it's not too long, and I get my name and inheritance back . . .'

The captain nodded. 'Thank you. I appreciate your forbearance.

It won't be more than a week or two, I promise you, then I'll bring two men with me to Hedderby and we'll arrest Tolson.' He pulled a notebook out of his pocket and scribbled on it, signing it with a flourish, then passed it to Jack. 'Will that do the trick legally?'

Jack read the deposition and nodded. 'It'll need to be witnessed.'

'Of course.' The captain rang the bell. 'I'll get the proprietor in to do it. He's a good fellow and will keep his mouth shut about what it says.'

'Thank you.'

As they walked back to the station afterwards, Jack said thoughtfully, 'I think I'll have a word with Hordle. He can keep an eye on Tolson, or whatever the fellow's real name is, make sure he doesn't try to sell your cottages and abscond with the proceeds.'

'Thank you for believing me from the start, Mr Burtell.' Gideon held out his hand and they shook solemnly.

'Shall you stay in Hedderby afterwards?'

'I don't know. It depends on my lass.'

'You've met someone, have you?'

Gideon couldn't stop himself from beaming at the lawyer. 'I have. And she's the grandest lass you ever met.'

17

When Dora answered the door she knew at once that Gideon was feeling happier by the expression on his face. Before she could say anything, Nippy pushed his way between them and began jumping up at the visitor, letting out little yelps of delight.

'I sometimes think he's as much your dog as mine.' Dora tried in vain to put a frown on her face. But she couldn't, not when Gideon was smiling down at her like that. 'Come in. It's freezing cold out here.'

'I need to talk to you on your own,' he said.

She took him into the kitchen and while he was greeting the family, asked Essie quietly if they could go and sit in the front room as Gideon wanted to talk to her.

'Yes, but leave the door open. I'll bring through some hot coals to light the fire or you'll freeze to death. Did you ever see such damp, cold weather?'

They had to wait for their chat until Essie had bustled round and by the time she left them Dora was feeling unaccountably shy. 'Did you – um – have a good day?'

'Mainly.' He was disappointed that his problem hadn't been resolved, but at least his identity had been proved and if he'd waited so long, he could wait a bit longer because he didn't want the clerk or Tolson to get away with anything. 'I want to tell you what I was doing today, and some things about me. I've been wanting to tell you for a while now . . .'

When he'd finished she could only stare at him in shock. 'Oh, Gideon, how terrible for you when you came back!'

'Aye, it fair knocked me sideways, I must admit. And we still haven't done anything official about it, but Mr Burtell is going to have a word with Mr Hordle in case that Tolson fellow tries to sell my cottages.' He hadn't dared let himself say *my* before, but he said it now – proudly.

'He might sell them without anyone knowing.'

'There are only two lawyers in town and he'd have to get one of them to do the legal paperwork. Anyway, it's only a week or two to wait, then things will be settled. He can't do much in that time.'

'I suppose not.'

'What this means is I'll not only have my own name back but a home to offer you.' He took her hand in his, raising it to his lips to kiss it. 'If you'll marry me, that is, love?'

She looked at him, her smile fading, her voice suddenly flat. 'You want to settle down?'

'I'd like a home of my own. Wouldn't you?'

She shook her head. 'Not to settle down in, Gideon. I meant what I said. I want to go on the stage with Nippy, and I think I can do it, too. With you, if you'll join me, otherwise . . .' She couldn't put that dreadful alternative into words, could only look at him pleadingly.

He was silent for so long she began to feel afraid, then he looked up and his expression made her heart sink. 'I'm not sure about going on the stage, Dora. Until I met you, it wasn't something I'd even thought about. Since you talked about it, I've been thinking and I'm not at all sure I *could* do it, get up in front of people, make a fool of myself, I mean.'

'You wouldn't be making a fool of yourself! You have a lovely singing voice.'

'Nice, but not special.'

She swallowed hard. 'We wouldn't be appearing as singers, but a dog act. Nippy and perhaps another dog, later.'

Still that doubt creased his forehead.

'I can't settle down, Gideon. I think I'd *burst* if I tried. Even waiting till I'm twenty-one is making me feel so frustrated!'

There was silence in the room then she stood up. 'I'm fond of you, more than fond, but I can't live like Essie does. I've always known that, but it's only recently I've seen how I can make another sort of life for myself.'

His voice was flat. 'With Nippy.'

'Yes.'

'And if anything happens to him?'

'I'll find another dog.'

A piece of coal slipped to one side with a sigh.

Gideon stood up. 'I don't know what to say.'

'Perhaps it's best to say nothing, then.'

But when he'd gone she made the excuse of feeling tired and went up to the room she shared with Edith, relieved when her sister didn't follow her. She slipped between the covers and allowed herself a few tears, then told herself fiercely to stop weeping. You couldn't have everything you wanted, could you? She'd found that out very young.

She loved him too much to agree to the sort of life that she knew would wear her down and ruin their relationship. Better stop things now than see their love wither.

In the morning, she got up early and found Essie yawning as she got the big stove burning. She might have known her step-mother wasn't fooled.

'Trouble, Dora love?'

'Gideon wants to settle down and I want to see some of the world.'

Essie spun round. 'You're not still thinking of going on the stage?'

'I *am* going on the stage one day, whatever you and Nev say or do. And if you turn Nippy out of the house, I'll go with him.'

Essie looked down at the little dog and then back at Dora and sighed in resignation. 'As if I could now. But at least promise me you'll talk this over with Marjorie when she next visits, work out how best to do it. You won't just – run away?'

Dora felt hope rush through her in a warm tide. 'Oh, no. I'm not ready yet and I definitely want to do things properly. Will you – do you have to tell Nev?'

'I don't keep secrets from him, love.'

'But he's completely against it. If he tries to take Nippy away from me . . .'

Essie shook her head, her expression sad. 'If you care so desperately about going on the stage that you'll stop seeing a young man you love, then I doubt there's anything we can do to stop you.'

Dora ran across the room, flung her arms round her stepmother and wept on her shoulder.

Essie patted her and let her have her cry.

When Dora pulled herself together, she gave her stepmother an extra hug. 'Thank you for understanding. I'd better get ready for work.'

'It'll be hard working with him, seeing him every day.'

'Yes.' She spread her arms helplessly and admitted, 'I've done hard things before, us Prestons all have, but I think this is the hardest.'

That morning the painters came in to start work on the inside of the Pride. The balcony was finished, but the seating wasn't in place yet, not until the walls had been painted and the floor varnished. Carrie and Eli stood watching the men set up their scaffolding and get out their brushes.

'It seems more real each week,' she said softly.

He put his arm round her shoulders. 'We can fix a date, start booking people for the opening now. I'll write to Bram and you can write to Marjorie. I'm hoping they'll save a week for us in July. We'll book some really good acts, make it a special week.'

'Are we still going to do the Saturday night concerts in the meantime?'

'Of course we are. They're profitable and people love them.' He grinned. 'So do I. Have to keep my hand in as Chairman, don't I?' Then his smile faded. 'But with the trouble we've been having in the town lately, I'm going to continue employing night-watchmen here. I'm not risking anything. I had all my dreams destroyed once when the old saloon was burnt down. No one's doing it to me again.'

'It's strange, isn't it? Both here and at the orphanage people have tried to spoil good things. I can't understand why they do it.'

'Because they're mad. And you're sane, not to mention practical and down-to-earth, so of course you don't understand them. Eh, love, you're the best possible wife for a dreamer like me.' He gave her a hug, picking her up and twirling her round, then winking at a grinning painter over her shoulder as he set her down.

Lucas and Gwynna walked round the orphanage arm-in-arm. They didn't say much, just looked at the bright, whitewashed walls and shining window panes, enjoying the finished creation. Thanks to the help of many townsfolk, they'd got the place cleaned up and ready more quickly than Lucas had ever dreamed possible, removing all traces of the damage.

'Are you ready to move in, love?'

She nodded, smiling. 'With just us two and Joe, we'll rattle round like peas in a barrel at first.'

'Yes. The sooner we find some children and other helpers the better. We could go along to the workhouse tomorrow if you like and see if there are any children without families who need a home. Mr Forrett's already spoken to them and you know how happy they always are to get inmates off their hands.'

'Not to mention *off the rates!*' she mocked.

He smiled. 'The Mayor seems to think of nothing else.'

There was a knock on the front door and a voice called, 'Anyone there?'

Lucas hurried down to the entrance hall to find two men staring round. 'Can I help you?'

'We've brought the sign.' He jerked one thumb towards the doorway and they all went outside to see the square wooden sign lying against the wall, ready to be hung to the right of the entrance. *Libby Forrett Children's Home*, it said in ornate gold lettering on a beautifully varnished panel of wood.

'It looks even better out in the open air than when I saw it at the workshop,' Lucas said. 'You've done a wonderful job on that lettering.'

'Can't beat Grandpa for lettering,' the younger one said. 'He can't do owt else much these days, what with his knees being bad, but he's still got a steady hand for the letters.'

They set to and within the hour the neat sign with its gold letters was fixed to the wall.

After the men had gone Lucas smiled at Gwynna. 'I'll go and see Mr Forrett, then, and tell him it's ready. Have you finished here? Good. I'll lock up.'

He walked across town filled with deep satisfaction. He and Gwynna both loved children and were sorry they hadn't started a baby of their own yet. Still, perhaps that was a good thing. It'd take a lot of hard work to get the orphanage going from scratch. Plenty of time to have their own family later.

When they'd turned the corner and strolled off down Market Street, a man who'd been standing behind a cart on the other side of the street walked briskly across and tried the orphanage door, glancing quickly round before ramming his shoulder against it. But the new door was too solidly built to be pushed in, so he went round to the side.

Here he tried the gates, ramming his shoulder against the nearest one. But again, it didn't give much. They built things too solidly these days. 'I'll need to bring an axe,' he muttered as he walked away.

He smiled all the way home, because he was looking forward to destroying something Forrett set such value on. He should have burnt the place down last time. Would do that this time.

Later, James walked round the building with Lucas and Gwynna, then went back outside to look at the sign. Pulling his hand-kerchief out, he blew his nose good and hard. 'Libby was a bonny little thing.'

Gwynna linked her arm in his. 'She was. And her name will never be forgotten now.'

'I'm going to have an opening ceremony. We'll invite the mayor and every dignitary we can think of, give the place a good send-off, eh?'

'That will be lovely.'

'We'll tie a big ribbon across the door and ask my wife to cut it and declare the place open.' Torn between happiness that the orphanage was ready to open and the sadness brought on by seeing his dead baby daughter's name on the wall, he walked off down the street, hands thrust deep into his overcoat pockets.

Benting and his family moved out of the overlooker's house two days after his dismissal. He'd been tempted to damage the place or at least leave it dirty, but his wife was so horrified at this suggestion that for once she stood up to him.

'No one's going to say that I have sluttish ways!' she declared, lips trembling, eyes welling with tears. 'My friends will see that everything's left clean and tidy.'

'Forrett doesn't deserve that.'

'Jack, *please!*'

And because she looked so white and ill, he shrugged. 'Oh, do what you want. But don't ask me to help, because I shan't lift a finger.'

She was as white as cotton rovings by the time she'd finished, even though she'd only supervised her friends. She kept clutching her chest, gasping when she tried to talk. He was starting to get worried about her.

'Are you satisfied now?' he demanded. 'You've tired yourself out for nowt, you silly fool.'

She was too spent to speak, even though she'd not done the actual work.

The cottage they were to live in was so small it reminded him of the home he'd had as a lad. His children started grumbling as they tried to put away their things and sort out the downstairs, so he gave the nearest one a quick backhander, which soon stopped the rest of them complaining, at least in his hearing.

When he caught Huey slipping out of the back door he hauled

him back. 'Where do you think you're going? There are things still to be done here, and you're not getting out of them. I want some glass putting in that broken window in the kitchen, for a start, so you can take the measurements – and make sure you do them properly – and go round to the glazier's for a piece of glass.'

Huey looked at the clock. 'I can't do it now, Dad. I have to see a man about a job.'

'What job?'

His son looked desperately in the direction of his mother and gave a quick shake of the head. Benting interpreted this, correctly as it turned out, to mean that the job wasn't one his mother would approve of, so he hustled Huey out into the back yard and repeated his question. 'What job? You didn't tell me about any job.'

Huey looked at his father's angry face and didn't dare do anything but tell the truth. 'Fellow I've worked for afore. He wants someone beat up good and proper. Me an' the lads have been doing the odd job like that.' He grinned. 'It pays a lot better than working in the mill yard.'

'Well, see you don't get caught. And don't agree to do anything on Friday night. I have something I need your help with myself then.'

'Oh? What's that?'

'Never you mind. I'll tell you on Friday.'

He went back into the house, not sure he approved of what Huey was doing. It could lead to trouble, prison even. But then Huey wasn't the sort to settle down to any regular job, Benting had known that for the past year. He'd been wondering what to do with him, because his eldest son was not only a surly lout, he wasn't nearly as clever as his next brother.

He looked round the kitchen and nearly left the house himself, but this place was all they had for the moment so it had to be endured. He'd written to Alicia Gleason to tell her what had happened and what her father was doing, and he was hoping she'd want him to take some action. He knew how to get into the mill, watchmen or not, could easily damage the machinery, though he'd not do any permanent damage.

Whatever she wanted or didn't want, he was inclined to deal with Forrett once and for all. A man of that age died so much more easily than a younger one.

But surely she'd want to do something about her inheritance? And before the new wife's belly swelled.

Dora hesitated at the edge of the market, then put up her chin and walked forward to the stall. Gideon was already there setting up and for once she was a little late.

He turned to look at her, frowning. 'Are you all right, Dora love? I was worried when you weren't here at your usual time.'

'I can make up the hours.'

'I'm not bothered about that but about *you*. You're upset. No, don't argue. I can tell you've been crying.'

She watched him run one hand through his hair, which he always did when he was worried about something. Had he changed his mind? Oh, please, let him have changed his mind!

'We didn't finish our conversation yesterday and – I don't think I made myself clear. I don't know how I feel about performing, so I can't say I'll do it. I've been thinking about that and what I suggest is, I help you train Nippy and just – you know – see how I feel about that side of things. There's one thing I do know, though, and it's that I don't want to lose you. Can we just take it step by step for the moment and see how we go? Surely we can work something out?'

She nodded, unable for a moment to speak even as joy ran warmly through her. She wanted to say his name, but couldn't even frame that one word. Then he pulled her into his arms and murmured her name very softly and something inside her melted. 'Gideon, oh Gideon, yes! I do want to stay together.'

She clung to him, heedless of who saw them and they didn't say anything, just held one another.

Then someone laughed nearby and a voice they recognised

said, 'Embracing in public? How shocking! Or is there something I don't know about you two?'

They broke apart and turned towards Declan, Gideon still keeping his arm round her shoulders.

'I was worried about something,' Dora said, 'so Gideon was comforting me. I'll – um – go and get some more water.' She squeezed his hand and moved away, unable to face any teasing at the moment because she felt too fragile. She had steeled herself to endure it as Gideon ended their relationship but for some reason, she hadn't prepared herself for him to want to continue it.

When she'd gone, Declan raised one eyebrow. 'Trouble between you?'

'A lot to decide. We had different ideas about what we wanted from marriage.'

Declan's smile faded. 'Don't marry unless you're very sure about each other. It's hell if you choose the wrong person.'

Gideon nodded. 'How are things going with you? Ishleen seems to have settled happily at Granny's. She's very quiet but she's lovely with Barney and Shanna adores him.'

His companion sighed. 'I'm still worried sick about Ruth. She hasn't settled, drinks up her week's money in a couple of days, then has nothing left and comes pestering me. I'm giving her the week's money bit by bit now, but every single day she's made a fuss because it's not enough.'

'I saw her staggering along the street yesterday afternoon.'

'Yes. It's a wonder she can find her way home when she's like that. She's not trying to hide her drinking now, goes into the lowest boozers. It's bad for the boys to see their mother like that.' Declan looked into the distance for a minute then shrugged. 'But that's my problem. You've enough worries of your own.'

'How's your mother?'

'Finding great comfort in looking after her grandsons. And the lads haven't been so well fed and cared for in a long time.'

'That's good, at least.'

After the market closed, Gideon turned to Dora. 'I'll walk you home and then we'll find somewhere in town to practise with Nippy.' He snapped one finger triumphantly. 'How about the back of the orphanage? Till the place opens there's no one there most of the time. I'll ask Lucas on the way home.'

He looked down at the dog, which had spent the last hour curled up against the wall and was now standing up, shaking itself ready to leave. 'A pity you can't help us clear up, young fellow.'

Nippy grinned at him, wagging steadily.

'Eh, he's the cleverest little dog I ever met,' a woman said, stopping to pat him. 'Here, lad. Have a bite of summat.' She broke off a bit of the crust of her loaf and offered it to the dog, but he backed away. 'Eh, what's up with him?'

'We've been teaching him not to take food from anyone but us. It's safer.'

'Well, to think of that!' She walked away marvelling.

Gideon stared down at Nippy. The woman was right. That animal *was* clever. But to base their livelihood on one little animal, who could so easily be killed and who wouldn't live nearly as long as you did, seemed very dangerous. If he did decide to do what Dora wanted – and he still felt nervous at the mere thought of going on a stage in front of a crowd of strangers – he'd insist they get another dog as well.

He realised she'd finished her work and was waiting for him to wheel the handcart full of equipment back to his lodgings. 'Sorry. I was miles away.'

'It's all right.'

She was quieter than usual. He wished he could say something that would bring back the cheerful companion whose company he'd enjoyed for the past few months, but he couldn't promise something unless he felt sure about it. And it was even harder to make a decision about his life with so many other things hanging in the air. At the moment he felt torn every which way.

One thing he was certain about, though. 'I do want us to find a way through this,' he said quietly. 'I'm quite sure about that, Dora love. But I won't make any promises until I'm sure I can keep them.'

'Nev says I'm being unreasonable.'

'You're telling me the truth about how you feel, what'll make you happy. And I'm doing the same. That's the only way to go on.' He let his words sink in then changed the subject to one more cheerful. 'Since the evenings are getting lighter now, how about we practise our tricks with Nippy tonight?'

Her expression brightened at once. 'Oh, I'd love that!'

'I'll be back for you after tea.'

She stood outside Linney's and watched him walk away. Surely his suggestion about rehearsing meant there was a real chance for them?

18

The next day was fine and quite warm. Tired of his wife's complaints about how ill she felt, Benting left the house. Then he wondered what to do with himself. You thought you'd enjoy life if you didn't have to go to work, but you needed money to do that, and he wasn't dipping into his savings for more than the bare minimum until he saw his way clear.

He walked up to the moors, stopping to look at the cottages where the fellow lived who'd employed his son to beat up Gideon Potter. The place was shut up, the curtains drawn and the garden needed attention. If he owned a house, he'd look after it better than that.

He went back into town, walking up and down so that he passed the end of the street where the orphanage stood several times, wanting to see when the place was left unattended. He also managed to find a vantage point in an alley to the rear, a place where he could stand on a pile of rubbish and keep watch on the back yard of the orphanage. But watching was all he could do, because men were going in and out of it still, clearing up the final bits of rubbish. In fact, there seemed to be people coming and going all day long. He didn't dare stay around too long in case someone noticed him.

In the afternoon they brought the furniture that had been stored at the mill and carried that inside. 'Well, it'll make a better bonfire with all that wood,' he muttered to himself. 'Just you wait, Forrett! See how the place burns. See how *you* feel when all your plans are set at nowt.' He walked away, still muttering to himself. The fire that had burned down the music saloon was what had given him the idea of burning the orphanage. Eh, that had lit up the night bright as day. Well, his fire would be just as big, make a fine show.

He still felt angry every time he thought of how much money Forrett was spending on a load of scruffy kids. They should put 'em to work as soon as they could, not send 'em to school. Life was hard and the sooner children learned that the better.

That night he used the spare key no one knew he had and slipped into the mill through the door at the rear of the cotton store. He took some of the oily rags from the engine room and also some cotton waste, not enough to make anyone suspicious, but enough for his purpose. At one stage a night-watchman walked through the room he was in and he hid behind a pile of cotton bales, amused. Call that keeping watch! Anyone could walk round a building. They should shine their lamps into corners, the stupid sods.

For a moment he toyed with the idea of setting the mill on fire, but somehow he didn't want to do that. Even though he'd been treated unfairly, he'd helped build this place up and he couldn't bear to see it destroyed.

When he got home his wife had fainted and was lying on the bed, too weak to speak to him. Not too weak to feed the latest baby, though. Ah, there was always something wrong with her. He was fed up with it. Fine wife she was these days!

The following day he saw Gideon Potter turn into the street and go inside the orphanage. He frowned and lingered at the end of the street, wondering what *he* was doing there. That fellow had a stall at the market and should be there, not gadding about town. What business had he with the orphanage or Forrett?

A couple of minutes later Lucas Kemp came out with his visitor and they unlocked the side gate with a big old-fashioned key, pushing it back with a loud squeal of the hinges. They were so busy talking that it was a moment or two before they went inside. They looked like two men who got on well with one another, friends even, Benting thought sourly. He'd been too busy working for Forrett to make friends. Given his all to that mill, he had, only to see himself cast off like a worn-out shoe.

He wished he could hear what the two younger men were talking about. He waited, getting strange looks from a few people walking past and scowling back at them till they looked away again. They should mind their own bloody business, people should.

When the two men came back out of the side gate, they were still smiling. To Benting's surprise, Kemp locked the gate then gave the key to his companion, after which he went back inside with a cheery wave.

Intrigued, Benting followed Gideon to the market and saw him brandish the key triumphantly at Dora, who beamed at him. What the hell was all this about?

What mattered to him was the key. If he could get hold of that, he could get inside easily. He didn't want to do anything noisy that would alert the police officer on night patrol to a break-in, nor did he want to break a window at the front of the building, because the sight of the smashed glass would also alert the police officer and he'd wave his damned rattle – noisy nuisances they were! – and bring folk running.

Fed up with walking round and round the town, Benting went inside the sleazy little pub just behind the market and found a seat from which he could watch that fellow's stall through the window. It made for a long, boring day and he got hungry enough to send the bar lad out for a pie, but the pub was the most convenient place for his purpose, so he continued to sit there, eking out his drinks sip by sip. He didn't want to be too befuddled to act.

At one stage the landlord came across. 'Didn't think you'd be patronising us, Mr Benting.'

There was just enough of a pause before the word 'Mr' to emphasise that Benting had come down in the world. He didn't say anything about that, couldn't afford to upset anyone, so bought the landlord a drink.

'Time hangs heavy,' he said, 'and there's summat to watch from here. It gets me out of the house till I find another job.'

'They say you'll be leaving Hedderby.'

'Who says?'

'Oh, people. Gossip. You know.'

'I may. Depends on what job I get.' He hadn't even tried to find one, because somehow he couldn't see beyond getting his own back on Forrett. Only when that was accomplished would he move on.

When the market began to close for the day, he watched carefully as Gideon and Dora packed up. Piddling little business, it was, selling hot drinks like that. He'd be scrabbling for every penny, that fellow would.

Benting admitted to himself that he was missing the mill more than he'd expected to: the busy machines making money, every minute occupied, not to mention the pleasure of being in charge and having people do what you told them. He scowled as he looked at Dora and remembered the way she'd defied him. Stupid bitch. She hadn't made much of herself. Look at her now, working outside in all weathers at the market with that scruffy little dog trailing her everywhere!

But Benting wasn't doing much better at the moment, either, because he was in charge of nothing now except his family, and a sorry lot they were. His wife hadn't been well since their move, Huey was becoming increasingly defiant and seemed to have grown taller and broader suddenly, and the other children avoided their father. A good thing too. What did he know about squalling brats?

Ah! He sat up straighter. Dora and her fellow were leaving. He gulped down the last of his beer and got up, nodding to the landlord and slouching out as if he hadn't anything pressing to do. In the street he pulled his hat down as far as it would go, hating the way people smirked when they recognised him. After following them two back to the Lanes, he watched as they left the cart in a back yard, then went into town again. They were going to the orphanage, he knew it. But why?

When they went through the gate, it squeaked dreadfully again, so he didn't dare follow them inside. He went to stand on the pile of rubbish in the back alley nearby and saw them playing with the dog. That was all they did. They didn't even have a bit of a kiss and fondle. What the hell was this all about?

Baffled, he prowled round the nearby streets, but everywhere he went, seemed to meet people who'd worked under him at the mill and some of them even called out to him. Not politely, either. In the end he went home. He'd come back into town after dark and oil that bloody gate. Next time them two went to the orphanage, he'd be able to follow them inside. They must be doing something else other than play with the dog. Probably they'd been waiting for somebody else to arrive, only he hadn't turned up. But who? And why? It baffled him.

When he got home there was a letter waiting for him from Mr Gleason, not Forrett's daughter who had written before, but her husband this time. It said there was nothing to be done now but accept the situation, and Gleason felt his wife had perhaps pushed her father too hard, been misinformed about how ill he was. They were sorry Mr Benting had lost his job and wished him well in finding another one.

With an angry roar Benting screwed the piece of paper up and hurled it into the fire. 'I'll do it on my own then!' he yelled.

'Do what, Jack?' his wife asked.

'Never you mind. But I'll get my own back, see if I don't. And where's my tea? My stomach thinks my throat's been cut, I'm that hungry.'

'It won't be long.'

He leaned back in his chair, but had to sit upright again to let his wife get to the cooking pot. You could only do stews or fry-ups when you had to cook on an open fire and he was sick of them already. He missed her apple pies. Though she hadn't made one for a month or two, she'd been that ill. Eh, this was a right old hovel. She'd never get better here.

When Huey came in, Benting took his son aside and reminded him to make himself available the next evening.

'I told you – I've got a job to do,' Huey protested.

'If you'd let me finish, I'd be able to explain that my job is also in connection with that fellow you're trying to nobble.'

'Gideon Potter?'

'Aye. What's he done to upset Shaw anyway?'

'Shaw didn't say, just that he wanted him killed and the quicker the better. Honest, Dad, he didn't say owt.'

'*Killed!* You're going to murder him?'

Huey shrugged uncomfortably. 'He'll pay me well if I do, only I can't rightly bring my mind to doing it, somehow.'

'I should think not. They'll come after you like hounds chasing a fox if you kill someone. Have you run mad? Tell Shaw to do his own killing.'

'But he's offering good money.'

'You won't need it when you're hanging on the gibbet, will you?'

Huey shuffled his feet.

'You can't do it, kill someone in cold blood.'

His son shrugged. 'I can try.'

'You will not! I'm not having it.' Was that relief on Huey's face? It was. 'Tell that Shaw fellow to do the job himself and stay away from him. I'm your father still and I'll look out for you.'

'How can you now?'

He cuffed Huey. 'I'm not finished yet by a long chalk. You just wait. I've a few things planned then we're leaving this sodding town. No wonder your mam isn't getting better, stuck in a place like this. Manchester, that's the place for a man like me.'

'Why haven't you gone there looking for work, then?'

He grabbed his son by the shoulder and swung him round. 'Because I've scores to settle. No one,' another shake, '*no one*, gets the better of me.'

Declan came home to find Ishleen talking to his mother. They hadn't heard him come in and he stood in the doorway for a moment, watching them. His mother was smiling in that way she did when she really liked someone, and Ishleen was speaking in that low, soft voice of hers which he loved to hear.

Then Shanna called out to greet him and the two women

turned round, stopping what they were saying to turn their smiles on him. If only . . . he cut that thought off.

'There you are, son. I've just invited Ishleen to stay for tea and she says she doesn't want to trouble us. Tell her it's no trouble. We like having our family to eat with us, don't we?'

'Please stay,' he said, his eyes meeting Ishleen's and seeing in them the longing he too was feeling. Surely he wasn't mistaken about that? And it couldn't be wrong to spend some time with her in his mother's company. No one could make anything of that. Well, no one except Ruth and she didn't matter.

He caught his mother staring at him open-mouthed and realised he'd betrayed himself. But he didn't care, gave her a slight shrug and a wry smile and then tossed Shanna up in his arms, making her shriek with delight.

'Well, all right then,' Ishleen said. 'I'll have to let Granny Horne know I won't be home for tea, though.'

'My sons can do that.' He turned and smiled at them. 'Can't you, lads? Won't take you a minute to nip round to Granny Horne's and tell her Ishleen is eating here with us tonight.' He spun a sixpence in their direction. 'And you can bring back some sweets for you and your cousin Shanna.'

'You're not to eat them till after tea, mind!' his mother called as they ran off.

He sat down, enjoying chatting with his mother and Ishleen. They said nothing important, but they were together and happy to be so. It was as simple as that.

When he got back after escorting Ishleen and her daughter home, his mother was waiting for him.

'I saw your face when you were looking at her. I hadn't realised . . . You'll not be committing a sin, son?'

'I'd never do anything to hurt her, body or soul. And if you think she'd become any man's mistress, you wrong her.'

She nodded. 'I know. I'm sorry it can't be.'

'So am I.'

'I saw Ruth today. She's getting thinner. She can't be eating properly. Maybe I should take some food round to her.'

'Don't. All she'll give you in return is a mouthful of abuse and likely let the food go mouldy while she sits drinking night after night.' He scowled down at the ground. 'She hasn't asked me about the lads, not once, only pestered for more money.'

His mother made a gentle tutting sound.

'I don't know what to do about her, Mam.'

'I don't think there's anything you *can* do, son. You've provided her with a roof over her head and money for food. I don't approve of married couples living separate lives, but in this case, for the lads' sake – well, I think you've done the right thing and so does Father Timothy.'

And there they had to leave it. But the memory of Ishleen's lovely smile threaded through his dreams and he woke filled with longing for her.

The first time Dora and Gideon went along to the orphanage yard after the markets closed, she showed him what she had taught Nippy so far.

He watched in amazement as the dog walked along behind her and she pretended not to know. Every time she twisted and turned, it moved quickly to stay out of sight.

'I need someone to say, "There's a dog following you, miss." Can you do that for me?' she called.

So he obliged.

They went from one trick to another, then she stopped and looked at him anxiously. 'What do you think?'

'I think you're doing really well. I hadn't realised how far on you were.'

Her face cleared and without thinking she flung her arms round him, then grew embarrassed and tried to step away. But he laughed and pulled her back into his embrace, kissing her soundly. When they stepped apart, both breathing heavily, there was a little yelp and they turned to see Nippy sitting with his head on one side, looking at them.

Gideon put his arm round her. 'You need to make some of

the tricks into a story, however simple, Dora. All the good dog acts I've seen do that.'

'I've never seen one of the top ones,' she said wistfully. 'But there's a dog act coming to the next concert, so we must watch it carefully.'

'Watch the audience, too. See what they like best.' He hesitated. 'There's another dog act performing in Manchester next week, a very well-known one, Eli said. Do you think your family would let me take you to see it?'

Her eyes lit up. 'You'll do that?'

'Yes.'

'If we had one of my sisters with me, it'd be all right, I'm sure, especially now that we're walking out together. Oh, I can't think of anything I'd like better! Can we come here tomorrow and go through it again, see if we can start working out a story?'

'Why not?' It gave him an excuse to spend time alone with her.

The next evening Benting followed them again. He'd oiled the gate and this time he was able to creep into the passageway after them. He was a bit worried the dog would hear him, but he stood very still and it was so excited about the tricks they were doing that it didn't even look in his direction. They were making plenty of noise, laughing and calling out to one another, enough to cover up any sound he made. He left after a while, amazed that she thought she could go on the stage. What fools them two were!

When he got home, he took his son aside and told him what he'd overheard.

'I could follow them into Manchester,' Huey said. 'Do it there. No one would know me.'

'Don't be daft. Someone will see you buying a ticket and getting on a train. How can I say you were with me then? No, you stay away from murder. Anyway, I need you to help get me the key to that gate and break into the orphanage. This time we're going to burn the place down, destroy it completely.'

Huey stared at him. 'Why?'

'Because I say so. Because it'll upset Forrett. I'll teach that bugger to throw me out of my job!'

Huey frowned. 'But no one will be paying you to do that, so why bother?'

'I don't need money. I've got plenty of that saved. This is to get my own back. And don't worry. I'll pay you to help me.'

In the kitchen, ear close to the door, Benting's wife pressed one hand to her mouth to hold back a cry. Things were going from bad to worse now and if her husband and son got taken up for arson or murder, how was she to manage? Only . . . if she warned people, that would also get the two of them in trouble. She crept back to the chair near the kitchen fire and picked up the baby, unbuttoning her blouse and putting it to suckle. Her head was aching and she felt faintly dizzy all the time, had to have help every day still.

She didn't know where to turn, she thought desperately. She and her children would end up in the workhouse at this rate.

There had to be something she could do, someone she could tell about this, someone who could stop him doing this dreadful thing. The room spun around her and she shrank down into the chair so that she wouldn't drop the baby.

When her husband came in, he shook her and then snatched the baby and gave it to Huey, before sweeping her into his arms and carrying her up the stairs. For a moment that took her back to when they'd been courting, but then she heard him puffing and wheezing with the effort, saw his grey hair and then saw her own pale face in the mirror.

She wished she was dead. She did. Rolling to one side, she began to weep, but he yelled at her to stop that and stamped off down the stairs, leaving her with one flickering candle and a baby crying with hunger because her milk was drying up.

John went to see Kath, but only stayed one night and refused to let her come back to Hedderby with him, which she'd been pleading to do for a while. 'I'm going to be busy and I don't want you involved,' he said.

'Doing what?'

'Getting rid of Gideon Shaw, that's what.'

'You'll be careful?'

'Course I will.'

'Can't we just – sell the cottages and leave without him finding out?'

'I've told you and told you. I can't do that until after I've got *rid* of him. If I sell the cottages someone will find out, for sure, because the only way to do that in Hedderby is through the local lawyers or by word of mouth. I don't want to draw attention to myself, don't want to risk the Army finding me. How would *you* manage if you didn't have me to look after you?'

'I wouldn't, John love. I'd have to take in lodgers or summat, an' I'd hate that.' She sighed. 'Nothing good ever lasts, does it?'

'This will. I'm going to make sure of that.' He tried to speak confidently, but he was finding it hard to nerve himself up to kill Gideon because he hated bloodshed. And as for Huey Benting and his friends, they'd proved to be all talk and no action.

But the following day Huey came round to offer to tell him where he could catch Shaw on his own.

'Why can't *you* do the job I wanted, if you know so much about him?' John demanded. 'I've offered you ten guineas. That's a fortune for a young chap like you.'

Huey wriggled uncomfortably and didn't say anything.

'Well, at least you've given me some information.' John fumbled in his pocket and took out two half-crowns, saw the disappointment on Huey's face and said, 'We'll do it tomorrow.'

'Dad wants me to help him at the orphanage on Friday.'

'Do you want to earn another guinea or not?'

That was more than his father would give him. 'I do. I'll see if I can get away.' But he'd not tell his father about his plans and anyway, he might get back before his father wanted to leave.

And as soon as he had enough money, he'd be leaving Hedderby and never, ever coming back. If it wasn't for his mam, he'd have left before now.

But every time he thought of killing Gideon Potter, something inside him shuddered away from it. He'd tried telling himself not to be a coward, but somehow . . . Ah, it'd be all right when it came down to it. He'd do it quickly, not give himself time to think about it.

19

The engineer went to see the deputy overlooker after the mill had got going for the morning. 'Someone's been in my engine room,' he said without preamble.

Thad looked at him in puzzlement. 'What do you mean?'

'I mean that between me closing the place down last night and coming in this morning to fire up for the day, someone came in and took a pile of my rags. If it's those night-watchmen doing it, you can tell them to leave my stuff alone from now on.'

'I'll go and ask them. They don't live far away and I could do with some fresh air.'

But both watchmen stoutly denied taking anything.

Thad went back to the engineer. 'Are you certain something's been took? Maybe it was just moved.'

'Of course I am! It was some blue checked material from a dress my wife wore when she were younger.' He stopped speaking to smile at some memory. 'She cut it down for our youngest and gave the bits to me for rags. She knows how I need rags. It used to make me smile whenever I used them bits, remembering how pretty she looked in the dress.'

'Oh.' Thad stood there for a moment, then admitted, 'I don't rightly know what to do about it. I don't see how anyone *can* have taken it.'

'Well, I know what I'm going to do. I'm seeing Mr Forrett and telling him someone's been where they shouldn't.'

'Do you have to? It's only a few scraps of rag, after all.'

'It's the principle of the thing. Besides, what if they tampered with my engine? Where would we all be then?'

He marched off to the office and banged on the door, explaining what had happened to his employer.

James frowned at him. 'You're sure these things went missing?'

'I'd stake my life on it, that's how sure I am.'

'Well, I think the night-watchmen would be telling the truth. I know those two from years back and they're as honest a pair as you're likely to meet.' He chewed one side of his mouth, then slowly put his thoughts into words, 'There's only one way someone could get in without being seen that I can think of – that side door near your engine room. And – there was only ever one person had keys to that apart from you and me. Benting. He gave me back his keys when he left, but what if he'd had copies made?'

The engineer looked at him in dawning understanding. 'But what would he want with my rags?'

'Were they clean or dirty ones?'

'Mucky with oil. When they're no more use to me here, the wife cuts 'em into scraps to light the fire with at home. They burn up real quick.'

They looked at one another and it was obvious that the same idea had struck them both. You couldn't live in a town where the music saloon had been burned down so spectacularly without being aware of what wicked men could do with fire.

'We'll have all the locks changed this very day,' James said grimly, not needing to voice his suspicions. Was Benting planning to come back and burn down the mill? He'd not have thought that of the man.

But then, he'd not have thought Benting would be disloyal to him, either.

He sent the office boy running to the locksmith's with an urgent note, then went across to tell Charis about it.

'You will be careful, won't you?' she begged, laying her hand on his arm.

He clasped the hand in his for a moment. 'Yes. And so will you, I hope? Tell the servants. No leaving outside doors unlocked from now on, even in the daytime. Tell them we've had pilfering in the mill. Are you going to see your mother today?'

'I was planning to.'

'Don't go down any side streets, just go straight there along Market Street and come back the same way. You'll be all right where there are plenty of people.' He let go of her hand and said simply, 'I don't want anything happening to you.'

'I could say the same thing to you, James.'

That exchange left both of them looking happy, in spite of the problems at the mill.

On the Friday evening, Mrs Benting gave a cry and fell down in a faint just as her family was starting to eat tea. Her eldest daughter, twelve years old and sensible with it, rushed to her help.

Benting sat and stared across the table. 'What's up with your mother?'

'She's been feeling bad all day,' Renie said. 'I told her to lie down but she wouldn't, said she had to get your tea ready.'

'And so she did have to,' he agreed, shovelling some more food into his mouth while it was hot.

Renie continued patting her mother's hand and shooting angry glances at her father and older brother, who were getting on with their meal and making no attempt to help her. 'She's fainted a few times lately.'

Fork suspended in mid-air, he looked at his wife, then put the food into his mouth and said indistinctly, 'Well, you'll know what to do then. You see to her.'

After another minute or two, Renie said, 'She's not coming to this time like she did before. Dad, we can't leave her lying on the floor. I need you to help me lift her up.'

With an aggrieved sigh, he went round the table and hauled his wife up, trying to sit her on a chair. But she only slid down, showing no signs of awareness at all.

'Do you think we should fetch the doctor?' Renie asked in a voice which quavered.

Benting opened his mouth to pooh-pooh this idea, then looked at his wife again. Her face was so white she looked like a corpse he'd seen once. And she'd been unwell ever since she had the baby. 'I suppose we'd better.' He turned to Huey. 'Go and fetch Dr Pipperday.'

'Me?'

'Yes, you.' Benting waved one clenched fist. 'How do you think we're going to manage without your mother? Who'll cook your tea then?'

His son crammed the rest of his food into his mouth and got up.

'Should we carry her up to bed, Dad?' Renie asked when Huey had left with a slam of the door.

'I suppose so. I'll carry her. You go up first with a lamp and pull the covers back.' He picked up his wife, surprised for the second time that day at how light she felt. When he got her up to the bedroom, he stayed beside her unconscious body, seriously worried now.

Dr Pipperday was there within a few minutes. He examined Mrs Benting and said, 'Ah!' as she began to regain consciousness.

'Is she all right?'

'No. She needs rest and good food to build up her blood.' He glanced sideways at the husband. 'And you'll need a wet nurse for that baby. Your wife's nearly dry now. She's been talking to my wife about it, worrying.'

Benting stared at him in shock, then looked down at his wife again. 'She's going to be all right, isn't she?'

'I don't know. She's very weak, been doing too much for a while now. Can you afford to get help for her?'

'We've been getting help. But I can get more if it's needed, someone to cook as well as clean.'

'I've just told you it's necessary. If you want to keep your wife alive, you'll have to let her rest. I can take the baby and let my wife find it a wet nurse, but *you* will have to look after your wife. She'll need careful watching tonight. Send out for some eggs and milk. Beat an egg up in milk with a bit of sugar and get her to drink some, a spoonful at a time if necessary.'

'But I was—' Benting broke off. No use telling the doctor he had intended to go out and burn the orphanage when he wanted everyone to think he was at home tonight.

'What's more important, keeping your wife alive or going out boozing?' Dr Pipperday asked scornfully. 'And don't give her any more children. She'd definitely not survive another confinement.'

When the doctor had gone, taking the wailing baby with him, thank goodness, Benting asked, 'Who does he think he is, telling me what to do with my own wife?' None of his children answered him and when he looked round he saw that Huey wasn't there.

'You'll have to help your mother,' he told Renie.

She looked at him anxiously. 'Who's going to get the children to bed then?'

'Can't they get themselves to bed?'

'Marty an' Paul can, but the others are too little. Can you sit with Mam while I get them to bed?'

'I suppose so.'

By the time Renie had done that, it was pouring down with rain. Benting looked sourly at the streaming window pane which was rattling in the wind. Not a good night for starting fires. Then he looked at his wife again. He didn't want her to die. How could she suddenly be so ill? She'd taken some time to recover after the previous baby, so he'd thought it was the same thing again. But now . . . well, he didn't know what to think.

Renie came into the bedroom and sat on the bottom of the bed, then burst into tears. 'What if Mam never wakes up? What'll we *do*?'

He'd been thinking the same thing and he couldn't find an answer for himself, let alone something to reassure his daughter. But to his relief she didn't seem to expect him to reply.

Oh, hell, he didn't need anything else to go wrong! Hadn't he enough to worry about already? His whole life was messed up. Damn Forrett! It was all his fault.

★   ★   ★

'It looks like rain,' Essie said as Dora and Edith got ready to go into Manchester with Gideon. 'Perhaps you ought to go another night instead? There'll be other dog acts coming.'

'I'll take Nev's umbrella,' Dora said desperately. 'Oh, Essie, don't stop me going! I've been looking forward to it for days.'

She exchanged glances with Edith and they nipped up to their room to get ready as quickly as they could. When Grace came to help them, the three put their heads together and Grace went back down, richer by threepence, to distract Essie's attention by breaking a plate.

The two older girls crept down the stairs, calling a quick goodbye from the hall and whisking out of the front door.

Essie looked up. 'I don't think they should go. I'll just—'

Grace pinched little Leah, who began to cry, and this distracted Essie for a few minutes, by which time it was too late to stop the outing.

Some time later, when Essie wasn't looking, Grace whispered, 'Sorry,' and gave her little cousin an extra cuddle.

Gideon, who'd been expecting to call at the house, looked surprised when the two sisters turned up at his lodgings and whisked him away to the station to take an earlier train. But he made no protest when they explained why.

Not until they had pulled out of the station did Dora relax.

He looked at her and Edith and shook his head with mock severity. 'You're a terrible pair.'

They giggled.

Long before they got to Manchester it began pouring down again, but they were lucky. Just as they arrived, the rain stopped. The streets were crowded, in spite of the damp weather, the pavements gleaming wetly in the light of gas lamps. So many shops were still open that Edith had to be dragged along because she kept stopping to stare in the brightly lit windows and comment on how they were set out.

When they got to the music hall, Gideon bought them the best seats, in spite of whispered protests by Dora at this extravagance, then they settled down to enjoy themselves.

The dog act was very clever and Dora watched it in breathless silence, sitting slightly forward in her seat. Gideon watched carefully too, but couldn't help stealing glances at the lass next to him as well. Her face was so bright and alive, full of intelligence and interest. Why had he thought she might want to settle down to just being someone's wife? Dora was – special. He hadn't met her sister Marjorie, who was part of a comedy act that was very successful, though he'd seen her in the distance. Now he came to think of it, though, she was the same: so full of life that heads turned to watch her pass by.

Dora had told him that she wasn't nearly as pretty as her sister Marjorie, but he thought she was. She wasn't a beauty as Lalika had been, but to his mind she was the most attractive young woman he'd ever seen – ever. There was something so vibrant and warm about her that— He realised suddenly that the show had ended and Dora was nudging him. 'Sorry. I was just thinking about something.'

'We have to leave now,' she said. 'They'll want to clean up for the second performance.'

It was raining again as they walked back to the station and she'd forgotten to bring the umbrella, but she was too interested in discussing the dog act to care about getting wet, so just pulled her collar up.

'Our Nippy's more lovable than that dog,' Edith said. 'He wins everyone round, he does. Look at how Essie cuddles him when she thinks no one's looking. He's clever too. I think he can do better than that dog. People will love him, like they do at the market.'

When they got on the train, they continued to analyse the other act, then Dora sat lost in her thoughts. Edith gave up trying to talk to her and settled back to watch the way Gideon was looking at her sister. It was very interesting watching people. She did it all the time in the shop where she worked. She'd never want to go on the stage like Marjorie and have to travel round all the time. What she wanted was her own shop, but it cost so much to set one up and although she saved what money she could, it wasn't enough for the sort of shop she wanted – a proper one in a good neighbourhood, one which sold everything 'and had lots of regular paying customers like the Emporium in Hedderby. Where she worked now, quite a few of the customers bought on tick and paid off when they got their wages, so they were always behind. She'd not give any credit at all, however bad times were. It was just giving money away, offering credit, because although some paid it back, others never did.

The train began to slow down and Edith watched Dora come out of her dream-like state and smile at Gideon. He walked the two girls home, then Essie had the three of them out of their damp outer clothes. They sat drinking hot milk and honey as they told the rest of the family all about the show. Gideon was part of the family now, she thought, and wondered whether Dora knew how often she turned to smile at him.

Aaah, it was lovely to see them. She hoped she'd meet someone nice one day, but not till she got her shop.

Lucas locked up the orphanage carefully. The two night-watchmen were there keeping an eye on things. They always slipped in singly during the last part of the afternoon, trying to look as if they were workmen and now he'd got them going round without lanterns, so that no one knew they were there during the night.

Today they'd come early because he and Gwynna were going to visit the workhouse to discuss which children might be suitable candidates for the orphanage. He hated that place, because it seemed to reek of unhappiness and misery. It was cruel to separate husbands and wives, especially the older ones, from whom there was no danger of unwanted extra children. And it upset him the way they treated the children in there, not letting them run about and play, acting as if they'd been naughty all the time, whether they had or not.

Matron came out of her office to greet them, keys jangling at her waist. She was wearing a fancy muslin cap with lace lappets dangling at either side, and a starched white apron with crochet work round the edges. 'Ah, Mr and Mrs Kemp. The children are waiting for you to inspect them, all except two who were naughty and who have lost their chance of a place in the orphanage as punishment.'

He and Gwynna looked at one another in dismay. Clearly the woman had been frightening the children already.

'We came to talk to you *about* the children, not see them,' he said. 'We wanted to discuss them with you, find out what they were like, how many there were.'

She looked at him pityingly. 'You're better seeing them for yourself. And the secret with pauper children is to decide how you want them to behave and treat them accordingly, not see what they're like. Yes, the only way to deal with such children is firmly. If you don't start out that way, you'll soon find yourself forced into it because they'll get up to mischief. Even keeping them clean is difficult, because they will dirty themselves and their clothes – and even their beds. Though I whip them good and hard for that.'

Gwynna took over. 'I'm sure you do your – um – best, Matron. But an orphanage is slightly different from a workhouse, isn't it? An orphanage is a *home* for such children.'

Matron's face took on an even more frozen expression. 'I had thought it a place where they could be trained for useful employment, before being sent out to earn their bread.'

Lucas squeezed Gwynna's hand and she kept her mouth shut. She'd never agree with this woman.

'I'll take you to the children, then you can inspect them. We've sent the older ones out to work, all except one who's lame. And I'd be grateful if you would not encourage them to misbehave while you're here.'

'We might as well see the ones you locked away as well,' Gwynna said.

'Not today, I'm afraid.'

It was Lucas who lost control. He stopped walking to snap in a harsh voice, 'If we don't see them, I'll go and fetch Mr Forrett and as he contributes greatly to the upkeep of this establishment, I don't think the superintendent will want to offend him. Where *is* the superintendent, by the way?'

Her expression was tight with disapproval. 'He's not well, I'm afraid. Shall we go?'

They followed her into a large, cheerless room, where about a dozen children of all ages were sitting on benches in two rows, arms folded. They jumped to their feet when the Matron came in and stood waiting, hands clasped in front of them now. They were wearing the rough clothing issued by the workhouse with a P for pauper on the right sleeve of each. Their expressions ranged from sullen to frightened to interested.

What upset Gwynna was how pale they were, as if they never saw the sunlight, and how thin, as if they weren't properly fed. She wanted to sweep them all into her arms and take them away at once. Instead, she and Lucas were ushered to chairs at the front and the children were brought out one at a time to be inspected.

Matron commented on each one's circumstances as if they were deaf. One lame girl was older than the others and seemed utterly subdued.

A little girl called Mallie wet herself when her time came to walk to the front and burst into tears. The look Matron gave her said there would be punishment that night.

Gwynna smiled at the weeping child. 'Never mind that, just come here and let us have a look at you. How old are you, dear?'

When every child had been brought out, Lucas asked, 'And the other two?'

The Matron elevated her nose. 'They're in the punishment room. You may see them there, if you insist, but they know they'll not be let out till tomorrow and I never go back on my word.'

Gwynna stood up but as she started to leave she saw the little girl who had wet herself crying against the skirt of a bigger girl and could bear it no longer. She marched across and picked Mallie up, cuddling her close, damp skirts and all. 'Shh, now. Shh.' She looked at Matron. 'We'll take this child with us now.'

The woman's mouth dropped open. 'But – you can't! She hasn't been signed out.'

Lucas stepped forward, standing between his wife and the rigid figure of the older woman. 'Oh, I'm sure we can go through all the formalities tomorrow. Come along, my dear. We'll just go and see the other two, then we'll take you to your new home.'

The lame girl, who'd been trying to comfort Mallie, shot him a quick, sideways look of gratitude, then lowered her eyes.

'I'll take her from you, love,' he said calmly and held out his arms to the child. But she cowered away from him.

'She's not heavy.' Gwynna began walking, but turned at the door to say to the others, 'We'll look forward to having you in the orphanage.'

The two lads being punished were locked in a windowless cupboard and one had clearly been crying.

Gwynna looked at Lucas and he rolled his eyes in resignation, then turned to Matron. 'We'll take these two now as well. We – er – could use some extra help getting the orphanage ready.'

She breathed in so deeply she seemed to swell with anger, but said nothing, only turned to the two lads to say, 'See that you behave yourselves or Mr Kemp will whip you good and hard.'

As they walked home Mallie fell asleep on Gwynna's shoulder. The two lads, who couldn't have been more than eight or nine, walked on either side of Lucas. One seemed cowed, the other was looking round as if he'd never seen a town centre before.

When they got to the house, they left the bewildered boys in the workshop in Joe's charge. It took only a few words to make him understand the situation.

'He's a clever lad, that one,' Lucas said as they went into the house. He looked at the child just waking up in his wife's arms and gave Gwynna a smile and shake of the head.

'I can't bear seeing children ill-treated,' she said as they went into the house.

'I love it when you get angry about injustice.'

She smiled but the smile faded very quickly. 'I know what it's like to be hungry and ill-treated. No one in our orphanage is going to suffer like I did as a child. And this one didn't wet herself on purpose but out of fear caused by *that woman*. Mallie can't be more than five, can she? Now, I need to get her clothes changed and we have to make up beds for those two boys. Goodness, I don't even know their names. Go and find out this minute!'

But first he kissed his wife's soft cheek and then, since the little girl was still clinging to her, kissed the child as well, which brought a flicker of surprise then a smile to her face.

20

The new overlooker and his family arrived in Hedderby by train and walked to their new home, carrying various bags and bundles. Samuel Newbold was a fresh-faced young fellow with a rather plain wife and four children, one only a babe in arms.

On their way to the overlooker's house, they walked up to the mill and Samuel popped into the office just across from the house to say that he'd arrived. James shook his hand warmly, introduced him to Thad and walked with him to the door. When he noticed the wife and young family waiting outside for their father, he swept them all into the house for a bite to eat.

'Eh, the master's changed since he lost that child,' Thad whispered to the man in charge of the yard. 'He'd never have done that in the old days.'

'Never hurts to be kind to folk.'

When the Newbolds arrived at their new home, the children ran from one room to the next, exclaiming at how big it was and how many bedrooms there were. Samuel and his wife walked round more slowly, arm in arm, smiling, then back to the kitchen where she burst into tears of joy at how big and modern it was.

Benting, who'd seen the dray stop outside his old house and guessed whose furniture it was, walked past twice, going into the pub for a drink between each survey of activity at his old home. Them sods hadn't much furniture, unless more was coming, and as for the children, they were running wild. *He* wouldn't have let his get in the way of the men carrying the furniture like that.

At dinner time he went back to the cottage. The contrast

between it and the much bigger overlooker's house brought bile
to his mouth.

The woman he was paying to look after things shook her head
and waved her hand to dispel the fumes of beer he was breathing
over her. 'You should have been here to talk to the doctor instead
of going out boozing,' she snapped.

He raised his hand to her automatically and she snatched up
a rolling pin.

'If you lay one finger on me, I'll walk out. I only took this job
to help your poor wife out because I know her from church and
feel sorry for her.' She waited until his hand had dropped to add,
'The doctor came and he said you've to go and see him as soon
as you can.'

'Get me something to eat first.'

'Aren't you going up to see your wife?'

'I'll see her after I've spoken to the doctor. Now, where's that
food?'

Lips tightly pursed, she got him some dry bread and cheese
and dumped the plate in front of him.

'Is this all you can find?'

'Aye, because it's all there is. An' I'll need some money to buy
food if I'm to make you all a meal for tonight.'

Grumbling under his breath he fumbled in his pocket for a
few coins, then gobbled down the bread and cheese before going
out to see the damned doctor. At this rate, he'd have to draw out
some more of his savings soon. His wife's illness was very incon-
venient, had already stopped him torching the orphanage.

Dr Pipperday left his meal to take his visitor into the back
room where he saw patients. 'I'm sorry, but there's nothing more
I can do to help your wife. She's markedly weaker than yesterday
and it can only be a matter of days.'

Benting stared at him in horror. 'She's *dying*?'

'I'm afraid so. Didn't you realise?'

'No. She's always been sickly.'

'I'm amazed she's kept going for this long, actually. It's a disease
of the blood, we think, and there is no cure.'

There was silence, then Benting pushed himself to his feet and stumbled out without a word. He didn't even look where he was going and when he found himself up on the edge of the moors, he looked round in surprise, wondering how he had got here. He went to sit on a rock, brushing tears away angrily. What good did tears do when everything you had cared about was being taken away from you?

It was all Forrett's fault. *He* had thrown them out of their home. She'd loved that house, had taken leaving it badly, that's what had killed her, whatever the doctor said.

A man came walking up the path, saw him and hesitated. It was the fellow who wanted Gideon from the market killed. Benting nodded to him and the man stopped to chat.

'Bit better weather today, isn't it?' the man said.

'You're the one as wants my son to kill that fellow, aren't you?'

Shaw looked round in alarm. 'Shh!'

'No one can hear us. But I'm telling you now, I'm not having it. It's one thing to bash a fellow for you. I don't mind Huey doing that – as long as you pay him for his trouble. But I'm not having him took up and hanged for murder. So do your dirty work yourself from now on.' He got to his feet and stumbled down the hill.

But he didn't go home, couldn't face his dying wife yet. Needed a few drinks to give him the courage.

Only, when it came down to it he had no desire to pour beer down his throat and after a couple of pots, he left the pub and took the long way home.

That evening Gideon and Dora again went round to the back of the orphanage to practise with Nippy. While they were doing it, someone walked round the corner of the building into the yard, which made Nippy bark, Dora squeak in shock and Gideon swing round quickly.

'Oh, it's you, Declan!'

'I was just walking Ishleen and her daughter home and we came to look at the new sign on the orphanage. We noticed the side gate was open and were worried that someone had broken in.'

Dora stepped forward, smiling. 'Why don't you bring them in? We need an audience.'

'What for?'

'Our dog act.'

As Declan went back down the side, Gideon scowled at Dora. '*You* might want an audience, but I'm not so sure I'm ready for it.'

'You'll be fine. Nippy always does his tricks better when you're with him.'

Declan returned with Ishleen and Shanna. 'Here we are, the very best of audiences.'

The little girl giggled and Declan swept her up into his arms, jiggling her around and making her laugh.

Gideon tried to hide his embarrassment at the thought that he might be making a fool of himself. Then Nippy jumped up at him and he bent to stroke his four-legged friend.

They went carefully through what they'd practised and to their delight, their audience laughed and applauded.

'I hadn't realised how good your Nippy was,' Declan said afterwards. 'That's not long enough for an act, but it's going to be a good one when you've worked it up.'

Dora dropped him an exaggerated curtsey. 'Thank you, kind sir.' She went to link her arm in Gideon's. 'We need a song to finish off with. Raife's writing one for us but he's not satisfied with it yet. He said he'll finish it by tomorrow, though.'

Some worry that had been hovering in Gideon's mind surfaced suddenly. 'You said the side gate was unlocked. I'd better not forget to lock it properly as we go out.' He went through his pockets, then checked them again before turning to Dora. 'I can't find the key. Have you got it, love?'

'No. If you remember, I tripped as we were coming in and dropped some of my things. You stepped forward to help me pick them up before Nippy could trample all over them. Perhaps you left the key in the lock?'

'I'll go and check that.' He walked off down the side of the building but when he returned he was frowning. 'It's not there. Are you *sure* you haven't seen it, Dora?'

'Certain.'

'Then someone must have taken it because I definitely haven't got it.'

The two men exchanged worried glances.

'We can't leave it open,' Gideon said.

'I'll call in at Lucas's house on the way home,' Declan offered. 'He's bound to have another key.'

'We'll wait here till he comes, keep an eye on things.'

'You'd be safer waiting in the street. It's getting late.'

Dora looked from one man to the other, feeling the undercurrents of tension.

Declan picked up Shanna and set her to ride on his shoulders. 'We'd better get you home, young lady.'

The two left behind picked up their things and went to stand in the street in front of the orphanage.

Dora shivered suddenly. The setting sun was throwing long shadows down the street and it seemed to her that one of them at the far end had moved. She stared in that direction and whispered to Gideon, 'Is that somebody down the end of the street?'

He followed her pointing finger, narrowing his eyes in an attempt to penetrate the shadows, but couldn't see anything moving there. 'I don't think so, but I'll be glad when Lucas arrives, I must admit.'

Just then there was the sound of footsteps coming from the direction of the main road. Gideon tensed and stared along the street at the outline of a tall man. Then the figure came closer and he saw who it was. He hadn't realised he'd been holding his breath until he let it out in a whoosh.

Lucas came striding up to them, looking serious. 'I've brought the spare key. You haven't found yours by any chance, have you?'

'No. I'm sorry about losing it. I'll pay for a new lock to be fitted tomorrow.' He saw Lucas start to shake his head. 'I mean it. I was careless and there's no reason you should have to pay.

Save your money for the children you take in.' He hesitated. 'Do you think this place will be safe tonight? I mean, if someone has the key . . .'

Lucas gave a grim smile. 'I'm sure it will, though I do want to lock the gate.' He turned and walked along the street with them.

Gideon didn't press him to explain why he'd said it'd be safe. He wasn't so sure, but the orphanage wasn't his responsibility. He felt uneasy tonight for some reason he couldn't fathom and had been relieved when the person who walked in on them proved to be Declan. He really should have locked that gate, was angry with himself for leaving the key in it.

Only when the three people had disappeared round the corner did the shadows at the other end of the street stir and a man walk out of them. He had the key in his pocket and patted it as he walked. Bit of luck, that. He'd come back later with the oily rags.

He looked carefully at the windows of the orphanage as he passed. No sign of lights inside, but he'd check carefully before going inside to make sure there were no night-watchmen around. He didn't intend to run any risks.

As he approached his home his steps slowed. He didn't want to go in. But there was nothing else he could do, so he opened the door and walked slowly through the front room. He could hear a child crying.

In the kitchen the woman helping them was sitting by the table cradling a cup of tea in her hands.

'I'm not paying you to sit and slurp our tea.'

She looked at him and tears welled in her eyes. 'She's gone.'

'Who's gone?'

'Your wife. Slipped away without us noticing, she did, and when I went up to see if she needed owt, she was gone.'

He stared at her in shock. 'Dead?'

'I just told you.'

'She can't be dead! The doctor told me she'd last a few days.'

'Well, she didn't. Renie's sitting with her. Grand little lass, that one is. I sent the other children out to neighbours.' She looked at him expectantly. 'Well, aren't you going to go up and see her? I'll lay her out for you later.'

He didn't want to see his wife's body, he definitely didn't, but he couldn't think of any excuse not to, so he climbed the stairs, feeling as if each one was a mountain.

Renie was sitting by the bed, holding her mother's hand and crying. She looked up. 'Mam wanted you. She called for you just before she died. Where were you, Dad?'

'I was seeing the doctor.'

'Not all that time you weren't.'

'I was upset, walked round the town and up to the moors.'

'You should ha' come home! I'll never forgive you for not being here.'

Sobbing, she pushed past him and went into the girls' bedroom, where he could hear her weeping. He looked down at the still figure on the bed. She hardly made a bump in the bedclothes, she was so thin. Why hadn't he noticed how thin she was getting?

She'd been a pretty little thing when he wed her, though that had soon faded. But she'd been a good wife and mother. He'd do right by her, give her a decent funeral.

And afterwards? What the hell was he going to do without a wife? He knew nowt about looking after children.

For a few minutes he couldn't seem to think, only stare down at the face he'd seen a thousand times, feeling as if he'd never really looked at it before.

Then his brain started working again, though slowly. He'd ask that woman to keep coming in to see to the house and meals, but only as a temporary measure. He'd start looking for a job once he'd dealt with Forrett. A man with his experience wouldn't have any trouble finding something. He was a good overlooker. And he'd have to find another wife, an older one whose belly wouldn't always be swelling. Men needed wives to run their homes.

He sighed and looked at the bed again. He'd not been a good

husband, and was sorry now that he'd shouted at her lately. None of his troubles had been her fault. It was Forrett who was to blame.

Late that night Benting slipped out of the house, taking his bag of oily rags and the tinder box. The key was in his pocket, banging against his thigh as he walked and he was looking forward to seeing that damned orphanage blaze up. It'd make as good a show as the music saloon had. He'd be glad to see it gone. If it hadn't been for this place being built and showing him that Forrett was losing his wits, he wouldn't have sided with Mrs Gleason and lost his job.

The streets were empty, but the moon was full enough to light his way. He walked as quietly as he could, not wanting to attract attention.

When he got to the orphanage he stopped outside and watched for a minute or two, but saw no signs of lights inside. Nodding in satisfaction, he unlocked the side gate, which swung back silently, thanks to his oiling it a few days ago. He wasn't feeling excited or nervous as he made his way round the back, just determined.

The windows at the rear reflected the dark outline of himself passing, with a background of clouds and moonlight. He tried them one by one, hoping to find an unlocked window, but no such luck. Wrapping one of the oily rags round his right hand, he thumped a pane with one fist, sending glass scattering. It wasn't big enough for him to climb through, but with a bit of effort he could get his hand in and unfasten the window.

It was awkward, though, and as he was pulling his hand out, he felt a slicing sensation and pulled his wrist away quickly, seeing the blood welling out of a long, deep cut. The blood looked black in the moonlight and he cursed as it dripped down his hand. He dabbed at it with a rag, but it went on bleeding, so with a muttered curse, he pulled off his muffler and wound that round his wrist.

Once inside, he paused to get his bearings, remembering with a grim smile the last time he'd come in here, the way he and

Huey had smashed things under the cover of the storm. It had been so satisfying to do that. He scowled. Huey should have been with him tonight, helping, but the young sod had slipped out earlier without saying anything.

He looked round. No furniture in this room. It'd be better to have something to get the bonfire going, so he went into the next room, where he found a couple of chairs. That was more like it. Setting down his pile of rags near the window, he pulled down the curtains to add to the fire. Then he opened the window to let in the air and make the fire burn brighter, after which he brought a chair across.

He got out the tinderbox and some shavings he'd brought for kindling and struck the flint several times without the shavings catching light. He paused to glare at the damned box. His wife had been the one who used it to light fires and she was better than him with it. She was too soft for her own good – *had been* too soft. Stupid bitch. Why did she have to die on him?

The kindling suddenly caught light and he laughed aloud.

Just at that moment someone grabbed his shoulder. He jumped in shock and let out a yell, dropping the tinder box. The burning shavings fell on to the oily rags, which caught fire. He began to struggle with his opponent, desperate not to be taken up by the law, trying to keep the other man away from the fire so that it had a chance to catch.

John Shaw glanced at the clock and wished time would pass more quickly. Huey sat in the cottage kitchen with him, fidgeting about and asking stupid questions he'd asked several times before.

When John could stand that no longer, he shouted, 'Sit still and shut up!' It was clear that the youth was too nervous to do the job himself, but he would be there to help, that was what counted, because in spite of the damage to his hand, Gideon was still a tall, sturdy man. It might take two of them to subdue him.

To John's intense irritation, his companion fell asleep suddenly, looking much younger with his face all relaxed. When the clock struck midnight John let out a grunt of relief and shook Huey awake. 'Time to go.'

'What? I – oh, yes.' He stood up and yelped, hopping about. 'My foot's gone to sleep.'

John curbed his impatience and waited until Huey pronounced the foot all right for walking again, then led the way out.

At the front door he stopped to pick up a club from the umbrella stand and thrust it at the lad. 'You take this one.' He picked up the other one he'd made for himself, hefting it in the air. The root ball at the end of the stick had hardened nicely in the fire. With a curt, 'No talking from now on, mind!' he led the way out and down the lane into town.

'What if—'

'*Will* you shut up, dammit!'

As they were nearing the centre of the town, a bell suddenly began pealing out. On and on it went. Lamps came on behind closed curtains, voices called out and doors opened.

'What the hell is going on?' John exclaimed.

'That sound's coming from the orphanage,' Huey said. 'I didn't know they had a bell. I wonder why they're ringing it.'

Praying for patience, John moved back into the shadows and watched as a nearby house door opened and a man came out, running towards the sound. When several men had done this, he nudged Huey. 'We might as well go and see what's happening. We'll not get our job done tonight with all that row going on, that's for sure. Let that club hang down and no one will notice it.'

Just as he was about to move out of the doorway, another man ran past them in his shirt sleeves. It took a minute for it to register who this was, then he exclaimed softly, 'That's him! I wonder . . .' Then, as Huey hadn't moved, he dragged the lad on. Gideon kept up a brisk pace and the two following him were hard put to keep up.

Neither of them saw the woman who ran along the street after them, clutching Gideon's coat in her arms. But she saw them, recognised them too, because she'd seen Shaw a few times at the markets, seen how he scowled at Gideon. It was soon obvious from the way he suddenly came to a halt and moved into a doorway when Gideon stopped to speak to someone that he was following her fellow lodger. And why was he carrying a club?

She slowed down, staying behind them, watching Shaw just as carefully as he was watching Gideon.

When he got to the orphanage, Gideon found people clustered in front of it, while an acrid smell of burning came from the rear.

Lucas was at the front door, fumbling with the lock, so Gideon shoved his way through the crowd towards him, feeling sure this had something to do with him losing the key and feeling desperately guilty about that. 'What can I do to help?' he asked.

As the front door swung open, Lucas turned and said urgently, 'Stop people coming inside. Thanks.'

Gideon nodded and stood blocking the doorway, shouting out in his loudest sergeant's voice, 'Stay back till we see what's happened. Stay back, there, please!'

Inside, Lucas followed the smell of smoke and found one of the watchmen sitting on a chair holding his head while the other was finishing beating out a fire with his coat. A lamp was on the floor beside them with its shutter open, and showed a wet dark patch of what looked like blood nearby. Another lamp had been set down just inside the door.

'Are you hurt?' he asked the man sitting down.

'That sod who broke in cracked a chair over my head while Tom here was ringing the bell.'

'Did you recognise him?'

'Aye. Benting, the fellow as used to be overlooker at the mill.'

'You're sure?'

'I am that. I worked with him for years. I'm sorry we didn't manage to keep him here, Mr Kemp. He struggled like a madman an' I just couldn't hold him.'

Lucas looked at the smouldering pieces of wood. 'You both did well. It was more important to ring the bell and put the fire out.' In hindsight, they'd needed three men here tonight, not two. 'Is the rest of the place all right?'

'I've not checked yet, but I didn't smell any smoke or see any sign of light from other fires, just this one. Benting broke in through the window of the next room so he probably didn't have time to do mischief anywhere else.'

'I'll go round the building quickly now.' Lucas picked up one of the shaded lamps and opened the shutter to give more light, then went back to the front hall. He found Declan there.

'Everything all right?' Gideon called from the doorway.

'Benting broke in and tried to set the place alight. My watchmen stopped him but he escaped. I want to check the rest of the building.'

'All right if I tell people that?' Gideon asked. The ones near him were already spreading the word about who had done this.

'Yes.'

At the back of the crowd Ishleen was watching the man and lad who'd been following Gideon. She knew the lad. It was Benting's son. And the man looked vaguely familiar, but she couldn't quite place him until he turned his head and the light from someone's lantern caught his face full on. She stayed where she was, chatting to a woman she knew from the markets, but all the time she kept her eyes on those two. They were standing there, still looking as if they were watching Gideon, still holding the clubs. Why?

The police sergeant made his way through the crowd, dressed any old how, with a uniformed constable behind him, probably the one who'd been patrolling the town. A short time later Gideon came to the door again and called, 'It was Benting. He tried to set the place on fire, but he failed. You may as well go home. We're going to close the doors and the police will stay here with us till morning. There'll be nothing else to see.' He suited the action to the words.

She could have called out and gone inside with him, ought to have given him his coat because it was a cold night, but something told her to keep watching John Shaw.

He glared at the big doors and turned away. Huey slouched

after him, keeping his head down and a muffler round the lower part of his face.

She followed them, keeping a good distance back, glad she still had her felt house shoes on because they made no noise. It wasn't hard to see where they were going because other people dispersed quickly, peeling off into various nearby streets, talking excitedly. Doors closed behind them with one bang after another.

Her only worry as the streets emptied was keeping herself out of sight.

When the two men started up the lane that led to the moors, she stayed where she was, not daring to go any further. There was nowhere to hide up there and no one to call to for help if they turned on her.

Should she go back and mention the men to Gideon and Declan now, or wait until the morning? She couldn't make up her mind as she turned back towards the town, but her shoes were wet where she'd trodden in a puddle and she was shivering. She swung Gideon's coat round her shoulders and hurried back to Granny's. She'd tell him in the morning.

21

When the two men returned to the cottages, John Shaw turned to Huey and said, 'We'll do it tomorrow night, then.'

Huey nodded and decided to go back home, wondering what had happened to his father, and if it really was his dad who'd tried to set the orphanage on fire. If so, the old man had mucked things up and serve him right for always thinking he knew best how to do anything.

'Come back here quick!'

John sounded upset so Huey ran back to the cottage. The front door was still open but there was no sign of anyone. Cautiously he took a step inside and heard someone moving in the kitchen. Looking over his shoulder to make sure no one was sneaking up on him from behind, he crept along the hallway and looked through the door.

He was shocked to see his father, lower arm covered in blood, confronting John with a knife in his hand. He didn't know what to do, looked from one man to the other in dismay and stayed where he was, away from that knife.

'Look, Benting, I'm not going to turn you over to the police,' John was saying in a low, coaxing voice. 'I'd not do that to anyone. I just want you out of my house.'

'Where would I go? It'll be morning soon and too many people know me. If I stay here till tonight, I can sneak into town and get on a train. Huey can go back home and fetch me some clothes and stuff, then he can buy me a ticket.'

His father was speaking faster than usual, face ghastly white under the sweat and dirt, eyes like deep holes in his face, burning with a wild light. Huey took an involuntary step backwards. If you asked him, his dad had run mad.

John looked across the room. 'Don't go away, lad!'

And somehow, Huey didn't dare disobey.

John came across to shut the door behind him then turned back to Huey's father. 'I'll help you on one condition, Benting.'

'Oh?'

'You kill Gideon Potter for me.'

'How the hell am I going to do that? I won't dare go into town.'

There was silence for a moment as John's forehead creased in thought. 'What if we lure him up here?'

'How the hell do we do that?'

John grinned, but it made Huey shiver, because it wasn't really a smile, more the gloating expression of a man who was going to do something bad and was enjoying the thought of it. 'We capture that lass he's so fond of. He'd do anything to save her. Your son will get her up here, then when he comes after her you can kill him for me.'

'Kill him your damned self!'

'I daren't be seen to be involved or I'll lose all this.' He gestured round him with one hand. 'The police will be looking for you and you'll have to get away, so it'll not matter to you. We won't let the lass see me, so she won't know what's really going on. You can tie me up before you go and I'll claim I had nothing to do with it.' He leaned forward and said slowly and emphatically, 'Do you want me to hide you – or not?'

Benting nodded reluctantly.

'Then do as I ask. Afterwards I'll give you some money to help you and your son escape.'

Huey stared unhappily from one man to the other. He didn't want any part in this, the sight of the blood on his father's arm made him feel sick, but he knew better than to say so. All he could think of was that the minute he saw his way clear, he was going to run away and leave them to do their own dirty work.

Benting muttered something under his breath, plucking absently at the blood-stained muffler that was wound round his arm. 'All right, then. What choice do I have?' He looked down at the makeshift bandage. 'You'd better help me wrap this up properly if you want me to help you. I cut myself on the broken glass.'

'Your son can do that.' John stood up, averting his eyes from the bloody strip of material with a shudder.

Benting sat down suddenly, clutching the edge of the table.

'Are you all right?'

'I will be when someone's seen to this an' I've had a rest. I just feel a bit dizzy like.'

At a head jerk from John, Huey went over to help his father, horrified at how bad the gash was. It began bleeding again as he tried to clean it up and it wouldn't stop for ages. In the end his father shoved him away with a curse for his clumsiness.

'You'll have to help me tie it up, Shaw. He's that clumsy he's only making it worse.'

John hesitated then did this. It seemed to the lad that he turned pale when the blood smeared all over his fingers. After he'd finished, Huey's father stumbled into the front room and lay down on the sofa, closing his eyes. John was too busy washing the blood off to watch him.

'You'd better get what sleep you can, lad,' he said as he wiped his hands. 'You've got a busy day ahead of you.'

It was all right for some, Huey thought rebelliously as he tried to get comfortable on the floor. These old men should do their own dirty work and not make others do it for them. But if he ran away, his dad might come after him and even weak and injured, he still terrified Huey.

Gideon managed only two hours' sleep after the arson attempt, because he stayed at the orphanage for a while talking to police and helping clear up the mess. But it was a market day, so he still had to go to work.

Ishleen came downstairs while he was eating his breakfast with Granny in attendance. 'Is everything all right at the orphanage now?'

'Yes. They can repair the room where the fire was. It's just the floorboards that are damaged, mainly. The watchmen put the fire out quite quickly.'

'Eh, it's a crying shame,' Granny said, as she'd been saying ever since Gideon got up.

'There were two men following you last night.'

He stilled, staring at Ishleen. 'Oh? Are you sure about that?'

'I am, yes. And they were carrying clubs.'

'Do you know who they were?'

'I do. Benting's son and that Shaw fellow who lives in the cottages up on the edge of the moors. They couldn't have been involved in the fire but I was a bit worried about what they wanted with you. I followed them afterwards, when everyone went home, and they both went up the lane to the cottages, but I didn't dare follow them up there.'

He pushed the plate away, losing his appetite suddenly. 'You're sure they were following *me*, not just going to look at the fire?'

'They were definitely following you, but I don't understand why.'

After a moment's thought he told them, explaining that only Declan, Dora and the lawyer knew who he really was.

Granny gaped at him in shock. 'Eh, Gideon, lad! And to think you've been living in my front room. Why, you're rich.'

He shook his head ruefully. 'Hardly rich.'

'I'd think mysen rich if I owned four cottages.'

Ishleen said urgently, 'You'll be taking extra care of yourself from now on, won't you, though?'

'Oh, yes.' He glanced at the clock. 'I'd better go now. Thanks for the warning, Ishleen.' He took the cobra head walking stick with him to market. You didn't need all your fingers to hit someone hard with that.

When Dora got up, she found everyone still discussing the night's happenings, though Carrie and Eli had gone to the church hall to start getting ready for the evening's show. She ate her breakfast and hurried off to the market, where people could talk of nothing but the attempt to burn down the orphanage. They were all amazed that it was Benting who'd done it.

Gideon listened to the talk but said little until they were alone behind the stall. 'Benting got in through the side gate with my key, Dora. It was all my fault.'

'Mine too.'

'No, I was the one who left the key in the lock. I feel bad about that. Anyway, it's just the one room damaged, thank goodness, and we know who did it. That fellow won't be able to hide for long, either. His face is too well known. Someone in the town will see him and then he'll be captured and put in prison.'

'The sooner the better,' she said with a shiver, remembering the time she'd had to fight Benting off at the mill.

When the day's work was finished, Gideon escorted her home. They both kept a watchful eye out for anyone following them but didn't see anyone acting suspiciously.

'Are you working at the church hall tonight?' he asked.

'Yes. I have to change quickly then get down there.'

'I'll wait and walk with you to make sure you're all right.'

'There's no need.'

'I like to make sure you're all right, love. Then I'll come to the second concert and take you home again.' He smiled. 'It's no hardship. I enjoy your company.'

She smiled at him, but her thoughts were on other things. 'There's a dog act tonight, with an old man. It won't be nearly as good as the one in Manchester. Patrick's been staying with us at Linney's and his dog's lovely. It's called Duke after the Duke of Wellington because Patrick served in the Army once, till he'd done his twenty-five years. I'll introduce you to him after the show. You'll be able to talk to him about military things.'

At the church hall she was kept busy helping get the refreshments ready to serve. When the first session began she waited eagerly for the dog act, stopping work to watch it carefully. Patrick looked tired, hardly able to lift one foot in front of the other, and he looked even older on stage, somehow. The dog kept looking at him in puzzlement as if he'd not done something right. Even so, Duke was very clever and no one booed them.

Just before the second act she took some cups of tea through to the performers and found a group of them huddled round a body lying on the floor, all talking excitedly. It was Patrick. Duke was pacing to and fro behind the circle of people, whining loudly.

Dora set down the tray and went to look at Patrick, asking, 'What's the matter? Is he ill?'

The man kneeling beside him said in a hushed voice, 'He's dead, love. Just dropped down dead at my feet. Can you fetch Mr Beckett? We'll have to get the body moved. We've a show to put on.'

She looked down in horror at Patrick, who had been chatting to her only two hours ago. 'How can you be so heartless?'

'Because that's how things are on the stage, love. The show has to go on, whatever happens backstage. It's what Patrick himself would want, we all would.'

Shaken, she ran off to find her brother-in-law. Then Eli and one of the singing minstrels carried the body out. The dog followed his master so Dora went too, keeping a hand on Duke's collar. What was going to happen to the poor creature now? she wondered.

They laid the old man down in a storeroom at the rear of the church hall, in among old hassocks and broken chairs.

'I'll have to write to his agent, see if he has any family,' Eli said. 'In the meantime I'll send for the undertaker and he can keep the body for us.' He looked down as the dog whined. 'What are we going to do with Duke, though?'

'I'll look after him.' Dora stroked the dog, who knew her since he'd been staying at Linney's. Duke turned to flash a quick lick over her hand, then looked back at his master's body. 'He and Nippy get on all right.'

In spite of the gravity of the situation, Eli grinned suddenly. 'And Essie? How are you going to persuade her to take in another dog?'

She rolled her eyes, appreciating just how difficult this would be. 'I don't know. But we can't just turn him into the street, can we? He's a clever animal, valuable.'

'All right. I agree we can't turn him loose.' Eli sighed. 'That leaves me an act short for the second show, though. I suppose I can get some local singers to come and fill in tomorrow, but there's nothing we can do about tonight. I'll have to ask the performers if any of them can sing an extra song or tell another joke.'

An idea suddenly came to Dora and she gasped, clasping Eli's arm in her excitement. 'Why don't Gideon and I go on with Nippy? People will understand that we're just trying it out for the first time, if you explain to them why we're filling in so suddenly.'

He looked at her dubiously. 'Are you up to scratch yet? I've asked you a few times if you want me to see what you're doing, but you've said no.'

'We've got about half an act put together, so it'll be shorter than they usually are. And there's only one way to find out if we're up to scratch, isn't there?' She took a deep breath. 'Me and Gideon can do it, I know we can.'

'Let's go and see what he thinks.'

But when she beckoned Gideon out of the hall and told him what she'd suggested, he stared at her in horror. 'We're not ready to perform in public yet.'

'People will understand, I know they will.'

He opened and shut his mouth then said in a hoarse voice, 'I can't do it. Not yet, not till I'm *sure* everything about the act is all right.'

She looked at him with tears starting in her eyes. 'You have to. It's our big chance to try things out, don't you see?'

'But . . .' He had faced danger and death without flinching, but the thought of going on stage in a hall crammed with people who didn't hesitate to show their opinion of acts they felt weren't good enough . . . well, it filled him with blind terror and that was the truth. 'I'm sorry. I just can't do it yet,' he repeated, shaking his head and taking an involuntary step backwards.

She glared at him. 'Then I'll do it myself. I'm not afraid. Why, half the audience is made up of people I know, and they know Nippy too, from the market. They'll be happy for me to have a go.'

As she flounced off, he looked pleadingly at Eli. 'Don't let her do it.'

Eli looked back at him thoughtfully. 'People will enjoy it if I tell them they're the first people ever to see Mr Nippy doing his act. If you're not going to be able to go on the stage – and I wouldn't blame you for that, because some folk simply can't do it – it's best Dora finds out now and gets herself another partner. I'm sorry if that sounds harsh, but it's better to face things squarely.'

Gideon swallowed, not knowing what to say. But he still felt cold and clammy at the mere thought of getting up on that stage.

'Look, the second show is starting in a minute or two. Can you keep an eye on the body for me till the undertaker arrives? It's out in the storeroom at the back.' Eli turned and walked away, leaving Gideon standing there.

He went slowly out to the storeroom, suddenly becoming aware that he wasn't alone. The dog was following him. When they got to its master's body, Duke whined softly and laid its head against the dead man's hand.

Gideon felt so sorry for the poor animal he forgot his own worries for a moment or two and bent to stroke it. 'It's a bad do, isn't it, lad? Eh, you're a big one, a lot bigger than our Nippy.'

Duke pushed itself against Gideon, as if he needed the human contact, so he continued to stroke the animal's long, soft coat, feeling himself calm down as he talked gently to Duke. He heard applause and the distant sound of Eli's voice. The first act must be going on stage.

A man poked his head round the door of the storeroom. 'Ah, there you are. Is that the deceased?' The undertaker came in and studied the body. 'He went peacefully, you can always tell. Shall we take over here now?'

'Yes.' Gideon led the dog away. For a moment Duke strained

against the hand on his collar, then with a sigh he allowed himself
to be led out. They walked slowly out and Gideon turned into
the nearby church yard, the dog padding along beside him. When
he sat on a raised grave, Duke sat on the ground at his feet and
pushed his head into his hands.

As a cool, damp wind blew round them, Gideon realised with
a start that he'd been sitting there for some time and was chilled
through. He didn't know how much time had passed but hurried
into the hall, terrified of missing Dora and Nippy.

'She's just gone on stage,' one of the serving girls whispered
to him.

He went to the side door that led on to the stage, only then
realising Duke had come with him. Well, there was no time to
take the dog away, so he gestured to the animal to sit down and
stayed where he was, hidden by a big potted plant, watching
Dora. She was completely at ease, explaining to the audience that
she couldn't find Nippy. The dog was playing its usual trick of
standing behind her skirt and already they were laughing and
calling out to her.

Shame flooded through Gideon at his own cowardice and he
squared his shoulders. He had the same feelings as when he'd
been facing enemy fire, but he wasn't going to leave her out there
alone so he let her finish that first part of the act, then strode on
to the stage while the audience was applauding, waiting till they'd
quietened down to stop in pretend shock.

She swung round and gave him a quick smile, but didn't hesitate, simply carried on with what they'd worked out so far as an
act.

Only when they'd gone through their small repertoire of tricks
did he become aware that they were not alone on the stage. Duke
had come out to join them and was sitting at the side, seeming
to be waiting for his turn.

Dora glanced at the animal, then whispered, 'You look after
Nippy. I know what to do.' As Gideon took the smaller dog to
the side of the stage and told him to sit, she walked to the front
of the stage, waited till the audience was quiet and announced,

'This dog's owner died suddenly tonight. He's used to coming on the stage. I don't know if he'll do any of his tricks for me, but I'd like to give it a try if that's all right with you?'

They applauded furiously, shouting encouragement, and the dog got up and went to the front of the stage to woof three times, as if this was a cue. That made them applaud even more loudly.

Dora started doing one of the tricks she'd seen performed earlier in the evening and Duke joined in. She only remembered two or three tricks, so stopped after that and muttered, 'Sit!' To her relief the dog did. She looked down to Eli and nodded.

He banged his Chairman's gavel and stood up. 'I think we should put our hands together for a brave pair of performers and their new dog act. They weren't going to put it on stage yet, but they didn't want you to be missing an act. You'll never forget this night, ladies and gentlemen, because one day Mr Nippy and Miss Dora will be famous, and you were here the very first time they went on stage.'

The applause was mixed with whistles and shouts and stamping feet, and they had to come back on stage a couple of times with the dogs to take extra bows.

When they finally got away, Dora flung her arms round Gideon and he held her tight, shuddering.

'I nearly died of fright,' he whispered. 'That was the hardest thing I've ever done in my whole life.'

She gave him a look of glowing love. 'It'll get easier and look – unless someone claims him, we've now got two dogs for our act, Mr Nippy and the Duke.'

He couldn't resist that look in her eyes. He wasn't sure he would ever be as good as she was on stage, but he'd try his hardest for her sake, because he wanted very much to make her dreams come true. 'I'll walk you home now, shall I?'

'And come in with me to help persuade Essie to let me have another dog?' she pleaded.

At the door, he put out one hand to stop her. 'Look, why don't I take Duke home with me instead? I'm sure Granny won't mind and I'll enjoy his company, to tell you the truth.'

The family at Linney's oohed and aahed over the idea of their Dora performing on the stage, and none of them there to see her, except Eli, Carrie and Raife.

'You should have sent someone to fetch us back,' Essie said reproachfully. 'We'd have gone to the second show instead of the first, if we'd known.'

'I didn't know myself until the last minute. I wasn't even wearing a special stage dress, because there wasn't time to come home and change. That poor man died so suddenly and then – it just happened.' Dora beamed at them. 'I loved it, though, absolutely loved it. And Eli wants us to do it again tomorrow night. *And* he's going to pay us for it.'

Nev looked at Gideon shrewdly. 'And what about you, lad? Did you love it, too?'

He shook his head. 'I was terrified.'

They all laughed, thinking he was exaggerating, but he wasn't.

He pleaded tiredness and walked slowly home, with the dog on its leash. He was accompanied by Declan who just happened to be waiting outside for him, saying he'd been taking a stroll because he couldn't sleep. But it seemed to Gideon that Declan was keeping an eye on him. Had Ishleen said something to her cousin about the men she'd seen following him? He really liked Declan and Ishleen, thought it such a shame that they couldn't marry when they were so clearly in love with one another.

When Gideon and Declan had walked away from Linney's, John Shaw scowled after them from the alley where he'd been hiding. 'What did that Irish bugger have to be hanging around for? We could have nobbled Potter without any trouble, wouldn't have needed the girl.'

Huey was glad about how things had turned out. The longer this went on, the more certain he was that he didn't want to be part of killing anyone.

'Well, we'll just have to find a way of getting hold of *her*. Potter will soon come running then. Let's go round the back and see if the dog's out there.'

They walked along the lane at the rear of Linney's and stood peering into the yard, bobbing down out of sight when the back door opened.

'Be a good boy, Nippy,' Dora said.

As the dog scampered out to relieve itself, someone called from inside the house and she went in, leaving the door open and light streaming out.

'Here's our chance,' John hissed. 'Here, take the sack and throw it over him.'

Huey climbed up on the wall and Nippy stared up at him, growling in his throat. The lad looked down on the dog, which had grown up to be an alert little thing. By a lucky chance he chucked the sack over Nippy first go. He jumped down and grabbed the bundle before the dog could wriggle out from under the sack, passing it to John then clambering quickly back over the wall.

As the two ran off down the lane, Shaw chuckled. 'That were well done. She'll do anything to get her dog back, that one will. I've seen her with it and you'd think it was her baby, the way she treats it.'

Huey had a sudden memory of his mother bending over the new baby, her face filled with tender love, and a pang shot through him. 'We're not going to hurt the dog, are we?'

Shaw stared at him. 'Not till after she's come to us, we're not. After that, you can cut its throat.'

Huey knew by now to keep silent when Shaw gave such orders. He didn't like the man, resented the way he'd been treated by him during the past day or two and wasn't looking forward to running off with his father, either. Let alone *he* hadn't done owt against the law, unless you counted stealing a dog tonight or a few little fights – and everyone he knew got into a fight or two. He didn't want to spend the rest of his life under his father's thumb.

The dog was wriggling in the sack and managed to get its sharp little teeth round one of his fingers. He yelped. 'The damned thing just bit me.'

Shaw laughed. 'Well, you'll get your own back on it later, won't you? Now, let's shut that thing up in the outhouse, then I'll write a note to *her*. You can go back into town and find a way of getting it to her.'

'How the hell do you expect me to do that?'

'I don't know and I don't care. But you'd better do it if you want me to help your father to escape.'

As he walked slowly and reluctantly into town with John's note to Dora stuffed into his pocket, Huey seriously considered running away. But he had only a few coins and there were no trains in the middle of the night, so he couldn't. He didn't want to go home, either, now his mother was dead. It still upset him to think that she'd gone, would never give him a hug and tell him he was her dear, naughty lad again.

He went round the back way to Linney's and couldn't believe his luck when he found Dora out in the back alley, calling to someone else who was also searching for Nippy. He didn't want her screaming out so waited till she'd gone a bit further along the alley, then grabbed her. Putting one hand over her mouth, he tucked her under his arm and dragged her along. She kicked and wriggled desperately, but he managed to keep her quiet until he got a bit further away.

Judging that he was out of earshot of her family, he stopped and shook her to make her listen, then said in a low voice, 'We've got that Nippy of yours. If you want to see the dog alive, you'd better not scream.'

When he took his hand cautiously away from her mouth, she sobbed but didn't make any loud noises.

'I'll pay you anything you like to bring him back. Please don't hurt him,' she pleaded.

'The man that's got him says you've to come with me. That way, you can see the dog and we can – um – talk about money. So you'd better keep quiet and hurry up. The man isn't very patient.'

He could see her considering this and tensed, ready to grab her again.

'You promise me Nippy's all right?'

'Yes.'

'Why are you doing this?'

'For the money.'

'I'll come. But I won't pay you anything if you've hurt him.' She finished on another sob.

He couldn't believe she'd be daft enough to risk her life for a dog, but John had known she would. He was clever, that one was, but squeamish with it, went pale at the mere sight of blood, the silly sod. Well, Huey didn't like blood either, but he wasn't as bad as John was. And his dad could kill Gideon Potter if he wanted, but Huey wasn't going to do it. Killing a dog was one thing – people killed them all the time and no one would lock him in prison for that – but killing a man would bring the police chasing after him and they wouldn't stop till they caught him. Mind you, it'd be harder to kill such a clever dog. He wished he had one like that.

Keeping hold of her arm he marched Dora at a brisk pace up towards the cottages and when she tried to say something, told her to shut up.

Nev poked his head out of the back yard gate and called out into the darkness of the alley behind the houses, 'Dora! Where are you, lass?' But there was no answer. He called again then hurried back into the house. 'She didn't answer.'

They looked at one another, frowning. 'She said she was just going a few steps down the alley to call for him,' Essie said. 'It's not like her to go further without telling us.'

Carrie stood up. 'I'm going out to look for her. She shouldn't be out there on her own at this time of night.'

Eli stood and caught hold of her arm. 'You're not going out on your own, either, love. In fact, it'd be better if you women stayed at home and us men went out to look for her.'

'You're right. We'll go straight away and I'll give her what for when we find her for worrying us like that.' Nev walked purposefully towards the back door.

'I'm coming too,' Ted said. 'If anyone's hurt my sister . . .'

'You go with Nev. Raife can come with me,' Eli said. 'We'll split up and go in different directions.'

When the door had closed behind the men, the women looked at one another. 'I don't like being left behind,' Carrie muttered.

'I think you and me should go out and look for Dora as well,' Edith said mutinously. 'Men think they're the only ones who can do anything.'

'They're a lot stronger than you lasses are, that's why.' Essie began to clatter pots around, then stopped. 'But you could go and tell our Gideon. That's only just down the road. *He* could join in the search. He'd want to.'

'Good idea.' Carrie bounced to her feet again. 'And just let anyone try to stop us.'

They were out of the house and clattering down the street within the minute, arriving at Granny's house breathless, to bang on the door and call his name.

Gideon peered through the window of the front room where he slept, and came to open the door, staring at them in shock. 'What's the matter?'

'Dora's missing. She sent Nippy out into the yard and when she went out to get him, he wasn't there, even though the gate was locked. She went out into the back alley to look for him, just in case he'd wriggled out somehow, only she vanished as well. The men are out looking for her and we thought you'd want to help.'

'I do. I'll get dressed and come with you straight away.'

The three of them went back to Linney's. 'No use me going out till I know where the others have looked,' Gideon said, but the way he paced up and down the kitchen showed how worried he was, how anxious to do something.

A short time later the men came back, to report no sign of her in the streets nearby.

'We'll divide up the town and carry on searching,' Eli said. 'I can't believe she's gone so far on her own. Something must have happened to her or to Nippy. She wouldn't leave him if he was hurt. She thinks the world of that dog.'

The men got ready to leave again and this time Carrie insisted on going with Eli, making it three pairs of searchers. They agreed to come back an hour later to report progress.

'And if we've not found her, we're going to knock up the police sergeant,' Gideon said.

'There'll be no need to knock him up by that time,' Essie pointed out. 'It's nearly dawn now.'

When they got to the cottage, Huey stopped and said to Dora, 'I need to cover your eyes. Hold still and remember your dog if you're tempted to call out.'

She let him use a dirty handkerchief to cover her eyes, but he did it clumsily and she could see a little from beneath it.

'Start walking.' She hesitated but he gave her a shove so she moved cautiously forward, stumbling over the doorstep and hearing a door slam behind them.

John poked his head out of the kitchen to see who'd just come in by the front door, the wolf smile coming on to his face again as he saw who it was. He put one finger to his lips and pointed up the stairs.

When Huey looked at him in bewilderment, he moved close and whispered in the lad's ear, 'Lock her in the front bedroom. Tie her up to a chair first. I'll get you some rope.' He went back into the kitchen and came out again with a piece cut off the clothes line, which he thrust into Huey's hand.

'Go up the stairs now,' Huey said loudly to Dora. He shoved her forward and when she half fell over the bottom step, hauled her to her feet and said, 'Go on.'

Dora felt in front of her with her foot and began climbing the stairs, too afraid of them hurting Nippy to protest. At the top she put her foot on a stair that didn't exist and stumbled forward. Huey laughed and shoved her forward again. Before she realised what he was doing, he'd tied her arms behind her and shoved her down on a bed. She still had the handkerchief over her eyes and was terrified that no one had even mentioned her dog. Surely they hadn't killed him? If so, why did they want her?

She shouldn't have come. But then she'd not had much choice, because Huey was much stronger than she was.

The minute she heard a key turn in the door, she rubbed her face against the bedcovers and got the blindfold off. But it was very dark and she could only see the dark shapes of a few pieces of furniture. She waited a minute for her eyes to get used to the dimness and swung her feet off the bed, finding it hard to sit up with her hands tied behind her. Now that the room was quiet she could hear Nippy yelping and barking somewhere. Relief shuddered through her. He was still alive then.

She had to find a way to escape and save him. Huey Benting had tried to kill him once.

'How did you manage to capture her?' John asked when he came down.

Huey shrugged. 'I fell lucky. She was out in the back alley looking for that dog, so I just grabbed her, then told her we'd got hcr dog and she come along all peaceful.'

'Well, done! You can go and kill that damned dog now. I shut it in the outhouse, but it's been yelping and barking. The neighbours have banged on the wall twice about it.' He mimed cutting his throat and thrust a sharp knife into the lad's hand. 'Hurry up. You can do it while I write another note for Potter telling him we've got his lady love. You can wrap this new note round a stone and chuck it through his bedroom window. He sleeps on the ground floor at the front in Granny Horne's.'

'Why don't you do it?'

'I told you, I don't want to be seen.'

'My dad, then.'

'He's asleep still. That man could sleep through a battle, never seen anyone like him.'

'Can I get myself a cup of tea first?' Huey asked. 'I'm tired and thirsty.'

'You can have one when you come back from taking the note. Now go and kill that damned dog. Its howling is driving me mad.'

Huey took a candle and went out at the back, guarding the

flame with one hand and holding the kitchen knife in the other. He didn't want to do this, was sure it'd bite him if he tried. For a little dog, it was very brave. Who'd have thought that scruffy little pup would have turned out so well? He looked back at the house and scowled. He was fed up with being ordered around.

When he opened the outhouse door and held up the candle, the dog took a step towards him, not growling this time, but whining as if to ask what was going on. He closed the door behind himself, fumbled for the knife and took a step forward.

Nippy held his head on one side and gave a tentative wag.

Huey stopped and brandished the knife but the dog wagged again. He couldn't bring himself to stab it when it was trying to be friends. He'd seen it with people at the markets. Everyone liked Nippy. Even his friends did now. They'd thump him if he killed the dog. But Shaw would thump him if he didn't kill it. 'Stop doing that,' he muttered. 'I don't want to kill you, but I have to.'

As he stretched out one hand to catch it by the collar the dog thought he wanted to shake hands and held out its paw. It seemed to smile at him. Dismayed, he took a hasty step backwards. The dog darted across the shed, picked up a stick and dropped it at his feet.

The hand holding the knife trembled. He tried to nerve himself for a quick stab, but he couldn't, he just couldn't.

'It's all very well for you,' he said. 'But if I go back and he hears you barking again, he'll thump me, and he's a big fellow, nasty with it too.'

The dog brought him another stick.

Then the solution suddenly came to him. If he let it go, it would go back into town, then there wouldn't be any more barking. He stepped to one side and held the door open. 'Go on! Get out.' He aimed a kick at it which it avoided easily, then watched as it rushed out of the shed and vanished into the darkness.

He stood there for a moment longer then slowly grinned. He'd got rid of the dog, hadn't he? He couldn't imagine John or his father coming out to check on the dead body of an animal.

22

Someone came to the front door of Linney's and banged the knocker hard.

'Peep out of the parlour window and see who it is before you open it!' Essie said at once.

Edith did so. 'It's only Ishleen.' She went to open the door.

Their friend came in, looking anxious and carrying a crumpled piece of paper. 'Is Gideon here?'

'No, he's out looking for Dora.'

Ishleen held the piece of paper out to Essie. 'Someone threw this through the window of his bedroom, wrapped round a chunk of cobblestone. I'm not very good with the reading, but if it says what I think it does, he needs to know at once.'

Essie smoothed it out and read the smudged words aloud:

Potter,

If you want to keep that lass of yours alive, come up to the moors by the lane that leads past those cottages and don't bring anyone with you. If the police are called in, you'll never even find her body.

There was a moment's horrified silence, then Edith exclaimed, 'Who could this be from? Who'd threaten our Dora? I can't—'

Ishleen interrupted her. 'Never mind that. We need to get this to Gideon quickly. Do you know where he is?'

'He and Raife were searching the centre of town. Shall I run down and see if I can find him?' Edith volunteered.

'I'll come with you,' Ishleen said at once. 'Two are safer than one. It's still dark out there.'

They left without another word, leaving Essie with the two younger girls, who came to sit near her for comfort.

'Our Dora will be all right, no one really means to hurt her, I'm sure. And she's a sensible lass.' But Essie's words lacked conviction and she hugged Lily close as the child began to cry, blinking her own eyes furiously.

Ishleen and Edith ran down to the town centre and risked calling out for Gideon. Footsteps came pounding towards them and he ran out of a side road into Market Street with Raife panting along some distance behind.

'Has she been found?' he asked eagerly.

'No. But someone threw a message about her through your bedroom window. It's bad news.' Ishleen held the piece of paper out to him and he moved over to stand under one of the gas lamps near the Town Hall.

He read it in silence, then read it again, looking at them with an anguished expression. 'Even if I go, there's no guarantee she'll be safe. They could kill us both, probably intend to.'

'Do you know why they want you?'

'I can guess. It has to be the impostor. He wants to get rid of me and he's made a few attempts already.'

'What do you mean by "the impostor"?' Edith asked.

He explained briefly and she looked at him in amazement.

'You've been in Hedderby all this time without getting your aunt's cottage back? How could you stand it?'

'You have to have proof to take property off someone. That fellow had my belongings to prove he was me, but I had only a few bits and pieces left, nothing to show who I really was – until recently. I've got my proof now and we're only waiting for the Army to take action. If they'd acted more quickly, we'd not have had this trouble because *he* would be safely locked up.'

'What are we going to do about Dora, then?' Raife asked. 'If you go to them, you'll be in danger. Only we can't leave her in their hands, can we?'

'I'll have to go, otherwise I'll be putting Dora's life at risk, but I'll scout round the place first and see if I can surprise them.'

'You should take the police with you, son.'

'I daren't. If that fellow sees anyone else with me, he'll kill Dora for sure.' Gideon started walking. 'I just need to pick up a few things from Granny's first.'

James Forrett sighed and looked at the police sergeant, then at the fire-damaged room. 'Well, I suppose we'd better go home now. If we leave the two watchmen here, everything should be safe enough. Benting won't try twice in one night, especially if he's been injured. It's nearly dawn now. I can find some other men to send across as soon as the mill starts up. Hang the yard work, we need to keep this place safe.'

The sergeant nodded. 'And meantime I'll send my men out to look for Benting. He can't have got away by train because there aren't any trains in the middle of the night. I'll have a man at the station before the milk train arrives so he can't catch that. I don't reckon he can have walked far, because if the puddle on the floor was anything to judge by, he was bleeding like a stuck pig.'

'He must be hiding out in someone's house,' James said, frowning in thought. 'But which one? I've a good mind to—' He slapped a hand down on his thigh. 'I'll do it!'

'Do what?'

'Close the mill and send all my operatives out searching. There's enough of 'em to visit every single house.'

The sergeant goggled at him then chewed his thumb for a few seconds. 'That'd only work if we divided up the town and did this properly. I've a map and list of streets at the station.'

'Go and get it then, and I'll stop my engineer from firing up the steam engine.' James gave a wry smile. 'I'll still be paying them, and I've no doubt those lasses will enjoy a day away from the spindles.' His expression was very determined. 'We have to capture Benting as quickly as we can because I reckon he's run mad and who knows what he'll try next?'

He stared at the sergeant as another thought occurred to him.

'What about his children? Has anyone thought of them? If he's out causing trouble, who's looking after them? Some of them are quite little still. I don't like to think of them going hungry. It's not their fault they've a father like that.' He sighed and added quietly. 'And I won't have them suffering for it.'

All the way back to Granny's the two women tried to persuade Gideon to get help before going after Dora, but in vain. Each of them kept an eye out for the other searchers so that they could send them with him, but the streets were disappointingly empty.

'Gideon, please don't rush off like this,' Ishleen pleaded.

'I'm not giving him time to hurt her.' He pulled a short knife in a leather sheath out of a drawer and fitted it into the side of his boot, muttering, 'You should have taken this off me when you took everything else, Tolson! If you've hurt one hair of her head, I'll be sticking it into you.' Then he picked up the cobra-headed walking stick and hefted it in his hand. 'Or thumping you with this.'

He strode out of the house and the two women followed him along the street, running to keep up. He turned briefly to say, 'Go back!' then continued walking.

The big dog slipped out of the half-open door and set off after them.

Ishleen moved faster, tugging at his arm to slow him down. 'There are dry-stone walls running alongside that lane, Gideon. Edith and I could follow you on the other side of them, then you could call out for help if you needed it. They couldn't kill all of us.'

He didn't even slow down. 'You'd do better to find Declan and send him after me. He'd be the one most capable of helping me. A man like Tolson wouldn't hesitate to hurt women.'

She saw how stubborn his expression was and stopped walking, nudging Edith to do the same. Not until Gideon was out of earshot did she say, 'Go and fetch Declan, tell him to get after us as quickly as he can.'

'After *us*?'

'Whatever Gideon says, I'm going to follow him. I may be able to help, if only to distract them. I have to try.' She set off running again, desperately worried about Dora's safety as well as Gideon's. That lass had helped her when she was nearly dead, and if Ishleen could help her now, she would.

At the bottom of the lane she clambered over the wall and started moving along it. But she had to slow down on the rougher ground and was worried that she was falling further and further behind Gideon. She kept her body bent so that she'd be hidden from anyone in the lane and that slowed her down even more.

Gideon stopped before he came to the cottages and slipped through a gate to crouch behind the wall and observe everything carefully for a minute or two in the grey light of the false dawn. As he did so, a small body hurtled into him and nearly knocked him over. Nippy began licking him, yipping with delight.

'Shh. Shh, now.' He picked the dog up, held it in his arms for a minute, caressing its wiry coat, then set it down. Pointing, he said sternly, 'Go home!'

The dog went a few paces, turned round and looked at him pleadingly.

'Go – home!'

Nippy trotted off but once he was out of sight he stopped again, going back to peep at Gideon who was now approaching the cottages from the side, trying to remain hidden.

Another dog came trotting up. Duke sniffed at the smaller animal and Nippy went instantly into a subservient position, lying on his back, belly exposed. Satisfied, Duke gave him a quick lick of approval then set off after Gideon with Nippy following.

From behind the wall, Ishleen saw them and risked calling, 'Here, boy! Duke, come here!'

Duke stopped again, looking round for the owner of the voice, which he recognised.

She moved to a gap in the wall and patted her skirt, repeating, 'Here, boy!'

Both dogs walked across, standing looking at her for a moment before moving right up to sniff her thoroughly and recognise her as a friend. Then they sat down and stared up at her as if to ask, 'What do we do now?'

She didn't know what to do, because Gideon had gone round the back of the house, still trying to stay out of sight. The trouble was, she was sure she'd seen the curtain of the front room twitching. And if they'd seen him coming, they'd be waiting for him.

When Dora wriggled off the bed and stood upright, she began to search for something to free her of the rope which bound her hands behind her back. By that time the faint light of early dawn was filtering through the window, and as her eyes were now used to the darkness she could study the room in more detail.

It didn't take her long to realise that the only possibility for getting the rope off was a rough brick fireplace. Maybe if she rubbed the rope against one of the brick edges, it'd fray enough for her to free herself. She had to try that. There was absolutely nothing else to help her in this room.

It was very difficult to move her hands about accurately behind her back, but she kept at it, sawing the rope on the rough edge of the bricks again and again.

She was starting to despair of anything happening when she felt a strand break, then another. Her arms felt like lead because of the awkward, half-crouching position so she rested for a while, but as soon as she could, she started again. She knew there were other people living in the adjoining cottages and hoped at the very least to attract their attention before the men could silence her. But she wouldn't do that until Gideon arrived. She was worried sick about him and Nippy. She intended to shout out and warn him. They weren't going to kill her man if she had anything to do with it. Or her dog.

When the rope at last parted, she groaned in relief but it was a few moments before she could move her arms properly again. She was terrified Huey or his father would come upstairs to check on her and didn't dare move any furniture to prevent the door being opened because they'd be sure to hear her.

When he'd dumped her on the bed, Huey had warned her gruffly that he'd come and knock her out if she made any noise. But then he'd left without checking anything except that the rope round her wrists was secure. It seemed to her that he couldn't get away from her quickly enough.

The first thing she did was check every inch of the room and furniture properly, but she found nothing that might help her get the door open, no possible weapon to defend herself with, either. The place smelled musty, as if it hadn't been used for years, and although there were spare sheets in the drawers, there were no personal possessions or ornaments anywhere.

Tears came into her eyes when she closed the last drawer quietly, but she refused to give way to despair, so went back to stand by the window and keep watch. It looked out on to the back of the cottages, where there was a communal yard with a row of outhouses at the far side of it. Everything had looked dull and grey when she first freed herself, but now sunrise was painting the clouds. As she watched the whole sky seemed to fill with glorious light and beyond the low huddle of buildings, the clouds above the moors slowly turned red and gold.

She couldn't help wondering if it was the last sunrise she'd ever see.

Suddenly she stiffened as a figure darted from the side of the house to move behind the outhouses. As the man peered out from the opening in the middle of the row of outhouses, she recognised Gideon. Well, she'd know him anywhere now.

Had he come to rescue her? If so, he'd need other men to help him. She'd glimpsed Benting sleeping on a couch through the poorly tied blindfold and then the impostor. That didn't surprise her. It was he who stood to gain most if anything happened to Gideon.

And she who would lose most! Oh, please, don't let them hurt him!

She pressed her face against the window and waved her hands, willing the crouching figure to look up at her, but he didn't. All his attention was on the back door of the cottage.

He didn't see the man who crept round the side of the cottage after him, a cudgel in his hand.

But she did! She tried to slide the lower half of the window up, but couldn't budge it. She looked round for something to break the glass with, but the only chair in the room was a heavy one and even as she raised her fist to hammer on the window, the second man crept up behind Gideon and raised the cudgel.

Some instinct seemed to warn Gideon because at the last minute he swung round, raising his walking stick to counter the blow. The attacker jumped backwards and yelled, 'Come and help me, you fools!'

Dora gasped in horror as Benting came stumbling out of the cottage, brandishing a knife, with a bloody cloth tied round his arm. Then she stared in puzzlement as Huey followed his father out. He looked round and then, instead of helping the two older men, he ran away round the side of the house. His father bellowed after him, but he didn't even turn his head.

As Benting turned back to help the impostor capture Gideon, Dora put one hand up to her mouth, letting out an anxious moan.

'If you don't do as we say, we'll kill your lass,' Shaw threatened. 'Come inside the house this minute.' He cast an anxious glance at the other cottages.

'If I do that, you'll kill her anyway and me with her,' Gideon replied, keeping the stick poised ready to hit out at them.

'There are three of us here,' Benting said. 'You'll not get away.'

Gideon raised his voice and called out loudly, 'I see only two and one of them injured, so I'll chance my luck. I know how to fight.' He hefted the stick to emphasise his words.

The door of another cottage opened and a voice called, 'What are you doing?'

They all looked in that direction to see a man standing at the door of the second cottage.

'We've caught a thief,' Shaw said quickly. 'Help us tie him up then we can hand him over to the police.'

When Ishleen saw the impostor come out of the front door and creep round the back of the house after Gideon, she knew it was time for her to do something. Calling the dogs to come with her she clambered over a broken bit of wall and began running towards the cottages. She slowed down as she went towards the side, walking on a soft grassy strip of ground so that her footsteps would make no noise. The dogs stayed behind her, as if they knew not to go ahead and spoil the surprise.

A figure ran round the corner towards her, nearly bowling her over. Huey Benting. She recognised him by sight.

He yelled in fright and put out one arm to fend her off, speeding up once he'd got past her. She watched in open-mouthed astonishment as he vanished down the lane, then she turned back, determined to help Gideon.

As she rounded the corner, she saw him held at bay by two men, one armed with a cudgel, the other with a knife. She heard the impostor say to another man standing in a cottage doorway, 'We've caught a thief.'

'That's not true!' she cried, running forward but keeping out of range of their weapons. 'He's *not* a thief. He's come to rescue his lass from these two.'

As if on cue, Dora began knocking on the window, hammering with all her might and calling out to them.

'See!' Ishleen pointed up to the bedroom window. 'There she is.'

The neighbour had been staring open-mouthed at the sight of the woman and two growling dogs. When he heard sounds from above, he edged out of his doorway, keeping a wary eye on the group of men, and looked up at the window of the end house.

Shaw seized the moment when everyone's attention was distracted to swipe his cudgel at Gideon, knocking him sideways, then he ran off round the cottages. Seeing two men coming along the lane towards him, he turned and headed for the moors, cursing under his breath as he ran up the slope beyond the cottages.

The dogs started after him, but Ishleen called, 'Heel!' in as loud a voice as she could manage, knowing it was one of Nippy's commands. To her relief, both dogs stopped, quivering as if they wanted to run after the fleeing man.

Benting also turned to run but he staggered and spun into a wall, holding on to it as if he was dizzy. The knife he'd been holding fell to the ground.

The neighbour stepped forward to stand beside him. 'Shall I keep an eye on him, missus, while you let that lass out and tend to this fellow?'

'There may be someone else inside,' she said.

'Nay, there were nobbut three on 'em, and the missus saw the lad run off down the hill just now.'

Ishleen picked up the club Benting had dropped, hurried into the cottage, going straight up the stairs and unlocking the door of the back bedroom.

When Dora saw who it was, she burst into tears and fell into her friend's arms for a minute.

'Come on down, love. Gideon needs our help. He's been hit on the head.'

'Who's that?' Declan asked as a figure came flying down the lane towards them, not even seeming to notice them. He grabbed the runner's arm and the lad let out a yell of pure panic as Declan swung him round to face them. 'It's Benting's son!'

Huey realised who had hold of him and began to struggle wildly, yelling, kicking and punching, but he was no match for Declan and Kevin Reilly, who soon subdued him.

'What were you running from?' Declan demanded. 'And you'd better tell us the truth or we'll hand you over to the police.'

Huey looked from one stern face to the other and sagged in visible despair. 'No, don't do that! I didn't want to be in any of it. They made me! She's all right, just tied up. I didn't hurt her, I didn't.' As their grim expressions didn't change, he added desperately, 'I didn't even kill the dog. I let it run off.'

'Who's tied up?'

'Dora Preston.'

'Have you seen Gideon Potter?'

'He turned up just now. They're going to kill him. It's not fair to blame me for that. I didn't want to do it so I ran away. Let me *go* or my dad will come after me!' He began to struggle even more wildly and almost got away from them.

With a grunt of annoyance, Kevin punched him on the chin and watched as he fell senseless. He bent to tie Huey's hands behind him with the lad's muffler, then used his own to tie his feet, working rapidly, then stepping over the unconscious figure. 'Sounds like we'd better hurry up.'

The two men set off again up the lane.

As the women helped Gideon and Benting into the cottage, Declan and Kevin turned up.

Declan's first thought was for Ishleen. 'Are you all right?'

She nodded. 'It's Gideon who's hurt, though not badly, and we've got Benting, though the impostor ran away.'

They sat Benting on a chair in the corner and he sagged down in it, his face white where it wasn't dirty, his whole body speaking of defeat.

'I doubt it's any use going after the other bugger,' Declan said. 'I never saw anyone run so fast and I'm not a good runner, myself.' He looked down ruefully at his heavy, muscular body.

'Me neither,' Kevin agreed.

'We'd better let the police know about him. Will you do that, Kevin, and I'll stay here?'

'Yes.' He grinned as he stood. 'It's all downhill to the town.'

But as he reached the first houses, he found a party of spinning lasses searching every dwelling in that road for the fugitives. They told him that Forrett had sent all his employees out to search the town.

Kevin chuckled at their high spirits. 'Benting's been caught and the other fellow ran off across the moors, so you can go back to work now.'

'I'm not in a hurry,' one replied with a saucy smile. 'We'll go up on the moors and see if we can find him. He can't hurt four of us. If we do find him, we'll sit on him till help comes.'

'It's the police who'll be doing the hunting.'

But they went off anyway, glad of an excuse not to return to the mill.

Kevin went on to the police station to report what had happened and had to explain about who Gideon really was.

'We have to catch that other fellow,' the sergeant said with a frown. 'Tolson, did you say his real name was?'

'Yes. He may be making for the village where his mistress lives. I followed him there once.'

The sergeant asked stiffly, 'You didn't think to tell me about all this before?'

'Gideon's lawyer – Mr Burtell – advised him to keep everything secret till he could prove who he was.'

'Hmm. Well, I'll send two men to see this woman. In fact, I'll go with one of them myself on the next train. My rank will make the village constable do as we ask and keep a watch out for Tolson.' He pulled his watch out of his waistcoat pocket and looked at it. 'The next train leaves in half an hour. Excuse me.'

Gideon refused to go back into town and instead took possession of his aunt's house, looking round nostalgically at the pieces of furniture, many of which he recognised. Dora stayed with him, so after exchanging glances, Declan and Ishleen did as well.

'Just to be sure he's safe,' Declan whispered to Ishleen. 'That fellow might come back.'

'Sure, he can't be so stupid!'

The four of them walked slowly round the house. It needed a good cleaning, not to mention a great deal of fresh air to blow away the smell of the clay pipes to which Tolson had been addicted, to judge from the broken ones lying to one side of the hearth.

'I remember this,' Gideon said, pointing to the clock. 'It always had such a loud, cheerful tick.'

'It needs winding up.' Declan picked it up and looked for the winder key, which was nearby on the mantelpiece. He inserted it, but couldn't turn it.

'Let me.' Gideon smiled. 'There used to be a trick to it if I remember rightly.' He tipped the clock slightly to one side then back again, seeing a mental picture of his aunt doing exactly that. The key turned a little more and the back popped open, to display a soft leather bag tucked in among the machinery.

He let out an exclamation and pulled it out. 'This was mine. I had it on the ship coming back. I kept my savings in it.' Opening it, he tipped a pile of guineas on to the table, counting them quickly and sighing in relief. 'He hasn't spent much. I'll put this in the savings bank tomorrow.'

They went upstairs, Dora shuddering at the sight of the main bedroom, which was in far worse state than downstairs, the sheets grey with long use and a sour smell coming from a pile of dirty underclothes in one corner.

'I'm getting a new mattress before I use this room,' Gideon said grimly.

They went on to the attic, where a trunk lay open. Inside bright colours gleamed.

'My wife's saris,' Gideon said in a choked voice. 'I hate to think of him pawing through them.'

'We'll soon put them straight,' Ishleen said soothingly. 'Are you going to move in here?'

'In a day or two. First I'm going to get the place cleaned from top to bottom.'

'We can do that for you,' Dora said.

He turned to smile at her, putting one arm round her shoulders and taking hold of her hand with his free one. 'I'll find someone else to do the heavy scrubbing, love. You can't go on the stage with red hands. Anyway, I've money now, so there's no need for you ever to do dirty chores.'

She smiled at him. 'I'm not frightened of hard work.'

'I know, love. But nonetheless we'll get someone else in.'

'Is no one else hungry?' Declan asked. 'Because I am. I think it's about time we went back into town and got our breakfasts.

We're supposed to be working today. We can lock this place up and ask the neighbours to keep an eye on it.'

In fact, when they spoke to the woman next door, she at once volunteered her own and the next neighbour's services to clean the place out.

'I've been itching to do that since poor old Mrs Haskill passed away. She'd have been horrified to see what he's let it get like.'

'Do that and we'll forget your rent this week,' Gideon offered. 'Your friend's too.'

Her beaming smile said she was pleased with that bargain. 'And I'll take the spare key off the back lintel too,' she said. 'We don't want to leave the place unlocked. Though I can't see him coming back, can you?'

Her cheerfulness brightened the morning and made things seem normal again after all the trouble they'd seen.

'We'd better get down to the markets. Can't let people down, can we?' Gideon moved towards the door. 'I'll just lock up and be with you in a minute or two.'

When they went outside, the two dogs were sitting there waiting. They frisked around them as they walked down the hill, adding to the wholesome normality of the now sunny day.

'Will the police catch him, do you think?' Dora asked.

'Bound to,' Gideon said, though he wasn't sure of that. Tolson was a cunning devil.

23

When all the mill lasses had gone out searching, James went to find his wife and told her about Benting's children.

'We can't leave them there alone,' she said at once.

'Well, I'm not bringing them here. Maybe we can pay a woman to look after them.'

She looked at him and smiled. 'You've forgotten something.'

'What?'

'You have an orphanage. They're as good as orphans now.'

He blinked, then shook his head, both amused and surprised. 'I suppose so.'

'Shall we go and see Lucas and Gwynna? They're the ones who'll have to look after them. I know the orphanage isn't officially opened yet, but if some of them are quite small they'll need looking after.'

'Get your coat and hat, then. We'll do this together.'

They went first to Lucas's house, catching him and his wife at home, with a row full of children standing in the kitchen as Gwynna examined their hands for cleanliness.

'Can we have a word in private with both of you?' James asked, looking with approval at the neat and tidy children.

'I'll keep an eye on this lot and give them their breakfasts,' Lucas's uncle said.

Gwynna led the way into the front parlour and there, James explained about Benting's children.

'Doesn't it matter that he tried to burn your orphanage down?' Lucas asked, amazed at the man's generosity.

James shook his head, then gave him a twisted smile. 'It's strange how things turn out, isn't it?'

'We must go round to see the children straight away,' Gwynna said.

When they got to the small house in the lanes, they found two very young children sitting clutching one another in a corner, while an older girl was folding some women's clothing and an older lad was playing with some bits of wood, which he was building into a neatly constructed wall.

The older girl looked at them in alarm. 'We haven't done anything wrong, Mr Forrett!'

'Nay, who said you had?'

'Have you found my dad?'

'They're out looking for him.'

'What about our Huey?'

'They've found him. The police have him locked up.'

Tears ran down the girl's face. 'Huey didn't want to help Dad. But Dad belts him if he doesn't do as he's told.'

'What are you doing there?' Charis asked.

Renie gestured to the pile of clothes. 'I thought we could take some of them to the pawn shop. That's not wrong, is it? Mam can't use them now and there's no money in the house, so we haven't had anything to eat today.'

Gwynna went across to put an arm round her. 'Why don't you all come home with me? I'll give you some food.'

'Thank you. But what will we do tomorrow?' Renie's eyes filled with more tears. 'Mam told me to look after the little ones if anything happened to her, but I don't know how.'

'You know Mr Forrett is opening an orphanage?' Gwynna said, still keeping her arm round the girl. 'It's for children like you who haven't got families to look after them.'

Renie pulled away. 'I've heard about those places. They're like the workhouse, treat you badly, whip you if you do anything wrong.'

'Not our orphanage. I promise you: we don't whip children. And if you don't like it there, you can leave, I promise you.'

Renie looked at her, still suspicious. 'What will Dad say?'

'He won't say anything. He'll be in prison for trying to burn down the orphanage. They've caught him as well.'

'Oh, no!'

Gwynna tried to distract her from that sad news. 'I'm going to need your help, because we're only just starting the orphanage and we need to get all sorts of things ready. You'll be the oldest girl there and you'll be helping me with the little ones.'

Renie gave her a suspicious glance, then the youngest child began to cry and ask for a piece of bread and she went to cuddle it for a minute before looking back at Gwynna and saying grudgingly, 'We could give it a try.'

'Come and see where you'd be living. I'm sure you'll like it and we can all move in this very day.'

As Gwynna led the way out, Lucas picked up one small child and Charis the other. Then they went by way of the workshop to collect the other children, because Gwynna didn't want them feeling left out in this first view of the orphanage.

Charis was talking to the little girl she was carrying and James watched her, bemused. He hadn't known she was good with little children.

As he trailed behind, looking at the motley group of children, a lump came into his throat. Fancy Benting's own children being among the first to take refuge in the orphanage the man had tried so hard to destroy. Fate played some strange tricks on you sometimes, it did that.

He paused to look at the sign outside the front door of the orphanage, with his dead daughter's name on it, nodded to it then followed the others inside.

By that time Gwynna was working her usual magic. He'd never seen anyone as good with children as she was. And Lucas was just as good with the older lads.

The sergeant and his man interviewed not only Kath Capley but her neighbours and the station master as well. It was obvious that Tolson had not been there. They gave all the information to the village constable, then returned, grim-faced, to report to the Chief Constable that they'd lost the villain.

Afterwards Sergeant Hankin went round to see Gideon at the

market and the two had a long chat. But neither could come up with any ideas about where Tolson might have gone.

'You'd better be careful,' the sergeant advised.

Gideon looked at him. 'From the way he committed his crimes, Tolson is incompetent as well as squeamish, but even he isn't stupid enough to return to Hedderby, let alone to that cottage.'

The sergeant grinned. 'You'd be surprised at how stupid some criminals are. We had one let out of prison recently who'd been boasting to his fellow inmates that he was going to steal things from the place where he'd worked the very first night out. And he did try, but we were waiting for him.'

'I don't think Tolson is that stupid.'

'Well, he hasn't been all that clever so far. He's had months to get rid of you and hasn't managed it. But be careful. You really ought to stay on at Granny's till he's caught.'

'And what if he's never caught? No, I'm moving into my aunt's cottage as soon as it's been cleaned. Two of the women in the other cottages are doing that for me and they said they'd be finished tonight. They've been around all the time, so they'd have seen Tolson if he'd come back.'

Dora walked up the hill with Gideon at the end of the afternoon carrying a basket of food provided by Essie, while he carried his stained canvas bag of clothes and possessions, plus another bag, because he'd purchased quite a few new things.

As Nippy and Duke frisked around them, he said, 'Are you still determined to go on the stage, Dora love?'

She stopped, looking at him apprehensively. 'I thought *we* were going on the stage together. You haven't changed your mind about it, surely?'

'I was hoping you had.' He waved one hand towards the cottages. 'We'd have enough money to live on if we were careful, without needing to traipse round the country.'

She shook her head, tears coming into her eyes. She didn't want to lose him, but couldn't lie to him. 'I'd never be happy staying at home and looking after a house. How would you feel if you had to do that all day? You know you're bored with working at the market already, and that's much more interesting than most women's lives.'

He was silent for a few more paces then said quietly, 'What about children? Don't you want any?'

'Eventually, I suppose.' She sighed. 'I'm like my sisters there. I had enough to do with babies when I was growing up, and now Essie's bringing up three of them so I'm still surrounded by them. That sort of life isn't what I want, Gideon. I'm sorry, but it's simply . . . not enough.'

They walked the rest of the way in silence, neither daring to say anything more on that subject, not wanting to spoil the sunny evening.

The cottage doors stood wide open and the whole of the interior was clean, the windows sparkling, the fires laid ready to light.

The woman next door popped her head round the kitchen door. 'It's all ready for you. We're still airing the place out, though. It smelt that strongly of pipe smoke. But we've kept an eye on it for you, made sure *he* didn't come back and sneak in.'

Gideon called, 'Thank you,' and went inside.

'It'll be lovely to have a place like this to come back to in between shows,' Dora offered when his silence continued.

'Mmm.'

He was avoiding her eyes. Was he going to change his mind about their act and insist on her staying at home if they got married? Some men would, but she hadn't thought Gideon was like that. She could feel tears rising in her eyes, so said hastily, 'I'll just nip upstairs and check that they've made up your bed properly.' She ran quickly up the stairs and into his bedroom, wiping her eyes once she was out of his sight.

As she went through the door someone grabbed her. She tried to shriek but a heavy hand covered her mouth, the fingers digging into her cheek.

'Shut up and stay still or I'll cut your throat, you stupid bitch. I've nothing much to lose now.'

Fear shivered through her and she stood perfectly motionless, making no further attempt to struggle.

'We're going to walk down the stairs, you an' me,' that harsh voice whispered in her ear. 'And I'll have this knife at your throat all the way, think on.'

Tolson was dishevelled and unshaven, as if he'd been sleeping rough, but what terrified her most was the knife that lay on the soft skin of her neck, such a thin barrier between life and death.

She had no choice but to move with him, hating to have his body pressed so close to hers, afraid that a misstep on her part might make him jerk his arm and kill her.

When they got to the door of the kitchen, Gideon turned round, saying, 'Dora, I—' He stared at her in horror.

'Don't move until I tell you to, Gideon bloody Shaw,' Tolson ordered. 'Or she'll be the one to suffer. It's very easy to make her bleed. See.' He pressed the tip of his knife into Dora's throat and she felt a warm trickle run down her neck. 'Yes, she does bleed easily, doesn't she?'

Gideon stood utterly motionless.

'Now, sit down, nice and easy like.' Tolson watched as Gideon obeyed him. 'Put your head down on the table and your arms behind you. She's going to help me tie you up and heaven help you both if you make a wrong move.'

'What do you want?' Gideon asked.

'Money. You've took what I had hid in the clock. Where is it?'

'In the bank.'

'Well, I'll take whatever I can find to help me get away, and she'll be coming with me. Not that you'll know it because you'll be dead. But if you do as I say, I'll keep her alive. She's a tasty morsel, be a pity to kill her.'

Gideon raised his head to glare at him.

'Put your head down, I said! If there's any trouble, I will kill her. It takes a lot to make me shed blood, but two nights out on the moors, jumping at every sound, got my anger up good and proper against you.' He edged backwards, dragging Dora with him. 'Use your right hand to get the washing line out of that top drawer. Don't make any sudden moves.'

She did as he told her, pushing the contents of the drawer around as she searched. 'It's not there.'

He risked a glance sideways at the drawer. 'Them damned women must have moved it. Well, it must be here somewhere and your fellow's not going to move an inch while we search, are you, Shaw?'

'Not an inch,' he agreed.

Late that afternoon, four soldiers got off the train at Hedderby, very smart in immaculate uniforms, under the charge of an even more resplendent Captain Darrow.

He asked directions to Jack Burtell's rooms and the five of them walked along Market Street to the other end, the men following their officer in twos.

Jack was delighted to see them. 'You're ready to take action?'

'Yes. We got the clerk at headquarters yesterday and with a little persuasion, he confessed everything. Now, before we do anything else, we want to catch Tolson, who is, by the way, a deserter.'

'I'm afraid he's run away. He kidnapped my client's young lady and tried to lure Gideon to his death, but it went awry and in the confusion Tolson escaped. We've got his two fellow conspirators locked up, awaiting trial, though one of them's very ill, but nobody has any idea where Tolson is. He was last seen running off across the moors. I checked the village where his mistress lives myself, but he's not been back there. The village constable is keeping an eye out for him, just in case.'

'Damn!' The Captain thought for a minute then said, 'I should think he's living rough. I would in his shoes. Perhaps we can find a shepherd or someone who knows the moors to help us look for him. We can't go back without at least trying. He may have stolen food or left some clue to his whereabouts.'

'Well, I'll direct you to Gideon's cottage. It's easy enough to find. He's moving in this very afternoon. The impostor left the place in a mess, so he had to hire two women to clean it from top to bottom.'

With Tolson still close beside her, Dora continued to search the various drawers, doing it as slowly as she dared. Only as she was turning to the final set of drawers, the ones in the dresser, did she see Nippy and Duke hovering in the doorway. Tolson hadn't noticed them and she quickly made the hand signal that told the dogs to hide.

When she opened the next drawer, she said conversationally, 'It's getting a bit chilly now. Can we shut the back door?' She'd noticed that he was looking cold.

'Aye, but do it careful-like.'

Again they edged round the room together and she stretched out her hand to close the back door. As she did so, the blade was at its furthest from her throat so she risked ducking down, screaming, 'Nippy! Nippy!' She flung herself under the kitchen table as she did so, hearing the dogs start to growl as they moved forward quickly, on the alert.

Gideon sprang to his feet, picking up a kitchen chair to protect himself from the knife.

As Tolson yelled a string of obscenities at him and brandished the knife, two furry bodies hurled across the kitchen. Before he had realised it, they were on him. Nippy bit his leg while Duke grabbed the arm with the knife, an action Dora remembered suddenly from the act with his former master. She continued to crouch under the table, not wanting to get in the way.

Duke's effort gave Gideon time to hurl the chair to one side and grab the hand with the knife. The dog let go of that arm, but as the two men struggled Duke seized the opportunity to bite Tolson and hang on to the back of his thigh.

Yelling in pain, the man let go of the knife and before he could do anything else, Gideon punched him in the jaw, a clumsy punch with his left hand, but enough to floor the man, upon which Duke leaped for his throat.

The dog didn't bite into the man's skin, but he was a big animal and had the throat between his jaws, keeping up a low, rumbling growl in his throat.

Tolson yelled in fright, calling, 'Get him off me! Get him off!'

When the knife fell, Dora scrambled out crabwise from under the table and snatched it up with a moan of relief.

At that moment the back door opened and the man from next door poked his head inside, goggled at what he saw, then rushed to help Gideon drag Tolson to his feet.

'We need something to tie him up. Did you find that washing line yet?' Gideon asked Dora, not taking his eyes off his captive.

'It was in the very first drawer, but I pushed it to the back and pretended I couldn't find it.'

He beamed at her. 'That's my clever lass.'

She passed him the rope and Tolson was soon fastened tightly to a chair, with Duke sitting beside him, growling every time the man so much as twitched, while Nippy stood at the other side, echoing the growls and looking equally eager to have another bite.

There was a knock on the front door and Gideon turned round warily. 'I'll answer that, Dora.'

He opened it to reveal Captain Darrow, who said, 'Ah!' when he saw Tolson. 'You found him, then.'

'He found us, sir.'

'We were coming to arrest him today, but Burtell told me he'd escaped.'

'He was stupid enough to come back. In fact, he's not a very clever conspirator at all.' Gideon introduced Dora to the captain, then the soldiers were brought in to take Tolson into custody.

'You'll be needed to give evidence at his trial,' the Captain said. 'The man's a damned deserter, as well as a criminal.'

'I'll be happy to do so, sir.'

'You were a good soldier, Shaw. It was a sad day when that accident happened.' He nodded at Gideon's damaged hand.

'I thought so at the time, but if it hadn't, I'd never have met Dora.' We'll invite you to the wedding, sir.'

*　　*　　*

Only when everyone had gone did Dora fling herself into Gideon's arms. 'I thought he was going to kill you.'

'I was more worried that he was going to kill you.'

They leaned back a little to stare into each other's eyes.

'Oh, hell,' he said suddenly. 'Nothing seems to matter except that we're alive. If you're so keen to go on the stage, we'll do it – though I don't think I'm very good at that sort of thing.'

'Oh, Gideon, do you mean it?'

'Of course I do. I'd never lie to you, never.'

As they began to kiss one another, someone nudged Gideon. He spun round, shoving Dora behind him instinctively, then laughed as he saw Duke and Nippy sitting wagging at them.

'They're a grand pair of dogs,' he said. 'It'd be a shame not to let them perform for people.'

She looked outside at the warm reflection of orange light from the setting sun. 'We're late for supper. Essie will be wondering what's happened to us. We'd better set off.'

'Only on condition that you'll marry me as soon as it can be arranged.'

Her loving smile was answer enough, but he felt the need to seal the bargain with a few more kisses, which delayed them still further.

As they were strolling down the hill into the glorious sunset, arm in arm, she stopped suddenly. 'I know what we can do with the market stall.'

'Oh?'

'Give it to Barney and Gran.'

'Good idea.'

But the way he was looking at her said his mind wasn't really on such mundane matters. It took rather longer than usual to get back to Linney's, because they kept stopping to kiss or tell each other the things that lovers always do.

When they walked into that big kitchen full of family, Gideon felt a sense of coming home. He put his arm round Dora's shoulders and announced, 'We're going to get wed as soon as we can.'

After that it was an uproar as all Dora's sisters kissed him and all the men shook his hand.

Even the dogs were not missed out, because Essie saw that they each had a big plate of scraps.

'Perhaps things will go right now,' she said as she served a fine meal to everyone. 'The orphanage is opening and the Pride is nearly finished.'

'And you're all invited to the opening night,' Eli said. He turned to Dora. 'By which time you'll have got your act ready, I presume?'

She nodded.

'Then I'd like to book you.'

She pointed to Gideon. 'You'll have to ask my manager. He's dealing with the money side of things.'

'She always did hate doing sums,' Carrie said.

Dora pulled a face at her, then bent to stroke Nippy and Duke. 'I don't think I've ever been so happy in my whole life.'

Essie had to wipe a tear from her eye at that, and tried to conceal it by going over to get the apple pie which was keeping warm on the stove top and telling Gracie sharply to get some small plates out.

Epilogue

The orphanage was opened the following week by the Mayor. James fretted around so much that morning that Charis took him by the shoulders and held him at arm's length.

'Calm down, James. Everything's going to be all right.'

He put one hand up to cover one of hers. 'We've had nothing but trouble so far. I can't help worrying.'

'Well, let me tell you something that'll cheer you up, at least I hope it will.' She blushed a rosy pink as she added softly, 'You're going to be a father again.'

He stilled. 'You mean . . .' He couldn't go any further. Out came the handkerchief and he made several trumpeting noises into it before he dared put it away, by which time his face was red and his eyes suspiciously bright.

'You are happy at the news?' she asked anxiously.

'I couldn't be happier.' He pulled her close for a big hug and said into her ear. 'Best thing I ever did, wedding you, my lass.'

They stayed like that for a minute or two, then she pulled away. 'We'd better finish getting ready for the opening.'

The street in front of the orphanage was crowded with people. The orphans already in residence were lined up neatly to one side, big ones standing behind the little ones, all with strict instructions not to fidget, backed up by the promise of a big piece of cake each if they behaved themselves.

Dressed in their best, Lucas and Gwynna stood on either side of Mr and Mrs Forrett to greet the Mayor, who was wearing his official robes and chain, with an old-fashioned hat on his head with a brim full of dyed red and black feathers. He made a short speech, cut a ribbon and allowed himself to be led round the building. As he and the other dignitaries of the town made inroads into the refreshments, the orphans had their own feast next door.

'A very laudable act, Mr Forrett,' said the Mayor, unaware of a smear of cream on his chin.

'I don't like to see children in need.'

'They looked very neat and tidy,' the Mayor's wife added graciously.

Gwynna exchanged smiles with Lucas. They could both guess how quickly that tidiness would vanish as the children ate their feast then played under his uncle's supervision.

The remark she would cherish most from today had come from an old woman, shabby but tidily dressed, who had been standing near the front. 'It shows the folk in this town have got good hearts, a place like this does. I hope no orphan ever wants a home again in Hedderby.'

Dora was excited that the grand opening of the Pride music hall was to happen in four weeks' time. She and Gideon rehearsed most days, even if they had to wait until after the markets closed sometimes.

Members of her family came to watch and offer their opinion, but it was Raife's suggestions which helped most. And his song, finally finished, was a masterpiece, with a catchy chorus of the sort that encouraged audiences to join in. He'd already told them to find a music publisher and sell him the song, then they'd make an ongoing profit from sales of sheet music.

Her sister Marjorie was to perform on opening night with her husband in their comedy act, which was now topping the bill in all but the largest London theatres. The Prince of Laughter, they called Hal, and it suited him because he had a gift for making people laugh the minute he stepped on to the stage.

And it was in doubt until quite late whether Eli's cousins Bram and Joanna could make it. Nowadays they were top of the bill anywhere they played and were booked up months in advance.

But at the last minute there was a cancellation due to fire damage at a theatre, so they too would be able to come back to

Hedderby for the opening night and meet the man who would be their new relative.

When the music hall building was complete, Eli invited all his family and close friends to come and view it. As he and Carrie showed them round, Gideon grew quieter and quieter.

'I can't imagine myself getting up on that stage in front of a hall full of people,' he confessed to Dora.

She looked at him anxiously.

'I wish we hadn't listened to Eli, wish we were married now.'

She smiled. 'I don't. He's right. It'll make our debut even more special.'

The day before the opening, Eli opened the new music hall to members of the public, who were allowed to walk through it on a path chosen by him. Golden cords fenced off other parts, but he lit the gas so that the gilding and painted cameos along the edge of the balcony and in the entrance showed to best effect.

He hadn't realised that just about the whole population of Hedderby would take advantage of his offer, and had to send out for members of the family to help keep the people moving through.

Dora stood near the stage next to Gideon, accepting congratulations on their coming marriage as well as the beauty of this 'palace of entertainment'.

'I helped dig out the foundations,' one man said proudly.

'Eh, I've never seen such a place,' said a woman whose clothes were almost rags, but whose eyes were bright with the marvels she was seeing.

They'd no need to ask people not to touch, because the inhabitants of Hedderby were as proud of 'their' music hall as Eli had one day dreamed they would be.

'My man doesn't drink as much when he's got a show to see, and he brings me too,' a middle-aged woman with a careworn face said. 'We can't afford to come tomorrow, but we're saving up for next week.'

'Here,' Gideon said suddenly, thrusting some coins into her

hand. 'Have this one on us. Dora and I need some luck for our first performance.'

She looked down at the coins with tears in her eyes, unable to speak for joy. Then she gave him a big hug, with another for Dora, and walked out with a handkerchief in her hands.

'You're a kind man,' Dora said.

'If you can't help people like her, it's a poor look-out.'

'Not just her. I heard what you did for Huey Benting.'

He looked flustered. 'I don't like to see a lad of his age going into prison. Besides, the Army will make a man of him – or break him. It'll give him a choice, at least.'

'I wasn't sorry his father died of his injuries. He was a horrible man, treated the lasses in the mill shamefully.'

'Cheer up!' a voice said loudly in her ear and she turned to see Declan and Kevin standing there. 'All ready for the wedding, Gideon?'

'Can't wait.'

'We'll be here tomorrow, clapping.'

He couldn't hide a shiver.

When the morning finished and the last person had walked through the Pride, Dora hurried home to make her final preparations for her wedding the next morning.

She slept soundly, woke up to Nippy licking her face, with Duke standing panting happily behind him. She got up to enjoy a big breakfast.

'Aren't you nervous?' her little sisters asked.

'No, not at all.'

And she wasn't. She walked down the aisle on Nev's arm, proud to be marrying Gideon, knowing she was looking her best in a new dress of cream silk with three tiers of flounced skirts belled out over a crinoline, the outfit a present from her sister Marjorie.

Afterwards she and Gideon ate some of Essie's food, then walked up to their cottage for a quiet hour or two before the performance.

As the afternoon passed, she grew quieter and quieter.

'Is something wrong, love?' Gideon asked.

She looked at him, then nodded. 'I never thought I would be, but I'm nervous.'

'*You* are? You're never nervous.'

'I am today. I've forced you into this, and if we don't go down well, we shall be shamed in front of everyone in Hedderby. And I can't bear the thought of that.'

With a laugh, he pulled her into his arms and kissed her soundly. 'We'll not fail, love, not with our two friends here.'

Nippy and Duke seemed to know he was talking about them and came across to press against them.

There would be one performance only that evening, a grand gala show to which all the dignitaries in the town had been invited. People were crammed in so closely it seemed as if there was a sea of faces.

But the audience was in a mood to be pleased, applauding every act.

When it came their turn to go on, Dora took a deep breath, stroked her stage dress, a soft harebell blue, with a slightly shorter skirt than usual showing her trim ankles and allowing her to move quickly when she had to.

Before they went on stage, Eli stood up and made an announcement in his booming voice. 'Ladies and gentlemen, we not only have a new act here tonight, our very own Mr Nippy and Duke, but we have a newly-wed pair to assist our canine stars. I give you . . . Mr and Mrs Gideon Shaw!'

People cheered and cheered again as Dora and Gideon walked on stage, a dog on either side of them. Then they walked off and as soon as the big hall was silent began their act. Nippy hid behind Dora's skirt, Duke leaped effortlessly over obstacles and through hoops, and when the act was over, both dogs sat quietly as Dora and Gideon sang the song written specially for them: 'Me and my little furry friend'.

When they were finally allowed to leave the stage, Dora flung her arms round her new husband and gave him a sound kiss, before allowing the other performers to come and congratulate them on a successful debut.

As they returned to their dressing room, Dora looked at him challengingly. 'Well, can you stand this sort of life, Gideon?'

'With you by my side I can stand anything. But I must say, these fellows behaved themselves beautifully . . . and it was lovely to hear the applause. So yes, I think I can stand it.'

Eli had the final word at the party held on the stage afterwards. He stood with his arm round his wife and said, 'I once thought I'd like to make my hall the pride of Lancashire, and I still do want that. But even more, I want to make it the Heart of the Town, a place where everyone in Hedderby can come for a decent night's entertainment.'

'You've done that already, lad,' Raife said with a smile. 'And you've pulled the whole family into it, too.' He looked round the crowded foyer. 'Who's going to tread the boards next?'

The five unmarried young Prestons hastily denied they had any desire to follow their two sisters on to the stage.

'You never know,' Raife said, slipping a titbit to Nippy, then another to Duke. 'You never know what will happen in the future.'

CONTACT ANNA

Anna Jacobs is always delighted to hear from readers and can be contacted:

BY MAIL

PO Box 628
Mandurah
Western Australia 6210

If you'd like a reply, please enclose a self-addressed, business size envelope, stamped (from inside Australia) or with an international reply coupon (from outside Australia).

VIA THE INTERNET

Anna has her own web domain, with details of her books and excerpts, and invites you to visit it at
http://www.annajacobs.com

Anna can be contacted by email at *anna@annajacobs.com*

If you'd like to receive email news about Anna and her books every month or two, you are cordially invited to join her announcements list. Just email her and ask to be added to the list, or follow the link from her web page.

Heart of the Town

ANNA JACOBS

Heart of the Town

HODDER

Copyright © 200⟨ by Anna Jacobs

First published in Great Britain in 2006 by Hodder & Stoughton
A division of Hodder Headline

The right of Anna Jacobs to be identified as the Author of the Work
has been asserted by her in accordance with the
Copyright, Designs and Patents Act 1988.

A Hodder & Stoughton Book

2

A CIP catalogue record for this title is available from the British Library.

EAN 978 0340 84077 1
ISBN 0 340 84077 3

Typeset in Plantin by
Palimpsest Book Production Ltd, Grangemouth, Stirlingshire

Printed and bound by
Mackays of Chatham Ltd, Chatham, Kent

Hodder Headline's policy is to use papers that are natural,
renewable and recyclable products and made from wood grown
in sustainable forests. The logging and manufacturing processes
are expected to conform to the environmental regulations
of the country of origin.

Hodder & Stoughton Ltd
A division of Hodder Headline
338 Euston Road
London NW1 3BH